Message Deleted

Message Deleted

K. L. SLATER

MICHAEL JOSEPH

PENGUIN MICHAEL JOSEPH

UK | USA | Canada | Ireland | Australia
India | New Zealand | South Africa

Penguin Michael Joseph is part of the Penguin Random House group of companies
whose addresses can be found at global.penguinrandomhouse.com

First published 2024
001

Copyright © K. L. Slater, 2024

The moral right of the author has been asserted

All characters in this publication are fictitious and any resemblance
to real persons, living or dead, is purely coincidental

Set in 13.5/16pt Garamond MT Std
Typeset by Jouve (UK), Milton Keynes
Printed and bound in Great Britain by Clays Ltd, Elcograf S.p.A.

The authorized representative in the EEA is Penguin Random House Ireland,
Morrison Chambers, 32 Nassau Street, Dublin D02 YH68

A CIP catalogue record for this book is available from the British Library

HARDBACK ISBN: 978–0–241–67844–2
TRADE PAPERBACK ISBN: 978–0–241–67845–9

To Mackie and Francesca Kim

Prologue

June

The street is quiet as the red digits on his watch change to 23:01. The house is situated in West Bridgford, a leafy suburb lying immediately south of Nottingham, the kind of area often described as 'highly coveted' by estate agents.

The residents of this affluent part of the city are safely inside their brick-built fortresses with their flatscreen televisions and American-style refrigerators. Shiny new lease cars are parked up on well-maintained driveways while sophisticated home security alarm systems await activation. The things that make them feel safe. Untouchable.

He's been watching the family inside for thirty minutes now from behind a cluster of bushes and small trees that provide a good barrier from the road. A thick covering of cloud completely obscures the moon and this one is a waxing gibbous, he thinks. Currently gifting him with a reassuring cloak of darkness.

Today has been a hot one. After a day spent travelling, he is clammy and desperate for a cold beer. Ideally, something stronger. Now, the unbearable heat has faded, affording a milder night for the task ahead.

He adjusts the night-vision goggles and scans the area around the house. No movement. The only disturbance so far has been a bull terrier on a late-night walk that caught his scent. The animal had growled, thrust a chunky snout into the undergrowth, and he had frozen, held his breath, until its owner cursed and pulled the beast back.

The property he's interested in is slightly smaller and less impressive than the others on the street. A swept narrow path blends into a short run of paved steps leading up to the front door. It almost feels like an invitation to enter . . . but he knows he would not be welcome. A small front lawn is edged with neat borders that house popular perennials such as achillea, hollyhocks and hardy geraniums. He'd plucked a leaf from the cherry laurel hedge when he walked past earlier. Now, he splits its soft, shiny skin and rubs it between his fingers, inhaling the sweet, light scent of an English garden he wishes was his own. Soon, he'll be heading around the back of the house, and that tells a different story altogether.

He's already spent hours in this overgrown back garden. He knows the family's routines almost as well as his own. The way the woman switches on the replica art deco glass lamps after dark, bathing the downstairs rooms in a pleasant amber glow. Sometimes, when the child has gone to bed, they leave the television off and pour a drink, talking together. Sometimes it's just a coffee, on other occasions perhaps a finger or two of something stronger served on ice in one of the heavy, cut-glass tumblers she takes from the old-fashioned mahogany cupboard by the window.

It might start off amicable, but it nearly always ends in accusing glances and bitter, angry faces.

Last weekend they fired up the barbecue on a small area of paving amongst the overgrown weeds and grass. He waited until nearly midnight before he could enter the back garden and, from the shadows, observe the two of them in the lounge.

Earlier in the day they had taken the child for a sleepover

at a friend's house a fifteen-minute drive away, so they were alone. It was clear they'd had far too much to drink. The French doors were ajar and a noughties playlist continued to boom. By then he was familiar with the perimeter of the garden and easily avoided tripping the motion sensors on the outdoor lights.

He'd moved closer, using the bushes as cover. A lamp bathed the oblong room in a subtle glow. Two grey leather sofas faced each other like sentries across a cream wool Berber rug patterned with charcoal diamonds. At the far end, integral bookcases with clean white lines flanked an Adam fireplace.

The woman had stripped down to her underwear and began to dance around the room, taking messy gulps of gin and tonic. She'd laughed, wiped her wet chin with a careless hand as she performed her suggestive moves. Her husband had watched with a strange look on his shadowed face: a curious mix of longing and what looked like revulsion.

He'd reached out, caught her hand to pull her closer, but she'd shrugged him off carelessly, turned her back. He'd jumped up then and caught both her arms like capturing a butterfly, unclipped her bra, and they'd lain together on the rug. Lights on, doors open. He seemed completely oblivious to anything or anyone around them, but her eyes were open and staring unblinkingly at the ceiling until it was over.

His overriding reaction had been one of disappointment. He had previously thought better of her. If anything, their behaviour had further convinced him that he was doing the right thing. It convinced him he would take what he wanted despite what it might cost him.

23:08 now.

The street feels relaxed, the heat imbuing the air with a kind of looseness, as if everyone has breathed out for the weekend.

He brings his fingers to his mouth, tastes the bittersweet leaf sap with the tip of his tongue.

Summer makes everyone less vigilant, doesn't it? The sun, the drink, the general feeling of wellbeing, of living life to the full. So often doors are left open, alarms forgotten.

Nobody ever really thinks anything bad will happen to them. Not in a place like this.

I

Saffy

Thursday

Saffy walks into the reception area of Glassworks IT and waits for the receptionist to finish a call. Behind the curved, blond wood desk, a Karlsson clock hangs on the wall. Saffy is five minutes early for the interview – had aimed for ten but the bus was late.

'Saffy Morris,' she says when the receptionist puts down the phone. 'I have an interview for a data manager position at one o'clock.'

The woman, Saffy thinks, is probably in her late twenties. She has blonde hair scraped back into a smooth ponytail and very full lips. While she locates her details on the screen, Saffy looks around at the features of the old mill and its tasteful refurbishment. There is a large, arched window with dozens of small square panes and a high ceiling that allows the natural light outside to warm the panels of exposed brickwork.

'Here we go, got you,' the receptionist says. 'Take a seat, they'll call you through when they're ready.'

Saffy ignores the big squashy sofas and chooses a cosy bucket chair in the corner where she can see the door. She puts her handbag down on the polished wooden floor and smoothes her dress. Breathing quietly and deeply, she lengthens her outbreaths as she'd been instructed to do in a yoga class. Back when she used to take part in that sort of thing.

She picks up her handbag and cradles it on her lap. The minutes tick by slowly and Saffy imagines how it might feel to work here. She shifts against the low back of the stylish boucle chair, stretches her toes against the tightness of the navy suede stilettos she borrowed a week ago from Leona. They are half a size too small but smarter than anything she owns.

Through the high, arched window, the sky looks bleak, a skein of dark clouds sweeping past, buffeted by the wind. It's warm in here, too warm. She considers slipping off her jacket, but then she'll be all flustered if they suddenly call her in for the interview.

She pulls out her phone and opens the notes she's made on the company to focus her mind on the interview.

When her mobile phone suddenly lights up in her hands and her ex-husband's name flashes up on the screen, she starts. There is no other visitor in the foyer, but Saffy stands up and walks over to a small alcove. Away from the main seating area and reception desk.

'Neil? Is everything OK?'

'Yes, everything's good here. Fox is fine. I was calling to see how you are, how you're doing with the job situation.'

'Oh, you know. I'm getting through it.' She rakes her nails up and down her pale forearm, leaving bright red tracks. 'I'm just at an interview now, actually. A place called Glassworks IT. On King Street. Do you know it?'

He perks up. 'Really? I don't know it, but best of luck and all that.' A beat of silence, then, 'Listen, I've been thinking about what you said. About Fox.'

The receptionist looks over and Saffy turns away from her, stares up at the arched window and imagines the summer rain that will soon be falling all over the city. 'Are you saying . . . I can have him this weekend?'

'I'm saying, maybe you have a point.' Neil pauses. 'It's just . . . keeping him the whole weekend is quite a jump from your usual Sunday. That's what I'm concerned about.'

'I'm ready, Neil.' Saffy has been trying to convince him for months and now she feels so close to succeeding, she is almost shaking.

Neil falls silent, the way he used to whenever he had an important decision to make. It had been one of the things that had driven her crazy in the end. She needs to spend some proper quality time with Fox and feels a twist of panic at the thought that Neil might change his mind and back off again. This might be her last chance to convince him.

'If I felt it was too much for me, I'd be honest and tell you, Neil. You know I would.' But he probably *doesn't* know that. Since they split up, they've both reverted to who they used to be right at the beginning, when there were still lots of things they didn't know about each other. Back when there had been a glorious attraction that sparked between them like fireworks.

To give Neil credit, he doesn't have to allow Saffy even a day a week with Fox. He was granted full custody by the family court two years ago when their son had just turned one.

Back then Saffy didn't know how she was going to look after herself, never mind a toddler. Neil had taken Fox without a second thought, and she had been so grateful to him because even though there were lengthy stretches of time when she spent full days in her pyjamas, streaming box sets back to back, unaware of whether it was day or night, there was never a moment's doubt in Saffy's mind that her son deserved so much better than she felt able to give him. The scars ran deep and they had irrevocably changed her from the inside out.

In those days, Leona was her rock. Her best friend never stopped trying to pull Saffy out of the deep, dark hole that threatened to swallow her up. These past few months, Saffy had been trying to do the same for her. But she knew something was off. Knew Leona well enough to easily see through her platitudes of 'everything is fine'.

And then last week, Leona told her what had really been going on with Ash. And now, finally, Saffy understands what it must have taken for her friend to finally confide in her.

The court's decision to grant Neil custody of Fox was the catalyst that forced Saffy to get the help she so badly needed. Six months passed in a blur, but once her GP was satisfied she'd stabilized on her medication and she had a confirmed programme of therapy in place, Neil allowed her to see Fox weekly in the form of a supervised Sunday afternoon visit at his mum's house.

'So can we try it and see how we go? Nothing needs to be set in stone yet,' she says now to Neil. 'All I'm asking for is a chance.'

When her health had improved further, Saffy began working as a barista. Just a few hours a week at a local coffee shop before she started a full-time job. Neil would drop Fox off at her bedsit on Sundays where Saffy would look after him unsupervised. She always made the most of it. They baked cookies and cakes and stuffed their faces until they felt sick. Daubed gaudy masterpieces on big sheets of paper on the kitchen floor with their fingerpaints and then papered the walls with them. On warmer days, they'd often take a picnic and homemade lemonade to the local park and eat it from an old tartan blanket spread across the grass.

Neil doesn't have to allow any of this, but he does. And for the past few months since his work schedule has increased, instead of asking his fiancée, Mira, to step in to help, he has turned to Saffy. Back on her feet, in full-time work and renting a decent house, Saffy has picked Fox up from nursery every Thursday and given him tea before Neil picks him up after work just after six. He adores Fox, but he isn't a natural father. 'I don't want any more kids,' he'd told Saffy. 'I couldn't imagine loving another child as much as Fox.'

'All right then, let's give it a go,' Neil says now. 'If you promise to let me know if it starts to feel too much.'

'Yes, I will. Of course I will.' The bottom of her back feels damp and her hands are trembling.

'OK, I'll bring him over first thing Saturday and pick him up on Sunday around teatime.'

'Thank you.' She wants to say more about how much this means to her, but the moment passes. 'I'll see you later.'

They end the call and Saffy feels a smile like the heat of the sun spreading over her face. She thinks this is how it must feel when things finally take a turn for the better. When you get through the worst of everything life throws at you and manage to claw your way back out the other side.

It's Thursday too, so she'll be picking Fox up from nursery later. It's turning out to be a good day after all.

'They'll be calling you through any moment.'

Saffy glances past the receptionist at the clock. The panel are running ten minutes late. Nothing can dampen Saffy's spirits now, and she needs this job. She walks back to her seat. She's here today for the interview not because she is out of work, but owing to the fact her current job as a data manager is under review due to company reorganization. Getting her life back on track depends on her working full-time, so it's a worry. Her job forms a big chunk of the routine she has built around herself to keep busy, to leave as little time as possible for her mind to dwell endlessly over what happened three years ago.

She blinks, forces her thoughts away from that night. She'd like to call Poppy, but at the age of twenty-two – eleven years younger than Saffy – her sister gets increasingly frustrated when Saffy checks in with her morning and night to make sure she's safe.

She looks around, searching for distractions, her eyes pausing on the receptionist who is now staring intently at her computer screen. And then she spots the pinboard on the far wall and the large printed sheet at the side of it.

It's one of those posters she's been trying to avoid looking at for the last couple of weeks. The ones the police have plastered all over town, warning people to be vigilant after a couple of pensioners were attacked in their homes. It doesn't take much to bring Saffy's trauma back, now it feels like the city is currently drowning in a crime wave. She crosses her legs and her foot starts to jig. She can't tear her eyes away from the heavy black font that screams out from between the two top curled corners.

DO YOU RECOGNIZE THIS MAN?

A blurry, pixelated image is all they have. A powerfully built figure dressed in black. His face turned away from the camera as he hurries away. It could be anybody really, but this CCTV snapshot is the biggest clue yet.

POLICE ADVICE.

A list of suggestions. Anyone who keeps an eye on the news headlines knows them off by heart.

Lock your doors.

She'd told her to keep them locked.

Keep your phone close by.

Her sister had left her phone on the bedside table.

Set the house alarm if you have one.

Saffy's heart beats fast and hard against her breastbone.

There had been no house alarm.

An explosion of muted laughter permeates through the closed door of the interview room. Sounds like it's going well in there for someone. Saffy reaches into her handbag for her bottle of water, taking a sip before dropping it back. Her phone screen lights up again. Dreading it is Neil saying he's changed his mind, she takes a breath and studies the screen. No text from Neil but there's a notification for three WhatsApp messages. All from Leona. She frowns and reads the messages once, twice.

> Can't speak
> Don't text or call
> Pls just come

Three short messages, sent in a panic.

> Can't speak . . . Don't text or call . . . Pls just come

The tight thread of fear she carries everywhere unravels inside her. She can sense the danger dripping from every word Leona has written. That awful stuff she'd told Saffy last week about her marriage. The way she'd looked, like she was fading away in front of Saffy's eyes. Her grip loosens; the phone slips and falls into her lap.

'Sounds like they're nearly finished in there,' the receptionist says, pulling Saffy from the screen. 'Sorry for the delay.'

> Don't text or call
> Pls just come

Saffy looks up and nods vaguely at her.

When she picks up her phone and looks back down at the screen, the message thread is still open but something has changed. She swipes out of the app and back in again to try and recover the words, but the messages are no longer there.

In their place are just three short lines.

This message was deleted.
This message was deleted.
This message was deleted.

2

Saffy

Saffy stands up and waves her phone to get the receptionist's attention. 'Sorry, I need to just step outside to make an urgent call.'

The sculpted eyebrows beetle together. 'You'll probably miss your slot if you do.'

Saffy is about to ignore her when she remembers what the messages had said.

Can't speak . . . Don't text or call

She tries to slow her breathing, resist where her thoughts are trying to go. There's a column of heat building inside, scorching her chest and her throat.

Saffy takes a long breath, in . . . and back out again. There might be a simple explanation. It could be a joke, a silly whim, and Leona had pressed send by mistake. She'd deleted it quickly, hoping Saffy didn't see. Maybe it's nothing.

But then she thinks again of what Leona confessed to her in the bar last week, when she finally spoke the awful truth about what Ash was doing to her. What he was putting her through on a daily basis. That's when the panic Saffy has been hiding pushes to the surface.

The door to the conference room suddenly opens and two men walk out. They are talking as they shake hands, the younger one laughing loudly, showcasing astonishingly white teeth. The senior-looking man wears a well-cut navy suit and consults a paper in his hand.

'Saffy Morris?' he says, looking back up as the other candidate leaves. 'Sorry to have kept you waiting.'

She hesitates. Should she just leave and find Leona, or stay and do her best to get this job for herself? For Fox and Poppy, too. To provide a safe family home for them both. She slips the phone back into her handbag. She can't respond to Leona's message now and maybe that's a good thing. The doubts are flooding in and conjuring up a thousand scenarios.

'Ms Morris?'

Saffy really needs this job. She needs it to pay her bills and remain solvent. To keep her life on track so she's able to care for her son. She stands up.

'Thank you,' she says and follows the man in the suit across the reception area towards the interview room. Her feet propel her forward, but her head starts to spin. Who is she kidding? Leona would never send her a text like that as a joke. In fact, she's never sent Saffy an urgent message like that in the entire time they have been friends.

'Take a seat,' he says, opening the door and ushering her in. 'I'm David Dewsbury, the CEO of Glassworks IT, and these are two of my colleagues. Our Head of Personnel . . .'

His voice fades out as Saffy thinks back to her night out with Leona last week. When it was time to leave, Leona had reached to get something off the table. Her sleeve had pulled back and revealed a small circle of bruises around her bony wrist. The marks were at the stage of fading slowly and looked like soft smudges of blue-black ink. They had looked as if they might have been there for a while.

The CEO clears his throat and she suddenly realizes she is still standing and the room has gone deathly quiet. 'Is everything all right, Ms Morris?'

The two men and one woman are staring at her. She hasn't yet acknowledged them. She has zoned out as if they don't exist.

'Ms Morris, are you feeling all right?'

Nausea pulses through her and she grips the back of the chair.

'I'm so sorry,' she says. 'I'm not feeling too good. I – I think I need to leave.'

The CEO frowns. 'I'm sorry?'

The other members of the panel sit quiet and still.

And Saffy runs from the room.

The instant she's outside the building again, she checks her phone but there are no more messages. Leona had asked her not to call or text, just to go directly to the house. And the quickest way to get there is by cab.

The rain that had threatened when she arrived is now arrowing down in drenching sheets. She has no umbrella, and within seconds, her shoulder-length brown hair is sticking to her face and forehead. Her dress and jacket are already soaked through, and she pulls at the fabric where it sticks to her skin.

She starts to run towards the taxi rank at the end of the road, passing a newspaper stand. She slows down and glances at the afternoon headlines on the local news. She doesn't read the news, it's another trick to keep the flashbacks at bay.

A man pushes by her, mumbles an irritated apology. She turns away from the stand, the beat of the rain on her face as she comes to, remembers where it is she's supposed to be heading.

Leona. She must see her, must make sure that she and Rosie are safe.

By the time she reaches the taxi rank, there are already a

few people waiting there. Still shaky, she finds a space under the corrugated plastic and steel shelter, turning her back on the rain. Closest to her, a young mum stands with her little boy. He has red hair and blue Paddington wellies. He looks about three, the same age as Fox.

The bored child takes an interest in Saffy, as if he can sense the buzz of panic that surrounds her. He breaks away from his mother's side and stands directly in front of her, staring blankly at her mud-splattered tights and shoes.

'I should've put my wellies on like you,' she says, causing the boy to turn away and step back towards his mum, burying his face into her side. Her hand presses down reassuringly on the top of her son's head, a faint smile playing around the corners of her mouth.

Saffy squeezes her toes up inside Leona's ruined shoes, feels the squelch of rainwater across the seam of her tights. She lowers her eyes and watches her fingers twist against each other. In the corner of the shelter, a small pile of filth has gathered over time. Cigarette nubs, mud, wrappers.

People are glancing at her now, sensing waves of something unpleasant rolling off her that makes them shuffle a little further away.

And just like that, the breath catches in her throat and she is back there again. His masked face pressed close to hers. Panting like a dog.

His hot breath. The sour, unwashed smell of him.

3
Saffy

A cab pulls into the taxi rank and Saffy rushes forward. It is not her turn. There are others who were here before her, but she needs to get away. She must get away this second to escape the memories that are rushing in. Not just from the attack but before that, too. The secret shame she carries with her like a millstone every single day.

She can't go down that road. Not today.

Nobody objects to her jumping the queue. Blank faces regard her silently as she clambers inside the car.

She gives the driver Leona's address and checks her phone. No new messages.

Inside, the cab is dry and warm despite wet footprints on the floor. The door closes with a heavy, reassuring *clunk* as she sinks back into the seat and squeezes her eyes closed. Every sinew, every tendon in her neck and shoulders feels taut and sore.

The driver watches her through the rear-view mirror – blue eyes and tanned, weathered skin and an explosion of deep, crinkled lines at the corner of each eye. She looks away, stares into space repeating the contents of Leona's deleted messages in her head.

. . . Don't text or call . . .

Saffy has to pick Fox up at three fifteen from nursery so she must leave herself plenty of time. Going to the house is

17

the right thing to do, she knows that now. Leona would never have reached out if it hadn't been important.

They've drifted apart a bit in the last couple of years, but Saffy still knows her friend better than anyone. She knows the heart and core of Leona, knows about the hidden scars from a painful childhood largely spent in care. She knows her friend would never joke like this. Not after everything they've been through together.

The rain-lashed cab window provides a semi-opaque screen, and Saffy lays her hot cheek against it, staring out at the skittish raindrops and the streets beyond. It's early afternoon and there is more traffic on the road than she expected. People are keen to get home to their families, their kids. Perhaps reading those headlines and realizing the city is not a safe place.

City living, attracting people who were prepared to spend silly money turning their homes into fortresses. Security companies were amongst the biggest winners, newspaper headlines fostering a boom in demand for alarm systems, panic button installations and mace sprays. Businesses boosted by the scaremongering on all the social media platforms. *Scaremongering*. She'd called it that too, until Poppy was attacked.

At last, the driver turns into Leona's street. She pushes a twenty-pound note at him and says, 'Here will be fine, thanks.'

Outside, the downpour has receded to a drizzle. The air feels cold and Saffy stands under a thick grey sky for a moment, looking at Leona's executive detached house with its red-brick exterior. They'd bought this house soon after they married and Leona had confided in her that she'd suffered sleepless nights because of the size of the mortgage they'd had to take out.

'My old place was so much cheaper, but Ash didn't want us to live there. He wanted something bigger.'

Something fancier.

Saffy has visited here a handful of times in the past year, trying to keep up the contact with her best friend and her goddaughter. Eventually, she realized it was causing problems for Leona because Ash didn't want her here.

The hedged front garden features a small, neat lawn with colourful planting around the borders. Two cars are parked on the driveway. She looks up at the bedroom windows and at the front room with its traditional bay. All seems quiet.

She walks up the block-paved driveway, glancing into the cars as she passes. She can see the cream leather front seats in Ash's sleek black BMW. The interior looks immaculate. In Leona's little orange Toyota Aygo, empty water bottles and what looks like Rosie's school reading folder are scattered across the back seat.

She clutches her phone tightly in her hand. There are no more messages from Leona, but Saffy is debating whether she should call her now she's here. Tell her she's just outside? But that would mean ignoring the instructions in Leona's deleted messages.

Can't speak . . . Don't text or call

Saffy thinks she might call the police, but then wonders what she might say. *My friend messaged me and then deleted it?*

She's at the front door now. Before she can overthink it, she takes a breath and rings the doorbell. If there's no answer, she'll go around the back. If she can't get a response there then she will call Leona, regardless of what she said in her message.

Saffy pulls at the neck of her dress despite the cooler weather. Her breathing feels too shallow as the moment of truth approaches. She steps back and peers in through the bay window, but the room is empty. She rings the doorbell again. A car crawls past and, instinctively, she turns to look.

The driver raises a hand in greeting and she recognizes Leona's neighbour, Tania, who once called round for a cup of tea and a chat in the days when Saffy visited at the new house more regularly. If she needs to run for help, it's good to know Tania is home just across the road.

She rings the bell again and someone calls out from inside the house. Not in an alarmed way, just like you might shout out to others to get the door. Saffy steps forward and pushes on the off-chance the door is unlocked when it suddenly opens and Leona appears. For a split second, she just stares then smiles. 'Saffy, it's you!'

Saffy looks at her, searching for red-rimmed eyes, a puffy face or trembling hands. But there is nothing.

She cranes her neck and looks over Leona's shoulder into the house. The television is on somewhere inside, the volume set too loud. The smell of cooking drifts in the air, accompanied by the chink of crockery from the kitchen. Shoes are piled untidily under a radiator and muddy footprints have dried across the light oak laminate floor.

Leona frowns. 'Is everything OK, Saff? You look . . . I don't know, a bit stressed.'

'What's wrong?' Saffy hisses, low enough that she hopes Ash can't hear. 'Come outside for a minute . . . Can we talk in your car?'

Leona gives a little shake of her head and a half-hearted laugh. 'What do you mean?'

She's acting normally, and Saffy is desperately trying to find a non-verbal sign she might be sending, something that gives her a silent clue. Leona has on skinny jeans and a longline leopard-print tunic top. An outfit Saffy has seen before. The fabric of the once-snug top now bags at her neck, drapes in loose folds over her hips. Her feet are bare, toenails painted pink. Her arms hang down at her sides, hands gently curled. She appears relaxed enough, not like a woman on the edge of something. And it's then that Saffy spots it, the sign she's been waiting for. Leona is not wearing her wedding ring.

Leona leans forward and looks beyond her, at the road. 'Nothing's happened, has it? Is Fox OK?'

'I got your messages,' Saffy says, her voice lower still. 'I came as quickly as I could.'

'Saffy, are you feeling all right?' Leona glances over her shoulder, back into the house, before reaching out and touching her arm. Then she says, 'I'm really sorry, Saffy, but I don't know what you're talking about.'

4

Saffy

Saffy and Leona last met in the city, a week ago. Their meet-ups had dwindled over time from weekly to maybe once every six weeks – it's true they both have busy lives, but Saffy knows the real reason Leona holds back. Ash doesn't like her going out and he doesn't like her having friends. A few months ago, he'd even finally convinced Leona to give up her nursing career. A job she loved and excelled at. A job she'd spent years in training for.

Saffy and Leona have always been the kind of friends who tell each other everything, right from their first day at secondary school when Leona tripped and sprained her ankle. The teacher had asked Saffy to take her to the school office and from that moment they were like sisters; they laughed, cried, hugged each other through the best and the worst times. Years later, when Saffy and Poppy needed supporting after the attack, Leona was there for them both every step of the way.

But just as Saffy started to get back on her feet, Leona, who'd been on her own since five-year-old Rosie's father abandoned her while she was still pregnant, met Ash and that's when everything changed. And it changed quickly.

Leona drastically cut down the amount of time she spent with Saffy. She made every excuse under the sun as to why she couldn't get out as much, but Saffy wasn't fooled. She knew the real reason for her withdrawal. One day about eighteen months ago, after they got back from a holiday in Mallorca, Leona told her that she and Ash had got married out there.

'Ash wanted a quiet day with the minimum of fuss,' she'd said, giving Saffy an apologetic smile. Rosie had stayed home with Leona's mum and they'd asked the hotel staff to act as witnesses. The news hurt, but Saffy bit her tongue because her friend looked so pale and thin. The Leona she knew had always worn bright colours and tight clothes. This Leona always seemed to be in a baggy grey tracksuit or in clothes that no longer fit her properly.

'I'm sorry,' Leona said again. 'It's just the way Ash wanted us to do it.'

'Are you happy?' Saffy had asked, desperate for her friend to see how controlling he was, how much he'd taken over her whole life.

Leona had paused, looked wretched for just a moment, but then she'd taken a breath and smiled. 'Of course I'm happy.' She blinked before adding, 'I do wish you and Rosie had been there with Poppy and my mum. But Ash felt it was best this way.'

Saffy had reached out and touched her shoulder gently. Even through the thick material she could feel the lines of her bones. And that had been the end of it. They never talked about Ash or their relationship again.

Until last week when Leona had messaged unexpectedly asking Saffy to meet up for a drink.

They'd met in a favourite bar and Saffy was watching the door when she first arrived. Leona's dark hair – usually so thick and full of body – looked flat and barely brushed. Her skin dry and flaky. What had happened to her beautiful, full-of-life best friend?

Leona spotted her right away and waved, awkwardly

weaving her way through groups of after-work drinkers. Her eyes darted around, as if checking out every face in there.

'Sorry,' she'd said without meeting Saffy's eyes. 'Bus was late, and it's just been one of those days.'

'You're here now, so relax.' Saffy pushed her cocktail closer and Leona picked it up and took a deep drink.

'Passion fruit martini, my favourite,' she said. 'I've been thinking about you, Saffy, about how we should catch up more. Are you and Poppy doing OK?'

'We're both fine,' Saffy said, swallowing down the tight knot in her throat and closing off that line of conversation. She didn't want to rake up the past tonight. She wanted to focus on Leona and why she'd asked to meet up.

Leona nodded and took another big gulp of her drink. Her shoulders dropped and she closed her eyes briefly. Saffy could see two pale half-moons of concealer under her eyes that she must have forgotten to blend properly, but it wasn't enough to disguise the dark circles anyway. 'That's better.' She held up her glass. 'Cheers!' she forced.

Saffy asked how Rosie was doing at school and Leona asked how the job hunting was going.

'I've got an interview next week for a data manager vacancy,' Saffy told her. 'Are you missing the hospital?'

And that's when Leona's face crumpled and she just cracked open, like an egg revealing rotten insides. Everything came spilling out all at once and it was messy and upsetting.

Saffy stares at Leona now in disbelief. *I'm so sorry, but I don't know what you're talking about . . .*

Leona looks back at her from the doorway.

'Three messages sent and then deleted,' Saffy murmurs, watching her face.

'Have you been drinking?' Leona says.

Saffy regards her with narrowed eyes. Leona's hair is lank and her eyeliner a little smudged. Apart from that she seems calm, put-together.

'I haven't been drinking, I'm just doing what you asked. You needed help and here I am.'

Leona throws her hands up, sighs and steps back. 'I haven't a clue what you're on about, but you'd better come in. You look soaked to the skin.' She ushers her inside and Saffy can hear water running and the television still blaring in the kitchen, at the end of the hallway.

Leona glances down at Saffy's feet, at the sodden suede pumps Leona has loaned her.

'Sorry about the shoes,' Saffy says. 'I'll replace them.' Leona waves her offer away and beckons her into the front room with the bay window.

Saffy follows and as Leona pushes the door to but doesn't fully close it, she can see her phone poking out of the back pocket of her jeans. 'So, tell me again why you're here?' Leona folds her arms.

'I got your messages, just after one o'clock. They said something odd like, *Don't call, can't talk. Just come.*'

Leona stares at her blankly. 'You're joking, right?'

'I got them just before I went into the interview. So I left early, grabbed a cab and came straight here.'

'You walked out of your interview?' Leona presses her fingers down on top of her straight black hair. 'Look, I don't know who it was that texted you, but it wasn't me. I've had a crazy busy day. Rosie has been off school today with a tummy ache, then I had to pick up food for dinner. We're celebrating Ash's big promotion at work. I'm sorry, Saffy, but I haven't messaged you at all today. I haven't had the time.'

'Look!' Saffy takes the phone out of her handbag and opens the chat between them, turning the screen towards

26

her. 'See, it says you've deleted them now, but I read the original messages before they disappeared.'

She watches as Leona takes the phone and scrolls up and down the thread of their chat. She reads the 'this message was deleted' notes and her eyes flick up to the top of the screen to check it's from her number. Then she swipes up to exit the app and hands Saffy her phone back. 'Well, I didn't send you any messages. That's all I know.'

'Can you show me your phone?'

'Saffy, this is ridiculous,' Leona whispers under her breath, sliding her phone out of her jeans. She glances over her shoulder as loud, canned laughter from the other room echoes down the hallway. She taps her phone screen and holds it up in front of her. 'See? Nothing there. I don't mean to sound off, but please, can we just let it drop now? You're being weird.'

Saffy takes the phone from her and studies the screen. It's open at the same message chat thread except it is now Saffy's name and her photo at the top of the screen. The last time they'd exchanged a text was yesterday morning when Saffy asked what she had planned for the day and mentioned her nerves building over today's interview. Leona had texted back saying Ash had just got a big promotion, and regarding the interview, she'd replied: *Good luck*. There is no trace of today's messages on there, nor anything to say any messages have been deleted, either.

'Maybe someone sent the messages from your phone and then deleted them,' Saffy says carefully.

'Yeah, maybe someone erased the "message deleted" notes, too,' Leona snaps. Then her voice softens. 'Or maybe you just made a mistake, Saffy.'

'I didn't make a mistake. You've seen the deleted message notifications are still on my phone. I can –'

Leona holds up a hand. 'I know you've been worried about what's happening at work and seeing Fox more. I get that. Do you want to come through and say hi to Rosie? She'd love to see you.'

The two women stare at each other for a long moment. There's a gigantic elephant in the room and Saffy is unwilling to continue ignoring it. 'I didn't make a mistake, Leona. I got those messages from your phone. *Your* number. If you can't talk, I just need to know that you and Rosie are OK. Just a simple yes or no will do.' She glances at the door. 'You only need to say the word and I can have you both out of here in record time.'

'Saffy, I know you mean well, but you're acting a bit crazy. I mean, I've told you nothing is wrong, you've even seen my phone. You're mistaken, OK? Can you just accept that?'

Leona starts to edge towards the door. She clearly wants Saffy to leave now and that's not like her. It's not like her at all. Something is wrong, she can sense it drifting in the air between them like an ill wind.

Saffy feels her shoulders stiffen. 'Can I take a look around before I go?'

'Why? Look, this is getting out of hand. I –'

Leona flinches as behind her, the door flies open and a tall, broad shape looms up from the dim hallway. Ash places his hands on Leona's shoulders. He's had his hair cut shorter since Saffy last saw him a couple of months ago and it looks as though he's trying, unsuccessfully, to grow a beard. 'Everything OK, honey?'

Leona's voice takes on a new, upbeat tone. 'Yes, everything's fine. Saffy was just passing.'

'And so you thought you'd bundle her in here?' Ash looks at her, his brown eyes twinkling. 'Saffy, I've got to say you look stressed, mate. Everything OK?'

'Everything's fine thanks, Ash.' *Mate*.

He looks at Leona and back at Saffy. Neither of them speaks. The room is papered in an oppressive teal wallpaper with a botanic gold print. The walls feel like they're closing in and cutting out the light, restricting the air in Saffy's throat.

'So then, what's new?' Ash says finally.

She looks at Leona, seeking guidance as to whether it's safe to mention the messages. The reason she's here. Leona's eyes meet hers before she looks away. 'Saffy was just passing nearby,' she says carefully.

'I thought I'd pop in and say hi.'

'Right, well don't hide away in here. Come and have a drink with us. Say hello to Rosie.'

'It's fine if you haven't got the time, Saffy. We can make it another day.' Leona steps back. 'I know you said you can't stay long.'

Leona has had every chance to tell her there's a problem before Ash even knew she'd arrived. She's said nothing at all and yet . . . something feels off in the energy between these two.

'I'd love to have a drink with you,' she says, looking at Ash. 'Thanks.'

'We're celebrating, has Leona told you?'

'Yes,' Saffy says. 'Congratulations on the promotion.'

'Thanks. Long overdue, but they finally realized I'm their biggest asset.' He winks playfully, his mouth stretching into some semblance of a self-deprecating smile, but they both know he totally means it. 'It's good you can stay a while and help us celebrate though. Come through to the kitchen.'

He signals for Saffy to follow him out of the room. She glances at Leona as she passes and she could swear her friend gives her an almost imperceptible shake of the head. Maybe,

Saffy thinks, she should have refused Ash's offer, but it's too late now. And there's not just Leona to consider in this.

'Look who came to say hi, sweetie,' Ash's voice booms as he strides into the kitchen.

Rosie looks up from watching her cartoon, a smile instantly blossoming on her sweet face when she sees Saffy. It has to be said, she doesn't look remotely unwell.

'Auntie Saffy!' she sings out and jumps up from the small sofa in front of the TV. At least someone here is happy to see her. 'Is Fox here, too?' she asks, straining her little head to peer behind Saffy.

'Not today, sweetie, but he's staying over at the week-end. Maybe you and Mummy can come over and we can watch a movie.' As she says it, it occurs to her that it would be a brilliant way of getting Leona out of the house. Who knows what Leona might say without Ash breathing down her neck.

She feels a pinch of regret as Rosie embraces her, wrapping her small, warm arms around her hips. She wishes she could see more of her. Maybe she should push to take her to the park once a week like she used to. As her godmother, she has a right to see her, surely? Now Fox is going to be around more, it's the perfect time.

For the first three years until she went to nursery, Saffy was an integral part of Rosie's life. That is, before Leona met Ash. Saffy would often take Rosie to playgroup and the park, look after her when Leona was at work. It was therapeutic for her; this bright little girl was a balm to her troubled soul. A reason to get out of bed each day.

Before she had Fox, Saffy would sometimes sleep over at Leona's house when Leona worked a night shift at the hospital and Neil was out entertaining overseas clients. Rosie also adored Poppy and she'd come over to Saffy's, where the two of them would spend hours together, making bead jewellery, watching TV, singing karaoke.

And then Leona met Ash. Very quickly, Saffy saw a lot less of her friend and even less of her goddaughter.

Rosie was the result of a brief, disastrous relationship Leona had with Harris, a man she met on a training course. He was a doctor, he told her, in the UK only briefly for medical training, but she fell head over heels in love with him. That was always Leona's way. She'd go long spells without being in a relationship and then meet someone who would become 'the one' virtually overnight.

Within a matter of weeks, she was researching visas and regulations to follow Harris back to the small Greek island where he lived alone in a white house covered in purple bougainvillea that overlooked the ocean. He'd painted it all so beautifully over expensive meals out and candlelit nights in.

Saffy had met him a bunch of times and had a bad feeling but Leona, true to form, didn't want to hear it. 'Can't you be happy for me?' she'd snapped. 'Just this once?'

She'd found out the truth when his Greek fiancée contacted her. They'd been together for six years and were planning to get married that Christmas and hopefully start a family. They lived in a crumbling basement flat in Athens and it turned out he wasn't a doctor at all, but a health assistant.

'Red or white, Saffy?' Ash asks, holding up a bottle in each hand.

'Just a soft drink for me thanks, Ash. I'm picking Fox up from nursery in just over an hour.'

Rosie pulls away from her and jumps up and down. 'Mummy, Mummy, can I show Auntie Saffy my new bedroom?'

She senses Leona stiffen beside her. 'I don't think Auntie Saffy has the time, darling, and she's seen your bedroom before.' Leona gives me a tight smile. 'It's not really new. Ash just painted it pink.'

Rosie looks affronted. 'And I've had new bedding!'

Despite her polite refusal, Ash hands Saffy a glass of wine with a smirk and she places it down on the worktop. He winks at his stepdaughter. 'Sure, pumpkin, take her up,' he says to a whoop of delight from Rosie. 'Saffy, are you going to stay for tea?'

She's never known him to be so friendly. It's quite unnerving now she's aware what he's capable of. At least she knows where she stands when he's being an unsociable so-and-so. When she first met Ash and looked at his face – a handsome face, she can't deny that – it was like stuff was happening behind his eyes. Almost as if he were projecting an image to people to showcase his genial, gregarious personality, but really that was just a cover for darker rumination that was happening inside. Of course she has never mentioned this to Leona. But standing here now, Saffy gets that same feeling, like looking into the eyes of a predator.

'Thanks for the offer, but I need to get off soon.'

'Leona's making her famous Tuscan chicken bake.' He laughs. 'Just saying.'

'Saffy's probably forgotten all about it,' Leona says, her voice faint. 'It's been a while.'

'I could never forget your Tuscan bake, Leona.' Saffy smiles. 'Thanks for the offer, Ash, but I can't stay. I'll take a peek at Rosie's bedroom and then leave you all in peace.'

She watches as Leona breathes out, but she can see her features are still etched with a subtle tension. Saffy should know.

It's the expression she's had from her early teens when she was trying very hard to hide something but not quite pulling it off.

5

Saffy

'I choosed the paint and new bedding all on my own, Auntie Saffy.' Rosie chatters on adorably as they head out of the kitchen. Whatever might be wrong in this house doesn't seem to be affecting her. 'I got lots and LOTS more toys than you've ever see'd!'

Rosie continues to babble as they climb. Saffy catches bits about school and how her friend might be coming to play next week.

On her last visit here, Leona and Ash had been in the house about six months. They'd been about to start redecorating and making the place their own. Now, the stairs carpet is a plush silvery-grey colour and the wallpaper features a pretty feather design. But as soon as they reach the top step, it feels to Saffy like they're stepping into a different house altogether.

The old wallpaper has been stripped off and it is not a clean job. Ragged tongues of dry, yellow backing paper hang off the walls and it looks as if it's been like this a while. The plush carpet does not extend up here. The whole landing is green underlay underfoot, the carpet grippers exposed and lethal-looking nails upended, just waiting for Rosie to step on them with her little bare feet.

It's like the money ran out suddenly and they just stopped right in the middle of it. Which is puzzling seeing as Ash is doing so well at work.

Saffy is led to a door bearing a pretty 'Rosie' nameplate. The room is painted in a bright pink with Disney princess bedding. There is only underlay on the floor in this room too, although a couple of small scatter rugs have been placed; one next to the bed and the other in the middle of the room.

Rosie turns to look at her, beaming. 'This is MY bedroom, Auntie Saffy!'

'Wow, I love the colour! And that beautiful Disney bedding . . . This is the best room ever, Rosie!'

'Mummy says I can have a pink carpet soon.' She points to a short rail in the corner holding dresses and other garments. 'And a new wardrobe, too.' Underneath the rail, small tops have been folded in a pile on the floor with loose socks and underwear beside them.

'You can sit on the bed if you like and I'll show you all my toys.' Rosie eyes her hopefully and Saffy will not disappoint her.

'I can't wait!' She places her hands on the windowsill and peers down. Rosie's room looks out over the back garden. In contrast to the front of the house, the grass is wild here, the borders strewn with dandelions. It clearly hasn't been cut for weeks while the neighbouring gardens either side are neat and maintained.

'You get out the toys, and I'll just pop to the bathroom.'

Rosie nods happily and begins to arrange the soft toys around the floor in an arc next to the bed.

Saffy steps out on to the landing and pauses a moment, listening. She can hear voices and the clattering of glasses and plates down in the kitchen. She creeps down the landing to the slightly open door she knows leads to Leona and Ash's bedroom. This space is a little bigger. There's a beige carpet in here with a heavily flattened pile. The substantial oak fitted wardrobes are dated but still serviceable. Despite this, piles of clothes lie everywhere. Toppling into each other and covering every surface and large areas of the floor.

The curtains are drawn, the bed unmade. Saffy walks across the room, peeling the edge of the fabric away to look out of the window. The view is the same as Rosie's, but the windowsill is littered with rubbish. Half-full cups of cold, skinned coffee, old receipts and screwed-up tissues.

Saffy moves back to the middle of the room, looking for something, anything that might give her a clue as to why Leona would send messages crying out for help then delete them and deny it. There's so much stuff lying around in here, it's hard to pick out the detail. It doesn't look wrecked, as if they've had a physical fight. It's just in serious disarray.

The Leona she knows – *knew* – always liked to keep things reasonably tidy. Downstairs, this house looks smart. It is organized and functional, exactly how Leona likes to operate. But up here it's a different story.

If Ash is doing so amazingly at work, then where is the evidence of that?

Saffy can still hear the two of them talking and moving around downstairs, so she moves over to the other side of the room, taking less care to be quiet. A small pile of women's magazines sits on the floor next to Leona's side of the bed. She spots a small yellow sticky note amongst the pages of a magazine tucked underneath. She opens it at the marked page and peers closer at an article entitled: '*Are you being emotionally controlled?*' She squeezes her eyes shut briefly and moves on. The top of the chest of drawers is cluttered with dusty toiletries, a couple of the brightly coloured silk scarves Leona favours, costume jewellery and a small pile of loose change.

Saffy pauses as something catches her eye, shining behind a bottle of hand cream. She steps forward and looks a little closer, her heart beginning to race as her fingers reach out. *It can't be.*

'Everything OK up there, you two?' Leona's voice calls from the bottom of the stairs. Saffy jumps back as if she's been scalded and rushes out of the bedroom, pushing her hand into her jacket pocket.

'We're fine,' she calls back. 'Rosie's just showing me her soft toy collection!'

Saffy hears a thumping noise above her and then footsteps start to climb. She darts back inside Rosie's bedroom where her goddaughter is just placing a white teddy bear in a little tea-party tableau. Quickly, she sits down on the bed, touching her pocket just as Leona appears in the doorway.

'Looks like you two are having a lovely time.' She looks around the room.

Saffy beckons her to come in. 'Leona, are you sure everything is OK?'

She opens her mouth to speak and then immediately clamps it shut.

'You're doing a great job here, Rosie,' Ash says, suddenly appearing behind Leona in the doorway. His stature dwarfs her, his hand resting on the back of her neck. It could resemble a touch of love, but Leona's face is scrunched up, her body tense. 'Have you told Auntie Saffy all their names?' he continues.

'Not yet, I've been getting them ready while she's been out.'

'Out?' Ash says.

'To the bathroom,' Saffy offers.

'You were gone ages, Auntie Saffy,' Rosie says with a small frown.

She laughs off Rosie's comment and reaches for one of the toys. When she looks up again, both Leona and Ash are staring at her.

Ash slides his arm around his wife's narrow shoulders and pins his dark eyes to hers.

Are you being emotionally controlled?

'We'll leave you to it then,' Leona says slowly.

Rosie hands her a fluffy pink bear. Saffy smiles and takes it, and when she looks back, both Leona and Ash have gone.

6

Saffy

Saffy sits with Rosie in her bedroom, trying to listen for any raised voices downstairs as she is taken through an endless narration of names. Just before she's about to embark on a third recital of their names, Saffy shuffles to the edge of the bed.

'I have to go and pick up Fox from nursery soon, Rosie, but I'll call to see you and Mummy again very soon. I promise.'

'Can I come?' Her face lights up. 'I like playing the ship game with Fox.'

Saffy has never heard of the ship game, but her heart squeezes. Rosie loves him so much and yet they hardly see each other. 'You have to stay here to celebrate Daddy's new job. But I'll ask Mummy if she'll bring you over to play with Fox at the weekend. How's that?'

Her small body sags. 'Why is my mummy sad?' She begins to stroke the fur of a grey seal.

'*Is* she sad?' Saffy ducks her head in front of her face, so Rosie is forced to look at her. She blinks and puts down the seal and turns to pick up a caramel-coloured lion with enormous black, empty eyes.

'She cries when Daddy is mean,' she says simply. Rosie was only three when Leona met Ash and now she calls him Daddy with ease.

It feels wrong to try and get information out of a child,

39

but what choice does Saffy have? If Leona sent the messages earlier and then changed her mind about involving Saffy in whatever is happening here, then maybe she should just accept that. Leona only has to say if she wants her to back off. But Rosie . . . well, Rosie is different.

'Have Mummy and Daddy been arguing, sweetie?' she says carefully.

A raft of emotion travels across her tiny, forlorn face. She nods but doesn't speak. Saffy thinks about the mysterious tummy ache she's complained about. Maybe what's happening between Leona and Ash is affecting her after all.

Saffy glances at the door to check Ash has not silently returned. She reaches forward and strokes her goddaughter's hair. Thinks about the item she found on the chest of drawers that is now tucked into her pocket. 'What happened, Rosie? Can you tell Auntie Saffy what made Mummy sad?'

She takes a big breath in, her narrow chest rising with the effort.

'Daddy stayed out very, very late and when he came home, he shouted and it waked me up. Mummy cried.' Her face begins to crumple, and Saffy reaches for her hand and gently squeezes it.

'Don't get upset,' she says, her heart thumping at the thought of having to explain to Leona that she's been questioning her. 'Do you know why Daddy stayed out so late?'

'I don't know,' she says in a small voice. 'But Mummy got angry when he wouldn't stop drinking the wine and it was horrible.'

Saffy stands up. 'It sounds as if it was really upsetting, Rosie. Tell you what, let's go downstairs and I'll help you take a few toys down to watch cartoons with you before I leave to pick up Fox. How's that?'

'Thanks, Auntie Saffy!' Her worries alleviated for the time

being, she jumps up, causing the circle of toys closest to her to skittle over.

Downstairs, Rosie runs into the kitchen and turns the volume up on the now muted television. Leona glances at Saffy, and Ash turns to the sink, dipping his hands into soapy water. Saffy piles soft toys on the small sofa next to Rosie before walking back into the hallway. She opens the Uber app, pushes away thoughts of her dwindling bank balance and what might happen if she doesn't get another secure job soon, and orders a cab that is currently twelve minutes away. That should leave her plenty of time to get to nursery with a few minutes to spare.

Back in the kitchen, Rosie is happily absorbed in her cartoon and Saffy walks over to the small island where Leona is chopping salad. She keeps her eyes on the small, sharp knife as it cuts effortlessly through the purple and green leaves, the wet, gleaming blade hitting the wooden board with a regular dull thud.

Leona's phone is face down on the countertop, away from the food prep area. It would be pretty easy, while Leona was distracted, for Ash to swipe it off as he walked by, send three short messages in the hallway, delete them and return the phone with Leona none the wiser.

But why on earth would Ash want to get Saffy over to the house? He's spent most of his time ensuring she keeps away. No. That can't be right.

Lowering her voice, Saffy says, 'Neil's letting me keep Fox for the weekend. Will you bring Rosie over to visit?'

Leona nods but doesn't stop chopping. 'I'll speak to Ash, see what we've got on,' she says quietly.

'Just for an hour or so. The kids can play, and we can have a glass of wine . . .' She hesitates. She needs to make clear that Ash is not invited. 'We can have a good chat. Just the two of us.'

Leona stops chopping and squeezes her eyes shut momentarily. An expression that smacks of regret. Of perhaps being in a dilemma.

Saffy stands very still, canned laughter from the television filling her ears. It was a loaded suggestion and she shouldn't have said it. Not here, not now.

'What was that?' Ash seems to loom up from nowhere again, butting into their conversation.

'Saffy was just saying she's got Fox at the weekend.' Leona scrapes the chopped, damp leaves on to a plate. 'I was just thinking, it would be lovely to pop over for an hour with Rosie.'

'The three of us, you mean?' Ash leans forward to open the wine cooler, meaning Saffy has to move out of the way to avoid his arm pressing against her leg.

'I . . . Yes, course. If you'd like to come,' Leona says quickly.

'Oh, I'm sure Saffy doesn't want me intruding on your little *chat.*' His tone is incongruously bright and jolly.

'Not at all, the three of you would be very welcome,' Saffy says, thinking about the dark smudges that are concealed under Leona's cuff.

Ash peers into the cooler and then closes the door without touching anything. He doesn't move away, so Saffy takes another step back.

'We'll have a think and let you know, if that's all right,' Leona says. She picks up the knife and starts to scrape tiny green flecks from the chopping board. 'I know Ash was planning to do a bit more celebrating this weekend.'

Ash laughs. A hard, hacking sound. 'You make it sound like it's all about me.'

'It's amazing what you've achieved.' Leona wipes the blade

of the knife with a cloth and resumes her scraping. '*You're amazing, Ash. I'm so proud of you.*'

It must be exhausting, constantly treading on eggshells, trying to avoid your partner having a narcissistic meltdown and everything that brings with it.

Cruelty. Disrespect. Bruises.

Ash presses his face closer to Saffy's. 'I was going to suggest you and Fox might like to join us at the weekend, but then I forgot you rarely go out these days. Still battening the hatches at the first sign of dusk, Saffy?'

'Ash!' Leona hisses and glances over at Rosie, who is still absorbed in the TV.

Ash knows her family history, knows what happened not that far from here on a cold December night three years ago, just a couple of months before he met Leona. But, so far as she knows, he hasn't got a clue about her life now.

'I just meant that's why I was so surprised to find you'd dropped by today,' he adds.

When neither Ash nor Saffy speaks, Leona says, 'It's lovely to see you, Saffy. I'm so glad you came by. Rosie often asks about you and Fox.'

She's pushing the words out, saying all the right things. But her voice is monotone and she's still scraping the now pristine chopping board. Clutching the handle of the knife so hard, it's becoming difficult for her to use.

'Hey, I'm only kidding, mate,' Ash looks at Saffy. The winning smile and twinkling eyes are back. 'Hardly go out myself these days.'

Leona turns to him and their eyes meet for a moment or two.

Daddy stayed out very, very late.

Ash walks over to the sink and picks up a dishcloth. While

he's there, he pours himself another goldfish-bowl-sized glass of dark red wine and takes a gulp.

'Well, let me know anyway . . . about the weekend. It would be lovely to see you all.' Saffy hooks her handbag strap over her shoulder. 'I'd better get going to pick Fox up from nursery.'

Leona puts down the knife and squeezes Saffy's arm. 'I'm so pleased for you . . . about having Fox over more. It's brilliant news.'

'Yeah, it's great news,' Ash says, his dark eyes boring into Saffy's. 'Must feel like you've got an awful lot of making up to do with the poor lad.'

Leona opens her mouth to say something and Saffy squeezes her hand, ignoring Ash completely. 'I'll see you soon,' she says. She kisses the top of Rosie's head and then walks out of the room.

On the way to nursery, Saffy puts her hand into her jacket pocket and touches the item she removed from Leona and Ash's bedroom. It was such a shock to see it there and her instinct had been to shove it into her jacket pocket.

It feels cool and fluid against her fingers but she doesn't remove it. Not here in the cab. Not until she feels ready to see it again without getting emotional and she's had the time to properly consider what it might mean.

7
Saffy

Saffy reaches into her damp handbag, pulling out her phone. She turns away from the rain-lashed cab window, finds the number on her recent calls list and presses it. It is snatched up after one ring.

'Yeah?'

The morose music she seems to favour these days is turned down.

'Poppy, it's me. You said you were going to call at the house later for your textbooks.'

'Yeah.'

'I'm on my way to pick up Fox from nursery but I've just called to see Leona.'

A beat or two of silence then, '*And?*'

The words all rush into her throat at once before falling out in one big mess. 'I'm really worried about her, Poppy. Rosie too. I think there's something odd happening there.'

'What're you talking about?' Poppy sighs. 'Odd how, exactly?'

Saffy's promise of confidentiality to Leona echoes in her ears.

'I'll explain when I see you. What have you been up to today . . . more online lectures?'

'Haven't been online. I'm trying to write my essay, remember?'

The English essay. The one she's been given extra time to do by her tutor.

'Is your door locked?'

'What?' She sounds distracted.

'Have you locked your door?'

'Yes!' Then, 'I think it's locked . . . yep, I'm sure it is.'

'Can you check?'

'Christ, Saffy. I told you I'm not putting up with this any –'

'Just check, Poppy. Please.' After deferring her course after the attack, Poppy resumed her degree the following September, moving back into student digs, an old house converted into four student flats.

If she's at her desk or lying on her bed then it's just a few paces to the door and the extra bolt lock Saffy fitted herself.

'Hang on.' A chair scraping on the hard floor. Muttering and huffing. She pictures the small pine table they'd picked up from a second-hand store, scattered with her paperwork, and the MacBook Saffy is still paying for will probably be open on there. Just a regular afternoon on an ordinary day. Except anything can happen if the door is unlocked.

Poppy picks up the phone again. 'It's locked. Satisfied?'

'I'm just looking out for you.'

Her voice softens a touch. 'There are three other students living here, Saffy. They'd come if I screamed.' For a second, she sounds so vulnerable, as if she's on the edge of tears.

Saffy's breath catches in her throat, and for a moment or two, she can't speak. Her sister seizes the opportunity to flip back to her default defence. Being angry.

'I've told you not to constantly mother me. I'm not a kid any more. Jeez, just chill, can't you?'

It's true Saffy still thinks of her as a young girl, although she's now in her second year at Nottingham Trent University. Poppy hates it when she acts like their mum used to. Saffy has tried to explain countless times that she doesn't even know she's doing it. Before their mum died, she made Saffy

46

give her her word that she'd take care of Poppy and keep her safe. She intends to keep that promise no matter what.

'I'm sorry. I just need to know you're safe,' Saffy whispers.

'I know, and I am safe. I'm not scared any more, Saffy, and you shouldn't be, either. We both need to live our lives. You live yours and I'll live mine, yeah?' She's trying not to rush off the call, but Saffy senses she's keen to bring their conversation to an end.

The cab slows to a stop in traffic and someone walks by, folding a newspaper. Saffy is distracted, catching sight of the black, weighted words of the headline: *City's Crime Rate Soars*.

She sits there rigid, liquid fear trickling down her spine.

When she looks back down at her phone, she sees that Poppy has already ended the call.

8

Poppy

Poppy rolls over on to her side on the bed, props herself up on an elbow and looks down.

She'd met the guy in a bar last night. It was late when he'd made a beeline for her, then plied her with expensive cocktails when her housemates shared a cab back. Had some corny line about coming straight from the airport and walking into her life. It was timely enough after an apparently promising recent relationship had turned out to be a bit of a damp squib and finished a few weeks earlier.

Harry was her 'type', Poppy supposed. Good-looking in a wild sort of way, quite a bit older than her with a lot of swagger. Which she tended to like. But there was something different about him. Something *dangerous* that made her tingle.

'Come on, tell me who that was on the phone,' he says, smiling. He doesn't seem to care that his teeth need brushing or that he's desperate for a shower, and Poppy kind of wants him all the more for that.

'It was my sister. She's eleven years older and likes to check up on me from time to time.'

'And what was she worried about?'

'Oh, something and nothing. She's obsessed with the news headlines.'

'Tut, tut . . . you didn't even check the door as you claimed,' he says with lazy admiration. His fingertips trace gently over the smooth curve of her hip and down into the dip of her waist where he digs them in firmly, causing her to wince. 'Disobeying your sister like that. I can see I'm going to have to watch you.'

'It was too late to check the door,' Poppy says. 'I already let the dangerous man inside my room.'

He grins and presses his face close to hers. 'You have no idea.'

She smells sweat and his stubble grazes her chin as he starts to kiss her, his hot tongue probing.

The squirming starts in the pit of Poppy's stomach. She squeezes her eyes shut and endures the feeling. She allows herself to float away to the faraway place where she feels safe and removed from everything and everyone around her.

Where she can forget about who she is and what happened to her.

9

Saffy

There's been an accident on the outskirts of the city and so the cab's progress is unusually slow. She starts to fret about getting to Fox on time. Saffy takes her Thursday responsibility for Fox very seriously. As with most other areas of her life, she has stringent plans in place to ensure nothing can go amiss.

The traffic, the grey sky and the never-ending rain seem to permeate the car. Saffy doesn't want to open the window, so she's forced to breathe in the thick, oppressive air.

She'd like to ask the driver how long he thinks the journey will take now, but he's been on the phone since picking her up outside Leona's house. He's speaking in low, serious tones in a language she doesn't recognize, his eyes pinned to the road.

After driving freely for five minutes, the cab slows, caught up in yet another snarl of traffic. But Fox's nursery is located just a couple of streets away now.

'Here will be fine, thanks.' Saffy leans forward and taps on the glass before getting out and walking quickly to the road where the nursery's entrance is located.

As usual when she approaches, a few heads turn before looking quickly away again. Nobody has spoken to her or acknowledged her and yet, by the way they send meaningful glances to each other, they all seem to recognize that this is Fox Cardle's mother.

You know, Fox Cardle, who is being raised by his father because his mother is so lacking.

She imagines that's the sort of thing they say about her, these young, glossy mothers with their permanent lip liner and eyelashes thick as yard brushes. '*Russian* lashes,' Poppy sighs and corrects her whenever she comments on them.

Saffy doesn't need anyone passing judgement on her, because she knows what she is. She's the mother who isn't a proper mother, the mother who was too weak to protect her only child and put his needs before her own.

But that was then and this is now, and Saffy is going to make it up to her son. She will be the best mother any woman can possibly be.

When the doors open on to the play area at three fifteen, she surges forward with the other parents. Fox is one of the first to be ushered out by the teacher, his shock of white-blond hair making him easy to spot.

Saffy has left it too long to push through the crowd of adult collectors and now Fox must wait until the teacher hands over other children before supervising his handover.

'Mummy today, Fox,' Saffy says brightly, ruffling his hair when it's her turn.

'He's doing so well, Ms Morris,' the class teacher tells Saffy. 'He loves looking at picture books and he tells me you read a story to him every night at home, so well done! He's got a new book to take home today.'

Saffy forces a smile and takes Fox's hand. 'That's brilliant. Thank you so much!'

She guides her son away from the crowded area, an ache beginning in her stomach. She didn't know nursery gave Fox books to take home. Neil hasn't mentioned it. She smiles down at him.

'Choc choc?' Fox says hopefully, looking up at her with wide blue eyes.

'After tea,' she kisses his smooth, warm cheek. 'You can have some chocolate after tea.'

'Me want choc choc now.'

She takes his hand and distracts him from the subject of candy by setting a challenge of who can be first to spot the bus as it comes around the corner.

'Me spot bus!' He jumps up and down when the bus appears. 'Me win.'

When they get seats and the bus trundles off, Saffy pats his folder and says, 'You are doing so well looking at books! Who reads stories to you at Daddy's house?'

'Mummy.' Fox beams and looks up at her, his eyes searching her crestfallen expression before he corrects himself. 'Mummy Mira.'

Back home at last, she turns up the heating, makes Fox a drink and sits him in front of the TV for a few minutes while she pops upstairs and strips off her damp clothes.

She hangs her jacket up without emptying her pocket, hooking the coat hanger on the back of her bedroom door. It's still not the right time to face her feelings about what she found in Leona's bedroom. There is a chance she might dissolve and she can't afford for that to happen when her young son is here.

For speed, Saffy wraps her warm dressing gown around her and goes back downstairs to make Fox's tea. She peers around the door to see him happily drinking his juice and staring at the bright, noisy television. She puts some whole-wheat pasta on to boil and takes out the dish of vegetable sauce she made from scratch for him yesterday.

They chatted about all sorts of things during the bus ride

home: *PAW Patrol*, Neil's neighbour's new pug puppy, the sandcastle he built at nursery today . . . Saffy should feel full and warm inside, but since he mentioned *Mummy Mira*, a tentacle of ice has coiled itself around her heart.

Mummy Mira. Are they serious? Saffy has known about Mira for a while, but she and Neil aren't married yet. Mira is just Mira. Fox doesn't need another mummy.

Saffy makes herself a strong coffee and takes it into the living room. She laughs with Fox in all the right places at his current favourite cartoon, but she feels so restless and is not as invested as she'd usually be.

A message notification pops up and a blip of panic pops in Saffy's chest in case it's from Leona. But it's from Neil.

Meeting delayed. Might not get to you until 7 or bit later. Sorry.

That's OK with Saffy. It's only four o'clock now and more time spent with Fox is always good news. She'd like to start planning their weekend, decide what it is they're going to do – what they'll eat and the places they will go. But her mind is still full of Leona and Rosie and her visit to the house. The deleted messages.

Fox doesn't want to stop watching *PAW Patrol*, so she decides to be lenient with her sitting-at-the-table-to-eat rule and brings their pasta meals in on trays with plenty of kitchen roll to mop up any of Fox's spills.

The rain starts up harder again, spattering noisily at the window. Unenthusiastically, Saffy chews her food and stares at the water-streaked windows, inhaling the deep, nutty aroma of the coffee.

'Eat your pasta, sweetie.' Fox stares at the TV, ignoring his food. She loads up a fork and he opens his mouth, his eyes never leaving the screen. She wonders if Mummy Mira does the same for him.

Saffy does not drink her coffee. She's shaky enough and needs to snap out of this spiralling anxiety. Despite her worries, she still has blessings to count.

Leona appears to be fine, after all the drama. Saffy got to see little Rosie, and in a couple of days, she'll have Fox with her for the entire weekend. She is going to give him the best time, away from the fear and unidentified threats hovering over her. She'll keep him safe and it will be the start, she hopes, of a new beginning. An important first step towards her and Neil properly sharing custody of their son.

The sound of the front door opening startles her. She glances at the wall clock and sees it's past five. Poppy rattles her keys and calls out, 'Only me!'

Her sister often pops back home and Saffy encourages it. She walks into the kitchen now, shrugging a frayed denim jacket from her narrow shoulders. As usual, her shoulder-length dark blonde hair is woven into two neat plaits. Poppy wears flared jeans and platform sandals, and a skimpy, knitted top clings to her petite frame. Her fingernails are painted in a glittery purple. She looks like she just blew in via a seventies disco portal.

'Oh, hey dude!' Fox looks up and grins, reciprocating Poppy's high-five before his eyes search out the cartoon again. She raises an eyebrow at his food tray and turns to Saffy. 'What happened to your weird obsession about only eating at the table?'

'It died a death when Bluey the dog turned my son into a zombie.' Saffy sets her own tray aside and stands up. 'You OK? I'll make us some coffee.'

'Yes, Saffy, I'm OK. Look!' She dances in front of Saffy, waving her hands in the air for dramatic effect, silver bangles jangling. 'I survived the afternoon, despite your massive panic that the door might not be locked.'

Her top rides up an inch or two and Saffy spots an angry red patch on her waist.

'What's that mark?'

'I walked into the corner of my desk.' Poppy follows her stare and gives her skin a quick rub. 'No need for you to worry about security any more, anyway. We've all agreed we'll be more vigilant with the front door and stop leaving it off the latch. With the city's crime rate supposedly shooting up and everything.'

'Oh God, is that what you've been doing?' Saffy's fingers flutter up to her throat.

Poppy groans. 'Everybody does it! We all know each other from uni, so we're always popping in and out of each other's houses.'

'Did you get your work done?'

'What?'

'Your essay. That's what you've been doing all day, isn't it?'

'Oh yeah, right. It's coming on well. Nearly finished.' Poppy looks down at her phone.

Saffy turns on the tap and starts to fill the kettle. 'Hey, can I ask you a question?'

'Oh God. What now?' Poppy places her phone face down on the side and folds her arms.

'It's nothing bad. I just want to know how you delete a message once it's been sent.' Saffy opens the app on her phone.

'Go on,' Poppy says with a flicker of interest.

'So, if you send someone a message on, say, WhatsApp and then delete it –'

'You'll get a notification saying, "Your message was deleted." And the other person gets one saying, "This message was deleted."'

'But can you delete *that* message, too?'

'Sure. Look, we can try it.' Poppy taps for a few seconds on her phone and Saffy gets a notification ping on her device. The message reads: *Test.* She opens it up and shivers as the message disappears before her eyes. Replaced by the words: *This message was deleted.*

'And now, I can delete that message on my phone, too.' Poppy shows her the screen as she deletes the words: *Your message was deleted.* 'See, no trace I sent anything at all!' she says triumphantly. 'Why do you want to know, anyway?' Poppy grins. 'What are you up to?'

'Nothing!' Saffy looks away. 'I just wondered, that's all.'

'Yeah, right.' Poppy snorts and throws her a knowing look. Turning around, she opens the fridge door and stands staring into it. From behind, she's so slender. After the attack she'd curled up into a ball and wouldn't stop screaming for anyone but her big sister. Now, Saffy wants to wrap her arms around her, insist she moves back in with her. But no matter what she does, or what she says, she always feels these days like she can never quite reach her.

'Neil's agreed I can keep Fox at the weekend,' Saffy says. 'Two full days, unsupervised.'

'That's cool.' Poppy plucks out a yogurt, studies the label before replacing it and closing the fridge door. 'I'm out on Saturday but the three of us could do something together on Sunday if you like?'

'I'd love that!' Saffy's heart lifts a little. 'Where are you going on Saturday night?' She spoons instant coffee into the mugs.

A beat of silence. 'Oh, just around a few of the student bars in town. It's someone's birthday who lives a couple of houses down from ours. Another student.'

Saffy bites the inside of her lip and turns to face Poppy.

'I saw Leona and Rosie today. I've asked them to come over this weekend to see Fox.'

'Sounds good. So why are you acting weird about it?' Poppy starts to peel a Babybel from the fridge.

'I'm not acting weird. It's just . . . I think there's something wrong with Leona. With her relationship.'

Poppy is just about to bite the cheese but lowers her hand. 'Oh? What makes you say that?'

'I saw them today, her and Ash, and . . . I think there's something she's not saying. So I thought if I get her over here, away from him, she might feel more relaxed in talking about it.'

Poppy puts her snack down untouched on the side. 'You know, you really need to stop interfering in people's lives, Saffy. Why do you constantly feel you need to save the world?'

'It's not that . . .'

'It's *exactly* that. It must be so exhausting being you, that's all I can say. Have you ever considered giving yourself a break? And giving everyone else a break while you're at it?'

Saffy turns to look at her sister, for the first time realizing she thinks it's an option. 'Poppy, don't you think that if I could, I would? I can't help worrying.'

'Still, I don't know what your problem is with Ash.'

Saffy pops a three-cheese pizza in the oven for Poppy's tea while Poppy takes her coffee through to sit with Fox. She cuts a few tomatoes into tiny chunks and drizzles them with olive oil and balsamic vinegar. She smiles when she hears hoots of laughter in the other room.

Saffy keeps getting pains in her chest when she takes a deep breath in. The stress of what happened at Leona's house, and now the worry about Poppy's safety, is pulling her down like a physical thing. For a moment she almost calls Neil to ask him about the 'Mummy Mira' thing. But she must keep a level head and that means avoiding speaking to Neil while she feels emotional. She'd felt so positive before the interview when everything seemed to be falling into place. Now, the familiar cloud of anxiety is hovering again.

She adds seasoning and puts the dish of tomato salad in the fridge to marinate for ten minutes.

Today has dredged up so much insecurity. She feels like a feather in a storm, whisked back to the past then hurled into imagined future horrors.

'You must learn to forgive yourself, Saffy,' her therapist once said. 'Or the guilt will rob you of finding any joy again.'

Saffy hadn't recognized it at the time, but it turned out the therapist was right. Slowly, very slowly, she felt able to hold her head above the water. Just for a short time at first. She looked around and saw a world she had almost forgotten about. It had been a shock to realize that while she'd been struggling beneath the water, life had carried on as normal around her. There were people in the real world who still cared about and needed her. Her son, and for a while – at least until things fell apart – Neil. She still had Poppy and back then, they were both still very close to Leona. Saffy realized she had tried to do the best she could at the time. And through the discomfort, she kept coming back to that thought. Kept trying to forgive herself.

The doorbell ringing startles her and the whole kitchen looks hazy. The pizza! She rushes over to the oven and sees she has set the temperature dial far too high.

'Get the door, can you, Poppy?' she shouts, grabbing a tea towel and wrenching open the oven.

'Coming!' She hears her sister rush along the hallway as the doorbell rings again.

Saffy pulls out the circular baking tray and groans, although it could have been worse. The edge of the pizza is blackened, but thankfully, the middle is still OK. She hears voices coming from the hall and quickly shoves the tray on the hob to cool. It sounds like Poppy has already let the caller inside.

She walks into the hallway, wiping her hands on the tea towel. 'Everything OK?'

But Saffy can see there is a definite problem. Two women in trouser suits are standing in the hallway holding up identity cards to Poppy.

A bolt of panic almost winds her. *Leona.*

Poppy's face is creased with concern. 'They say they need to speak to you, Saffy.'

Dropping the tea towel, she rushes forward. 'What is it? What's happened?'

The short officer in the navy suit with the red hair starts to make introductions. 'I'm DS Rose MacFarlane and this is my colleague, DI Fatima Shah. We're here to . . .' Her voice fades as a whooshing noise floods Saffy's ears.

'Has something happened to my friend?' she manages to say. 'Leona Bannatyne?'

Stone-cold fear pools in her chest. She turns at a shuffling noise behind her as Fox appears in the doorway and says, 'Who is it?' When he sees the detectives, he falters and steps back again.

'My son.' Saffy flutters her fingers in Fox's direction. 'Has something happened?'

Shah, tall and slim in a well-cut grey suit, glances at Poppy's panicked face. 'Is there somewhere we can talk privately?' she says in a clipped voice.

'Through here.' Saffy looks at her sister, sees the shadows that cross her pale face. 'Poppy, take Fox into the kitchen and put the television on in there. The pizza is ready, salad in the fridge.'

Fox stares at the detectives with wide eyes. He looks up at Saffy for reassurance, gripping briefly on to her top as

Poppy scoops him up into her arms and heads for the kitchen.

'Mummy won't be long, darling. You stay with Pops,' Saffy calls to him but he buries his face into Poppy's shoulder.

She leads the two detectives further into the house and through to the living room. She picks up the remote control and turns off the blaring television.

Her insides feel like liquid but somehow her legs manage to keep her upright.

Saffy has no idea what it is they're here to tell her, but she can tell by their grim expressions it's bad. It's something very, very bad.

10

Saffy

Saffy closes the living room door behind the detectives. 'Please, sit down,' she says, her throat dry and sore. 'What's happened?'

There's something odd about the way they're both looking at her. There are no sympathetic expressions or considerate gestures.

Shah fixes her flinty eyes on hers, and Saffy can almost feel the hostility rolling off her. 'Ms Morris, back in the hallway you asked us if something had happened to your friend, Leona Bannatyne. Why did you instantly assume that?'

'I've been dreading something like this happening.' Saffy can hear the desperation in her own voice.

'Something like what, exactly?'

Wrapping her arms around herself, Saffy says, 'I don't know.' She does know, of course, but she's not sure if the two officers are aware of what's been going on in Leona's marriage.

MacFarlane says, 'Ms Morris, where were you between one and five p.m. today?'

Unnerved by her stern tone, Saffy sits up a little straighter. 'I left a job interview just after one o'clock and got a cab to my friend Leona's house. I stayed a while and then got an Uber back to the nursery to pick up Fox. We got the bus home.'

MacFarlane's pen hovers over a notebook. 'So you arrived back here at what time?'

'About four, I think. Maybe slightly later because of the bus.' They've been here for a few minutes and they're yet to tell her the reason for their visit. 'What's happened? Is it Leona?'

'We are here regarding Leona Bannatyne, but this also concerns her husband, Ashley Bannatyne, and their young daughter.'

Saffy feels so sick that she let Leona so easily convince her she was fine. She *knew* something was wrong. She could feel it and yet she had left her and Rosie to deal with a potentially dangerous situation. 'I thought Leona was in trouble, that's why I went over there.'

'Oh really? And why did you think that?'

Her mind is working overtime trying to second-guess what has happened and to make sense of the uncomfortable vibe of hostility she is getting.

'I was waiting for my interview when I got three Whats-App messages from Leona asking me to go over to the house. The messages were immediately deleted, so I thought maybe it was a mistake. But she's never done anything like that before and I was really worried about her, so I jumped in a cab and went over there.'

'Can you show me your phone?' Shah says.

Saffy reaches for her phone on the coffee table and opens Leona's message thread. 'There were three short messages, as if she'd sent them quickly, in a panic. Leona sounded scared and was asking for my help. But this is all it says now.'

Shah takes the phone from her and peers at the screen before handing it back. 'So all three messages were deleted and yet you still rushed over to the house?'

'It was a shock to get a plea for help out of the blue like that. Before the messages were deleted, I mean.' Saffy's cheeks feel hot. 'I was in no doubt that Leona was in trouble. I thought there might be a reason she'd had to delete them.'

'What kind of reason?' MacFarlane looks up from her notebook.

Saffy looks at her. 'Can you just tell me if Leona and Rosie are OK?'

'If you could answer our questions for now, that would be really helpful,' the detective says. 'Can you talk us through exactly what happened when you arrived at your friend's house?'

Saffy swallows, trying to relieve her dry mouth. 'Leona came to the door and she looked surprised to see me.'

'Yet you claim she'd sent messages asking you to come?'

'Yes. I asked to see her phone but there were no messages on there, no notifications that she'd deleted any, either. Leona didn't seem to know what I was talking about.'

'Did you go inside the house?'

Saffy nods. 'I insisted on having a look around to make sure she and Rosie were OK.' She looks at them both in turn. 'I'm Rosie's godmother.'

'Was there any reason in particular you were so worried about Leona?'

'She'd been having problems with her husband, Ash, and . . . well, the messages sounded urgent.'

'What sort of problems?' Shah says.

'Issues of control. That sort of thing.' The stuff Leona told her at the bar last week was personal and she had sworn Saffy to secrecy. She wants to know a bit more about why they're here before she considers breaking her friend's confidences.

'You didn't think to call her before rushing over there?'

'One message specifically said not to call.'

'I see. What exactly did the messages say?'

Saffy thinks for a moment, trying to recall the exact words. 'They said: "Can't speak . . . don't text or call . . . please just come."'

'But then Leona deleted them almost immediately without explanation?'

'Yes. But . . . I thought she might've done that because she was worried about Ash seeing what she'd written.'

'Could I see your phone again?'

Saffy pulls out the phone from her dressing gown pocket and offers it. 'As I've said, there's no trace of Leona's messages on there now. Just the notifications she'd deleted them.'

MacFarlane takes the device from her. 'It would be useful for us to take a good look at this. If you're happy for us to do so?'

Saffy hesitates. 'How long will I be without it?'

'Shouldn't be too long. I can confirm later with our forensic tech people.'

Forensic tech people . . . Don't they believe her story about the messages?

'Could I just text my ex-husband? He needs to know where –'

'It's best the phone isn't used again. Keeps it simple for forensics. Perhaps your sister could contact him on your behalf?'

Saffy nods and MacFarlane pops the phone into a small plastic bag and seals it. It's probably smart not to involve Neil in the confusion yet anyway, Saffy thinks. Not until this has all blown over.

Shah says, 'Ms Morris, had Leona told you she was afraid of her husband?'

'Not exactly, but there have been signs,' Saffy says. 'Signs that worried me.'

'Can you elaborate?'

'Well, she'd stopped looking after herself, stopped going out and seeing friends. Last week when I met her for a drink I saw bruising on her wrist. They looked like finger marks to me, as if she'd been gripped too hard.' Shah waits, seeming to want more. 'I've got no real evidence because Leona tends to defend Ash every time I try to talk about him.'

'Did you see Mr Bannatyne when you went to the house?'

'Yes, but –' A fresh wave of panic rolls over her. 'I'd rather not say anything else until you tell me what's happened. Sorry, but I think I have a right to know.'

The detectives look at each other and MacFarlane clears her throat. 'Officers were called out this afternoon by a concerned neighbour who noticed the front door of the property was wide open for some time with a smoke alarm continuously going off.'

'A neighbour who is also a witness to your visit,' Shah adds.

Saffy's voice emerges too high. 'Are Leona and Rosie OK?'

'I'm afraid the Bannatyne family are currently missing. All three of them.'

'What? But . . . where can they be?' she whispers.

'We're rather hoping you might be able to help us with that.'

'But how do you know they didn't just go out?' As Saffy says the words, she considers Leona's Tuscan chicken in the oven, Rosie watching TV, the glasses of wine to celebrate Ash's promotion. They hadn't been planning on going anywhere.

'When officers arrived, the house was in disarray. Furniture knocked over as if there had been a struggle. Car keys, passports and phones were still present, and a significant amount of blood was found.'

She watches Shah's mouth moving but her voice fades out. *Blood.* Leona and Rosie, missing?

Saffy looks at her. 'I don't know what's happened,' she says faintly, looking out of the window. It's nearly six now, still light, and the rain has finally stopped.

Shah's lips thin. 'We need you to come down to the station with us to answer a few more questions, please.'

'What? I can't do that now!' Saffy looks down at her dressing gown. 'I have my son here . . . and I need to help search for Leona and Rosie.'

'There is an official search in hand, Ms Morris. Both at their property and in the wider vicinity. It's more important that you assist us in other ways in our enquiries. Is there anyone you can contact to look after your son while you're away?'

Neil's concerned face looms into her mind's eye and she pinches the top of her nose. 'Poppy, my sister, can look after him, I suppose.' But when Neil comes to collect Fox, he'll find Saffy isn't here and the place is crawling with police. Saffy turns to challenge the detective, her face burning. 'If I don't come to the station, what are you going to do . . . arrest me?'

MacFarlane tips her head to one side and regards her thoughtfully. 'Put it this way. It appears you were the last person to see Ashley, Leona and Rosie Bannatyne before they disappeared. That makes you a significant person of interest in what is now officially a missing persons investigation.'

11

Poppy

When Saffy leaves the house with the two detectives, leaving the front door on the latch for the search officers, Poppy stands back from the window and watches as they all get into the unmarked police car. There's movement in various gardens over the road. They don't miss a trick around here. Neighbours finding reasons to come outside to check out the garden or fetch something they've 'forgotten' from the car.

When the car containing Saffy pulls away, a large white van begins a slow reverse into its spot. There are uniformed police officers inside, no doubt big and burly and keen to rip the house apart.

Poppy loves her nephew to bits, but the last thing she wants is to be stuck with a three-year-old kid for the entire night. She was supposed to be meeting Harry again.

Saffy had been crushed to leave Fox but she'd had no choice. The detectives said Poppy and Fox had to leave the house right away too so the search could take place, so what the hell is she going to do with him?

'Where my mummy gone?' Fox says in a small voice.

'She'll be back soon, dude.' Poppy pulls on Fox's jacket at the bottom of the stairs, opens a game on her phone and gives it to him. Then she picks him up and bolts upstairs into the spare bedroom Saffy has earmarked as Poppy's own space.

'Sit there a minute, little man.'

'Why?'

Everything was always *why, why, why* with this kid. 'Just while I grab my bag. You play the game, yeah? Help Sonic collect all the little gold rings.'

Poppy knows Fox isn't allowed to so much as touch mobile phones by Neil or Saffy, but this is a bit of a crisis. And in a crisis, you do what you must, right?

Fox is quickly pulled in by the bright colours and hypnotic music and Poppy hauls out from under her bed the large empty backpack she bought for Leeds Fest last year. The textbooks she'd originally come over to get are on her dressing table in two neat piles, but she ignores them. There's something far more important she needs to get out of this house and with the police already pulling up outside, she's got maybe a minute or two tops to do it.

She pulls out shoe boxes from the bottom of her wardrobe until she reaches the large, shiny black one right at the back.

Poppy pulls the tape from around the edges of the lid and lifts the tissue paper containing the delicate jewelled flip-flops inside. Next, she snatches out the thick folded envelope at the bottom. Poppy opens it and takes out a small silver phone.

'That Pops's phone?' Fox slides down from the bed and pads over to her.

'Hey, Pops is busy. You go and play your game for a minute.' Fox does not move.

She fills the rucksack with textbooks and freezes when she hears the front door open.

'Hello?' a deep voice calls out.

Fox looks alarmed and takes a step closer to her.

Poppy begins frantically piling the shoe boxes back into the bottom of the wardrobe.

'I'll be down in a moment!' she calls out, wiping a sheen from her forehead with the back of her hand.

'Who is it, Pops?'

Heavy footsteps start to climb the stairs and, having replaced the last shoe box, Poppy stands and closes the wardrobe doors. She brushes down her jeans, adjusts her top and pats her hair before picking up Fox. When the middle-aged, uniformed police officer appears in her doorway, a little red-faced and out of puff, Poppy is casually slotting the last two books into her backpack, praying she looks cool and unruffled.

'Everyone must leave the house.' He frowns, looking around the bedroom. 'Who are you?'

'I'm Poppy Morris. It's my sister's house. This is Fox, my nephew,' Poppy says, giving him her most winning smile.

She jiggles Fox in her arms. 'I'm looking after him until Saffy – that's my sister – gets back from the police station.'

'I see.' The officer's eyes are glued to the rucksack. 'What have you got in there? You should have been told that nothing is permitted to be removed until the house search has been carried out satisfactorily.'

'Oh, it's just textbooks,' Poppy says nonchalantly.

'Phone,' says Fox, pointing to the bag.

'Phone is on the bed, see, Fox,' Poppy says, aware it's not *that* phone he is referring to. 'I just called in for textbooks, but then the detectives rocked up and I didn't even have a chance to get them.'

'I'm afraid you'll have to leave them.' The officer presses his lips together. 'You can come back for them when we've finished.'

Poppy's face falls. 'Oh no, I can't do that. I mean, without them I'll fail my assignment. I've left revision until the last minute and . . .' She bites her lip, delighted when she feels tears prickling in her eyes. She looks up at him. 'Oh God, why do I always mess everything up?'

The officer walks over and crouches down by the rucksack. He picks out a couple of books. 'History of Art, eh? My niece is studying the same course.'

Poppy lowers Fox to his feet and he clings to her leg, his eyes glued to the police officer's duty belt; specifically, the silver handcuffs.

'I bet your niece is completely organized. Not a failure like me.' She lowers her eyes and inspects her short purple nails half-heartedly.

'Not according to her mum, that's my sister. She leaves everything until the last minute, too.' He takes out a couple more books and peers into the rucksack, sliding a flat hand into the large interior pocket that Poppy knows to be empty, thank God. At Leeds Fest last year, she'd used it to store a small plastic bag containing three ecstasy tablets.

The police officer stands up again, grimacing as his knee clicks. He grins at Fox and pops out the handcuffs. 'Want to take a closer look, buddy?'

Fox shrinks back, pressing his face into Poppy's leg.

'He's really shy with strangers,' she says, glancing at the backpack.

'Go on then.' He jerks his head towards the door. 'You can't take anything else, but I'll let you off with the textbooks. Good luck with your assignment.'

'That's so cool, thank you!' Poppy's face lights up. She reaches for her phone off the bed and grabs the heavy bag, swinging it on to her back. Holding Fox's hand, they walk carefully downstairs, past the coat stand and several surprised officers standing in the hallway.

'I've checked the bag, she's good to go,' she hears the

officer say as he walks downstairs. She heads for the front door, a relieved smile playing on her lips.

Outside, there are more officers standing in small clusters, including two who have their backs to Poppy as she emerges from the house.

Fox looks around. 'What they doing, Pops?'

She squeezes his hand. 'It's OK, they'll be gone soon.'

As they walk towards the gate, Poppy sees an officer talking on his phone and she slows her pace.

'Yeah, we've got officers inside doing the search and we're about to sweep the neighbours here, see if we can verify any sightings of her returning to the house. Right, OK. That's good.'

He ends the call and Poppy hovers behind with Fox.

'What's happening at the Bannatyne house?' his colleague asks.

'Forensics are still ongoing, and the team are door-knocking on the street, asking for CCTV.'

Poppy shifts her position to accommodate the weight of the rucksack on her back and the officer who was on the phone suddenly turns. He looks at her first and then down at Fox. 'Who are you?'

'I'm Saffy's sister. I just came back to get my stuff. I spoke to the officer inside.'

He looks at the bulging rucksack on her back. 'What have you got in there?'

'Just textbooks. I need them, I have an exam coming up.'

He glances at his colleague. 'Unpack the bag, please.'

'What? My bag has already been checked!'

'What he want, Pops?' Fox says in a worried tone.

The other officer speaks in a low voice. 'If she's already been checked out, we haven't got time for this. We need to get this street canvassed soon as we can.'

'I know, but . . .' The officer who was on the phone looks at Poppy's rucksack and sighs. 'Go on then, get off. But don't come back until you've had confirmation we're all finished.'

Poppy nods and walks down the drive, ignoring the curious glances of passers-by and the neighbours across the road. The bottom of her back feels damp. That was a close call; quite a thrill in getting away with it.

When they turn the corner of the street, Poppy stops to catch her breath, wiping damp palms on the front of her jeans. She's done it, thank God. She managed to get it out of the house.

She takes a breath and calls Neil. 'Hey, it's Poppy. Listen, something came up and . . . Saffy's had to go out. I've got Fox.'

'She's had to go out where? I texted to say I was running late but it wasn't too bad in the end so I'm on my way.'

'It was kind of an emergency and so she had to leave Fox with me.'

'Where has she gone?'

'I'll tell you when I see you.' Poppy hesitates. 'It's complicated.'

'I'm five minutes away from the house now, so see you soon.'

'I'm not at the house,' Poppy says quickly. 'I'm waiting for you with Fox on the corner of the street.'

'Why aren't you in the house?' Neil says immediately.

Poppy hesitates. 'Like I said, it's complicated.'

'Christ,' he sighs. 'Everything is always complicated when it comes to Saffy.'

Not for the first time, Poppy found herself wishing that Saffy and Leona had never become friends. But their friendship was nearly older than Poppy was herself and she had heard the tale of how they met a hundred times.

12

Leona

'Mum is making macaroni cheese for tea,' Saffy said excitedly as the two girls walked home together after school. 'She makes the best macaroni cheese.'

They were in Year Nine at St Luke's and were pretty much inseparable apart from when they were in different ability classes for Maths and English.

'If you stopped telling yourself you're no good at it, you'd learn really quickly,' Leona had told Saffy several times. But her words always seemed to fall on deaf ears.

Saffy's house was further from the school than the council-run River Crest where Leona lived. A children's home that was nowhere near the river.

'Oh God, oh God . . . don't look now but it's him.' Leona began walking faster while staring at the ground. 'Over there. He's watching us.'

'What? Who?' She heard Saffy run a few steps behind her to catch up.

'That boy at school. Wes. The one the other girls are always talking about in class.'

Leona took another crafty look, saw him leaning back on the wall and dragging on a cigarette. He was thirteen like them, but he looked older. He looked like trouble. In a sexy way. But she'd never say that to Saffy.

'Just keep walking,' Saffy snapped. 'He proper fancies himself, that one. He's not even that good-looking.'

Leona kept moving but she managed to glance over at Wes and give him a little coy smile.

'This is our street,' Saffy said after they'd been walking about twenty minutes. She turned into a quiet road full of pebble-dashed council houses. Most had neat gardens but the homes were concrete and blocky.

'Your house looks really nice,' Leona said, taking in the clean white nets that hung halfway down the front window and the door painted in a glossy cream colour. It was the kind of welcoming house Leona had always dreamed of living in with her very own family who cared about her.

'It's OK, I suppose,' Saffy said, pushing her key into the Yale lock. 'I wish I still had my big bedroom though.'

The front door opened and the girls stepped into a hallway that smelled of polish. Leona followed Saffy's lead, slipping off her shoes and coat and placing her school bag close to the bottom of the stairs. She watched as Saffy stood still and inhaled, her face looking suddenly troubled.

'Mum?' she called.

'In here.'

The girls walked into a narrow, long room separated by internal glass-paned doors. Leona saw a small dining table and chairs beyond them. In here was the TV and a three-piece velour suite.

'Mum, this is my friend, Leona.'

A small woman with short, dyed red hair and a pale complexion sat on the sofa, cradling a small, whimpering girl of about two in her arms.

'Hello, Mrs Morris,' Leona said. 'Thanks for letting me come round.'

'Hello, love.' She glanced briefly at Leona and then glared at Saffy. 'Poppy's not well again,' Mrs Morris said sharply. 'You'll have to nip up to the chemist and get her some Calpol. I've rung ahead and explained I can't get out. They said you're allowed to collect it this once.'

'We'll go and get it now, Mum. Poor little Pops.' Saffy stepped closer and wiggled her fingers at the toddler.

'I've told you not to touch her!' Mrs Morris slapped Saffy's hand away. 'It's probably the germs you're bringing in from school every day that make her so sickly.'

'Sorry, I forgot, Mum.' Saffy glanced at Leona. 'We'll go to the shop before we have our macaroni cheese.'

'What? I haven't had time to slave over a stove! I've been worried sick about this little mite all day and all you're bothered about is stuffing your face.'

'I didn't mean . . . Sorry, I just thought –'

Mrs Morris rolled her eyes at Leona. 'You'll get to know that Saffy's a selfish girl. Always has been. You can rely on her to get nothing right and everything wrong.'

Leona bit her lip and looked away.

'Mum's just a bit stressed,' Saffy explained as they walked to the chemist. 'She always worries that Poppy is ill even when she's all right.'

She went on to explain her dad had suffered a big heart attack and died before Poppy was born. 'I think Mum is scared Poppy might get ill and die, too. Mum is scared about a lot of things.'

They picked up the Calpol and headed back to the house. In the living room, Mrs Morris hadn't moved but Poppy was now fast asleep. 'You can't watch TV or you'll disturb her. Go up to your bedroom, but no banging about or loud music.'

'Come on,' Saffy said to Leona. 'Let's go upstairs.'

They walked to the end of the landing and she opened the last door. Her bedroom was tiny, smaller even than Leona's room at River Crest. There was a single bed in here, pushed up against the wall, and an upside-down wooden box with a lamp on it that served as a bedside table.

'Where are all your things?' Leona asked, looking around. 'Your wardrobe?'

'My clothes are in Poppy's bedroom.' Leona followed her down the landing again. Saffy opened the door to an oasis of pink: a plush, raspberry carpet with matching pale pink bedding and curtains and pristine white bedroom furniture. Soft toys adorned every surface and the pendant light was fashioned as a pastel-coloured hot air balloon.

Saffy walked over to a triple wardrobe and opened the single door. 'I keep my stuff in this bit and I have the bottom two drawers, too.'

'Poppy's got a lot of space and a big room given she's just a toddler,' Leona murmured, looking around.

'It used to be my room but Mum said the baby needed to be next to her so she can make sure she's safe.' Saffy looked wistfully around. 'Mum says I shouldn't mind Poppy having all the nice things. That would just be selfish.'

'Yes, but you deserve nice things too,' Leona said, not sure why she felt troubled by Saffy's words.

13

Saffy

In the police car, Saffy feels hot and can't seem to get enough breath into her lungs. Poppy had assured her Fox would be safe, but where will they go while the search takes place? She checks her watch: 18:35. What will happen when Neil arrives to pick him up?

Just as he'd finally agreed to Saffy having Fox over more, too. What rotten timing. Why hadn't she asked Poppy to just lie, cover up for her, just this once? All she can do now is pray her sister will use her head and somehow keep the truth from Neil about where Saffy has been taken.

The detectives had asked if they could conduct a search of the house. 'We can get a warrant, but then things drag on. This way, you can get back to normal much quicker.'

Saffy didn't need to think about it, and she had nothing to hide. But as soon as she'd given her permission, they'd done away with their softly, softly approach, brusquely told her to get dressed because they'd be leaving right away. Then they'd whisked her away like a common criminal when the search team had arrived outside and told Poppy she and Fox must vacate the property immediately.

'Can't she stay in the house with my son?' Saffy had pleaded. 'He's only three and I don't want them both wandering the streets. I need to know they're both at home, safe, or I'll never rest.'

But the detectives were in no mood for leniency. 'Everyone must leave the house,' Shah had said blankly.

Saffy stares out of the window now at the dull, unremarkable sky and the nondescript wet pavements lined with shops and people walking. Talking on their phones, talking to each other, drinking coffee from recyclable cups . . . living their lives. Just as Saffy was doing this morning when the biggest problem she faced was getting through the interview for a new job.

The car moves quickly now, switching to a faster road that will take them directly to the police station. There, Saffy will be questioned about what might have happened to her best friend, her goddaughter and Ash Bannatyne.

At the police station, Saffy is led into the building through a side entrance and she is grateful, at least, not to be paraded through the public foyer. She follows MacFarlane down a stark, narrow corridor with a tiled floor and harsh fluorescent lighting.

At the end, the corridor opens out into a bigger space where a duty sergeant stands behind a desk organizing paperwork.

'Evening. We've brought in Saffron Morris for a voluntary interview regarding the Bannatyne family disappearance,' MacFarlane says, indicating Saffy should step forward.

The uniformed officer is young and efficient. He takes Saffy's details and politely asks her to sign some paperwork.

'You're entitled to legal representation during the process. Will you be requiring a solicitor for today's interview?'

Saffy swallows. 'Am I under arrest?'

'No, you're free to leave at any point. However, depending on the information disclosed during the interview, which will be recorded, it may lead to further actions.'

Saffy doesn't have a solicitor on speed dial like people seem to have in the crime dramas she now tries to avoid watching. Either that or they are allocated a disinterested duty solicitor who usually manages to do more harm than good. And it's not like she has anything to hide.

'I don't need a solicitor,' she says.

The detectives leave and Saffy sits down on a hard plastic chair. There are no windows in this part of the building. The desk clerk is in his mid-twenties and looks lean and fit, as if he is no stranger to the gym. Saffy imagines he can't wait to get out of this claustrophobic environment at the end of his working day. With no natural light and no fresh air, it's not the healthiest of places to spend a full eight-hour shift.

After about ten minutes a new female officer she hasn't seen before appears.

'Ms Morris? Come with me, please. The detectives are ready for you.'

Saffy is beginning to wonder if she should have accepted the offer of a brief, even if it is just a duty solicitor. But it's too late now. Besides, she just wants to get this over and done with. Go home and make sure Fox and Poppy are OK. She wants to get the house back to normal after the search team have ransacked it.

The interview room is a short journey back down the corridor. The officer opens a door on the right and Saffy steps inside. Predictably, it's another poky and airless room. There are two long fluorescent tubes on the ceiling and the glare feels too bright for such a small, bare space.

The two detectives, Shah and MacFarlane, sit side by side behind a light oak table. Both have a slim stack of paperwork in front of them.

'Ahh, Ms Morris. Is it OK if we call you Saffron?' Shah has slipped off her grey jacket and a printed lanyard swings in front of her crisp, white cotton blouse as she waves her arm inviting Saffy to sit.

'It's Saffy,' she says, heading for the padded chair.

'Saffy? OK, good. Are you happy for us to record the interview? Just so we don't have to worry about making lots of notes when we're talking.'

'That's fine.' Saffy isn't going to be saying anything that she might regret. Besides, she has already told the detectives everything that's happened.

She laces her fingers together on her lap. About thirty minutes have passed since she left the house and Fox must surely have now been collected by Neil. Saffy wonders if, by some miracle, he doesn't yet know she has been taken to the police station for questioning.

MacFarlane starts the digital recorder and documents those present. When she speaks directly to Saffy, her voice sounds confident and no-nonsense.

'Firstly, thank you for coming in today, Saffy. You'll be aware by now that you are the last known person to have visited the home of Leona, Ashley and Rosie Bannatyne, who live on Musters Road, West Bridgford, and who are currently missing. Because of this, you are regarded as a person of interest in the investigation of their disappearance. Do you understand?'

'Yes,' Saffy says.

'In addition to this interview, you have agreed to officers conducting a search of your property and vehicle. For the tape, can you confirm this is correct?'

'Yes, that's right.'

'When you got to your friend's house, after you'd received the now deleted messages, Leona answered the door to you, is that correct?' MacFarlane says.

'Yes.'

'And how did she seem to you?'

'Leona didn't look upset at all, which I found odd. She seemed surprised I was there and when I mentioned getting the messages, she said she didn't know what I was talking about. I went inside and she showed me her phone. There was no trace on there of the messages she'd sent, but I didn't quite believe her. Something just felt off.'

'When you were inside, you saw all three members of the family and interacted with each one?' Shah says.

Saffy gives a faint frown. It seems an odd thing to ask. 'Yes, I spoke to all of them. Leona, Rosie and even Ash.'

'So, I have a specific question to ask you, Saffy. Did you notice any obvious injuries on any one of them?'

'What? No, of course not . . . I would have said!'

She suddenly feels panicky and upset. The detectives' expressions, their super-formal behaviour . . . *the blood they'd found*.

'You're certain about that?'

'I'm certain none of them had any injuries. That I could see. And . . . nobody looked in any pain.' Saffy hesitates. 'But I just thought, what if Ash *had* hurt Leona and that's why she sent the messages? Then he forced her to cover the injury up in some way and delete the texts?'

'Let's not speculate,' MacFarlane says smoothly. 'It's important we stick to the facts.'

'OK. Well, I didn't see any injuries while I was there. I wish to God I *had* spotted something because I'd have rung the police immediately instead of just leaving the house.'

'Indeed, I'm sure you would have done.' MacFarlane gives her a tight smile.

14

Poppy

They're standing on the corner of Saffy's street where the busier main road joins at the bottom. Poppy has chosen to wait next to a lay-by that Neil can easily pull into but it's a noisy spot with so much passing traffic.

'Auntie Pops, I'm cold,' Fox complains, pressing closer to her.

'Not long now, Big Ears. Your dad will be here any minute.' Poppy pulls Fox's bright yellow woollen hat further down over his reddening ears. 'OK. You take black cars, I'll take white. First one to five wins. Let's go.'

Fox's face brightens as he points up the street. 'Black one, I win!'

She grins. 'Four more before you get the winner's crown, hustler!' She turns just as Neil's dark grey Lexus slows and pulls into the lay-by. 'Hey, look who's here.'

'Daddy!' The car game instantly forgotten, Fox jumps up and down as the Lexus comes to a halt.

Neil gets out and walks around to the pavement, scooping Fox into his arms and swinging him off his feet. 'Hey, buddy. Let's get you in the car and we might just have time to watch some TV together before bed. How's that sound?' Fox gives an approving whoop as Neil opens the back door. He turns to Poppy. 'Two minutes and then we can have that chat.'

Poppy kisses her nephew and while Neil straps him in, she

shifts from one foot to the other, wondering exactly what to tell him to minimize any problems for her sister.

Poppy was fourteen when he and Saffy met. She knows him well enough to have seen the cold flashes of temper. The way his jaw sets when he makes his mind up about something. Neil knows her well, too. He knows her better than Poppy would like.

Neil shuts the door, straightens up and turns around to face her, his expression stony. 'OK, so cut the crap, Pops. Where is she?'

Poppy takes a breath. 'Something urgent came up and Saffy had to go out at short notice. It's totally cool because I was there to –'

Neil's nostrils flare with impatience. 'You might as well just tell me. I'll find out the truth anyway so unless you want to make things worse, you need to tell me now.'

She feels heat channel into her face. 'Leona and Rosie are missing. Ash, too.'

'What?'

'The police came round to the house to tell Saffy. She was cooking tea and . . . well, it was a terrible shock.'

'Why did the police want to tell Saffy? She's been telling me she doesn't get to see that much of Leona and Rosie these days.'

'I'm not sure. You can ask her when you see her.'

'I've called her a few times to let her know I'm on my way. Her mobile phone is off and I've left a message on her landline.'

Poppy looks at the pavement. *The police took Saffy's phone.*

'We have an agreement that she's contactable at all times when she has Fox.' Dark shadows flash in his eyes. 'Where is she, Poppy?'

'The police asked her to go to the station to answer a few

more questions,' Poppy admits, her fingers twisting together. 'They . . . might have taken her phone, I guess.'

Neil looks at her. The engine noise and fumes of a constant stream of cars fades into the background as they stare at each other. 'This gets worse. Why do the police want to question Saffy and why would they take her phone?'

'They said she was the last person to see the Bannatynes before they went missing.' Neil opens his mouth to ask something, and Poppy raises a hand. 'That's honestly all I know, Neil. Making sure Fox was safe was Saffy's only priority. It wasn't a problem because I was there and –'

'But what if you *hadn't* been there? If she'd been alone with Fox, then what?'

'You think the police would have forced her to leave a three-year-old home alone?' He was seriously getting on her nerves now. 'Saffy hasn't been *arrested*. She had a choice whether to go with them, and as I was around, she was keen to help with their investigation.' They both glance back at the car as Fox bangs on the glass from the inside, screwing up his face impatiently. 'Her best friend and goddaughter have disappeared. Course she's going to do whatever she can to help.'

Neil frowns, unconvinced. 'When you see her, tell her to call me right away, will you? She needs to be honest with me, keep me informed.'

'Sure thing.' Poppy waves to Fox as Neil starts to walk away. 'Oh, and Neil?'

He turns and raises an eyebrow.

'Maybe you ought to show Saffy the same courtesy in keeping her informed. When are you going to tell her *your* news?'

'Like I said. That's none of your business,' he snaps before getting into the car and slamming the door far too hard.

15

Saffy

The detectives sit silently, waiting for Saffy to speak. She swallows. The interview is getting steadily worse for her. They clearly think she has something to do with the entire Bannatyne family disappearing, which is ludicrous.

'There was no sign of any blood when I was in the house,' she says carefully. 'No blood and no injuries.'

Leona had seemed a little jumpy when Ash asked Saffy to stay for dinner. Ash himself had been relaxed and friendlier than he'd been for ages and little Rosie, although she'd got upset upstairs, had seemed happy watching cartoons in the kitchen when Saffy left. There had been no hint of violence earlier. If there had, Saffy would never have left her friend and goddaughter there.

But then there are the awful things Leona told her a week ago. The misery one human being can exert on another is both shocking and heart-breaking. Saffy had struggled to control the sadness and fury that had swept through her that night when she saw her friend's pain.

'Any other signs you can think of that, with hindsight, were possibly red flags?'

Saffy tilts her chin and looks up, thinking. There's a big crack running down the centre of the ceiling and the corner of the room is thick with dusty cobwebs. 'There's the stuff she told me last Friday night.'

MacFarlane confirms the date.

Saffy thinks for a moment, then nods. 'Leona texted me and asked if we could meet for drinks. It was a nice surprise as it's unusual for her to instigate a get-together. I'm normally the one who pushes to keep in touch.'

'And so you agreed to meet with her?'

'Yes. We decided on the Hockley Arts Club at seven p.m. It's one of our old haunts in town, back when we saw each other all the time.'

'Tell us about that night.'

'I got to the bar first, bagged our favourite corner table there and ordered some drinks. When she came through the door, I remember thinking how awful she looked. Thin, ungroomed . . . Leona always prided herself on her appearance. In the old days, we used to joke that she wouldn't even put the bins out without a full face of makeup.'

A terse smile passes over Shah's lips. She says, 'How did she seem in herself?'

'OK at first. A bit nervy. I spotted some bruises on her wrist.' Saffy touches her own forearm to show where the marks were. 'I asked her about them, and she suddenly just opened up. Told me some very disturbing things about her marriage.'

'What sort of things?'

'Awful stuff. I mean, I already suspected for some time Ash was a bully, a controller. She told me there were rules she had to live by. If she broke these rules even accidentally, then there was a punishment to pay.'

MacFarlane leans forward, a new intensity lining her face. 'Can you give us an example?'

'Ash had told her she needed to cut down on food. He did the grocery shopping online and carbohydrates were banned . . . for Leona, at least. No bread, pasta, rice or potatoes. Only low-fat versions of foods. No cheese or cream. The list

90

went on. She said it had been happening for a couple of months and I saw the results of it when she walked in the bar. Her clothes were hanging off her.'

'You mentioned a punishment if a rule was broken?' Shah says.

'If she was found to have "cheated", as he called it, then she was made to fast until the test strip result was satisfactory.'

'I'm sorry . . . test strip?'

'If you continuously starve your body – like you might, say, on a very low-calorie diet – your body enters a metabolic state called ketosis. It burns fat instead of glucose. I learned about it once when I tried a fasting diet.'

'I get it.' Shah nods.

'You can freely buy test strips from Amazon which change colour when dipped in urine and you can't really cheat. Ash gave her a five-hundred-calorie daily allowance and that was every day until she'd got down to a size six. There wasn't a big margin for snacking.'

'Jeez.' MacFarlane cursed under her breath. 'Did she challenge him on this or was it something she'd just grown to accept?'

'She'd accepted it. She said he'd convinced her she was fat. But she was worried about her daughter. Although he didn't ban Rosie from certain foods, he kept them in a locked cupboard that only he had a key for. Not the message you want to be sending a child. Rosie got school dinners during term time, Leona said, as if it wasn't a problem.'

'It must have been quite a shock for you,' Shah says. 'Out for drinks one minute and then hearing this harrowing confession the next.'

'Yes,' Saffy says. 'It really was.'

'What was your reaction? When she told you all this?'

Saffy looks down at the table. 'Sadness, fury . . . I felt hopeless. I tried to talk to her about leaving him. I said, "Pack up your stuff when he's at work and you can both come to live with me. If we go to the police, he can't hurt you any more."' A noise of frustration escapes her throat. 'She sat and listened, nodded her agreement here and there. She said she'd been keeping a record of his abuse in a journal. I told her not to wait too long to do something about it, but I could tell she'd switched off. It was like all the fight had left her.'

The detectives glance at each other.

'Did it occur to you to take matters into your own hands, Saffy?' MacFarlane asks, tapping the end of her pen on the paperwork in front of her. 'What you've just described, it counts as serious emotional and physical abuse. Abuse that a child is also witnessing. Did you at any point consider that Leona might no longer be mentally able to make a judgement about her own safety and that of her young daughter?'

'Of course I did!' Saffy feels heat channel into her face. 'But when your lifelong friend tells you something in confidence, something you've suspected and been trying to get to the bottom of for the last year or so, it's not easy. I felt torn. Torn between doing the right thing and making it even worse for her.'

'Making it worse in what way?'

'Well, it's always been clear to me Leona has no intention of leaving Ash. If I'd gone to the police, she'd probably have excommunicated me rather than kicked Ash to the kerb. I am Rosie's godmother. I need to maintain a connection with Leona for her sake.'

'You've never tried to speak to Ash yourself about his treatment of Leona, either before or after your meet-up last week?'

Saffy shakes her head. 'Leona would have hated that, and she'd have hated me for trying. Ash has destroyed her self-esteem, you see. Leona has started to believe the lies he tells her about herself. She thinks she's fat, lazy and incapable. That's what he's doing to her every day of every week. He's hiding in plain sight and taking her apart bit by bit.'

Saffy touches her cheek with the back of her hand. It feels hot and clammy.

'It must have made you very angry, hearing how Ash was treating your friend,' MacFarlane says carefully. 'Maybe you feel angry at Leona too, for putting up with it.'

Saffy looks at her steadily. 'Angry with him, yes. But not with her. I admit I'm frustrated and I worry about what Rosie's seeing behind closed doors. I really do.'

'Maybe you felt frustrated enough to try and do something about it,' Shah says bluntly. 'Some might say you could hardly be blamed for that.'

Saffy feels rigid with indignation. 'I understand you have to explore all angles, but it's fairly obvious what's happened here, isn't it?'

Shah raises an eyebrow. 'Is it? Perhaps you'd like to enlighten us.'

'I'm surprised you need it after everything I just told you. It's pretty clear that Ash has done something bad. Forced Leona and Rosie to go with him somewhere, hurt them. Where in the house was the blood found?'

Saffy wonders if it might have been upstairs, in their bedroom. She thinks about the contents of her jacket pocket at home. She won't admit to snooping around their bedroom just yet. Not until she's thought it through.

Shah says, 'For what reason would he force them to go somewhere?'

Saffy looks at the detective and wonders if she's being

purposely obtuse. 'I don't know. Maybe he hurt Leona and had to get her out of the house. Maybe, in view of what Leona told me last week, she'd finally had enough and come to her senses. Told him she wanted out of their controlling relationship, that she was taking Rosie and leaving and he exploded. Hurt her.'

It was baffling how this stuff hadn't occurred to them yet. How they're hell-bent on suggesting Saffy herself might have something to do with their disappearance.

'And yet you've said that when you arrived at the house, Leona acted perfectly normally,' MacFarlane chips in. 'She had every chance to tell you there was a problem but didn't.'

'Perhaps because she's afraid of him.' Saffy looks from one detective to the other. 'Abused women don't just ask for help, right? You've got a poster up in the station foyer showing ways people can reach out if they're in trouble.' The detectives look back at her. Surely she shouldn't need to spell this out; it's like teaching your grandmother to suck eggs. 'I admit I've felt angry and frustrated watching my friend suffer. But that's the extent of it. It hasn't crossed my mind to act on those feelings.'

'Right-o. Well, we might well need to revisit some or all the points we've just discussed at some point quite soon,' Shah says, straightening the papers in front of her and picking up the top sheet. 'Now, I want to bring the timeline forward to this afternoon.'

Saffy shuffles uncomfortably in the hard seat. This 'chat' they've talked her into is exhausting and she doesn't like the accusatory direction it's taking. Maybe she should get a lawyer after all, but if she changes her mind now then it's only going to look suspicious. She wants to get out of here, get back home and smooth things over with Neil.

94

'You visited the Bannatynes' house because of the deleted messages asking you to do so. Is that correct?'

Saffy goes through the whole story again.

Shah reaches down to a small table at the side of her, picks up a small, sealed cellophane bag with some writing on it. She places it on the table in front of her and Saffy sees it contains her confiscated phone. Now taken as evidence in their investigation.

'So all we have here are three notifications that some messages were deleted,' MacFarlane says smoothly.

'Yes, deleted at the sender's end as I said. But the notifications remained on my device.' Saffy bites her tongue to avoid snapping further, but it's so frustrating. Why do they find this particular point so hard to grasp?

Shah picks up the questioning again. 'So, you had your interview before leaving Glassworks IT?'

'No. I couldn't focus, said I felt unwell. I headed for the cab rank and that's when I saw the headlines everywhere about the city's crime level warnings. I panicked, started worrying something had happened to Leona. I . . . I have a severe anxiety problem.'

'We know the history of what happened to your sister, the attack, and we can touch on that later. For now, I want to stick with your visit to the Bannatynes' house,' Shah says without a scrap of empathy. 'Seeing those headlines reminding you of past trauma must have made you feel far more upset than usual,' she continues.

Saffy shrugs. 'I was already upset and worried about Leona's messages.'

'How did Leona seem?'

'She looked fine. Better than when we'd met up last week. As I mentioned, she seemed confused as to why I'd just turned up at the house because I hadn't visited her there for months, and she said she didn't know anything about the messages.'

The old guilt she carries in her bones stirs as Saffy thinks about their shared past. Growing up so close, like sisters. Saffy knew Leona better than anyone and vice versa. What she'd give to have done better by her friend back then . . . to be someone Leona could have relied on and trusted to do the right thing.

Instead of the lie Saffy had chosen to hide behind that day and had been trapped in ever since.

16

Leona

Leona sat in front of her makeshift dressing table under the window. She'd pulled a stool up to her bookcase and propped a small mirror up against the wall.

She studied her reflection and sighed. Two new angry red spots had appeared out of nowhere.

Usually Leona and Saffy would be putting their makeup on together, with Saffy advising her on the best colours for her eyes and how to pluck her eyebrows.

But she knew better than to involve Saffy in her makeup routine tonight.

Leona leaned forward and looked down. When Saffy had suggested that Leona move in with her and Poppy after the death of her mum, Leona had jumped at the chance. Her room overlooked a small car park and also the factory behind the house. There were offices upstairs and sometimes she liked to sit and watch the office girls sitting at their desks, busying around. To Leona, it all looked a bit meaningless. People at school, Saffy included, didn't seem to have a clue what they wanted to do for a living. She'd always known, though, that she wanted to be a nurse. Strange really, she didn't know where the knowing had come from. Leona just wanted to help people who were in need. Simple as that.

Leona looked around her small, cramped bedroom with

its woodchip wallpaper and dull, worn carpet. It wasn't much but it was home in a way none of the children's homes had been.

She was happier than she'd ever been in her life, and no small part of that was the fact she had a date tonight with Wes Sharpe, the dreamy sixth-former at school, now captain of the senior football team and the object of desire for most of the girls in her class.

'Make sure you come on your own,' Wes had said when she'd accepted his invitation to go to the cinema. 'Don't bring that weird girl you always hang around with.'

Leona had frowned. 'You mean Saffy? I won't bring her, but she's not weird!'

'You sure about that?' He'd given her a look as he'd laced up his football boots, sitting on the wall at the end of the field. 'She's literally stalked me for about a month. Every time I've come out of the house she just "happens" to be walking by. My little brother met someone at the park who asked him lots of questions about me . . . guess who? Your friend.'

'Really? What sort of questions?'

Wes had snorted and shrugged his shoulders. 'Do any girls come to the house, has he heard me talking to girls on the phone? That sort of thing. She obviously thinks I'm some kind of player.'

'And are you?' Leona had grinned.

'No way. But even if I was, it wouldn't be any of her business. I had to tell her to get lost in front of my mates last week when she came skulking round us.'

Leona had felt shocked. She and Saffy had talked about her date with Wes and she hadn't been particularly impressed by him, but she hadn't said anything about checking him out. But Saffy was very protective of her. Sometimes, it felt to

Leona like she was trying to take a mum's place not only with Poppy, but with her, too.

Leona sighed and opened her makeup bag, took out the items she only used for a special night out. Some Rimmel foundation and blusher, a Boots No.17 eyeliner, a small palette of eyeshadow and a wand of mascara that Saffy had given her last Christmas. She stared into the mirror. Apart from the spots, her warm skin tone was smooth and even. Her mid-brown eyes were bright and her lips full. Maybe it wasn't going to be so hard to look passable for her first-ever date after all.

She plucked her eyebrows as best she could, following the natural curve of them as Saffy had shown her. She winced as she gave each tough, wiry hair a good tug to remove it. Next, she applied the foundation with her fingers because she didn't have a sponge. Then she turned her attention to her eyes, applying a layer of beige eyeshadow all over the lid before contouring the eye socket in a smoky grey. Finally, after applying a couple of flicks of eyeliner wings and a coat of mascara, she blinked and studied her face in the mirror.

Her eyes seemed bigger and brighter and the foundation had done a pretty good job on her spots, although it was a shame she hadn't got any concealer.

Leona allowed herself a little smile. All in all, she looked passable.

She dressed in the nearly new Biba denim jumpsuit she'd found in a charity shop on the High Street and fastened some white beads around her neck and a couple of colourful bracelets around her wrist.

She glanced at the ornate wooden box beside her bed. It was the only thing she owned from her old life, the only thing she had that used to belong to her mother. Now, Leona used it for small items such as hair bobbles and slides, and the odd piece of jewellery. At school, she'd used it to keep her stickers in and her stash of Bazooka bubble gum balls.

Heading out, she walked to the bus stop at the bottom of the hill and waited for the 342 that was due in six minutes.

She stood playing Snake on her phone when a movement across the road caught her eye. She looked up just in time to see a short figure dash down an alleyway between the houses.

She put her phone away and walked a few steps up the road, peering into the dark, narrow space but seeing nothing. Then she caught sight of a red dot in the distance, getting bigger by the second. She returned to the stop, boarded the bus, paid her fare and went upstairs. As she took a seat near the back, she looked down on to the alleyway, just in time to see Saffy emerge, her face concerned as she leaned against the wall to watch the bus drive off.

17

Saffy

When she emerges from the police station, it's seven forty-five and still light outside. The weak sunshine is a relief on her cool, pinched face. Saffy stands on the steps for a few moments and breathes in fresh air to dispel the stale, dusty environment of the interview room.

Before she left, the detectives told her the search of her house had been completed and that she could go back there. But she feels so lost without her phone. She'd glimpsed it, bagged up as evidence during the interview, but they still haven't told her when they are going to be finished with it. The only choice she has is to buy a new one in the meantime so she can communicate with Poppy and Neil.

She sees a bus pull into a busy stop over the road and rushes over to join the queue for a ride into town. Other people join the queue after her and within seconds she's in the middle of a burgeoning crowd, surrounded by bodies. Surrounded by people she doesn't know.

They're standing so close she feels at risk. If someone had a knife, they could stab her right now and she'd never even see the danger until it was too late.

You'll never know when I'm coming but I give you my word. I will.

The queue shuffles forward and takes her with it. She pulls off her scarf and unzips her puffer jacket a little.

Before today, she has managed to keep herself in a little bubble of certainty and safety by always having her phone with her. Going to work, coming back home, doing most of the shopping – especially grocery shopping – online. Locking all the doors and activating the alarm before bed.

If you discount the fact she often lies awake half the night thinking about the mistakes of the past, about her need to see Fox more, worrying about Poppy's safety – usually all three – then she has found a way to survive. A way to keep her head above water and the wolf from the door. But that was before Leona and Rosie went missing.

Now it feels as though her glass walls have shattered and, here in this queue full of strangers, she is about as exposed as she could be.

During the police interview, Saffy got the distinct impression that the detectives don't trust her story and are searching hard for a motive that implicates her in the Bannatynes' disappearance.

She'd agreed to the police search immediately because she'd had nothing to hide. She had assumed the detectives' attitude would change when that search was completed, but that hasn't happened. If anything, it feels like the noose is tightening. Were they so desperate to prove her guilt that they'd found something that could be used to somehow make everything worse?

Saffy had been constantly on the defence in there, guarding against being tricked into saying something by one detective that the other would then try and latch on to.

The crowd surges forward again and now Saffy is the fourth or fifth passenger away from the boarding step. She has a sense of overheating, of burning up, and suddenly it's all too much. She turns and tries to push her way out of the queue, but the people around her are so focused on boarding the bus, they push back even more determinedly.

'Please, I need to go.' Her breathing is shallow and erratic.

She feels light-headed. One woman in front of her glances at her face, sees the panic and steps aside. Others follow suit until suddenly, she is ejected from the queue. Saffy stands there on the edge of the crowd, slightly bewildered. It's a serious wake-up call. In that moment she recognizes that she has created a safe world around herself that has efficiently disguised the fact that she is too anxious and stressed to board a busy bus alone for a ten-minute ride into town.

She abandons the idea and, instead, forces herself to start walking to the next stop where it will be much quieter and she can wait for a later bus. The sky is still bright behind the thickening cloud. The birds are singing, and Saffy feels sick to her stomach as the feeling of being in control of her own life continues its slide away from her like melting wax.

She ends up walking all the way, calling at a Tesco branch and buying the cheapest pay-as-you-go phone she can find. When she gets home about forty minutes later, Saffy feels her shoulders drop when she sees there is no sign of the police forensic team, no police tape, nor curious neighbours lurking.

The front gate is wide open. She walks up the short path and slides her key into the front door. 'Hello?' No answer. Poppy wouldn't have known when to expect Saffy back and has probably returned to her student digs after Neil collected Fox. She only prays he arrived after the search was completed and is none the wiser.

In the hallway, which is neat and bears no obvious signs of an invasive police operation, Saffy shrugs off her jacket and boots. The house smells different. Even if she hadn't known the police had been inside, she thinks she would have sensed something wasn't quite right.

In the kitchen, though, it's a different story. Some of the cupboard doors have been left wide open and the contents of others strewn over the work surfaces. She fills the kettle, flicks it on and heads for the living room. It's then she sees the landline answerphone is flashing on the small hall table and when she gets closer, Saffy sees that there are six answerphone messages waiting.

She presses a button and the messages begin to play. The first few are from Neil.

'Hi Saffy, it's me. Can't seem to get you on your mobile phone. Ring me, can you?'

'Me again. You're a hard woman to get hold of today.'

The third message starts. Neil again, only sounding slightly more irritated.

'Hello? Are you there yet?' Silence, then, 'Please yourself.' The call ends.

The fourth message is from Poppy. 'Hi Saffy, you not back yet? I tried to cover for you, but Neil knows you're at the police station and . . . sorry, but I might've let slip the police took your phone. God. Nightmare.'

Fifth message. Neil. 'What the hell is going on, Saffy? Poppy says she thinks the police took your phone when they carted you off to the station. I need you to get in touch as soon as you get my messages.'

Then the final, sixth message, also from Neil, that makes her blood run cold.

'If you still want Fox this weekend then you'd better call me in the next thirty minutes with an explanation, otherwise our arrangement is off.'

That last message came in nearly an hour ago.

She snatches up the phone and presses '3' to redial.

'Hello?' The call is answered.

'Neil! I'm so sorry you couldn't get me. My phone is . . .'

'Poppy says the police have taken it. Is that right?'

'It's not like that . . . I'll be getting it back soon. I've just bought another but I haven't set it up yet. Use Messenger if you need me before tomorrow.'

His voice dips lower. 'What's happened, Saffy? Are you in trouble?'

'No! Absolutely not. The police just wanted to ask me a few questions, that's all.'

'About Leona's family disappearing?'

'Yes. But . . . is Fox OK?'

'Fox is fine. While he's here at home with me, at least.'

Fear strikes into her heart, and she takes a moment to steady her voice. 'He's going to be fine with me too this weekend, Neil.'

'If you still want to see him then I need to know what's happened. Poppy was worried, I could tell. She tripped herself up and then tried to backtrack.'

Saffy makes a quick calculation of her chances of keeping the arrangement with Neil about Fox. If she carries on her current trajectory of denying anything is wrong, Neil will probably just stonewall her and downright refuse. Her chances of getting Fox at the weekend right now are probably about 5 percent, tops. If she tells Neil the truth? Maybe her chances might rise to 10 percent, but they're not going to really improve until the police interest in her dies down when the Bannatynes return home. *If* they return home.

'Hello? You still there?'

So Saffy tells him. Gives him the bare bones of what has happened. She doesn't share the confidential information Leona entrusted her with about her relationship with Ash.

'So you went over there after the messages were deleted and now you're the last person to see them before they went missing?'

'Yes. I dropped in at the house to visit and they all seemed fine. So now you can understand why the police wanted to talk to me. They're obliged to follow up on every lead. That's all it is.' Saffy pauses and waits for him to say something. When he remains quiet, she continues. 'The thing is, I'm desperately worried about Leona and Rosie. I could do without all this hassle, Neil, and the last thing I want is to –'

'Saffy,' Neil says, his voice low and serious. 'Did you tell the police what happened?'

She squeezes her eyes closed and feels a pressure building in her chest. For a moment she feels winded and can't speak.

'Did you tell the police what happened last year?' he says, more stridently.

Saffy knows there's no point lying. Not to Neil.

'No,' she says, her voice little more than a whisper. 'I haven't told them anything yet.'

18

Saffy

Friday

It was the blood . . . the awful detail that changed every-
thing. That had infused her dreams. All night . . . stepping
over puddles of it everywhere as she fruitlessly searched
for Leona and Rosie. Where could they have gone . . . Were
they hurt, bleeding out somewhere waiting for someone to
find them?

When she opened her eyes, there was a beat when Saffy
felt like she was emerging from a bad dream before being
plunged back into stark reality. The nightmare is real and it
laced every second, minute and hour of last night.

Saffy's first job this morning is to set up her new phone,
but for now she snatches up her laptop and opens up Mes-
senger. She pulls herself up to a seated position, her back
cricking against the pillows.

Her heart drops when she sees a message from Poppy, but
nothing from Neil. She'd hoped for one of the placatory
'Try not to worry, we'll sort this out' sort of longer messages
Neil would sometimes send her during her *bad time*, as they'd
come to call it. One of those days when the past loomed
even larger than usual and she'd struggled even to see Fox.

But yesterday, Neil had been more annoyed than Saffy
had known him to be for a long, long time. Yesterday, Neil
had not shown much sympathy or understanding at all.

Before opening Poppy's text, she looks through social media and local news channels on X, but there is nothing beyond speculation and shock that this could happen in a sleepy suburb in Nottingham.

Saffy opens Poppy's message and sees she sent it at two o'clock this morning. Looks like she might not have slept well either, which will make her lectures tough this morning. Saffy had called her on the landline a couple of times and left a voicemail, too, before bed.

Sorry. Fell asleep last night. How did it go with the cops?

Saffy closes it without replying. No mention of how Poppy had dropped her in it with Neil. Letting slip the police had taken her phone when she might have just claimed to have lost it. Saffy had lain awake for hours during the night, in between her blood-soaked dreaming, staring up through the thick darkness towards the ceiling. She'd been completely unable to stop her mind from racing all night long. Like drawing circles in the sand. Getting precisely nowhere.

Her eyes sought out the dark shape of her jacket still hanging on the back of the door. She wasn't ready to look at what was inside her pocket. Not yet.

Sometime around dawn she'd finally dropped to sleep for a couple of hours, but now she still feels exhausted and out of it. As if she has a hangover, but it's been years since she's had one of those.

Still, she's awake now and her problems are back with full force. The truth of the matter is that Saffy is facing increasing interest from the police despite agreeing to a search, despite telling them everything that happened. And now there are Neil's veiled threats around whether or not he will allow her to have Fox tomorrow.

Her mind drifts to sweet Rosie, reciting the names of her

toys yesterday. Her confusion and sadness over the problems she sensed between her parents. And Leona . . . where is she right now? Is she terrified and injured? Is she even alive?

And the blood, the blood . . . The detectives wouldn't tell her how much blood beyond that ambiguous phrase, 'a significant amount'. They wouldn't tell her where it was in the house, as if they suspect she might already know. Her imagination provides a flashing scene of a violent struggle in the kitchen between Ash and Leona. A shove, a punch, a head hitting a sharp corner. Little Rosie terrified and screaming . . .

How can life change so completely on the turn of a coin? She'd taken a day off to attend yesterday's interview but this morning she'd have ordinarily been up and showered by now, running out of time to grab a bowl of cereal before getting the bus. Spending the whole journey wondering if she's about to become jobless. After speaking to Neil yesterday, she'd called in sick. Felt relief when her call went through to her boss's voicemail and she was able to leave a quick message.

It's only a temporary stay of execution. It's Friday, after all, and most minor ailments – including the stomach upset which she'd blamed for her absence – would surely be resolved over the weekend and she'd be expected back in her post on Monday morning.

Now the Glassworks job is off the table, she needs to keep her current income safe until this mess is all sorted out and life can return to normal. Which she'd believed wholeheartedly it would be until yesterday's police interview. Now, she isn't so sure.

Saffy gets out of bed. She can't allow herself to go down this soul-destroying road of *what-ifs* . . . she knows from experience it is the road to madness. She must try to be proactive, to think clearly and take useful action rather than submit to the illogical and dominating fear that usually rules her. She unhooks the jacket and carries it downstairs. In the kitchen Saffy makes herself a strong coffee and adds a splash of milk. Staring out of the window at the small lawn that needs a mow, she waits to properly come to her senses and get her thoughts in order. Face the possibility she's not going to be allowed to have Fox this weekend after all.

Yesterday when the police interview had ended and the tape had been turned off, DI Shah said, 'We'll be in touch again soon. It's highly likely there will be further questions we'll need to ask you.'

'What sort of questions?'

'Questions pertaining to the whereabouts of the Bannatyne family. It would be helpful if you don't stray too far from home.'

What could they possibly ask her that hasn't been covered already?

Saffy had replied, 'But I'm not under arrest?'

'No. You are not under arrest.' It felt to Saffy like there might be a 'but' coming. Or a 'yet'. 'But I strongly suggest you keep yourself available if the need arises for us to speak to you again.'

It feels like waiting to be shot. Moreover, it's odd they are focusing on her when all she's ever tried to do is to look out for Leona and Rosie. When she's given the detectives detailed information that might afford Ash a hundred motives for abducting his wife and young stepdaughter.

'Are you going to investigate the things I told you about Ash? If you find Leona's journal, it should prove everything I've told you. He's the one behind the family's disappearance, I can guarantee it.'

'Perhaps you should let us be the judge of that,' Shah said in a curt manner. 'We'll be in touch soon.'

Shah's comment had further inflamed the knot of discomfort that is lodged in Saffy's throat. Somehow her last phrase felt very much like a threat. A hint of what might happen if Saffy doesn't do as they say. How can the detectives possibly be more interested in *her* than pouring their resources into looking more closely at Ash? It doesn't make any sense.

Saffy knows one thing for certain. She made a big mistake yesterday in not engaging a solicitor. A mistake she won't be making again.

She takes a sip of her coffee before reaching for her jacket and slipping her hand inside the pocket. Gently, her fingers cradle the necklace she'd found on Leona's dressing-table and she closes her eyes for a moment. It feels so good to hold it again, but at the same time her throat burns with a quiet fury.

Back in the early days of Leona and Ash's marriage and not long after they'd moved into their current house, the two women had enjoyed a night drinking back at Leona's after a trip to the Broadway cinema. Ash hadn't been best pleased, hinted maybe it was time for Saffy to go home, but she'd had too many glasses of wine and took delight in ignoring his sour expression.

It was only when she'd got home and undressed for bed she realized she'd lost her mother's pendant. Despite the late hour she'd called Leona's phone and Ash had answered.

'A pendant?' he'd said. 'No, no. Nothing like that here, Saffy. Leona went up to bed and I tidied around and I'm sure I would have seen it. If we find it, I'll be sure to put it somewhere safe for you. OK?' She could sense barely concealed laughter bubbling behind his words. He wanted her to know he had it.

The next morning, she called Leona, who said, 'Ash spent ages looking for it last night, but it's not here, Saffy. He was quite upset for you, losing something with such sentimental value.'

Saffy looks down now at that very necklace, curled into the centre of her palm. She'd always suspected he'd taken it and now she knows for certain.

Saffy will tell the police and show them the necklace. Not a crime in itself, but it could be useful in helping them see what a cold, calculating kind of person Ash Bannatyne is. It might illustrate that he's capable of far darker deeds.

She places the necklace carefully on to the kitchen counter now, stretching out the fine gold chain and admiring the dark glitter of the gemstones.

Is it possible Leona had found the necklace at last and Ash had become angry? Leona might have sent the texts to Saffy and then thought better of it. Then, if Ash had found the necklace was missing after Saffy left the house, could he have become violent with Leona because of it? Big arguments can easily develop in fraught circumstances, particularly after a few glasses of wine. There are a thousand scenarios she can picture of what might have happened in that house yesterday, but none of them seem to fit quite right.

Saffy looks at the business card DI Shah gave her. Telling the detective about the necklace might also open a dialogue about the search and whether they have found Leona's journal. Before she can dither, she calls the number and punches in the extension at the prompt. It's only seven thirty but she can leave a message. The call is unexpectedly snatched up within a couple of rings.

'Shah.'

'Oh ... DI Shah, it's Saffy Morris here. I was going to leave a message.'

A beat of silence. Then, 'How can I help you?'

'I just wondered if . . . Is there any news on Leona and Rosie Bannatyne's disappearance?'

'Nothing yet,' Shah says brusquely.

'Did your officers search the house? I wondered if there was an update on that.'

A sigh. 'We've yet to review the house search results. We do have to sleep at some point, you know.'

'Yes, yes. Course. I know that. It's just that . . . did your officers find Leona's journal? She told me she'd recorded all the incidents when he'd –'

Saffy can hear the shuffling of paperwork. 'You've caught me just as I've arrived at my desk, so I need to go now. You'll hear from us in due course. Thanks for getting in touch.'

Saffy blinks as the line goes dead. She pushes the phone back into its base. Flashbacks of Leona scribbling in a small notebook jump into her head. Leona had also kept a journal during the two years she lived with Saffy and Poppy. She'd write in it religiously and then squirrel it away somewhere in her bedroom. Seven-year-old Poppy loved to spend hours helping her decorate the inside pages with coloured pens and tiny, stick-on jewels.

Leona had specifically told her she was keeping a record of Ash's abuse and yet nothing has been found.

That journal must exist . . . so where the hell is it?

Saffy takes her coffee into the living room and places the necklace carefully on the coffee table in front of her, sitting quietly to allow her mind to settle.

At this moment her problems seem insurmountable. Leona's disappearance and the lack of police focus on Ash is one thing, but there is something else equally pressing. Unless she wants to ruin her chances of having Fox stay over at the weekend, she needs to properly address what's happened with Neil. Speak to him face to face.

She mulls over the best course of action while she sets up the new phone that's been on charge all night.

Saffy knows from their time as a married couple – up until their divorce was quietly finalized late last year – that Neil has an aversion to risk. He is a senior partner in a very respected company that has been going for many years. His whole working world as an accountant is based on everything tally-ing up, an obsession with ensuring best practice is always employed and a preference for facts over speculation. In their marriage, that conditioning was always evident in his everyday life, and Neil would go to great lengths to assess risk and ensure he never made mistakes.

It hadn't occurred to Saffy at the time that he'd view his custody of Fox as another task to be allocated, delegated and solved efficiently. Mira would never have entered their lives if Saffy had been able to cope. Another entry on the never-ending list of stuff she had made a mess of leading to consequences that, ultimately, were her fault.

Neil was a classic over-planner and every activity had to be organized to within an inch of its life. In the days they were still a family, they never simply got up and took off for a family day out at the coast without a full appraisal of the traf-fic situation or a considered schedule of what they might do when they got there. Neil would fully research destinations before they made a final choice on where to go on holiday and he would write up a full itinerary for each day. There was no room for impulsiveness or time going to waste. It was the way he ensured he could always feel in control.

Saffy could kick herself for dealing with Neil's call in such an offhand manner yesterday when she knows full well how he operates. There is an urgent need now for damage limitation if she's to have any chance of keeping the week-end arrangements they have discussed for Fox.

While she waits for the call to Neil to connect, she stares at the small panes of coloured glass in the top half of the front door, the bright blue and blood-red distorting her view of the front garden.

She silently offers a prayer that her conversation with Neil will go well. When she's spoken to him, she'll turn her attention to piecing together what she knows about Ash Bannatyne. The police might be fooled by his successful businessman approach, but she isn't. The awful stuff Leona told her last week, the way he has been making her life a misery . . . Saffy feels certain it must be just the tip of the iceberg.

What has Leona's life really been like behind closed doors? Saffy has stayed away because of Ash, and in doing so, has failed her friend.

But no more. She knows Leona better than anyone and regardless of the detectives' misplaced interest in her, the last person to see Leona, she'll do whatever it takes to find her friend.

19

Leona

After spotting Saffy watching her, Leona tried to put her friend out of her mind as the bus trundled from the outskirts of Nottingham towards the city centre.

She stared out at the quiet streets feeling increasingly anxious about the night ahead. There were a few passengers up there with her on the top deck but Leona sat on the back seat, squirrelled into the corner, trying to stop telling herself that Wes was bound to be disappointed with their date.

The thing was, pathetically, she was almost eighteen years old and had never been on a proper date before. It had just been her and Saffy against the world, but this was it; she was off on a night out. A date with Wes, the best-looking guy in the sixth form.

Way before Wes had even spoken to her, Leona had seen the way the confident, most popular girls, with their perfect hair and made-up faces, sidled up to him at any given chance. Giggling and accidentally-on-purpose pressing their impressively full breasts against his arm.

Leona glanced down at her own flat chest and sighed. Patting down her black, wiry hair that seemed to have a mind of its own, she had assumed she'd never have a chance with a boy like Wes.

I can spot players a mile off,' Saffy had remarked just a

couple of weeks before when Leona had told her she liked him. 'You're too good for him.'

Leona always tried to remind herself it was because Saffy cared that she could sometimes say things without thinking. Leona wasn't used to people genuinely caring about her. Saffy was her first real friend and Leona knew she only wanted the best for her. But it was becoming more irritating every time it happened.

Leona had never been to this particular cinema before, so she wasn't sure where to go. But she needn't have worried. When the bus arrived at the terminus, Wes was waiting. He stood with his hands in his pockets, dressed casually in jeans and a black leather bomber jacket, scanning the windows, looking for her.

When she saw him, his bright, wide smile and perfect hair took her breath away for a moment. It didn't seem real that she was finally here, meeting the sixth-form heartthrob for their first date.

'Hey!' Wes walked over and kissed her easily on the cheek. 'Cool jumpsuit.'

Instantly, Leona fretted her Biba outfit was too much. Could he tell it was second-hand? Did it look naff? The sixth-form girls who flocked round him always looked like fashion models without the constraints of wearing school uniform. Their short skirts showed off perfect legs and their unbuttoned blouses were often low enough you could see their lacy bras. Leona felt like a clueless new-starter next to them.

'Thanks. You . . . you look great too,' she managed to say with a smile.

Wes bought them popcorn and Fanta and they settled into their seats to watch some newly released movie full of violence and car chases. It wouldn't have been her choice of film, but she was too hyper and nervy to focus on the screen anyway. Within five minutes of it starting, Wes slid his arm around her shoulders and Leona allowed herself to rest her head lightly against it. It felt like the most natural thing in the world.

A warm, safe feeling blossomed within her. Leona felt it rise from her pink-painted toenails to the top of her head. This was what feeling loved must be like, she told herself. She had never, in her whole life, felt loved and cherished, but she knew instinctively this was it. And she wanted more of it.

Saying that, Leona wasn't stupid. She knew Wes didn't *love* her per se, but his kindness and respect for the next couple of hours felt like a kind of love in its own way, and when the film with all its high-octane noise finally ended, Leona found she really didn't want the feeling to end.

After the cinema, they walked to a small but lively pub tucked away on a narrow street near the marketplace. 'My dad's mate is the landlord,' Wes grinned. 'We'll get a drink here no problem. No ID required.'

They stood at the bar for a short time until a small round table at the back became free. Leona sat down while Wes got the drinks in, the noisy conversation and laughter melting together to compete with the jukebox in the corner. The place was buzzing, and Leona loved every second. She felt so accepted; even better than being with Saffy. For once, she didn't feel like an outcast, the unwanted girl. She felt as if she had a right to be here just as much as everyone else.

Leona watched as Wes returned from the bar, trying not to stare at his broad shoulders and his firm, footballer's thighs that so amply filled out his tight jeans. When he got back to the table, he handed her a Bacardi Breezer with a straw. 'I got you tropical pineapple flavour.'

The drink was delicious, like nothing she'd ever tasted before. They began to chat easily about their lives. Leona was sketchy about her own background but she spoke briefly about her plans to train as a nurse. Wes seemed to have his future all mapped out. He enjoyed talking about his hopes and dreams.

'Football is the only thing I really want to do. I love it so much, I'd play for free but when I look at players like Steven Gerrard and Wayne Rooney with their big houses and fancy cars, I think: "Why can't I have that, too?"' She watched his face light up as he talked about his passion, his face animated as he made his point. 'Course, my dad's not keen. He wants me to go into the family business. He says hardly anyone gets to Premiership level, but why not me? I train hard and I'm determined to make it.'

'I think you will make it,' Leona said. 'Everyone at school says you're the best player by far.'

He stopped talking and narrowed his eyes. 'Are you just saying that, or do you really mean it?'

'Put it this way, if I had any money, I'd happily bet it all on you becoming a famous footballer.'

Wes laughed and took a swig from his bottle. 'You're sweet and funny, do you know that?'

By funny, she took it he meant silly, and she lowered her eyes, suddenly embarrassed. Wes slid a finger under her chin to tilt it up again. 'Hey,' he said softly. 'I like sweet and funny. I really like *you*.'

He'd kissed her then. Softly, on the lips. The noise of the pub faded into the background and for a few seconds, it was just the two of them together in their own little soft pink bubble.

After they'd finished their drinks, Wes walked her back to the bus stop where he kissed her again. This time for a little longer. His embrace felt caring and warm and she knew then that Saffy was wrong. Wes wasn't a player; he was the real deal and he'd chosen her to be with tonight.

Her heart sank when the bus appeared at the end of the road.

Tenderly, Wes placed his hand on the side of her face. 'I've loved tonight. Will you come out with me again?'

She nodded. 'I've enjoyed it too. Thanks for paying for everything.'

He laughed and touched the end of her nose. 'You're doing it again . . . being sweet. You're not like the other girls. They expect the earth.'

He stood and waved her off until the bus turned the corner again. Leona laid her head against the cold window, closed her eyes and tried to relive the moments of the evening she'd loved the most.

When she got off the bus, she felt as though she was dancing on air. She walked down the street and turned into the road where she lived now with Saffy and Poppy.

Soon she might even escape the deep-seated feeling she wasn't enough. Wes Sharpe had shown her another way to find affection and love, and she was already addicted.

20

Poppy

In her student digs, she lies on her side on top of the crumpled bed sheets and stares into a handheld mirror. One of her tight braids has come undone and dark blonde hair tumbles over her shoulder. It is soft and shiny, kinks with a natural wave. But Poppy can't bear to look at her hair any more. She pins it back, ties it up, braids it out of sight.

Afterwards, when she was in hospital, when she'd seen what he'd done to her, she had felt something splinter inside her. But she had no recollection of that moment. Something in her mind was protecting her and she felt glad.

Poppy puts down the mirror and turns her attention to the stuffed backpack on the floor beside her. She doesn't want to take out the textbooks yet, doesn't want to get any closer to what is hidden beneath the cardboard insert at the bottom of the bag.

She'd never admit it to Saffy, but what happened yesterday has unnerved her. After handing over Fox to Neil, she'd cancelled her planned night out with Harry, made some excuse about having to babysit Fox. She had told her flatmates she felt crap, like she was coming down with something, climbed into bed and drank herself into blissful oblivion. It was only when she woke in the early hours and couldn't get back to sleep, she realized she'd forgotten to check in with Saffy after her police interview. She'd rattled off a message and finally gone back to sleep.

Poppy holds up her hand and studies it in the grey light filtering through the small, square window at the side of her bed. Her hand looks the same and yet she knows it is not. It is different, like every inch of her is different. Inside and out. Despite her bravado, part of Poppy *did* die that night. The vulnerable part. The gullible, soft centre that really believed life might just turn out like the celebrity fairy tales she saw online. A life of travelling through glossy vistas, of sparkling cocktails and sunny skies. A life of parties and love and adoration from an array of handsome guys.

When she'd finally felt able to restart her degree after the attack, moving back into student accommodation, she'd felt exhilarated. Free at last from Saffy's claustrophobic monitoring and her obsessive need to know exactly where Poppy was and what she was doing every minute of the day. It had been an exhausting way to live. It had almost sapped the life out of her although it had somehow not quite succeeded in infecting her with the level of fear Saffy herself had.

Poppy's digs are just a twenty-five-minute walk from where Saffy lives now, on Trent Lane, if she takes the shortcut across Lady Bay bridge – or a thirty-minute bus ride that goes the long way around. No time at all, really, but reassuringly far enough to escape Saffy's preferred existence of isolation that she had tried so hard to pull Poppy into since the attack.

Saffy had called her a few times yesterday when she'd got back from the police station, but Poppy couldn't face talking to her. Couldn't stop worrying about what might come to light now the police were involved in their lives.

Poppy grabs the backpack and empties the textbooks out on to the floor before pushing her hand underneath the bottom insert and feeling around. Her fingers grip the unregistered phone she'd managed to conceal from the police yesterday before leaving Saffy's house.

She opens the message thread and deletes everything, including all the explicit photographs they had enjoyed sending each other.

She clicks on the short list of contacts and stares at his initials for a moment, a slideshow of flashbacks filling her mind.

Poppy blinks them away and looks again at his name. And then she presses *delete*.

21

Saffy

Saffy gets herself a glass of water and sits down at the break-fast bar in front of the laptop. Neil isn't answering his phone, so she's focusing on Leona for now. She opens her emails and searches Leona's name.

As a qualified nurse, Leona had to work some pretty anti-social hours. With Saffy working full-time during the day when Leona slept, they began communicating mostly by email.

Saffy scrolls down the list her search has generated and opens an email Leona sent her about Ash, not long after Poppy was attacked.

> You won't believe this but . . . I met someone at work! His name is Ash Bannatyne and he's a very successful salesman, not to mention good-looking and kind. The list goes on!! He takes me to the best restaurants and get this . . . he drives a Porsche Boxster!! He came into the hospital for an appointment regarding medical supplies and we got on like a house on fire. He asked me out and the rest is history! How are you and Poppy? Hope you're . . .

Saffy opens the next message sent just a couple of weeks later. Leona was never one to take it slowly when it came to boyfriends.

> I've told Ash all about you, my oldest friend, and he's dying to meet you! He says you sound lovely – obvs I've said nothing but good things about you and ignored what you're really like!! – ha

ha only joking, you know I love you. Anyways, if you like we could
pop over this weekend and bring wine? I know you're still not
getting out much and I've been really worried about you.

Saffy sniffs and re-reads that last sentence. Now, after all this
time, it looks as though Leona tagged it on for posterity after
all the banter. Saying that Saffy wasn't getting out much was
the biggest understatement of the year, because she was still
raw and increasingly depressed after the attack on Poppy, and
she wasn't getting out *at all* around the time of Leona's email.

Saffy looks up and stares at the plain white wall opposite
the breakfast bar. She remembers feeling chained to the
house like a prisoner; it was a state she had welcomed at the
time. The outside world terrified her, as did strangers of any
description including couriers or delivery drivers. But it was
damaging Fox. He'd become nervous and introverted and
Neil had sat her down to say unless things changed, some-
thing would have to be done.

Saffy remembered she'd replied to this particular email by
return and explained she wasn't feeling up to a visit that
weekend. Or any weekend for the foreseeable.

She scrolls past another few months' worth of messages.
She can recall feeling like death and reading Leona's effusive
and slightly surreal messages that were so full of life and
optimism for the future. Leona had always tried to cheer up
others by being jolly. It was a way of showing she cared, Saffy
had reasoned. But they felt like a mirror held up to her own
social anxieties.

Leona's relationship with Ash had intensified quickly and
Saffy, who at that time had been in the midst of what she
now knows to be a mental health crisis, had got the distinct
feeling, reading her emails, that there was no longer room in
Leona's life for her and Poppy. Not now that she had Ash.

She scrolls forward and the next message she opens is dated after Leona and Ash got married in Mallorca.

Ash has started a new job, working for a company called Mediden Global. They headhunted him, can you believe it? He's not just going to be a bog-standard salesman this time, it's a management role for their major sales projects in the Middle East . . . blah blah blah! The small print goes over my head, but it's all good and we're really happy together. How are you feeling? Is the . . .

Mediden Global. This is what she's been searching for: the name of his company. As far as Saffy knows, Ash hasn't moved on since landing this job and he's just had another promotion.

She opens Google and takes a sip of her water. The search results are there waiting when she puts down her glass.

She knows Ash uses his full name professionally, so she had googled *Ashley Bannatyne Mediden Global.* Several links are listed, all mentioning Ash's name in conjunction with the company name.

Now she's satisfied there is a definite link between Ash and Mediden Global, Saffy opens a new window and types in the URL address. A slick, professional-looking website loads and Saffy clicks on one of the buttons along the top: *Meet the Team.*

The screen loads with postage-sized photographs, clustered together by department and each one with the name of the staff member underneath. Saffy scrolls through to the Sales Team section and swipes past several sales managers, none of whom are Ash. She gets to the end of that section and then it's the turn of their HR staff to be featured. She checks the sales section again but it's clear that Ash's photo and name are not amongst them.

Back at the search pages, Saffy clicks on a couple links and spots immediately that although these articles allude to prospective sales drives into the Middle East and name Ashley Bannatyne as the Senior Sales Executive, they are all dated last year. There is nothing current, nothing new.

On the stroke of nine a.m., Saffy picks up her new phone and dials the main number under the 'Contact Us' details of the Mediden website.

It is after a couple of false starts and Saffy being given a different number when she remembers Leona had told her Ash worked for the Midlands branch, a woman's voice comes on the line. 'Can I help?'

'I'm trying to contact Ashley Bannatyne who is a Senior Sales Executive with Mediden. I have his business card and want to get in touch again with a sales query.'

'Bear with me a moment.' Saffy hears tapping on a keyboard before the woman says, 'I'm so sorry, madam. Ashley Bannatyne no longer works for the company. According to my records he left us three months ago. But if your call is regarding an order, I can put you through to –'

'No, no, that's fine,' Saffy says slowly. 'Thanks for your help.'

She ends the call and stares out of the kitchen window at the prickly gorse hedge that bears perfumed yellow flowers in the spring. Now it's reduced to spiky, bare branches, a warning to stay away.

Saffy has been out of the loop for a while, so there's a small possibility she hasn't been told that Ash has changed companies or lost his job and walked into another one. But it's the kind of information she would definitely have clocked and remembered if Leona had mentioned it. Moreover, they had been celebrating his big promotion yesterday. Granted, the company name hadn't been mentioned, but there was a definite sense of his career news being a continuation, a reward for work done. What had Ash's humble brag been, again? *Long overdue, but they finally realized I'm their biggest asset.*

The sort of thing you'd only say if you'd been working at a company for some time.

Saffy thinks about their house. The downstairs so homely and stylish and totally in keeping with a successful executive lifestyle. Set against the harsh surroundings of the upstairs: unwelcoming and fraught with danger and risk of injury for little Rosie.

She is certain there is no new company, no recent change of employer.

Ash Bannatyne is lying. Putting on a face to Leona, to his neighbours and even to the police.

22

Saffy

Saffy has in her head that since lockdown, Neil works from home on Fridays, but she could be mistaken or it's possible his schedule might have changed.

She's left messages, sent emails and there's only one thing for it now: she must go round there. Something she hasn't done for over a year. Saffy is sure Neil won't appreciate her turning up at the house without prior warning, but she needs to make him aware how important it is to her to have Fox tomorrow as they've agreed.

Outside it's bright and sunny and the forecast for the weekend is equally good. The possibilities of what she could plan for Fox feel endless, even with the shadow of Leona and Rosie's disappearance hanging over her. The local park, time together in the garden . . . Saffy's heart aches to spend a couple of glorious days with her son. A whole weekend with no need to clock-watch. No more Neil turning up ten minutes early to whisk him away before the traffic builds up.

It's only a few miles to Neil's house. She knows the twenty-minute bus ride like the back of her hand because she used to live there. Before it was Neil and Mira's house. They all lived there: Saffy, Neil and Fox; in the days when they were still married and had built a happy life together.

Before everything turned to hell one night just two weeks before Christmas, three years ago.

Saffy gets off the bus and walks down the long road,

wondering how many of her old neighbours still live there. They had never been overly friendly with the other residents on the street, but they'd usually get the odd barbecue invitation in summer. Saffy and Neil once held a Halloween party where everyone dressed up and brought their kids.

As she approaches the driveway, she slows her pace. There's a silver sports car parked in front of the house. Neil is a big Lexus fan and last time Saffy saw him, he pulled up in a sleek saloon. So this car must belong to his fiancée, Mira.

Saffy and Neil's marriage broke down after the attack on Poppy. Fox had just been a year old and Saffy had started to feel increasingly unwell and was being regularly treated by the hospital. They both agreed Neil should remain living in the house with Fox, and he rented Saffy a comfortable studio apartment close to amenities and a fifteen-minute walk away from the family home.

When Neil introduced Mira to her as Fox's nanny, Saffy had got on well with the slightly nervous young woman a good five or six years younger than herself. Slightly overweight and wearing grungy-style clothing, Mira's unremarkable features were dwarfed by heavy framed spectacles and an unruly mop of dark hair. She had listened attentively to Saffy's take on Fox's likes, dislikes and his routines. Mira had reassured her she'd be following Saffy's lead to keep things as familiar as possible for Fox. But Neil's regular updates as the months passed by seemed to suggest nothing but change.

'Mira's enrolled Fox into a few playgroups and clubs . . . Mira's overhauled our diet, we're eating so much more fruit and veg now.' Then: 'Mira's going to be staying over a couple of nights a week to help out with Fox on my early starts.'

Even through the fog of her heavily medicated depression and anxiety, Saffy had felt mild alarm. She'd clocked

Mira's infinite capabilities, so much more impressive than her own had been.

Saffy had suspected Neil would soon begin to resent an outsider imposing big changes on not just his son, but also his own routines. So it had been a big surprise when he'd told Saffy a few weeks later that Mira would be moving into the house with him and Fox. Just five months after her appointment.

'We have so much in common. Spending so much time together, we've grown really close,' Neil explained clumsily during an impromptu drop-in at her house. 'Fox loves Mira and . . . well, so do I. We're in a relationship.'

It had taken Saffy a while to come to terms with it: another woman being with her son more than she was. A creeping feeling of unease permeated her nights, managing even to pass through the defences of her prescribed sedation.

Then one day, Mira invited Saffy for lunch at a small, kitsch vegetarian café in town. Saffy had been unprepared for Mira's metamorphosis. Gone were the unflattering spectacles and baggy clothing. Mira had lost a lot of weight and had a new sleek hairstyle. It suited her. Stunning amber eyes and delicate features, previously swamped by outdated eyewear, popped from her smooth, blemish-free skin.

'I know it must have been a shock hearing about our relationship, but I want you to know I'll never try to be Fox's mum, Saffy,' Mira had said when they had ordered their drinks and food choices. 'I want to be a positive adult in his life. I hope he'll learn to trust me and that I can have a role in his upbringing, but I'm not looking to take your place in any way, shape or form.'

Saffy had been taken aback by Mira's straightforward manner, but she'd also respected her for it. She'd thought: *It can't be easy for her, either.* That exchange was over a year ago and since then, apart from fleeting glances, or the odd wave from the car, Saffy hadn't had another in-depth conversation with Mira. Neil recently announced they were engaged to be married.

Saffy opens her phone camera and peers into the small screen at her face. She never bothers with much makeup during the day. Mascara and a natural lip tint is about as good as it gets, but with everything that's been happening today, she hasn't given it a thought. She stares at the dark circles under her eyes and her slightly wild hair that refuses to be tamed by the over-stretched bobble struggling to keep it back.

She smooths her hair back the best she can with her fingers and teases out a couple of wispy bits at the side to soften the look. Then she walks up to the front gate.

Saffy rings the doorbell and waits. It's a new front door, she notices. It used to be a plain white UPVC one when she lived here, but it's been replaced by a dark grey modern design with three little diamonds of opaque glass along the top edge. The handle is now a long, polished sliver of brushed stainless steel that runs a third of the length of the right-hand side of the door.

She feels oddly pleased they've changed the door. The old one must have had indelible traces of her old life within it. The hundreds of times she'd spent opening and closing it while struggling with Fox's pushchair, stepping out and breathing in fresh air as they embarked on their frequent walks to the local parks in the crisp autumn sunshine. Coming home and snuggling up together on the sofa to read *Stick Man* with the log burner on.

For the first few months after the attack, Saffy thought she was coping. The fact her mental health was declining rapidly was the elephant in the room nobody wanted to talk about. Until Neil took charge.

The door opens and a radiant Mira stands there dressed in cashmere leggings and a loose knitted top. Saffy assumes she must be working from home today – Neil had mentioned some time ago she'd set up an online forum giving video instruction on 'Nanny knows Best' advice to parents – but she looks so relaxed, not like she's about to take part in a Facebook Live.

Her long, wavy hair is lustrous and glossy and her dark, smooth skin looks flawless. Saffy feels like a pasty-looking frump in comparison.

When she sees Saffy on the doorstep, Mira's perfect smile falters just for a second before she recovers.

'Oh . . . hi, Saffy, hi! This is a surprise, come in!'

'Sorry to just turn up like this, Mira,' Saffy offers.

'That's OK! Really . . . it's no problem.'

'The thing is, I desperately need to speak to Neil and he's not answering my calls. I keep getting his answerphone. Is he working from home today?'

Mira ushers her inside before closing the new front door. 'I have the same problem most days, Saffy. He's had to go into the office today and I do know he's in a meeting all this morning. That's the reason he hasn't got back to you yet, I'm sure. Let's go through to the kitchen.'

It's nice and warm in the house, but Mira pulls on a long, grey cardigan as they walk down the freshly decorated hallway. The rather grubby carpet that used to be here has been replaced by laminate flooring which runs throughout the house. Saffy passes the bottom of the stairs, recalling the pile of shoes that used to collect there until either she, or Neil, would finally give in and tidy them away. Now, there's a neat shoe rack by the front door that houses just one pair of Neil's well-worn Chelsea boots.

As she walks, Saffy cranes her neck to peer at the now

extended lounge. It's been completely redesigned in cool shades of white and grey with a big media wall containing an outsized flatscreen television and a modern oblong real-flame fire that sits flush to the wall. It looks like a completely different space to where she used to read to Fox, the floor strewn with his toys. Saffy has yet to see evidence of any of Fox's belongings here. Incredibly, she hasn't tripped over a single Matchbox car from the extensive collection he loves so much.

'Wow, the kitchen looks amazing, Mira.'

They've extended in here too. Wide glass doors and a glass apex allow the light to flood into what used to be a far smaller, darker space. Pale grey units line one wall with a run of glossy white on the other like something in an interiors magazine. It's all brought together by striking white and grey-veined marble counter tops.

Saffy feels gratified to see a colourful drawing pinned to the double American refrigerator. Mira follows her eyes and smiles, removing it and sliding it over the worktop to her.

'Fox drew this at nursery last week,' she says warmly, pulling mugs out of a cupboard. 'I thought it was so sweet.'

Saffy holds her breath and studies the picture. Fox has sketched Neil, himself and what is, without doubt, Mira, with her bouncy dark hair. They're all holding hands and standing next to the house – which is the exact same size as them. The sun is shining, the grass is green, and the sky is blue. When Fox's nursery teacher looked at this, she must have thought he has the perfect family.

Mira makes coffee quickly using a hissing boiling water tap and they move over to the squashy, stylish sofa in front of the glass doors.

'I know it must be hard seeing me on the picture, but Fox talks about you all the time, Saffy. He knows you're Mummy and I'm just Mira.'

Saffy feels a threatening prickle behind her eyes. 'Thank you for saying that. It means a lot.'

'Gosh, it's so warm in here,' Mira says, standing up again. 'I'll just open the doors a crack.'

Saffy nearly suggests Mira might as well slip off her wool cardi but stops herself. She watches as Mira moves over to the glass and opens the doors. The breeze blows in immediately, wafting her long cardigan open.

That's when Saffy sees it, so slight, she has to look twice to make sure it's not just a trick of the light. Mira's svelte, size eight outline has acquired a neat little bump.

Looking at her, Saffy estimates that Mira is probably about five or six months pregnant.

23

Poppy

After deleting the texts and contact details on her phone, Poppy feels a little calmer. More in control.

For the next hour or so, she focuses on getting ready to meet up with Harry again. Shower: tick. Hair tightly braided so she doesn't have to look at it: tick. She has carefully applied natural makeup in the interest of not looking as though she is trying too hard. But she reminds herself that Harry is not some fresher-year student at uni she is trying to impress. He looked pretty scruffy the other night in her bedroom, but when he's scrubbed up, he looks the biz.

Poppy dresses in a close-fitting black skirt that finishes just above the knee. Long boots and a black lacy vest top showing just a hint of cleavage toned down nicely with a silky overblouse. OK, maybe a little OTT for a late-morning coffee meet-up, but she is out to impress and this look is far classier than her usual boho mish-mash.

It's important she arrives looking cool and collected, so it takes no time at all for Poppy to decide the eight-quid Uber is worth it. During the longer than usual fifteen-minute journey into the city on irritatingly busy roads, Poppy enjoys the sparks of excitement in her belly that signal the fact she is again getting involved with an unsuitable man. She has nothing to back this up right now, but as with her last guy, Harry is all the more exciting because he feels somehow strictly out of bounds.

The Uber drops her off in the Lace Market and she walks around the corner to Victoria Street, checking out her reflection in the shop windows as she passes. She looks good and takes her time so that when she finally reaches the Cosy Club where Harry has booked them a table for brunch, she is a good five minutes late, which is what she wanted. Doesn't do to appear too keen.

Outside the club, a sandwich board advertises 'Today's Deal'. A mozzarella and pesto panini with a spiced pumpkin latte. Someone has drawn a coffee cup and saucer with tendrils of steam rising from it. Inside, it is pleasantly buzzing rather than crowded. Poppy scans the occupied tables and is a little put out that Harry is not here yet. A waiter takes her over to their reserved table and Poppy pulls out her phone, but she has no texts or missed calls.

Poppy raises her chin in defiance, sliding her phone back into her handbag. She reminds herself that, just like the others, this liaison won't go anywhere and nor does she need it to. She doesn't need a man – she is strong and independent, and if she only relies on herself, no man will ever be able to hurt her again.

After another ten minutes of waiting, she gets up and leaves. It really isn't cool to expect much from a guy. Today is more proof they are just passing distractions in a colourful life.

Poppy can't stomach going back to her digs and wallowing in her own misery, so she heads to the bus stop. She'll call at another café near her flat, a tiny place that's just opened and offers calorie-laden caramel lattes and chocolate flapjacks. She might even order a side of whipped cream with those tiny pink and white marshmallows piled on top. That will be more satisfying than any man.

Poppy begins to walk back along Victoria Street towards

the bus stop on Fletcher Gate. With each step, she feels her mood getting lower. She'd really thought Harry liked her. He'd even asked about her sister after Saffy's call on Thursday, seemed as if he was interested in Poppy's family and her life at uni.

The bump comes completely out of the blue. Poppy feels her knees buckle and then she is falling in slow motion. She wails, hands in the air as she goes down like a sack of potatoes and then, just as she should land in an unceremonious heap on the unforgiving asphalt, two strong arms break her fall and hold her there, suspended inches away from complete public humiliation.

A small noise of shock and relief escapes her throat as she looks up and stares straight into Harry's eyes.

'Got to say, I've never had anyone fall for me quite like that,' Harry grins as he hoists her back on her feet. 'I must be getting better at this white knight stuff.'

'Oh! I thought you were . . . I mean I thought you'd –'

'I got delayed, sorry. I was going to text you but . . . never mind, anyway. Let's get out of the cold.'

In the café, Poppy insists on getting the coffees to thank him for his impromptu rescue. While she's waiting, she turns to watch him sitting there, checking his phone and then running a hand through his hair as though he's as nervous to look good as she is. She carries the two lattes over to the table and slides one in front of him.

'Thanks. You were deep in thought back there on the street,' he says. 'I actually smiled and said hi from a few paces away, but you seemed hell-bent on colliding with me.'

'Stop!' She laughs, covering her reddening face with a hand.

He takes a sip of his coffee. 'Glad you made it and your sister didn't forbid you to leave the house.'

Poppy grins. 'I don't live with my sister any more!'

'I know, I'm joking, but . . . she calls you a lot, right? Keeps an eye on you.'

'Yes, but she's not my keeper.' Irritation pokes at Poppy's ribs. 'I refuse to let her infect me with her crazy fear.'

'Why is she like that? So scared of everything, I mean?'

Poppy swallows. 'It's a long story.'

Harry laughs. 'Hey, we've got plenty of time, right?'

'Well, it's Saffy's business, but let's just say she's still stuck on some stuff that happened in the past. Like I suppose we all are to some extent, you know?'

'Ain't *that* the truth,' Harry mutters, a shadow crossing his face.

She'd like to know the secrets of his past, but Poppy can't tell him the truth about what happened to her. She just can't. The invisible shield that keeps her safe would shatter into a million pieces, because Poppy's magic trick is to divorce herself from the reality of it. Treat the bits she can remember like a bad movie she once watched.

They order some food, chat about not much at all really, and then Harry says, 'Listen, we're running out of time now, but would you like to go for a meal another time . . . or a few drinks somewhere nice? I just feel like I really need to see you again when we can be together without watching the clock.'

'I'd love that.' She wants him. Feels a little breathless with it, and she loves this feeling when it comes. There is no time to play hard ball, she needs to get him pinned down. 'A meal and a drink would be amazing.'

He laughs. 'Are you free Sunday night? I mean, don't feel you have to say yes, but –'

That night in her flat, Poppy learned the hard way that it's not a given you'll live forever. Life isn't perfect and it can get cut short in the space of a moment, and that's why it's important to try and live it to the full. No time for regrets.

'That's cool,' she says. 'Sunday night is perfect.'

His phone pings with a text notification. He reads it and frowns before standing up, says, 'Sorry, I have to go now. Got all sorts of appointments I need to keep.'

When she stands up too, they look at each other and then he leans forward and kisses her lightly on the cheek. 'Until Sunday night then.' He presses his index finger lightly on her mouth. 'Our secret.'

'Our secret.' She grins without really knowing what the secret is.

But one thing is certain, Poppy thinks devilishly to herself. If Saffy could see her now with a guy like Harry, she would not be happy. She would not be happy at all.

24

Saffy

Saffy stands watching Mira by the open doors, momentarily frozen. She is still in shock at the realization Mira is pregnant. She is debating whether to mention her observation when Mira spins around quickly and catches her shocked expression. Saffy immediately averts her eyes, but too late. Mira's hand flutters to her belly.

'Oh,' she says, giving a little regretful smile. 'I see you've already spotted the obvious. It's just started to show this last couple of weeks.'

'Congratulations.' The skin around Saffy's mouth feels too tightly stretched. 'When is the baby due?'

'Thank you, Saffy. She's due late November,' she says, still cradling her bump as she sits down. 'I'm twenty-one weeks today.' She hesitates, looks a little awkward. 'I . . . I had my second scan on Tuesday.'

'Wow.' Saffy was right then. About five months. 'A girl! You both must be delighted.'

Mira relaxes, her face cracking into a wide smile. 'We really are. Neil is like a kid waiting for Christmas, he's so excited!'

'I bet he is,' Saffy says, and the stretched grin makes a return.

I don't want any more kids. I couldn't imagine loving another child as much as I love Fox.

He must have had a change of heart.

'A new baby girl is such super news for you both,' Saffy

147

says in a new, upbeat voice she doesn't recognize. 'A winter baby to welcome to the world . . . how lovely!'

'We'd always planned to have a child together, it just happened a little quicker than we'd anticipated . . . as these things often do. There's lots to think about now though, like where we're going to live.'

Saffy's ears fill with a low buzzing noise. 'You'll move house?'

'Look at this place!' She laughs and sweeps her hand around the large kitchen. 'It isn't big enough for a growing family. We want a decent-sized garden. I've always fancied the idea of moving to the country and . . .' She registers Saffy's concerned expression and stops short. 'Nothing has been decided yet, Saffy. I'm sure Neil will keep you fully informed.'

Saffy feels sick when she thinks about how they have the money to move anywhere; miles away in the country, even. Neil is a partner in his company. He can design a new working schedule for himself with minimal commute, no problem at all. They'll take Fox with them and because Neil has full custody, Saffy will have zero rights. No say in where her son might end up or how often she'll be allowed to see him. She'll be at Neil's mercy, and after everything that's just happened and how annoyed he is with her, that is an alarming thought.

Mira looks at her curiously and Saffy tries to shake off her catastrophizing. 'Have you told Fox yet? He'll be so excited to hear he has a sister.'

Mira gives her a tight little smile. 'We haven't told Fox, no. But we know we need to do that soon. He's a bright little boy and doesn't miss much.'

Is Mira really describing the traits of Saffy's own son to her? Like Fox is *her* child?

'And I think Neil was planning to tell you shortly, Saffy.'

Saffy opens her mouth to say something but words fail her.

Mira looks at her. 'He told me Leona and Ash Bannatyne are missing. And little Rosie, too . . . you must be out of your mind with worry.'

'Yes. Desperately so. All three of them, just vanishing into thin air like that.'

'Look, I hope you don't mind me bringing this up, but all these headlines about crime in the city, then the news about the Bannatynes, got me thinking how awful it must have been for you and Poppy,' Mira says, tipping her head slightly to one side and regarding Saffy. 'The attack, in Poppy's flat and . . . oh gosh, I'm making a hash of this. All I mean is, I think you're doing really well to try and be a good mum to Fox despite your . . . problems.'

'Thanks,' Saffy murmurs, slightly stunned by Mira's impulsive little outburst. The attack is the last thing she wants to revisit with everything else that's currently happening.

'How is Poppy these days?' Mira continues, undaunted. 'I don't know her well, of course, but Neil told me all about what happened. What you two went through and how Poppy might have died if you hadn't come back from –'

'Actually, Neil had no right to discuss something so personal and devastating without asking me first,' Saffy says stiffly. Mira looks mortified, but Saffy can't help it. Enough is enough and she has to bring this disturbing little violation of her privacy to an end. Mira needs to know she can't just bring Saffy's trauma up like this with no warning. As if she's discussing the weather.

'Forgive me, Saffy. I'm so sorry. I didn't mean –'

Saffy holds up a hand, feeling stronger in the light of the sudden shift in power. 'It's fine, Mira. Honestly. Please, don't apologize. Neil is the one who should have known better, discussing it so carelessly in the first place. It's not something I'd ever want to talk about openly.'

'I don't think Neil meant any harm by it,' Mira says, her tone a little less placatory. 'He said everything he's told me about what happened to you and Poppy is available to read online. And sometimes . . . well, I just thought it might help for you to talk about it with someone, you know?'

Saffy bites the inside of her lip. Mira is testing her patience now and treating her like a naïve fool. She feels certain Neil has included plenty of juicy recollections, like Saffy's middle-of-the-night meltdowns when she'd wake up screaming and lashing out. Maybe he's also mentioned the list of medications the GP prescribed, which included powerful sedatives and addictive anti-depressants. Or perhaps, over a glass of quality red, he chatted about Saffy's rejection of her son and her inability to provide even the most basic level of care for one-year-old Fox.

And none of the above *is available to read online*.

But Saffy takes a moment to breathe and remind herself that she is here to make amends to Neil for her earlier call. Primarily, she's here to rescue her precious weekend with her son. Not to pile yet more problems on to her already-overflowing plate of them.

Somehow, she manages to swallow her annoyance back down again.

'It's true that there is a lot of stuff online, but I'd have hoped Neil would understand it's still raw and very personal and I do struggle with speaking openly about it.' *Especially to someone I barely know*, she wants to add but resists the temptation. 'But honestly, Mira, not to worry.'

'Anyway, I apologize again.' Mercifully, Mira falls quiet.

It suddenly occurs to Saffy she might be able to use this opportunity to get Mira onside before Neil hears the full extent of what's happened from other sources. 'Going back to Leona and Rosie going missing, I was the last person to visit the house, apparently. Before a neighbour saw the front door wide open with the smoke alarm blaring for ages and rang the police.'

Mira's hand drops away from her face and she frowns. 'Gosh, you saw them directly before they disappeared?'

'Yes. I've already spoken to the police about it all. Yesterday. I've given them as much information as I can and answered all their questions.'

'They . . . didn't arrest you or anything?'

'No, no. I think they realize I had nothing to do with it.'

'You *think*?'

'Well, they haven't got any other information about what happened to the family yet. So until they find out exactly what's happened, they're keeping an open mind.' Cool air filters in through the open doors and Saffy shivers. 'I just hope they're OK, Leona and Rosie. I hope they're not in any danger. I don't really care about Ash.'

Mira glances at her phone on the low table. 'No response from Neil yet, I'm afraid. He's probably going to be ages in his meeting. I'm really not sure it's worth you waiting.'

'That's fine. I only called in on the off-chance I might catch him here.' Saffy pulls out her new phone and holds it up. 'I've texted him, so he'll have my new number.'

She picks up her mug and walks over to the window, to the new integrated sink and drainer installed there. In the exact place she used to prepare Fox's nutritious food from scratch, pouring the blended goodness into cubed trays for freezing. Lazy Sunday lunches, the homemade pasta sauces Neil used to say were to die for . . . all created here in this very spot.

'I'll tell Neil you called round and ask him to give you a

ring as soon as he can,' Mira says, giving her an odd look as she moves into the hall.

'That would be really helpful. I'm expecting him to bring Fox over to mine tomorrow morning.' Saffy places her mug on the side. 'Thank you, Mira. Thanks for the drink.'

Mira can't get the front door open quick enough, and when Saffy steps outside, she says a hasty goodbye before swiftly closing the door.

Saffy walks towards the bus stop in a bit of a daze. So much for getting Mira onside. She didn't seem that supportive, and Saffy is trying not to think about whether they'll want to relocate when Mira has the baby. It's as she's turning the corner on to the main road that Saffy has the idea.

Leona's house is only fifteen minutes from here. She could do a bit of a recce to see what's happening.

Saffy's not entirely sure why this thought is so appealing, but with each second that passes, she feels more and more of a pull.

She crosses the road to the other bus stop. The blue sky has dulled a little with clouds obscuring the bright sun of earlier. It seems so long since she's been in a warm climate, where she's looked up at a blue sky day after day and felt the sort of sunshine with the strength to sink down into her bones. Saffy hasn't been on holiday in years, since before Fox was born. Neil and Mira took him to Tenerife in the spring for a week. Saffy googled their hotel in a resort inspired by Disney and completely geared towards families with waterslides and non-stop entertainment for kids. Lifestyle photographs of good-looking parents lazing by the infinity pool with their cocktails.

It might be a little more difficult for Mira and Neil to do that next year with a newborn baby, Saffy thinks, a little spitefully, as she boards the bus, swipes her travel card and takes a seat.

When Leona had described her wedding to Ash in Mallorca, she'd talked about the pale, sandy beaches, the crystal-clear waters and lush greenery, and the intense heat. Leona had been head over heels in love with Ash back then, had thought she'd met her soulmate. Had she no inkling of his controlling nature when they'd wed? Why had Ash failed to tell Leona he was no longer working . . . or was it the case that Leona knew but had decided not to tell Saffy? They had become so insular and secretive.

The bus drops her a couple of streets away and she walks to Musters Road. The Bannatyne house is about halfway up, across the road from a small copse of trees and bushes.

Saffy pulls up her jacket collar and walks head down, past the house. Mindful of Tania, the neighbour who reported their disappearance, she moves cautiously until she sees that Tania's driveway is clear of cars. Then she speeds up and heads towards the cluster of trees.

It's been nearly twenty-four hours since her fateful visit here to check on Leona. There is a uniformed police officer stretching police tape across the front door. The tape affixed to the gate has already come loose and is fluttering in the light breeze.

The property might officially still be out of bounds but the house itself looks empty. Saffy suspects that the officer is there today in case a witness comes forward, or if the family unexpectedly return. The police are notoriously short-staffed and it's likely this officer won't remain in post for very much longer. Still, it's a waiting game. She realizes the risk is high for her to even be in the vicinity, bearing in mind the current police interest in her.

As she turns and hurries back towards the bus stop, Saffy thinks about the spare key tucked at the back of her bedside table drawer. When they'd first bought the house, she had still been picking up Rosie occasionally from school and Leona, who was still working at the hospital at that point, had given it to her in case of emergencies. As Saffy's visits grew less and less frequent, the spare key had slipped the mind of both women.

But now, Saffy thinks, at some point soon, if she needs it, that key could come in very handy indeed.

25

Poppy

Eight months ago, something completely unexpected happened to Poppy. It marked a new, bold step in fighting the fear that had threatened to overpower her after the attack.

What happened was also an event that risked everything around her turning to utter shit. A risk that was higher than it had ever been in her adult life.

But the thrill of it! That, to Poppy, was worth any amount of risk.

Last September she had begun her second year of study. Like most of her housemates, she had taken the mickey a bit. Brand-new student loan paid into the bank, student events all over the city and so much cheap booze, Poppy sometimes felt like she might drown in it.

Then all at once, about three weeks before breaking up for Christmas, a bunch of continuous assessments were imminent. Her tutor finally caught up with her, questioning Poppy's commitment to the course, and she'd had no choice but to cram in some revision before her appointment with the tutor – who, she had to remember, had the power to throw her off the course.

The day before the appointment, Poppy got in after a drinking session with her housemates at midnight. She simply could not face the university library, stuffed full as it was 24/7 with swots who followed the 'no phones, no talking' signs like their lives depended on it.

Instead, she'd taken herself off to the 200 Degrees coffee shop in Flying Horse Walk and ordered an almond milk spiced latte. She'd bagged her favourite table in the corner where she had a good view of the interesting new barista who, her flatmates had reliably informed her, bore more than a passing resemblance to Paul Mescal.

The assignment was based around the Renaissance painters and Poppy began sifting laboriously through the university's online art database for work by Donatello and Michelangelo, time slipping by without her noticing. The café was warm and bustling and she felt content in her little enclave with Billie Eilish playing in her AirPods. She'd forgotten just how much satisfaction she got from immersing herself in her studies and vowed to turn over a new leaf after she'd wriggled out of this sticky patch.

The tap on her shoulder came as a shock. She lurched forward and knocked her insulated paper cup clean off the table. There was only an inch of cold coffee left, but somehow it managed to spray everywhere, including all over the front of her dress and her laptop.

'Shit! Oh no . . .' she shrieked when the monitor flickered and then turned black. 'All my work . . .' She spun around, her eyes sparking. 'My tutor is going to throw me off the – oh, it's you!'

'Sorry! Poppy, I'm really, really sorry.'

Ash Bannatyne. Despite knowing him already as Leona's partner, because of the shock, she regarded him with new eyes as a stranger might. Saffy and Neil's marriage had broken down about eighteen months ago and Saffy was off men more than she'd ever been. Particularly when it came to Leona's husband, it seemed. But now, the echoes of Saffy's suspicion about Ash were silent. He was here, standing in front of her full of testosterone in a Paul Smith suit and a

five o'clock shadow. Jeez, she thought, he looked . . . *so edible.*
He also looked pretty mortified.

'Ash. What are *you* doing here?' Poppy said faintly, the fury
leaving her as quickly as it had come.

'Well . . . it's a coffee shop and so I came in for a coffee.'
He raised his full cup, his mouth stretched wide in a guilty
apology. 'I saw you sitting over here and thought I'd say hi . . .
and ruin your life. Sorry about all this.' He glanced down at
the blank monitor and her stained white dress. 'I guess I
made the wrong call.' He put down his cup and walked over
to the counter. The Paul Mescal lookalike handed him a
wedge of napkins, looked across at Poppy and winked. He
looked suddenly like a naff college student next to Ash's
mature masculinity.

Ash tried, ineffectively, to mop up the coffee beads pooled
between the buttons on her keypad. He began gingerly pat-
ting her dress with a napkin, leaning achingly close and
smelling deliciously of sandalwood. Then he said, 'I give up.
Let's head into town and sort this problem out.'

They called at a cosy little cocktail bar tucked away in
Eldon Chambers, a courtyard just off Wheeler Gate. Their
chat flowed easily and the thing Poppy liked the most was
that even without them agreeing anything, Saffy and Leona
weren't mentioned. Not once.

They laughed and laughed. Over Amaretto Sours, he told
her all about his job and the big promotion coming up soon
that he had his eye on and Poppy talked about her course and
her love of art. She didn't mention the fact she was at serious
risk of getting thrown off the course for failing to meet with
her tutor later. None of that seemed to matter. It felt as if
she and Ash were safely hidden from the outside world in a
glittery bubble only they knew about.

An hour or so later, Ash took her to AllSaints in Thurland

Street and insisted she try on a short, clingy, leopard-print dress he picked out.

'But I never wear leopard print,' she giggled in mild protest, the almond candy warmth of the cocktails still in her throat.

'Come on, just slip it on. Indulge me.' He slid an arm around her shoulders and nudged her gently towards the changing rooms where she shrugged off her denim jacket and the now ruined cheap white dress from Asos.

She picked up the new dress and inspected the label. Size eight and nearly two hundred quid! *Two hundred quid!* She loved AllSaints' clothing with its cutting-edge quirky styling and silky fabrics, but it was way beyond her student budget.

Poppy slipped on the garment and regarded herself critically in the mirror. Her skin tone instantly warmed against the caramel and golden tones of the dress. Far more flattering than the stark white or black she usually wore. The dark shadows from too many late nights seemed less obvious and her blue eyes popped against her blonde hair.

There was no doubt about it; the dress looked exquisite. It flattered her small build, her slim, shapely legs. She marvelled at how Ash Bannatyne instinctively knew that would be the case even when it had still been on the hanger.

She turned this way and that, admiring her tiny waist and pert boobs before stepping out of the cubicle.

Ash growled. A low, hungry sound that sent a thousand secret messages between them. All of which Poppy received and understood.

'Leave the dress on,' he said quietly, removing the tag for the payment desk. His fingers brushed the back of her neck, sending a shiver down her spine. 'It looks sensational.'

Poppy returned to the cubicle to get her jacket and laptop bag. She left the cheaper dress on the bench and turned to watch Ash's confident stride over to the cashier. Looking super-hot in his fancy suit.

For some reason Saffy hated Ash, and Leona didn't seem to appreciate him. It seemed to Poppy that Leona always seemed a touch aloof when she was around him. Her loss, Poppy's gain.

When she put her mind to it, Poppy knew she could have any man she wanted. Despite what had happened in her old flat, she refused to be a victim.

She was a courageous woman who could have whatever she wanted in life. And in that moment, Poppy knew she would have Ash Bannatyne. Whatever it took and whoever it hurt.

Her mind was made up.

26

Saffy

When she gets back home after casing out Leona's house and steps into her hallway, she's hit by loud music and the smell of food.

'Hello, Poppy,' Saffy calls at the kitchen door above the rich, smoky tones of Lana Del Rey. She surveys the work-tops, covered in vegetable peelings, wrappings and various pieces of cooking equipment. Cleaning as you go was never part of Poppy's culinary process. 'This is a nice surprise.'

'Oh, hi sis.' Poppy twists around from washing salad at the sink and turns down the music slightly. An open bottle of white wine stands next to half a glass that Poppy picks up now and takes a swig from. 'Thought we're probably due a catch-up so I cooked your tea. Aubergine parmigiana.'

When Poppy is under pressure, she takes refuge in being someone else. Right now, Saffy is seeing the Poppy who makes tea and aims to please – a rare sighting indeed. But today Saffy only wants to talk to the real Poppy. The young, vibrant woman who sometimes gets nervous and makes mistakes that she can't seem to admit to. The side of herself that Poppy tries to cover up at any cost.

'Lovely. But let's have a chat before we eat.' Saffy puts her handbag down on a breakfast stool and perches on the edge of the other one, instructing Alexa to stop playing music. Suddenly, there is just the hum of the fan oven to act as a buffer against complete silence.

Poppy takes another gulp of wine and holds up her glass. 'Want one?'

'Not yet. It feels like you've been avoiding my calls, Poppy.'

'What? No way! Not at all. I've just been . . . busy. Very busy.'

'Me too. I've been very busy trying to convince the police I'm innocent of any wrongdoing. Busy trying to fight to see my son this weekend because Neil is under the impression I'm about to be arrested.'

'He's not going to let you have Fox tomorrow?'

'I don't know. He won't speak to me. Today, it seems he's in the longest meeting known to man.'

Poppy's face falls. 'I feel responsible. I'm really sorry, Saffy. I did try to keep the truth from him about why you weren't there at Fox's pick-up yesterday, but . . . he has this way of keeping on until you say something and trip yourself up.'

Saffy recognizes the truth in that statement from the days when she was still married to Neil. He'd decide there was a problem in their relationship and question her at length until she'd somehow manage to say something that he'd then seize on as evidence he was right. 'It's not your fault, Poppy, we both know what Neil is like.'

When they first got married, Poppy was just sixteen and looked on Neil like a big brother.

'I properly tripped myself up. Somehow one thing led to another like stepping stones.' Poppy scowls. 'Neil can be such a dick at times. I told him . . . I said . . . oh, it doesn't matter.' She turns away.

Saffy puts her hand on her hip. 'Come on. You told him what?'

'I said, if he's so keen on honesty, maybe he should tell you *his* news,' Poppy says wretchedly. 'I'm sorry, Saffy, I should have told you already, but I didn't want to upset you. It's just that —'

'Mira is pregnant?'

Poppy's mouth falls open. 'How did you know?'

'I went round there earlier, to their house. To try and rescue my weekend with Fox. Last I heard, Neil was working from home on Fridays.' She sighs. 'He wasn't there, but I had a coffee with Mira and I saw her tiny bump.'

Poppy reaches for a glass from the cupboard, pours some wine and brings it over to Saffy. 'Shitty news, isn't it? Neil the hypocrite, he always said he didn't want any more kids after Fox.'

Saffy drinks some wine. 'How did you know Mira is pregnant?'

'I picked up a prescription the other day from the medical centre and the two of them were there, walking out of the antenatal clinic. Smiling at each other, Neil touching her bump, all lovey-dovey. Vomit-inducing.'

'Did they see you?'

'Oh yeah, I made sure they did.' Poppy grins. 'I walked over to them and I said, "Are congratulations in order?" Neil's face was a picture. He took me aside, started babbling that he needed to tell you himself, that the news could set you back. You know the drill.'

'When was this?'

Poppy shrugs. 'Beginning of the week. I said, "Fair enough, but you'd better tell her soon or I'll do the honours myself." He didn't like that. Told me to mind my own business.' An alarm sounds on Poppy's phone and she reaches to silence it. 'That's the food done. Sit down and drink your wine while I serve up.'

Saffy pulls out a chair at the small wooden table and sits down at one of the two place settings Poppy has prepared. She watches her sister now, busying around the small kitchen. Grabbing the oven gloves and taking out the bubbling stoneware dish. Years ago, they used to spend hours in the kitchen at the old house making fairy cakes together. Decorating them with sprinkles and those tiny silver balls.

Saffy knows she is often hard on her. But it comes from a positive place. A loving place of wanting to keep her from making wrong decisions or putting herself in harm's way. Sometimes it feels like overkill, now she's a young woman and living away from home, but Saffy can't stop herself. She just can't.

And now there's something bothering Saffy that isn't her business, but that she feels compelled to ask Poppy about.

'Let me get that for you.' Saffy takes the salad bowl while Poppy sorts out the plates. When they are both sitting down with the hot food on the table, Saffy pours them a little more wine and raises a glass.

'To us. We will survive.'

Poppy laughs. 'You're such a drama queen, Saff. Of course we'll survive. We always have, right?' She spoons a portion of parmigiana on to Saffy's plate and then serves herself.

'Are you OK, Pops?' Saffy says carefully. 'I mean, are you OK in yourself?'

Poppy helps herself to salad. 'Yep. I'm just dandy. Want some?'

Saffy shakes her head. 'It's just . . .'

'It's just what?' Impatience flickers over Poppy's face.

'Well, you said you were picking up a prescription. When you saw Neil and Mira at the medical centre. And I wondered if you were ill, or –'

'No, no. Not ill. Just routine stuff, you know?'

Saffy doesn't know. She collects a monthly prescription for her own medication from the GP surgery and none of her ailments can be described as routine.

'It's just I'd hate to think you were suffering alone. Dealing with something that I could maybe help –'

'Trust me, you can't help with this, Saffy.' Poppy puts down her fork and picks up her wine glass.

'I know it might *feel* like I can't help you, but –'

'It's for the contraceptive pill, Saffy. OK? Perfectly routine. Nothing I need your help with.'

Saffy stops chewing and stares at Poppy. 'You're in a serious relationship?' Poppy had never mentioned having a boyfriend at uni. She spends all her time with friends.

'No, I'm not in a serious relationship. I'm seeing someone, but we literally only just met.'

Saffy's head is buzzing. Her little sister is sleeping around.

'Poppy, if you're having unprotected sex then you're putting yourself in –'

Poppy puts her glass down so hard, Saffy wonders how the stem doesn't break.

'I'm not having this conversation with you, Saffy. End of.'

'But –'

'But nothing. I'm twenty-two years old. Back off.'

'I just . . . I'm worried about you. I –' She stops. She's been naïve, believing her little sister is an angel, a saint. When in actual fact she is clearly living a hedonistic life at university. That's the reality.

'Stop worrying. I'm not your responsibility any more, Saffy. Leona is not your responsibility. Stop worrying about bad things happening to other people and live your life. Please, just start to live your own life.'

'I was the last person to see Leona at the house. She seemed OK, but I should have acted on the weird feeling I had that things weren't right.'

'And done what? She's a grown woman. She had every chance to ask for help.'

'Ash was abusing her.'

Poppy rolls her eyes. 'You don't know that.'

'Actually I do because she told me herself. I saw bruises on her wrist. Why isn't anyone taking this seriously?' The police seemed uninterested in finding Leona's journal and now Poppy is doubting her. 'And there's Rosie to think about, too.'

'Rosie is Leona's responsibility, not yours. Mother trumps godmother when it comes to taking responsibility for kids, right? What's happened is not your fault, Saffy. Messages or no messages, it's just not.'

Saffy takes a sip of her wine and looks at Poppy. 'What do you think has happened to them?'

Poppy swallows. 'How should I know?'

'But you must have wondered. An entire family disappearing like that. A family you know well.' Saffy reaches over and touches her hand lightly. 'You can tell me the truth, Poppy. Let's be honest with each other. What do you think has happened?'

Saffy watches as Poppy twists her fingers. Straightens her cutlery. Pushes away her food. 'I don't know. I haven't got a clue.' Poppy stands up and picks up her plate. 'I'm not hungry any more.'

'Poppy, sit down. Let's talk. We –'

Saffy's phone starts to ring in her handbag. She jumps up and when she looks at the screen, she feels sick, hopeful and full of dread all at the same time.

'Neil? Hi. I've been trying to get in touch about arrangements for Fox tomorrow.'

'Yes, Mira said you'd just turned up at the house. That's what I'm ringing about.'

The feeling of dread was increasing. She is familiar with his no-nonsense tone.

'Congratulations, by the way,' she says brightly. 'Mira told me your baby news.'

'Thank you. I was planning to tell you when I brought Fox over in the morning but I'm afraid that won't be happening now.'

'What?' Her voice cracks and Poppy turns around at the sink to watch her. 'Why not?'

'I think it would be very unsettling for Fox to be around you with all the worrying stuff that's happening at the moment. Specifically, the police interest in you.'

A part of her acknowledges he's right, and of course, she only wants what is best for Fox. But to admit that to Neil would be to show weakness, and the only way to keep him from slamming the door completely on Saffy spending more time with Fox is to fight.

'I've given my statement to the police and that's the end of it,' Saffy says quickly, DI Shah's words echoing in her ears about keeping herself available for more questioning.

'That's not what I've just been told,' Neil says, his voice grave and uncompromising. 'The detectives have been here, Saffy. They had some searching questions about you and your relationship with the Bannatynes. They left me in no doubt that you are currently the prime suspect in their investigation and until that changes, Fox will be staying here at home. With us.'

'But –'

'I know it's hard, but all of us must put Fox first. He can't be in the middle of your chaos. You know that.' It's obvious to her that Neil is doing his level best to sound regretful but is falling some way short of achieving it. 'The minute the police drop their interest in you, then we can revisit our arrangements. I can't say fairer than that, can I?'

27

Saffy

Saturday

Saffy can't remember the last time she was out of the house at two in the morning. It's taken her just over thirty minutes to walk there, taking a few shortcuts and sticking to the shadows, dressed in dark clothing and black trainers. Her hair is pulled back into a ponytail and coiled tightly underneath a black woollen beanie hat, her hands encased in matching gloves.

No identifying features, nothing to stand out or catch the eye.

Yesterday, after Neil's devastating call effectively banning her from seeing Fox, Saffy found herself in a kind of temporary stupor. She slumped down on the sofa and closed her eyes. Poppy brought tea and water and tried her best to talk her sister up again. 'Don't let him grind you down, Saff. Fight him. Fight the police. Do it for Fox.'

But all Saffy really wanted to do was wallow in what felt like grieving for this lost weekend and future weekends Neil had robbed her of spending with her son.

Poppy went back home eventually, and the house fell silent and dark. The curtains were still open, the window looking out on to a dark patch of night sky too cloudy to see the stars. Saffy did not move. Her eyes remained closed although behind them she was far from sleep. Her mind raced, turning over the facts and then, close to midnight, the possibilities. What could she do to help herself?

The minute the police drop their interest in you, then we can revisit our arrangements.

That's what Neil had said and Saffy knew her only real option to instigate any meaningful change was to take a big risk. There had been nothing since her call to Shah. No updates, no communication one way or the other. They'd left her in limbo, just waiting for their next move. Saffy knew she had to do something to help herself. Shah had been uninterested in Leona's journal and yet it was a valuable piece of evidence that might make the detectives sit up and realize they had been focusing on the wrong person.

If she could find that journal, it would prove to the police that Saffy wasn't imagining it. Ash really was abusing Leona.

She opened up her laptop and looked on the West Bridgford Community group.

Concerns Over Local Family

The post gave brief details of an anonymous family of three that had apparently disappeared yesterday afternoon in broad daylight. No names were given in the main body of the post but the comments underneath were illuminating.

Leanne Morpeth They live on Musters Road, about halfway down. My niece goes to the same school as the little girl.

Tina Wendon What happened?

Leanne Morpeth Neighbour reported them missing. Front door wide open, smoke alarm screeching. I heard police are questioning a Nottingham woman who visited them yesterday. She must know something!

An uncomfortable crawling sensation started in her stomach. *She* was that Nottingham woman.

Leona's street is predictably quiet and, thanks to there being no visible moon and a number of streetlamps being out of service, it's darker than she'd imagined, but she's careful to stay in the shadows, away from any Ring doorbells. She has a small rucksack with her containing a flashlight and a small bottle of water.

Her heart is banging on the wall of her chest. She shouldn't be here. Shouldn't be risking getting in even more trouble with the police. The officer posted outside has gone but what if they have some other sort of covert surveillance on the front door? She can't risk being seen from the road.

So instead of walking down the street directly to Leona's house, she heads for a path, partly concealed by overgrown hedgerows. This, Saffy knows, leads around the back of the properties that line this side of the street. Saffy remembers their conversation about safety when Leona and Ash had first purchased it. They'd stood in what is now Rosie's bedroom and looked down at the back lawn.

'That path is a bit freaky,' Leona said. 'I don't like the fact that anyone can walk along the bottom of all our gardens, casing the joint. I'm going to ask Ash to put a bolt on the gate and I'll keep a close eye on Rosie when she's playing out in the summer. You never know, do you?'

Of course Saffy, more than most, knew that to be true. You never knew who might be out there and when they might decide to do you harm.

Now, Saffy pads soundlessly down that same path, the weak light from a lamp at the end providing just enough illumination that she can see where she's going without needing to use the flashlight. As she turns the corner at the end of the path, her feet scuff on a patch of loose gravel and the sound is startling as it bursts through the thick, still silence.

A dog barks a few gardens down, and she instinctively stops moving for a few moments until the blanket of silence falls again. Her heart rate settles and she starts to walk along the bottom of the gardens. A main road is adjacent to the other side of the path she's treading but it's in the distance, so Saffy can only just hear the faintest noise of traffic as the odd HGV rumbles through the night on its delivery journey.

Leona's house is the sixth one up from the shortcut path. Saffy passes the third property now with its six-foot high panelled fence and gate. She is unable to see the actual house, but others have just small fences or hedges, and she can see the outline of the backs of the properties with dark screened windows that remind her of blank, shadowed faces waiting for the morning light.

She reaches the Bannatyne property and stops walking. As Saffy had seen from Rosie's bedroom window, the narrow garden is fenced off with a gate, but each fence panel has the odd wooden slat missing as if broken or damaged in stormy weather. Through the gaps, Saffy can see the dark, looming shape of a plastic slide and swing about halfway down the overgrown lawn.

Beyond that, the house stands in darkness. Downstairs, the curtains and blinds are drawn but the upstairs bedroom windows are free of any screening. Two days ago, this place housed a family including her best friend and small god-daughter. What happened to them? Where are they this very second? Saffy shivers and stares at the larger of the two upstairs windows. To the left is Leona and Ash's bed-room where Saffy found her precious family heirloom tossed aside so carelessly, the fine gold chain beginning to tangle and knot.

Saffy waits thirty seconds and then moves across to the gate, stands on her tiptoes and reaches her hand over the top. Her grasping fingers soon find the bolt that Ash fitted days after they'd moved in. Initially, it is stiff and won't shift under her wiggles and twists, but with a little more effort, it finally works loose and cranks back with a jolt into its rusty casing.

She hears a dog barking again, a short flurry of alarmed yaps, and Saffy stops, waits, checks the sharp snap of the bolt opening hasn't alerted any of the nearby residents to her presence. The windows and gardens around her all remain safely shrouded in darkness, so she gently pushes the gate, which doesn't budge until she shoves a little harder. Saffy slips inside the garden and pushes the gate to but does not latch and lock it.

Sticking close to the overgrown bushes on one side of the garden, Saffy walks quickly up to the back of the house. The French doors have a single piece of police ticker tape stretched across them but the back door is clear. Leona only gave her a spare key for the front door so Saffy continues down the narrow path at the side of the house and waits just before the corner, scanning the road.

All is quiet on the street. There are no moving cars, no people. No lights on in any of the windows across the road. The only movement here is the odd untethered strand of police tape that has been too loosely attached to the gate. Saffy moves quickly across the front of the house and inserts the key into the lock. It turns first time, the door opens soundlessly and, moments later, she steps inside the house and closes the door behind her.

28

Saffy

The house is quiet and cold. The air thick and silent, creeping close enough to swallow her up, filling in all the tiny spaces around Saffy's body as if the place recognizes she does not belong here.

She gives her boots a cursory scuff on the welcome mat but does not remove them, nor her puffer jacket or hat. If she needs to get out fast, she can't afford to stop to put on outerwear. The house has had an army of search officers tramping through here, so it's doubtful she'll be leaving obvious footprints.

Saffy shrugs off her rucksack and, still wearing her thin woollen gloves, she takes out the flashlight and turns it on. Around her in the hallway are signs of this being a family home. Carelessly kicked-off shoes, a discarded man's jacket on the stairs, a striped scarf draped over the bottom banister post and here, by her foot, a small brown bear wearing a Fair Isle sweater and matching pom-pom hat. She reaches down and scoops up the bear, presses him to her face and squeezes her eyes closed for a second before forcing herself to place him on the bottom step and focus on the task she is here to do. *This* is how she will help Rosie. This is how she will convince the police they are wasting their resources on investigating Saffy.

She keeps the beam low and directs it at the floor as she climbs the stairs. The master bedroom is the logical place to focus her search. It's where Leona would probably be able to get a little time alone and have lots of places to conceal something.

She enters the bedroom. The curtains are open and she decides to leave them that way. The less change for the neighbours to notice, the better. She keeps the flashlight pointed down. The neighbours surrounding this house will all be on alert, fully aware of the family going missing and all the recent police activity here. She can't turn on the light for fear of attracting attention and can't risk someone seeing a flashlight bouncing around the room and calling the police.

The room looks pretty much the same as when she was in here a couple of days ago. Messy, disorganized and a complete mismatch to the face they were presenting publicly.

Saffy stands over the chest of drawers where she spotted the pendant two days ago. Shining the powerful beam of light down, she inspects the cluttered surface inch by inch.

It mainly consists of half-used toiletries, product boxes and old receipts that have been tossed there instead of being thrown away. A tangle of Leona's silky neck scarves, various items of makeup, a hairbrush, bobbles, grips . . . a mess, but nothing else of interest.

She opens the drawers one by one. Holding the flashlight with one hand, she rifles quickly through.

After hunting through drawers and cupboards, she moves to the wardrobe, kneeling down and shining the flashlight on to the floor amongst the heaps of shoes. But there is nothing.

Her heart leaps as she turns around to face the bed. She glimpses the edge of something wooden and ornate sticking out from under the bed that whisks her back in time.

Saffy sits on the edge of the bed and slides out Leona's prized wooden box, lifting it on to her knee. It's about twelve inches square and contains five long, narrow drawers, each featuring an intricately carved front-facing panel. The flashlight picks out the matching ornate carvings across the top and sides of the piece.

Saffy pauses a moment, remembering how this lovely item used to sit next to Leona's bed when she moved in with her and Poppy.

She opens the top drawer now and finds it empty. Same with the remaining drawers. Her shoulders drop and then she freezes, the memory of why the box seemed so special suddenly vivid in her mind. Magical, even.

She sits on the floor, leaning against the bed, and turns the box over, wedging it between her knees so the smooth back panel faces upwards. Holding the flashlight directly above it, she runs her fingertips under the bottom edge of the box. Perfectly smooth.

She adjusts the angle of the box slightly and runs her fingertips again along the bottom plinth of wood, this time on the inside edge, and there it is. A tiny protruding blob of metal.

A prickle chases around her body as twenty years suddenly dissolve. She is back in Leona's bedroom as she directs Saffy: *Pinch that little blob thing between your fingertips, that's it . . . now pull it.*

Saffy does so now and hears an audible click before the back of the box springs forward, releasing itself from the bottom edge. Gingerly, she prises it open a little further, hope flooding into her chest as she directs the beam of light into the secret panel. But her exhilaration dissipates when it becomes clear the journal is not in there.

Saffy pulls the back panel open a little more firmly and the light illuminates a folded wedge of paper. Perhaps a leftover from Leona's childhood; a crayon picture or one of the handwritten rhyming spells she used to be so keen on writing to manifest a puppy, or a foster family who really cared to replace the cold indifference of the children's homes she'd been raised in.

Saffy carefully removes the piece of paper and unfolds it. In the glare of the flashlight, she reads the handwritten letter.

Dear Leona,

Ignoring my calls and messages is not going to work. I'm coming back to the UK and I want to see my daughter. I know you're married to a dickhead but that's not my problem. Call me. Let's make this as easy as possible. Or make it hard on yourself. Your decision.

Either way, I'll be paying you a visit soon.

Harris

Saffy scans the note again. There is no envelope and no date so it's impossible to know when Leona had received it. She stares at the spidery writing. She barely knows a thing about Rosie's dad, Harris, just that their relationship was brief.

Saffy refolds it and sets it aside. She's about to push the panel back when she notices a long, thin piece of white plastic wedged so far to the side of the compartment, it would be almost invisible if the dazzling shaft of narrow light hadn't illuminated it.

She slips off her glove and, using her forefinger, she picks at the shard of plastic. When it loosens and falls free, she turns it so she can see the end of it and her breath catches in her throat.

It's a pregnancy test and it is showing a positive result. She distinctly remembers Leona telling her that Ash had never wanted kids. In his late twenties, after a girlfriend had falsely claimed to be pregnant by him and her aggressive brothers had called round to Ash's flat to 'encourage' him to do the right thing by her, he'd got himself a vasectomy before they'd even met.

'He regretted it later, but as Ash says, we have a daughter now. We've got Rosie,' Leona had said, her face shining with happiness.

As Saffy stares at the test strip, a scraping, metallic noise from the garden filters in through the window.

She freezes, then pushes the test strip into her rucksack pocket together with the folded letter. Slipping her glove back on, she snaps the back of the box closed again.

After a few seconds she gets to her feet and listens for more sounds, but there is nothing. Complete silence until . . . the scraping noise happens again.

Saffy tiptoes to the window next to the open curtain to peer down on the back of the house. She can't see anything, no movement, but just as she's about to step back, she sees the garden gate is open wide. Wider than she left it.

She creeps out of the bedroom and waits at the top of the stairs. The house is silent. Maybe the gate somehow blew open but . . . it's not that windy and the gate is stiff, having had little use. It had caught on the hard, packed earth when Saffy had pushed it to.

She starts to walk downstairs and then freezes mid-step as a dull thud resonates throughout the house, followed by the muted tinkle of broken glass.

Saffy can't move. Her feet are stuck to the floor and she is shaking. Someone is breaking into the house through the back kitchen or possibly the French doors. Silence again. Then a hard shove as a door gives way and footsteps . . . soft but still audible, coming quickly now into the house.

She looks around the landing, panicking, her eyes

searching for something hard, something sharp to save herself against this intruder or possible intruders. A new, awful possibility occurs to her. What if Ash is innocent after all and the family have genuinely been abducted . . . taken somewhere and killed? And now the murderer is back . . .

The noise has stopped.

Then, the unmistakable sound of an internal door opening downstairs, and Saffy braces herself, wondering whether to shout out or stay quiet, and then the footsteps are at the end of the hallway and the sound is getting closer and Saffy turns and creeps up to the top of the stairs and back into Leona's bedroom.

The footsteps start on the stairs, the steps creaking. She hears breathing, hoarse and noisy in the blanket of quiet, and Saffy reaches for a long, thin ceramic vase on the corner of the chest of drawers. The bedroom door swings open and a figure moves stealthily into the room.

Saffy steps back in shock, wielding the vase above her head, and then she looks at the intruder's equally shocked face and gasps. 'Oh my God . . . it's you!'

29

Leona

On Leona's eighteenth birthday, Wes bought her a beautiful silver necklace with a single, peardrop crystal hanging from it.

'It's for the tear of joy that being with you brings me, and the tear of misery that would fall if you ever leave me,' he'd said poetically.

'He'll have read that in a book somewhere,' Saffy had snorted when Leona repeated it and they'd had a giggle about him in that way only best friends can.

Saffy's weird behaviour over Leona's first date with Wes had lasted for a few weeks. She'd tried her best to convince Leona he was a player and she was making a mistake getting closer to him. But as Leona saw Wes more regularly and then one night snapped and told Saffy to mind her own business, she'd backed off. She now made the odd scathing comment as she'd done about his poetry skills, but disguised her dislike of Wes with humour. And Leona could handle that.

She had been dating Wes for six months now. After their first date at the cinema, Wes had asked her out the following week and then the week after that. They had started slowly seeing each other more and now they were closer than ever.

Leona loved being in a close, loving relationship. She wanted to spend every minute of every day with Wes and he said he felt the same. She'd met his parents and been delighted when his mum told her she used to be a nurse.

'It's a wonderful career and I think you would make an excellent nurse,' she'd said, and Leona felt encouraged and bolstered to achieve her dreams.

She spent a lot of time at his big family house on the edges of Wollaton Park. But now she'd started nursing college and had to find study time at nights and at weekends, it didn't leave much free time to catch up with Saffy.

That didn't stop Saffy trying to set up time together. She worked for a temping agency, going from office to office, filling in whatever they needed her to do. She hated her work and couldn't seem to settle. But she had no goals of what she wanted to work towards, either.

One day, Leona had come home to find Saffy sitting alone by the living room window. 'I miss you,' she told Leona, her eyes full. 'I know you have lots going on in your life but I feel like we're drifting apart and . . . I really don't want that to happen.'

'I understand and I promise I'll start spending more time with you,' Leona had said immediately, guilt nipping at her throat. 'But you should try and get out a bit more, Saffy . . . maybe you'll meet someone and then we can go out as a foursome. That would be fun!'

Saffy had not been keen. 'I don't want anyone else, I just want us to be like we were. Close.'

'I don't know why you don't find yourself some new friends,' Wes complained when Leona was down in the dumps about it later that day. 'She's dull and selfish. You can't be responsible for keeping her entertained.'

But they had been friends for a long time and Saffy had always been there for Leona; she couldn't just ditch her now that she had a boyfriend. Besides, she had other problems, too. For the first couple of months of dating Wes, Leona had endured snide comments and bitchy remarks from the girls who he'd told her followed him around college like puppy dogs. One girl even squared up to her when she was waiting for Wes to finish football practice.

'Do you ever wonder what he sees in you when he could have someone like me?' she'd snarled, a group of friends gathered around her, all carbon copies of each other. Bleached hair, false-tanned faces and heavy-lined eyes. 'He's only with you because he feels sorry for you!'

Leona prepared to defend herself but before she could do anything, Wes loomed up behind the group.

'The reason I'm with her is that she's a natural beauty and she's not full of spite and bitchiness like you, Meghan.' The girl's friends gasped at Wes's retort as Meghan's baby blues filled with tears and she hurried away.

Wes slid his arm around Leona and guided her away from the other students who were standing around taking an interest.

'You're my girl,' he said, holding her face in his hands. 'Don't let anyone tell you any different. You're mine now. You belong to me.'

30

Poppy

Poppy stops dead in her tracks and peers forward, trying to see through the glare of the flashlight. 'Saffy . . . is that you?'

'Yes, it's me!' Saffy hisses and lowers the beam of light. 'What the hell are you doing here?'

'I might ask you the same question.' Poppy pulls down the hood of her fleece and turns her phone torch off, her mind feverishly trying to come up with an excuse. She can't tell Saffy the truth: that she's here to recover something. That she's had to wait until the police have left the scene. That explanation would lead to a truth she doesn't want Saffy discovering.

Saffy narrows her eyes. 'You go first. I used a spare key to get in here that Leona gave me ages ago, but I heard you smash the glass. That's breaking and entering . . . you've broken the law!'

'You can't really point the finger. Neither of us are supposed to be here, right?' Poppy looks around the room as her eyes adjust to the dim light. 'The house is still a police-taped crime scene if you hadn't noticed. We've got to be super careful to leave no trace inside.'

Saffy steps closer and studies her face and Poppy wilts under the scrutiny. Saffy has always been able to tell if her sister is lying, which is one of the reasons Poppy avoids her like the plague whenever she's up to something that will set Saffy off on the warpath.

'This is my best friend's house and she's missing along

with my goddaughter.' Saffy's face is very close to Poppy's now. Close enough she can smell a hint of garlic on her breath. 'That's why *I'm* here, looking for something . . . *anything* that might give me a clue as to what happened to them. But you haven't seen Leona and Rosie for months – maybe it's close to a year. So now I'm asking myself, why are you here?'

Poppy swallows. 'I'm looking for something. Something that belongs to me.'

'What is it?' Saffy smells blood. 'What does Leona have that belongs to you?'

'I told you, I don't want to –'

'Answer my question, Poppy, because we need to get out of here. We could get arrested if a neighbour calls the police to report hearing breaking glass.'

'Or sees your flashlight beam dancing around,' Poppy snaps back, and then suddenly, it's hard to breathe as she finds herself in the grip of panic. Her throat tightens and she fights back tears. 'I . . . I could be in serious trouble. Please, just trust me, Saffy. I need to find what I've come for. Can you just leave and let me –'

'No way am I leaving you here alone.' Saffy reaches for her hand and grips it hard. 'Tell me what it is, Poppy. Why might you be in trouble?'

'I . . .' She feels the tears spill over and roll down her cheeks. 'Ash has a phone . . . we were texting each other. He has a second phone Leona doesn't know about.'

Saffy's face is pale, even in the low light. 'Why were . . . You and Ash, are you having an affair?'

Poppy lowers her eyes and nods, squeezing her eyes shut. 'Not any more. We were, but it's over. It was just a fling and we stopped seeing each other last month. But his other phone, it had pictures of me on it and –'

'You stupid, stupid girl.' Saffy's voice is low and cold. 'How could you do this to Leona?'

'I didn't plan it! It just happened by chance last November, we bumped into each other in town. In a coffee shop. Things just developed and –'

'You didn't get to know him too well, did you?' Saffy gives her a small, sad smile. 'Nothing happens by chance with Ash Bannatyne, Poppy. He'd have known exactly what he was doing when he "bumped" into you.'

Poppy shakes her head. 'You don't know him either. It wasn't like that.'

'Don't you start, too,' Saffy bursts out. 'I'm sick to death of the police constantly giving him the benefit of the doubt. I know who Ash Bannatyne really is, how he uses people. I know how he treats Leona.'

Poppy turns away, her eyes searching the room. 'I can't listen to this, your one-woman hate campaign. I need to find that phone. That's all that matters.'

Saffy grabs her arm and shakes it. 'This house has been searched, Poppy! By a forensic investigation team. If the phone was here, then the police will have it now.'

'No!' Poppy rushes over to the chest of drawers. 'He told me he kept it in his undies drawer. He joked that Leona never went in there.'

'You really think the search team won't have rifled through the drawers?'

Poppy turns on her phone torch and opens drawers until she gets to one filled with Ash's mainly black Boss cotton trunks and socks. She sifts through, then closes it and sits down heavily on the floor, a noise of frustration escaping her mouth.

Saffy crouches next to her and lays a flat hand on her upper back as Poppy sobs. 'Listen to me. Sshh. Poppy, listen my love. You've only got one choice here. You have to go to the police and tell them everything.'

'What? Are you mad?'

'If they have found the phone they'll pull you in anyway and it will look as if you've tried to hide something. The phone isn't here. They'll have it.'

'Oh God, no.' Poppy howls softly. 'I can't go to the police.'

'You have no choice. Why can't you go to them? Although what you've done is despicable, having an affair isn't illegal.'

Poppy blinks. 'No, but they're going to find something on the phone that's probably going to make me the next prime suspect.'

31

Poppy

Saffy stares at her. 'What do you mean? What are they going to find on that phone?'

Poppy looks away before mumbling, 'Photos. Ash asked me to do something but . . . I shouldn't have got involved.'

'Please tell me you're not involved in Leona and Rosie's disappearance in any way,' Saffy says, quietly at first. Then she starts to pace, her hand gripping her throat.

Poppy squeezes her eyes closed. She's made a big mistake opening her mouth like that to her sister. What was she thinking?

'Look at me!' Saffy snaps and Poppy looks up, bracing herself for the onslaught. She needs to bluff her way out and fast. 'We're standing here, in this house, without any authority to do so. A place that's covered in police tape, in the bedroom of a family at the centre of a major police investigation. Don't play games with me, Poppy. Tell me what you know.'

'Nothing. I mean . . . there's other stuff Ash said to me. About Leona.'

Saffy frowns. 'You said the police would probably look at you as a suspect. So what is it he asked you to do?'

'I should have just told the police on the day they went missing and I didn't.'

Saffy watches her. 'What did you do for him?'

'I don't want to talk about all this now,' Poppy says, resolved. 'But Ash wanted out of his marriage. You've always said he's a player, yet he told me he was almost certain Leona was having an affair.'

'That's rich, coming from him, isn't it?' Saffy says. 'Accusing Leona while he's enjoying an extra-marital affair himself. With you. A young woman nearly half his age.'

Poppy rolls her eyes. 'Yes, yes. No need to state the obvious, although I'm not half his age. But my point is that he *was* unhappy at that point, Saffy. He said that's why he'd started to play around. That he'd suspected she'd had someone else for a few months.'

'You'll be telling me his wife doesn't understand him next,' Saffy says bitterly. 'He's been possessive and jealous with Leona almost since the day they met. This is what abusers do; they tell themselves and other people a story that attempts to justify their diabolical behaviour.'

Poppy stares at her. 'No need for this conversation then, is there? If you've already got all the answers, I mean.'

'I didn't say that. What else did Ash tell you? Did he say exactly why he thought Leona might be having an affair?'

'He said he'd followed her when Rosie was at school and Leona thought he was at work. He hadn't caught her with anyone per se, but she hadn't been where she'd told him she was going. That sort of thing.' Poppy hesitates. 'He was affected by it. I mean, you could see it was eating him up.'

Saffy narrows her eyes. 'Still, doesn't sound like the kind of thing the police would blame you for.'

Poppy sighs. 'This one night, we'd had a meal, been to a club and were staying in a hotel, yeah? We'd both had enough but Ash carried on drinking back in the room and he said some things. Things that I just laughed off at the time.'

'Go on.'

'A month ago, when we were still together, Ash said he'd do anything to get rid of Leona so he and I could be together.

I said, "Are you talking about divorce?" and he shook his head, gave me this weird look.'

Saffy feels the colour drain from her face. 'What did he mean, do you think?'

'There's no "think" about it. He told me straight. Said he knew a man who knew a man who could make Leona disappear.'

Saffy opens her mouth and closes it again, aghast.

'I know, right? Ash said that was his only option as, if they divorced, she'd take everything in a settlement because of having Rosie to look after.'

'What did you say to him?'

Poppy pulls a face. 'Just laughed it off, didn't I? I mean, I couldn't do much else. He was drunk and I wasn't too far behind . . . I just thought he was kidding around.'

'People don't kid around about stuff like that, Poppy,' Saffy says darkly.

'Not in your world, maybe. You should hear some of the things my housemates say about –'

'Didn't it occur to you to say something? To me, or to –'

'To who? To Leona? "Hey, I've been screwing your husband for the last few months but I'm worried about your safety"?'

'Poppy! This is serious!'

'Yeah, I know that. Now they've gone missing, it's deadly serious, but it was just drunken banter back then. Me and Ash, we split up a couple of weeks later and I didn't give it another thought. Until Thursday afternoon, that is. And then I remembered what was on that phone.'

'If you'd told me the stuff he'd been saying, maybe I could have warned Leona.'

Poppy gives her a weak smile. 'Right, like I was ever going to tell you I was having an affair with your best friend's

191

husband. You would've spontaneously combusted right there in front of me.' She blows out air and stands up.

Saffy shakes her head. 'What Ash said to you is shocking. But what is it he asked you to do?'

'I don't think you're —'

'You do realize I'm their number one suspect at the moment in the investigation?' Saffy folds her arms. 'I'm the person they're most interested in right now. The police seem to be unable to grasp that Ash is capable of doing anything remotely dangerous. What did he ask you to do?'

Poppy squeezes her eyes closed and looks away.

'Fine. Sounds like the police will soon figure it out anyway, once they look at that phone.' Saffy's voice hardens. 'It will look better if you go to the police before they pull you in. They need to know what Ash said about getting rid of Leona.'

'I know,' Poppy says in a small voice.

'And if you won't tell me what he asked you to do, then at least tell them.'

32

Saffy

She's got cabin fever. Since she got back home Saffy has been looking around the walls, pacing in and out of rooms since the early hours, unable to sleep a wink. Trying, unsuccessfully, to escape the maelstrom of thoughts whirling through her head. To try and get them into some kind of order that makes sense.

She and Poppy had left Leona's house together. Crept across the back garden, closed and locked the gate again, ran along the shortcut alleyway and half-walked, half-ran home together. Miraculously, Poppy smashing the kitchen glass didn't appear to have disturbed the neighbours.

'I watched a video of how to break into a house quietly on YouTube. Wore gloves and wrapped my hand in a tea towel so it didn't cut me or leave prints.' Poppy shrugged.

Saffy had reminded her to pick up the tea towel on the way out.

When they got back to Saffy's around three a.m., Poppy wouldn't stay over. She insisted on going back to her student flat. It was clear she would rather be anywhere than under the same roof as Saffy. But before she left, Poppy had grudgingly confirmed she'd go to the police later this morning.

'Unless the police ask, I'm not going to volunteer that you've also been to the house,' Saffy told her.

She stops pacing and perches on the edge of the sofa,

staring into space. Something clutches at her insides, pulling and grasping. Unearthing bitter morsels from the past.

Saffy's mum, Linda, had been heavily pregnant with Poppy when Saffy's dad suffered a heart attack and died. Poppy hadn't been planned but her parents were both looking forward to welcoming a new child to the world and Saffy was excited to have a brand-new baby brother or sister. Her dad never got to meet his second daughter and somehow, even though it made no sense, Saffy always felt that her mum resented her for it.

'He would have loved her so much,' Linda would murmur after his death, watching little Poppy playing as a toddler. 'She's the image of him, and gentle and kind just like he was, too.' Maybe Saffy imagined it, but she often felt that buried beneath her mother's praise was an underlying criticism of her. As though she'd failed in ways that Poppy had already succeeded in. As time went on, their mother fostered a worship of Poppy that had never existed for Saffy.

Whatever the truth of the matter, there's no doubt that Poppy grew up confident and entitled in a way Saffy never did. Now she's an adult and – despite the trauma the attack brought to their lives – Poppy seems to have flourished and grown bolder. Particularly since she moved into her own flat.

The utter shock of Poppy breaking into the house like that in the early hours and confessing to the affair with Ash – Saffy felt shame, revulsion and fury. She has always told herself that Poppy is vulnerable and needs her protection, but Saffy sees now that she has been kidding herself. As if someone has removed a gauze from her eyes, she recognizes that she has managed, somehow, to become stuck, wedged in the past at a time when Poppy was a defenceless child. Saffy recalls her mother's hollow cheeks during her final days, her shadowed eyes and sallow skin, the endless, whispered pleas as she'd grasped Saffy's hand. And she had promised Linda that she would always take care of Poppy. That she would always keep her safe.

It's only now that Saffy understands her promise could only ever last until Poppy became an adult. You can try all you like to keep someone on a safe path, but as is their right of free will, they can step off it any time they like.

It's all such a terrible mess. The people Saffy cares about the most are all tangled up together with the people she despises. Poppy had stepped off the path and straight into the arms of Ash Bannatyne.

Her clandestine visit to the house was a disaster in terms of recovering Leona's journal. Her search was cut short by Poppy's arrival, but she now knows that Poppy and Ash had been having an affair. It had been a terrible shock, but Saffy privately acknowledges she is better off knowing. It's a troubling link to Leona's disappearance. A coincidence she cannot ignore.

Saffy realizes she barely knows her sister. Poppy has consistently lied and covered up her hedonistic lifestyle. Is she doing the same with her involvement with Ash Bannatyne? Does she know far more than she let on? Far from a bit of innocent snooping as she claimed, is Poppy directly involved in Leona and Rosie's disappearance in some way?

Saffy doesn't know the answer to all those questions. She only knows one thing: if Poppy is old enough to sleep around and embark on affairs with married men – the husband of someone who has only ever shown kindness and compassion to her – then she is old enough to take accountability for her actions. She is old enough to tell the police everything she knows, wherever that might lead.

Saffy's impulsive visit to Leona's house has also uncovered the letter from Rosie's biological father, Harris, who is back on the scene, and his brief letter makes it clear he is causing all sorts of problems for Leona. If Ash had somehow found out about him getting in touch – which Saffy assumes Leona tried to avoid by concealing the letter – it could have caused a major argument that descended into violence.

Poppy had said Ash was obsessed with the fact he thought Leona was having an affair. Could Leona have been secretly meeting up with Harris, Rosie's father?

And then there's the positive pregnancy test. There's no way of knowing when this was taken and, in fact, who it belongs to, although it's a safe bet it was Leona's own result, seeing as it was in her wooden box's secret compartment. Saffy's blood runs cold. It can't be Ash's child, so it follows she must be pregnant by someone else. Is it possible she and Harris have restarted their relationship and Ash found out about it?

Saffy sits for a few moments and considers her options. She wants to tell the police what she's found at the house, but she had no authority to enter a property that's still part of an ongoing investigation. Despite being the prime suspect in the Bannatyne family's disappearance, she hasn't really got a choice.

Saffy calls DI Shah's mobile and unsurprisingly gets her voicemail.

'Hi, Saffy Morris here. I have some new information that I think might help your investigation. Please call me back.'

When the detective returns her call, Saffy knows she'll have to confess exactly how she found this new information.

But now, there's something else that's filling her mind. Had Poppy really turned up at the house to find Ash's spare phone? Or had she gone there for another reason, perhaps to try and find something else that could give her away to the police? However painful it is to acknowledge, there is a distinct possibility that Poppy is involved in, or knows more about, the disappearance of Leona and Rosie. Saffy can't shake a particular thought that's now rattling around in her head with no way out.

If Poppy has been able to conceal her affair with Ash Bannatyne so easily, if she's been sleeping around while telling Saffy she's not interested in men, then what else might she have done that she doesn't want Saffy to know about?

33

Poppy

When they'd left the Bannatyne house, Saffy had wanted her to stay over, but Poppy wasn't stupid. She couldn't stomach any more interrogation. She just couldn't. Not tonight. Her head was in a mess, and she just wanted to get back to her flat. Away from Saffy's disapproving and wounded expression.

Saffy's view of others has always been black or white. Good or bad. Guilty or innocent. She's never had time for shades of grey, and Poppy had seen her face when she'd admitted the affair with Ash. She'd instantly become a fallen angel in her sister's eyes. But she'd have been the devil himself if Saffy knew what she had really done. Fortunately, Poppy had come to her senses and been able to talk her way out of it.

During her affair with Ash, Poppy discovered the real man behind the image makeover. She'd met men like him before. Many times. Men who played the 'big guy' with a successful career, constantly driven and with big dreams that they enjoyed sharing as if they'd already achieved them. A bit of a player with a fancy watch and a wardrobe full of sharp suits and designer logos. The same man who, underneath all the bluster, couldn't sleep for the constant fear that he would never amount to anything. And the closer he got to mid-life, the more risks he'd be willing to take to achieve the greatness he could almost taste. Before it was too late.

Men like Ash tended to underestimate young women who

looked like Poppy. During the first couple of months, they met several times a week for hot sex in hotel rooms Ash paid for. Rooms that started out as Executive Deluxe in the Malmaison before quickly sliding into bog standard at the Premier Inn. Poppy noticed, and she was both insulted and intrigued as to what had brought about the change in him.

When Ash took a shower, she searched his pockets. When he fell asleep after too much drinking, she went through his phone.

It didn't take Poppy long at all to discover Ash was a man who had a lot of secrets.

It didn't take her long to find out he was planning a better life that didn't include Leona. A life that didn't involve Leona's kid or Poppy, either.

She'd been a fool. Thought he'd wanted to be with her. Poppy hadn't realized the gravity of the situation and that's why she'd done what she'd done. Stupidly, she'd done what Ash had asked and, in doing so, had incriminated herself.

34

Saffy

Saffy has still not heard from DI Shah. On top of that, her calls to Poppy, who had promised when she left in the early hours to contact Saffy first thing, are going unanswered.

Frustrated, Saffy shoves her phone in her purse and heads for the door before she can overthink the situation. There is nothing in the house to eat and she's hoping to tempt Poppy over later for food and a chat. The feeling that she is being lied to has only grown stronger in the last few hours and she intends to get some answers whether Poppy likes it or not. She heads down the street to the Sainsbury's Local, a place she usually tries to avoid in case she bumps into someone she knows.

The shop is busier than she expected it to be mid-morning. Saffy looks along the ends of the aisles. What does she need? She didn't write a list. Poppy is always on a different health kick. Sometimes vegan, sometimes low carb. She can't go wrong, she thinks, with a bag of mixed salad leaves, vegetables for a homemade lasagne or maybe even a good-quality bought one, and perhaps some fruit and yogurt for dessert.

She makes her way over to the fruit display and finds a woman and her daughter – who looks around the same age as Fox – selecting items. The girl has a blonde ponytail and a sweet little pink-check dress with a white collar. Saffy watches the child, picking up one ripe pear after the other before inspecting it, finding a tiny imperfection and then replacing it to begin the process again.

The woman turns and pulls a regretful face at Saffy. 'Sorry. We're making a fruit salad for Granny's visit later and each piece has to be perfect!'

'Of course it does.' Saffy grins, thinking about how pedantic Fox can be with food. 'Don't worry, I'm in no rush.'

The woman starts to look away and then does a double-take. She stares at Saffy for just a couple of seconds too long, the smile sliding from her face before her expression darkens and she quickly turns her back.

'Come on, put the fruit down,' she chivvies her daughter along. 'We'll come back later. I just remembered there's something I need to do.'

Saffy frowns, watching as they move away from the fruit section, the woman glancing over her shoulder with the same dark expression. Surely not *everyone* around here knows about Saffy being questioned by the police over the Bannatynes' disappearance? Her neighbours, sure, but . . . not a stranger.

A young family walk by her, oblivious, and she tries to relax. It must be just her, doing her thing as usual and imagining everything out to be the worst-case scenario.

She thinks about her own family unit all those years ago. When her dad died, her mother's reaction had been one of paralysis. Her father had dealt with the money, house repairs, everything really, and Linda had looked after the day-to-day upkeep of the home and kids. She had no idea what to do without him, and so one day she just stopped struggling and did nothing.

Saffy pulls a paper bag from the dispenser and picks up a couple of courgettes. Instead of gradually learning to cope after her husband's death, her mother became more and more terrified that her beloved youngest daughter would be next. In order to protect Poppy, Linda became more and more insular. She stopped sending Poppy to school until the authorities intervened. The only time Linda relaxed and felt safe was when she and Poppy were at home with the doors locked and the curtains closed. So Saffy had to grow up fast, stepping in to mother Poppy, to buy groceries and make sure the electricity meter got fed regularly to keep the lights on.

Saffy weighs the vegetables, pops on the price sticker and places the bag in her basket. Next, she selects onions and a carton of mushrooms.

Linda's fear had infected Saffy on a cellular level. It was always with her, the gift that just kept giving. It was with her now. She looks around the shop. Everyone going about their business and not one person taking any notice of her whatsoever.

But ... what if? What if someone is watching her this very moment but she just can't see them? What if they all know that she, Saffy Morris, is the main suspect in the abduction of her best friend and her family?

She sighs and turns to watch the little girl and her mum, several bags of fruit safely in their wire basket.

Like her mother, Saffy has spent her whole life being afraid of the 'what ifs', but so much bad stuff has already happened and she's still standing. Terrified, not knowing what's going to happen, but nevertheless, still here.

When she's got everything she needs for tea, Saffy heads to the self-checkout and then falters in her stride. A woman further down the aisle is staring at her. She looks familiar and as Saffy draws closer, she sees it is Leona's neighbour, Tania. The one who must have reported her as the last visitor to Leona and Ash.

She raises her hand, but the woman turns and walks briskly towards the exit.

'Tania, wait!' Saffy calls out, striding forward. 'Hey! I need to speak to you!'

Her voice fades to nothing as she draws stares from nearby shoppers. She rushes down the aisle, dropping the basket containing her unpaid shopping on to the floor. She can still see a glimpse of the woman's grey coat as she reaches the door just as a new checkout opens and people surge towards it.

'Wait! I'm Leona's friend . . .' The woman does not turn and rushes through the automatic doors.

Saffy battles through the belligerent crowd. 'Excuse me!' she pleads with shoppers who stubbornly refuse to move, fearful of losing their place in the new checkout queue.

Saffy lets out a frustrated yelp and breaks through a roped-off barrier to get to the exit and somehow manages to knock a row of glass jam jars on offer, two of which fall and break, leaving strawberry jam oozing in her wake. When she finally manages to rush outside, she looks left and right and scans the people walking across the High Street.

But the woman is nowhere to be seen.

35

Saffy

When Saffy steps through the front door with her groceries, she feels exhausted. After a few fruitless minutes of searching for Leona's neighbour outside the shop, she braved the stares and under-the-breath muttering and brazenly went back into the store. Saffy apologized for the broken jam jars and picked up her basket from the place she'd abandoned it, paying for her goods.

Now, she's wiped out. When she closes the front door she sees the postman has been and nearly steps on the letters scattered on the hardwood floor. Saffy gathers up the three envelopes and takes them into the kitchen.

One is a utility bill, another concerns a near-neighbour's planning application for a conservatory at the back of their house. On the third one, Saffy's name and address have been handwritten.

She tears it open and takes out a single sheet of folded paper. Carefully, she unfolds it and flattens it out on the counter. She reads the short message once, twice, and the third time, she grips the worktop and sits on a breakfast stool, staring down at it in disbelief.

We don't want people like you around here . . . Everyone knows what you've done.

She grabs the envelope and turns it over. There is no

stamp; it has been posted through the letterbox by hand. She looks down the shadowy hallway towards the front door, visualizing one of her neighbours plotting and scheming about how to make her life a misery.

Doubts about whether to go to the police swirl in her head again. What if it makes everything worse? This note proves that, somehow, people seem to have found out what's happening. If the police believed Saffy had something to do with the Bannatynes' disappearance, surely they would have arrested her. It's unfair of people to start gossiping and speculating about what she might or might not have done.

Just then, her phone rings. She looks at the screen and sees it is DI Shah.

'Hi Saffy, I just got your message. Can you give me some idea of what you mean by new information?'

Saffy falls silent. She doesn't want to admit what she's done on the phone. 'I'd rather discuss it in person, if that's all right?'

A beat of silence then, 'Tell you what, we'll drop by. In about an hour?'

'I . . . Yes, OK. That's fine.'

Shah ends the call and Saffy stares at the wall. She's done it now. The detectives will be here shortly and she must tell them what she's found.

She just hopes her decision to be honest doesn't backfire.

36

Saffy

When the doorbell rings, Saffy is sitting in the kitchen. Trying to breathe. Trying to somehow settle her mind so she can make informed decisions again. It hasn't worked. She's opened a can of worms with the detectives but she can't see a way around convincing them of Ash's guilt without admitting that she has entered an active crime scene without permission.

She stands up, pats her hair smooth and walks into the hallway. The doorbell rings again. Seems DI Shah isn't in a patient mood today. Saffy pastes a pleasant expression on her face and opens the door to the two detectives.

'Thanks for coming,' she says. 'Come inside.' Shah and MacFarlane step into the hall and turn left into the lounge where Saffy offers refreshments. They refuse. 'What's happening in the investigation? Are you any closer to finding out where Leona and Rosie are?'

'We're following up on a number of leads,' Shah says, her voice detached.

'Surely there's something? Aren't the first twenty-four hours crucial in an investigation like this?' Saffy presses.

'Rest assured we're maintaining a sense of urgency with the case, which is why we're spending valuable investigation time responding to your telephone call.'

'We'll need to record what's said today as it may prove relevant to our investigations,' MacFarlane says, reciting the usual salient facts before starting the tape.

'I'm certain it will prove very relevant,' Saffy says, sitting down.

The detectives glance at each other.

'So, what is this important information you wish to impart?' Shah says.

Saffy takes out the plastic bag from her pocket and places it on the table.

Shah peers at the contents but does not touch the bag. 'What's this?'

Saffy pinches the top of her nose. 'I did something. Something silly . . .' She tails off, hoping to see an easing-off of Shah's unnerving formal attitude, but the detective remains poker-faced. This is the moment she's been trying to picture. 'I found these at Leona's house. Last night.'

'I'm sorry?' MacFarlane frowns. 'You're telling us you broke into the Bannatynes' house?'

'No! I didn't break in, of course not. I have a spare key. I used to collect Rosie from nursery on the odd occasion back before Ash waged his campaign to excommunicate me. I went back there to find Leona's journal that your officers failed to find in the search. I didn't find it, but I did come across a positive pregnancy test strip and a letter to Leona from Rosie's biological father.'

Shah gives her a hard look. 'Entry to the property remains prohibited as it continues to be an ongoing crime scene. This morning, a call came in to report a break-in at the rear of the house. A smashed window. That was you, was it?'

'I didn't smash a window.' Saffy reminds herself this is not a lie. She won't drop Poppy in it. 'I wasn't thinking straight . . .' She is making such a mess of this. 'I'm sorry. I didn't realize it was so serious. With me having a key.'

MacFarlane gives a wry smile. 'You didn't realize. Despite

the main entrance points to the property being clearly screened by police tape?'

'I thought if I went there, I could find evidence to prove to you that Ash is behind Leona and Rosie's disappearance!' she snaps. 'I told you all about his abuse of Leona, but it still wasn't enough to convince you he's done something bad to them.' Shah's face hardens further and Saffy knows she's gone too far.

Saffy begins to open the bag and MacFarlane puts up a hand to stop her. 'Don't touch the items.'

While her colleague slips on a pair of thin blue gloves, Shah says, 'Can you please disclose exactly where you found them in the property?'

'I found them under Leona's bed in a wooden box she's had for years. I remembered a secret compartment in the back and that's where I found these.'

'These were the only items in the box? No journal?'

'No. I didn't find the journal.' She stops short of saying she ran out of time because she was disturbed by Poppy.

Gloves in place, MacFarlane removes the pregnancy test strip and holds it in front of her. 'For the benefit of the tape, we're looking at a plastic pregnancy test strip showing a positive result. No date or identifying marks.'

Shah pins her eyes to Saffy. 'What do you think this means?'

'I think Leona is pregnant and she was hiding it from Ash!' she exclaims.

'And why would she do that, do you think?'

'Because it's not his baby. Leona told me Ash had a vasectomy before she met him,' Saffy says with some satisfaction.

Shah nods to MacFarlane who removes the letter and reads it out loud.

'Do you know Rosie's father, Harris?' Shah says.

'I met him a handful of times. In no way has he been a

father to Rosie; he abandoned Leona while she was still pregnant. Scurried off abroad somewhere, back to a fiancée that we didn't know existed.'

'Why do you think Leona may have concealed this letter?'

Saffy makes a noise of exasperation. 'It's fairly obvious! Harris is back on the scene and Leona might have struck up a relationship with him again. Surely you can join the dots. Leona might be pregnant with Harris's child!'

'That's rather a big leap to make, isn't it?' Shah gives a sardonic smile. 'The letter doesn't read in a particularly friendly way. Indeed, it implies Leona has ignored Harris, rather than encouraged his contact.'

'The letter has no date on it, so it could have been sent a while ago. I love Leona dearly but she's always been a pushover where men are concerned. She gets involved and falls in deep very quickly. It wouldn't surprise me one bit if she's got involved with Harris again. After all, she must have found him very attractive once. Before managing to marry a man who treated her even worse.'

'You certainly seem to have a very low opinion of Mr Bannatyne,' MacFarlane remarks mildly. 'Why is that?'

Saffy looks at her, aghast that she still sees fit to challenge her after all she's told them about his controlling nature and abuse of Leona. 'I know what kind of a person he is. I know what he's capable of and I've already shared that with you. What puzzles me is that, after everything I've told you, there still seems to be doubt in your mind as to what he might be capable of.'

MacFarlane gives her a tight smile. 'You seem to be under the impression you're the only person who knows the Bannatyne family, Saffy. The only person who has an opinion on the kind of husband and father Ash Bannatyne is. We are looking at all angles and speaking to all kinds of people and, it must be said, not everyone holds the same opinions as you do.'

Saffy is astonished. It's never occurred to her that the detectives have people telling them conflicting things about Ash. If they're speaking to his friends or colleagues – before he quit his job – then of course they'll have a different opinion because he's so good at projecting a certain image.

'All I know is that Leona herself told me what she was going through, and that's good enough for me.'

'Understood, but you're not concerned he's currently missing along with the rest of his family?'

'I'm extremely concerned about Leona and little Rosie but I'm convinced their disappearance is down to him.' Saffy hesitates and then says, 'I'm desperate to get them back safely, but when it comes to Ash . . . well, I'd be lying if I said I gave a toss. In fact, I'd be delighted if I never set eyes on him again.'

There's a split-second silent exchange between the detectives again and Saffy notes their lack of response to her remark before Shah begins looking animatedly through her paperwork. It occurs to her that the detectives seem to have a fresh energy about them today. They're all business rather than the slightly more relaxed manner Saffy has observed in their previous encounters.

'Is there any further information you want to tell us about?' Shah says efficiently.

Saffy takes a breath. This is it, the moment she gets a chance to convince the police to look closer at Ash. The exact moment when it's all on the line.

'I've got evidence that Ash has been lying to Leona about his job. He hasn't worked for Mediden for three months now, but when I called at the house on the day they went missing, they were supposedly celebrating his new promotion there.'

'Right, OK.'

She looks from one detective to the other. 'Surely, you'd agree that's quite a big omission to keep from your wife. I mean, why would he do that? What kind of trouble was he in?'

'Noted,' Shah says. 'What else?'

Saffy bites back her irritation and carries on. 'This might seem nothing, but a while ago I lost a pendant with great sentimental value at Leona's house. I always suspected Ash found it but decided not to return it and now I've been proven correct.'

Saffy opens her palm and shows the garnet pendant to the detectives. 'This is a unique piece that has been passed through the female side of my family for generations.'

'And this has precisely what to do with our investigation?' Shah says blankly.

'Well, it says a lot about the man. His duplicity. His slyness. I . . . I found it on the dresser in Ash and Leona's bedroom on the afternoon I visited. I wondered if Leona had somehow found it and it had caused Ash to blow up. That could be why she sent me the messages.'

'And yet you never mentioned entering their bedroom at the station yesterday,' Shah says, nodding to MacFarlane who produces a small, clear plastic bag. She holds it open and indicates for Saffy to drop the pendant inside.

'I know and I'm sorry,' Saffy says, allowing the fine gold chain to slip from her fingers.

'Do you have paperwork proving ownership of the necklace you removed from the house without the owners' knowledge?' Shah says, her voice cold.

Saffy looks over at the clear bag containing the pendant. She's made a big mistake just handing it over like that. 'I haven't got any paperwork. It was my mother's.'

'Was the item insured or left to you in a will?' Shah asks.

Saffy looks at her hands. 'No to both, but I think I have a photograph somewhere of my great-grandmother wearing it. You'll give it me back, won't you?'

'That depends. You broke into someone else's home and took it from there without permission. We have no reason to believe it isn't their personal property. It could become tricky to stake a claim on it without proof of ownership.'

Tears prickle behind Saffy's eyes. No matter what Ash Bannatyne does, the accusations slide off him like oil, but she can't give up now.

'Anything else?'

'No. That's it.' It feels like all her efforts have come to nothing. Saffy moves her seat back in readiness to stand. 'I'll leave all that with you.'

'Before you go, we have a query of our own,' Shah says and looks at her colleague.

'Following up on the *official* search carried out at this property,' MacFarlane says pointedly, 'we want to speak to you about a missing item in the kitchen.'

'Oh?' Saffy frowns.

The detective refers to her notebook. 'Officers conducting the search noted that a long kitchen knife appeared to be missing from the block on the worktop next to the oven. They looked in the sink, the dishwasher, the cutlery drawer and found no trace of it. Can you shed any light?'

'Really? I hadn't noticed. I haven't been doing much cooking.'

'We wondered if the knife had perhaps turned up?' MacFarlane says. 'OK if I go and check the kitchen?'

'Be my guest,' Saffy says, puzzled. The knife must be somewhere.

'Is there anything you want to add to what you have already said?' Shah gives Saffy a hard look.

Saffy thinks about Poppy's shocking revelation that she'd had an affair with Ash that only ended recently. Their reaction to date has been to doubt everything Saffy tells them and so she suppresses her original urge to be completely honest and open. Poppy must inform them herself of the things Ash said to her about wanting to escape his marriage.

'No,' Saffy says firmly, recognizing sounds of the dishwasher door being opened and closed again. 'I've nothing else to add.'

MacFarlane returns to the room and shakes her head quickly. 'No sign of the missing knife.'

'I'm sure I don't need to remind you that withholding information of any kind is considered a very serious matter,' says Shah.

'I'm not withholding any information,' Saffy says quietly. 'I just need you to find Leona and Rosie. That's all I want.'

37

Saffy

When the detectives leave, Saffy goes straight to the kitchen and stares at the Joseph Joseph knife block she bought in the John Lewis sale when she first moved in here. The long knife, one of five that usually sits next to the serrated bread knife, isn't there.

She looks in all the places the detectives mentioned had already been searched and it isn't in any of them. Saffy doesn't put the knives in the dishwasher because it can spoil the handles. She always leaves them by the sink to handwash after use. And she never puts them away in the cutlery drawer even by mistake; they go straight back in the block after being cleaned. The only thing she can think is that Poppy has somehow misplaced the knife, or maybe she borrowed it without telling Saffy. But the chances of that are almost zero.

Back in the living room, Saffy sits on the sofa and stares out of the window. She feels shell-shocked as the seriousness of the situation continues to dawn on her.

The detectives' attitude towards her has changed, she can feel it. There's a sense that they're getting closer to full-on blaming her for the Bannatynes' disappearance.

DS MacFarlane had turned to her in the hallway and said, 'Just so you know, Nottinghamshire Police are issuing a public appeal for information. This will be conducted by a series of press releases.'

DI Shah added, 'We're making you aware of this as you

know the missing family well and you were also the last person to see them, although of course you will not be named. But as you'll no doubt know from the attack on your sister nearly three years ago, the press can be very resourceful in finding out information. I think it's fair to say you may well be a target of increasing interest.'

The press. This was something Saffy had neither expected nor considered, but people talk and word gets around. The little girl and her mum at the supermarket, the neighbours who always seem to be doing something in their front gardens when the police call round. The very thought of it turns her stomach. The last thing she wanted was to draw attention to herself and particularly to Poppy. The last thing they both need is their own traumatic past looming large again.

Shah also added, 'In light of what you've told us, we'll be in touch later today to arrange for you to come into the station for more formal questioning.'

This would now be the time she'd have to confess to holding back crucial information. The worst possible time when she'd look very unreliable, not to mention guilty.

Saffy tilts the vertical blinds to a half-closed position. According to the detectives, there might soon be press lurking on the street. After the attack, Saffy had felt a prisoner in her own home. A gaggle of press had stood outside their old house day and night, haranguing her every time she emerged from the house to visit Poppy in hospital. So many demanding questions and not much empathy at a time of great stress and anxiety is how Saffy remembers it. Now she is not a victim but a suspect, and she imagines the press, if they come, will be more intrusive and aggressive, and she is not sure how she'll cope. She's not sure at all.

Her phone beeps with a text from Poppy. There is no written message from her younger sister, just a hyperlink to the *Nottingham Post*'s X account. Saffy clicks on the link and an article posted online just twenty minutes earlier opens.

LOCAL FAMILY OF 3 MISSING WITHOUT TRACE

Ashley and Leona Bannatyne and their young daughter seen by neighbour shortly before they disappeared.

Police officers found a pan of food burned to a crisp in the oven and half-full glasses of wine on the set dining table at the home of the Bannatyne family, and yet no sign inside the smart detached home of husband and wife, Ashley and Leona, or their five-year-old daughter, Rosie.

Their neighbour, Tania Torkard, who had spotted the family at home earlier in the day, became concerned at the prolonged sound of a smoke alarm and went outside to check. It was coming from the Bannatyne family home.

'I saw the front door was ajar but just thought they'd opened it to get some air in after burning food. But ten minutes later, nothing had changed,' Mrs Torkard told the Post. *'I walked over there and called out for Ash and Leona but there was no answer. It just seemed very odd because I knew they were home.'*

Both Mr and Mrs Bannatyne's cars were parked on the drive and Mrs Torkard had spotted a visitor leaving their property an hour or so earlier.

The couple had lived in the house for two years. The Post *understands that Ashley, 36, was a medical supplies sales director and Leona, 34, had only recently given up her work as a qualified nurse at the Queen's Medical Centre in Nottingham to become a full-time mum to Rosie.*

'I had this uncomfortable feeling that something was very wrong, I can't explain it,' Mrs Torkard said. 'I knew Ash and Leona reasonably well, but I didn't think it was my place to search their house. Instead, I decided to call the police.'

When officers arrived, there was no trace of any of the three members of the Bannatyne family inside the property or in the vicinity.

DI Fatima Shah of Nottinghamshire Police told the Post, *'We are extremely concerned for the wellbeing of this missing family that includes a small child. It appears all clothing and possessions, including bags and phones, have been left behind and there are no indications they planned to leave for an extended period of time. We are appealing to anyone who has any information or knows the whereabouts of Ash, Leona and Rosie to please come forward confidentially, so we can work to get this family safely back home.'*

The last couple of lines give details of how people can get in touch with the Nottinghamshire Police investigation team.

Saffy is about to close the window when another message notification appears from Poppy.

Read the comments online.

Poppy has copied and pasted several comments underneath from Facebook and X.

@JohnnyGGreen_73 Who was the visitor? That's who the coppers need to look at first.

@Anna_BGood I know someone who lives on that street. She said the visitor used to be the missing woman's best friend!!

@SalamandaPanda66 Too much of a coincidence I reckon @Anna_BGood. No smoke without fire!

@Anna_BGood According to my source police are questioning the visitor. Watch this space . . .

Saffy closes the message window and puts down her phone.

It feels like the noose is tightening around her neck. How do ordinary people like @Anna_BGood find out what's happening in a confidential police investigation? Has the neighbour, Tania – who Saffy saw pulling into her driveway – gossiped to other people living on the street, and have they in turn blabbed to people they know? Saffy herself has a direct link to the lead detectives in the case and has tried several times, in vain, to get any sort of update out of them.

You'll never know when I'm coming but I give you my word. I will.

A trickle of the old stone-cold fear traces around the back of her neck. She has found her strength and peace in anonymity and in ensuring she lives a predictable and fairly isolated life.

Is that all about to change?

38

Poppy

Later on Saturday evening, when the house falls quiet and she's sure all her flatmates are sleeping and she won't be disturbed, Poppy pores over the stories, the news articles, the sensationalist comments, and the numerous posts on social media.

They talk about the mystery visitor to the house before the family went missing and they express surprise that it was Leona's best friend.

Someone comments: *I went to school with Leona and her best mate was Saffron Morris. Wonder if it's her?*

Someone else: *Wasn't Saffy Morris the one whose sister got attacked?*

This stuff will never go away. Literally. Never. Go. Away.

But Poppy has promised her sister she will go to the police and confess to her connection with Ash before they analyse his phone and find out anyway. The last thing Poppy wants to do is speak to the two detectives who are hounding Saffy. She doesn't know if Ash Bannatyne and Leona are dead or alive. She doesn't really care.

But the kid, Rosie . . . she's a different ballgame. Like Fox, little Rosie has a one-way pass straight through to Poppy's heartstrings.

Poppy is not Mother Teresa. She's not a saint who is worried about going to hell. But the things he said to her about Leona . . . Poppy saw Saffy's shocked reaction. She can see how it's going to look to the police when she comes clean and tells them the full extent of what she knows and what she did against her better judgement.

All this drama, it's filling her head, her body. It's taking her over. All the drama and mystery and fear of something faceless and unknown . . . it's unlocking the hard, tangled knot that protects her, that's buried deep in the core of her.

Poppy can't stand the thought of talking to the police. She's been battling against it all day long and can't even think about fulfilling her promise to Saffy without echoes of the night of the attack flooding back. The flashing blue lights that filled the front room, the blurred dark green uniforms of the paramedics towering over her, the harrowing wails filling her head which she realized were coming out of her own mouth. Other details are mercifully out of reach in her psyche and Poppy is happy for them to stay that way.

A notification pings on her phone and Poppy opens and deletes yet another email from her tutor expressing concern over the recent lectures she's missed. Her hand is shaking slightly. She can't do it. She can't go to the police yet. Maybe Monday morning.

She needs a drink, but she's been trying to cut down after so many nights out. She has nothing in her room for emergencies, but needs must. She tiptoes downstairs to the communal kitchen and opens the drinks cupboard, kept stocked by the house kitty and used strictly on their movie nights. Poppy removes a half-full bottle of vodka and carries it back to her room under the cover of her big wool cardi.

She sits on the edge of her bed and unscrews the bottle, takes a sip of the slightly astringent liquid, relishing the burn at the back of her throat.

Only then does she unbraid her hair and fluff it out before tangling it in her fingers and pulling hard, ripping it free of the roots. She lets the clumps fall to the floor by her bed. In the morning, she'll add them to the soft balls of hair already in her wastepaper bin by the desk.

Poppy feels like bits of her are breaking off and dissolving. Her body feels numb and transparent, and sometimes she questions if she really exists at all. Sometimes, late at night when she is here alone, she wonders if the essence of who she really is perished three years ago at the hands of a stranger. A monster who wanted her to die.

Poppy sips more vodka and lies back, propped up with pillows, and she keeps on drinking until sleep eventually comes.

39
Saffy

Three Years Earlier

The office Christmas do was being held at some party venue in the city centre; unlimited food and drink with dancing on the tables. Not exactly Saffy's thing, but Neil had laughed and said, 'It'll do you good to let your hair down. Go and have a good time.'

Her job was only temporary, covering a maternity leave in a busy admin office, but they were a nice set of people and Saffy couldn't remember the last time she'd had a drink and a dance. It was just that she hated leaving Fox, soon to be a year old. Saffy knew Neil thought she was too clingy with their son and he was probably right. She'd even agreed to his suggestion she stay at Poppy's flat, which was much closer to the venue, so she wouldn't have to worry about getting home, or disturbing Fox when she came in. Poppy, on the other hand, was a bit of a night owl and she'd been surprisingly welcoming when Saffy mentioned staying over.

'Cool. You can sleep in my double bed with me and in the morning, I'll take you for breakfast at the new vegan café that's just opened around the corner.'

The night had progressed well, but about thirty minutes before the end of the entertainment, Saffy ran out of energy for dancing. She decided to leave slightly earlier to avoid the scrum for cabs outside the club a little later. She texted Poppy.

Poppy didn't reply but that didn't concern Saffy. Her sister had always tended to fall asleep in front of the TV.

In the cab, she dropped a text to Neil.

Everything fine, but decided to head back to Poppy's early. See you tomorrow.

It had been a shock to Saffy when Poppy moved into her student accommodation as she'd always assumed Poppy would continue to live with her and Neil. It was hard to let go, to stop worrying about her, but Neil was adamant. 'It's great she wants to spread her wings. You've done an amazing job, as you promised your mum you would. Now it's time for Poppy to live her own life.'

The driver dropped Saffy off outside, the headlights illuminating the ex-council house close to the university which had been converted into student flats, the ground-floor one being Poppy's. The front door led to Poppy's accommodation while the upstairs flat had its own side entrance. The road seemed darker than usual and when Saffy looked up, she noticed the streetlight outside the house wasn't working, leaving pockets of pitch-dark shadow. As she walked up the short path, she spotted the front door was slightly ajar.

She didn't panic at first, knew the bins were just around the corner at the side of the house. It was possible Poppy was taking the rubbish out. Instead of going into the house, she veered left to peek down the side.

Poppy wasn't down there at the cluster of wheelie bins. 'Hello?' she called out anyway, but there was no reply.

Cautiously, Saffy pushed open the front door wider and stood listening. The hall light was turned off, but she could see the amber glow of a lamp still on in the living room. That meant Poppy hadn't gone to bed yet and irritation poked at her throat. It was most likely her sister had taken out the rubbish and had forgotten to close the door properly.

Still, an uncomfortable sensation in the pit of her stomach continued to niggle. Saffy stepped inside the house, leaving the door slightly open behind her so as not to make a noise. She could see the kitchen was in darkness, too. Maybe Poppy had gone to bed early after all, in which case, leaving the front door open was even more unforgivable and Saffy would tear a strip off her in the morning.

She carried on walking down the hallway. The flat seemed unusually still, the air thick and dry. Something felt off.

Then she heard a strange sound.

The sucking in of air, or a low moan . . . it was hard to tell.

Outside the living room door, she opened her mouth to call out for Poppy, but something stopped her. The back of her neck prickled as her hand hovered over the door handle. She kept very still and listened, the feeling in her stomach worsening by the second.

At first, there was only silence again, but then she heard something else. A whimper. A low, menacing growl.

Saffy took a breath and then, very slowly and quietly, she pushed open the door.

40

Poppy

Sunday

She stands across the road from the police station and stares at the brutalist concrete architecture, stark and unyielding. Poppy is not looking forward to this.

Her knees feel weak and she has the mother of all headaches, having dreamed about the night of the attack. She'd woken with her head pounding from her late-night vodka drinking session.

When she'd opened her eyes, squinted against the filtered sunlight coming through the cheap, unlined curtains, something had changed. She was suddenly so tired of running, of distracting herself from the here and now. Yes, nearly three years ago she'd nearly died in an attack that she can't remember the details of, but she was here now. She survived.

And somehow, when she opened her eyes this morning, she knew that no matter how many people she told herself she didn't need, no matter how many men she slept with, no matter how much alcohol she drank to avoid facing her feelings . . . it had still happened to her. And it would never go away.

Poppy had cleaned her teeth, drunk a glass of tap water and then called the direct line for DI Shah that Saffy had texted her.

And the detective told her to come into the station right away.

In the empty station foyer with its scuffed floor and hard plastic chairs, Poppy is left waiting no more than six or seven minutes before a uniformed officer appears. He escorts her down a long, claustrophobic corridor to a small, impersonal room. There, she is introduced to DI Shah and DS MacFarlane, who she met at Saffy's house only very briefly the previous Thursday.

Poppy takes a breath to compose herself and sits down before taking out her water cooler bottle and holding it in both hands.

MacFarlane says, 'Thanks for coming in. May we call you Poppy?' Poppy nods and the detective reels off the necessary information for the benefit of the tape before turning to Shah. 'Ready when you are.'

'It's quite the coincidence that you happened to call us this morning, Ms Morris,' Shah says, picking up her pen before looking back at Poppy. 'We've just reviewed the findings of the search at the Bannatyne family property, and it's thrown up some very interesting information.'

Poppy takes a sip of water before forcing herself to look steadily back at Shah. 'Yes, that's what I'm here to talk about.'

'Really?' Shah raises an eyebrow. 'We're listening.'

'I had a brief affair with Ash Bannatyne. It started about eight months ago and finished a few weeks ago.'

'I see,' Shah says and writes something down. 'And it's only just occurred to you to tell us this?'

Poppy looks down at her hands. 'I thought, better late than never.'

'Indeed,' Shah says and falls silent.

'But then I suppose you already know that if you've found the phone he used to text me on,' Poppy adds.

'The forensic team did find a phone, yes,' MacFarlane says. 'On it were some photographs and text message exchanges between the two of you. Who was aware that you and Ash were having an affair?' Shah asks.

'No one.'

'Your sister? His wife?'

Poppy looks at Shah. 'Nobody knew.'

'Nobody knew to your knowledge,' MacFarlane clarifies.

Poppy bites back a retort. It's a waste of time arguing. She should just come out with the stuff Ash had said about Leona. Yet something is stopping her doing that. She feels intimidated, and for the first time, Poppy realizes the gravity of the situation. She realizes why Saffy is so worried about their growing interest in her connection to the case.

'Tell us a bit about how the relationship between you and Ash Bannatyne started,' Shah says.

Briefly, Poppy tells the detectives the story of their coffee shop meeting. 'Ash spotted me working at a table, I spilled coffee all over myself and there was this instant powerful attraction between us. It just happened, like it was the first time we'd ever set eyes on each other. Like we were complete strangers.'

'How did you conduct the affair, practically? Obviously, we've seen you communicated by phone, but where specifically did you meet and spend time together?'

Poppy shrugs. 'Bars and hotels mainly. Ash was quite romantic, took me for meals, bought me flowers, little presents. At the start at least. Then I noticed a change.'

'In what way?'

'Like, the fancy hotels turned into mediocre places and the meals and flowers dropped off. Soon it was a meet-up for a

231

quick shag and a "See you later, love. I'm off back to my wife."'

'I see. So how did the affair end?' MacFarlane clasps her hands together in front of her on the table and leans into them.

'I'm not one to hang around for long in relationships anyway, but Ash got . . . I don't know, distracted. You know, like he was always scrolling through his phone – his regular phone. He started disrespecting me. Treating me like an inconvenience, that sort of thing. For the first few months we were together, I thought he was different but turns out he's just your regular dickhead like all the others.'

'Must've made you pretty angry, being treated like that,' MacFarlane says carefully.

'Angry? I won't lie, I was furious for at least a week after.' Poppy gives a bitter laugh. 'But men don't get to treat me badly twice. Ash had become too much like hard work, so I kicked him to the kerb and got over it. End of.'

MacFarlane nods slowly, her face deadpan. 'So just to confirm, you're the one who finished it. The affair?'

Poppy shrugs. 'In the end, yeah, that was me. I won't put up with timewasters, it's a rule I have.'

Shah picks out a printed sheet from the folder in front of her. 'Poppy, I'd like to speak about the attack you suffered three years ago. Is that OK?'

Her fingernails press into the soft cushion of her palm. 'Sure, but there's nothing much to say. I got attacked, I survived and it left me refusing to take any rubbish from men.' Poppy looks from one detective to the other. 'I'm sure your case file will fill in all the gory details if that's what you're after. I still can't recall most of what happened that night.'

Shah puts down her pen. 'I'm interested in your reaction to such a traumatic event. It's . . . unusual to say the least.'

Poppy says nothing.

'Some people can become completely risk-averse as a reaction to severe trauma. They stop going out, try to pre-empt a thousand scenarios to avoid dangerous situations. But it seems you have come out fighting. It's an admirable response but, it must be said, quite an unusual one.'

Poppy feels validated by the detective's reaction. 'I'm lucky to have found strength from what happened, I suppose. My sister chose another path.'

'Your sister, Saffy, interrupted the attack?' MacFarlane says.

'Yes, she was staying over at mine after her work do and came back early. The attacker was still in the house.'

'Back then you were nineteen and had just started university?'

Poppy nods. 'I'd only recently moved into the flat after living with Saffy and Neil. I was so ready for my own space.'

MacFarlane says, 'Saffy was your legal guardian up to the age of eighteen, is that right?'

'Yeah, that's right. Our mum died when I was seven. Saffy took charge, ran everything like clockwork. She became my legal guardian and we got on OK. I mean, she was always quite strict because she gave Mum her word she'd look after me, make sure I was safe. As a kid, it felt like I was living with my jailer, but now I understand the sacrifice she made.'

'That must have been difficult for you.'

Poppy sniffs. 'I turned sixteen and Saffy still insisted on walking me to and from school. You can imagine how that looked. I became a joke. All my cool mates found other people to hang around with by the end of that term. So as soon as I started uni, I was out of the house like a shot. Got myself a cheap flat in a dodgy part of town and then the attack happened so I deferred my course for a year and moved back in with Saffy and Neil.'

'What was your relationship like with Saffy after that?'

Poppy thinks for no more than a moment. 'After the attack, Saffy changed. She became paranoid, terrified of what might happen if I so much as left the house on my own. Course, a year after the attack, we found out her mental health was deteriorating, and thankfully she got the help she needed.'

'We understand Saffy and Neil split up around that time, too,' MacFarlane remarks.

'Yeah. Sad really. Neil tried his best but there was nothing left between them in the end. Neil got custody of Fox, that's my nephew, and Saffy moved into a little bedsit. It was a difficult time for us all.'

'Would you say Saffy is in a better place now?' Shah asks.

'For sure. Don't get me wrong, she still worries too much and tries her best to keep tabs on me.' Poppy rolls her eyes. 'But when she recovered, she got a decent job and bought a shared-ownership house. The one you've been to. And she thinks the world of Leona and Rosie.'

'You're now living in student digs in Lady Bay, is that right?' MacFarlane says, consulting her notes.

'Yeah, I have housemates, a social life. Saffy and I get on OK. Better with a bit of distance between us.'

'Is it fair to say, do you think, that Saffy still has some serious unresolved issues linked to the attack?' Shah asks.

Poppy hesitates. Saffy was a pain for sure, but she was Poppy's pain. The slightest chance and these two are like terriers. They're already giving Saffy a hard time and the last thing Poppy wants to do is add to her problems.

'The attack had a profound effect on my sister. It's taken me a while to appreciate it, but Saffy's interference has always been based on love rather than just wanting to curb my freedom. She's not always done it the right way but I think all she's ever wanted to do is to protect me.' Poppy takes a deep breath. 'That's why I promised her I'd speak to you today. Tell you what Ash told me.'

Shah sits up a little straighter in her seat. 'Go on?'

Poppy tells them about Ash wanting out of his marriage. The things that had shocked Saffy.

Shah looks steadily at her. 'OK. And is there anything else you want to tell us about Ash and what you two spoke about?'

'No.' She doesn't like the detective's tone. As if she is testing Poppy in some way.

'Was Ash Bannatyne ever violent to you, Poppy?' Shah asks. 'Or did he speak or even hint about abusing Leona?'

'No to both. He was never violent to me. For a long time he treated me like a princess . . . until he got bored. I suppose Saffy told you he is a monster, didn't she? She thinks all men are, but she especially hates Ash because she blames him for breaking up her close friendship with Leona.'

'Does your sister hate Ash enough to do him harm, do you think?'

Poppy looks at her. 'Are you serious? She might dislike Ash, but she'd never hurt Leona or Rosie. Anyway, how on earth could one woman abduct three people on her own?'

'If she had help she wouldn't be on her own,' MacFarlane says slowly, leaning forward towards Poppy. 'Maybe two people working together could get the job done.'

She realizes now that they've been setting her up.

'What are you trying to say? Surely you don't think Saffy and I –'

Sweat pools at the bottom of her back. She's said too much. Said the wrong thing. She's managed to get Saffy into even more trouble.

Shah watches her thinly disguised panic and smiles. A tight-lipped, cynical smile.

'Let me make it a little clearer for you,' she says, her voice ringing out cold and clear in the small, airless space. 'We've asked you to tell us everything you know about the whereabouts of the Bannatyne family and you've given us very little. But the texts and photos on that phone suggest that you're far more involved in what's happened than you're letting on.'

Poppy's head begins to swim. 'That's not true.'

'We're just not sure yet if Saffy was involved, too,' MacFarlane adds.

'Saffy wasn't involved.' Rising nausea nibbles at Poppy's throat. 'I swear she had nothing to do with it.'

'Really? So can you explain the photographs of Leona Bannatyne you sent to him? Photos bearing a date stamp just weeks before the family went missing?'

Poppy sags in her seat, beginning to understand. The decisions she's made to help herself feel better, more in control – seeing whoever she likes without any concern for anyone else – those decisions don't happen in a bubble. They have consequences.

'Ash asked me to watch Leona when he was at work. I didn't think there was any harm in it, not really. I mean . . . I didn't think he'd do anything to hurt them.'

'What exactly did you do?' MacFarlane says.

'I watched the house for a little while . . . just a few mornings over this one week. Ash had got a covert tracker on Leona's car but he suspected that she deactivated the Ring doorbell when he left for work as he'd found he wasn't able to monitor any footage remotely during the mornings.'

'So, Ash asked you to spy on Leona?'

Poppy feels her face fall. 'It wasn't exactly spying. No binoculars or crazy stuff, just . . . watching. Ash wanted to know

236

if Leona went out on foot or if anyone came to the house.' Poppy looks down at her hands. 'I didn't do it for long and then a few weeks later we split up.'

MacFarlane stares at her. 'And what was your conclusion, after "watching" Leona's movements?'

Poppy squirms. 'I didn't see anything amiss. Not really. She did go out a couple of times but I didn't follow her or anything.'

MacFarlane narrows her eyes. 'And did you have to report back to Ash?'

'I snapped a few shots on my phone and sent them over to Ash and that was it, really.'

'*That was it,*' Shah repeats.

Poppy studies her short, bitten nails before looking back up at Shah. 'I know I was stupid, I see that now,' she blurts out. 'Ash told me he wanted us to be together, that he wanted to start a new life with me. But he needed evidence that she was having an affair.'

'And your aim was to provide that evidence by spying on Leona. What did you think he was going to do with it?' Shah presses her.

'I didn't know what was going to happen, if that's what you think!' Poppy cries, her eyes brimming with tears. 'There's no way I could know they might all go missing.'

'And yet,' Shah says, 'that is exactly what happened.'

41

Saffy

Saffy can't seem to focus on anything at all. She's constantly distracted by the very real prospect she could be summoned back to the police station with very little notice for further questioning. As DI Shah had hinted yesterday, it might well happen. On top of that she'd been unable to contact Poppy. One of her flatmates had answered the communal landline she'd called about an hour ago as a last resort.

'Who? Oh, Pops. Yeah. She's not here right now. Sorry, I don't know when she went out or where she's gone.'

It sounded to Saffy like she was being fobbed off but she wasn't about to hare over there as she would usually have done. If she learned one thing yesterday, it was that Poppy was old enough to make her own – albeit foolish – decisions in life, and so she must learn she also has to deal with their consequences.

As the hours tick on, Saffy turns to something else that's pressing and that she has been trying to avoid. Looking at her finances. She doesn't get paid for sick leave and with everything that's happened, she's had to take unpaid absence, which will be frowned upon. It will probably count against her in the final decisions on which jobs will go.

She doesn't want to go back there. Analysing and interpreting data like it's something that matters. Her job feels vague and senseless; part of another life back when she thought she had worries . . . little imagining how steady her life actually was.

Saffy has a little money put by. Not a lot. Just about enough, she judges, to survive for a couple of months if she has no income. She once read an article in a magazine that advised saving enough to be able to survive twelve months without any income. What planet did these financial advisors live on? Who could afford to save what amounted to a year's salary and keep it tucked away and forgotten about in case of a rainy day? Not her. Nor anyone she knew for that matter.

Saffy scrolls down her online bank statement and gives a heavy sigh. The energy direct debit has more than doubled in the last year and, thanks to the hike in food prices, her grocery bill is barely any lower despite Poppy moving out. After renting it for a while, she bought this house through a shared-ownership scheme so on paper only owns half of it. But her payment from her divorce, which was finalized quietly last November, covered a good deposit and meant she needed a smaller mortgage in the end.

Saffy logs off, closes the online banking window and stares at the wall. She can feel herself slipping. Only slightly, but each day it seems as if her foothold on solid ground wavers a little more, beckoning her into that unhealthy place she was trapped in a year after the attack, when Neil told her he must apply for full custody of Fox.

Fear has all but ruined her life. She has always had the distinct feeling that she must pay for being a bad person long ago. For the impulsive and perhaps pointless lie she told that grew bigger and lodged itself like a great black spider in the corner of her mind. And she feels no less afraid now than the night of the attack on Poppy. On the face of it an attacker who the police were convinced was an opportunistic thief who had assumed the house was empty. Despite the lights and television being on.

To Saffy, all that had never rung true.

No one was ever apprehended and after a year, it seemed to Saffy that everyone but her had forgotten about him. She most definitely hadn't. He stalked her days and nights, lived inside her head as if it had happened only yesterday.

Fear is so completely a part of who she is and what she does now, she suspects she might not know how to function without it.

Saffy takes a sip of her water, tipping her head like a bird when she hears what sounds like voices outside. She gets up and as she walks into the hallway, the landline rings.

She snatches up the phone. 'Hello?'

'Ms Morris? Saffy Morris? *Nottingham Post* here. Do you have any comment about –'

She cuts off the call and turns the ring volume right down. How do these people get ex-directory numbers? Is there nothing they can't find out about a person?

She walks into the living room and peers through the newly adjusted blinds.

There are people at the gate talking loudly to each other and shouting to a couple of dog walkers across the road. There's also a big white van parking up outside. The doors slide open, and two men emerge carrying formidable-looking camera equipment.

Saffy rocks on her heels and takes a step back, staring in disbelief. It didn't take long after the police appeal in the newspapers for the detectives' warnings to become reality.

Her skin crawls as she imagines what might come of it all. Once she – and possibly Poppy – are plastered over social media. She searches #MissingFamily online and it's everywhere, in one unofficial form or another, on all the social media channels.

Best friend of missing local mother, Leona Bannatyne, questioned by police . . .

And in the comments: *Her name is Saffy Morris.*

Ten minutes later, more press have arrived and there's now quite a gathering at the gate. Saffy creeps to the side of the window blinds and very slowly and, she hopes, discreetly, twists the plastic opener to close them a little further while still allowing light into the room.

Directly outside the house, two reporters walk slowly up and down, taking photographs, and then stand still, tapping away on their phones. In this new age of journalism, reports are uploaded directly online. Several neighbours are outside their houses, standing in twos and threes with intrigued expressions and folded arms, curious as to what or who the object of this sudden press interest is. Saffy assumes they'll soon have it all worked out.

A reporter opens the gate and walks up the short path, and she shrinks away from the window. The doorbell rings, its invasive shrill cry echoing through the house, setting her nerves jangling.

She stands, rigid, not daring to move an inch. It's crazy this stuff is legal; that they can hound a person like this. She feels like she is overheating. Sweat pools under her arms and at the bottom of her back. She's been here before. After the attack . . . everyone congregating outside, baying for information. Desperate to speak to Poppy. Hungry for more information about the female first-year student who escaped her attacker. Both she and Poppy had felt more like curiosities than heroines at the time.

The doorbell rings again and this time someone keeps

their finger on the button. The shrill screech fills Saffy's head so completely, it feels like her brain and teeth are rattling against her skull.

'Go away!' Saffy yells out, hands over her ears. 'Leave me alone!'

A woman's voice shouts through the letterbox, 'Saffy? Saffy Morris? Can we have a word?'

'*Go away. Go away. Go away.*' She whispers it over and over, crossing her arms and holding herself.

'Saffy?' the letterbox voice continues. 'Is it true you were the last person to see the Bannatyne family before they disappeared? What do you think has happened to them?'

Down at the gate, the men with cameras are taking photographs of the house, angling their equipment at the ground floor, then the bedrooms. They walk a little way past the gate and take photographs of the path that leads down to the back garden. A couple of journos are speaking to her neighbours, holding out voice recorders to capture their comments.

Saffy waits in the doorway of the living room and when she sees the two people at the door start to move away from the stained-glass panels, she runs back into the kitchen and slams the door shut behind her.

The doors and windows are locked. I'm safe. Nobody can force me to speak to them. She repeats the mantra silently.

For a few days after the attack, the press had gravitated outside the hospital where Poppy was being treated. Saffy remembers talking to herself to get through the long nights.

The house is all locked up. The downstairs alarm is activated. He would never dare to come back. We are safe.

Now, history is repeating itself and she is here again. Trapped in her own home and hiding away, praying to be left alone.

Saffy looks out of the window, sees the journalists at the door return to the growing crowd at the gate. They'll never go away until she speaks to them, makes them see she has only concern for her friend and goddaughter.

But would that further antagonize the police? Saffy has been advised not to speak to the press, but so much stuff has exploded online since then. Armchair detectives posting dubious and even libellous theories . . . How else are the reporters going to go away and leave her alone unless she strenuously denies all this crap?

Saffy walks to the front door and opens it. The crowd of press at the gate surges and they spill through the gate and on to her path.

'What do you think has happened to the Bannatyne family?'

'Have you been arrested?'

'Is it true you were the last person to see them?'

She walks down to meet them, holding her hands up to appeal for quiet. When the noise dies down, Saffy speaks.

'I've been friends with Leona Bannatyne since our school days. I'm godmother to her daughter, Rosie. There is a lot of unfounded speculation online but I want to make it clear, I have nothing to hide, nothing but concern for my friend and goddaughter's safety.'

'What about Ash? What about Leona's husband?'

The police, Poppy . . . nobody seems to get the type of man he is. Saffy's only loyalty is to Leona and Rosie. Why the hell should she protect the monster who ruled their family with an iron fist?

'Ash Bannatyne was abusing my friend, physically and emotionally, but the police don't seem to be connecting her disappearance with this fact.' They fall quiet again and for the first time Saffy feels listened to. Validated. 'She told me herself a week before they disappeared that she was afraid of him. Draw your own conclusions as to what might have happened. Now please, stand away from my gate and respect my neighbours' privacy.'

Saffy turns and starts to walk back up the path. Someone shouts her name and she turns to see the reporter who came to the door, and her cameraman.

'Saffy, please . . . can we just have a quick ten-minute chat? You can tell your side of the story, about Leona and Rosie. Someone might have seen something. Don't you want the three of them found safe and well?'

Saffy turns, resentment bubbling up into her throat. 'I'd do anything to find Leona and Rosie, but *him*? As far as I'm concerned, Ash Bannatyne can rot in hell.'

42

Saffy

Her decision to speak out makes everything worse.

The gaggle of press outside has doubled in the last hour and reporters are banging on the front door again. She hears the letterbox rattle and a man's voice bellow, echoing through the house.

'Have you got a comment? About what you just said on camera? Do you know you're trending on Twitter, Saffy? People want to hear more from you.'

She grabs her phone and opens up her X app, navigating to the *Nottingham Post*'s channel.

Local suspect 'hopes missing dad rots in hell'

The ten-second video starts to play automatically and here's the reporter, asking, '. . . don't you want the three of them found safe and well?'

The camera pans around quickly and in an instant Saffy is there, outside her front door, arms folded as she snarls, 'I'd do anything to find Leona and Rosie, but *him*? As far as I'm concerned, Ash Bannatyne can rot in hell.'

The same clip has been shared again and again until it seems to be echoing in her head, in this room, throughout the house . . .

'Oh no,' she whispers.

Her comment is all out of context. They've cut the bit where she talks about Ash abusing Leona. About him ruling the household with an iron fist. And she looks like a crazy woman, a *guilty* woman.

Her phone begins to ring. She's got two numbers programmed into it. One is Poppy's and the other person is calling her now. Neil.

'Neil! I've been trying to speak to –'

'Saffy? What the hell is going on . . . have you lost your mind?' he demands. 'Your video is all over the internet, effectively telling the nation how much you hate Ash Bannatyne and hope he rots in hell. Do you realize the danger you're putting yourself and Poppy in? Not to mention Fox.'

'What about Fox?' She suddenly feels panic about her boy. 'Is he OK?'

'Fox is fine, but this crazy stuff you're spouting online . . . this stuff won't go away, Saffy. It will stick around and be there for Fox to view himself when he's older. It's there for the mothers of his little nursery friends to see and to question whether they want their kids playing with the boy of a woman who conducts herself like this. Don't you see? Your reckless behaviour has implications for us all.'

'Have you finished?' she says quietly. 'I've been waiting hours for you to get in touch and it's taken this to convince you to pick up the phone and speak to me.'

'Saffy, listen to me. This has all got out of hand. The Bannatynes are missing and social media is already rife with discussions about you being the last person to see them and whether you might have something to do with their disappearance. Now you've given the police a gift, a reason for them to delve deeper into your reasons for despising him.'

Even though she's dying inside, she questions who the hell he thinks he is, speaking to her like that as if Ash is an angel and she's a . . . she's a –

Neil's annoyance breaks through her distraction. 'And

actually, no. I haven't finished. Not by a long way. This is a courtesy call to tell you that the second I come off this call, I'm calling the police to tell them about that letter incident last year. It's highly relevant to their investigation and –'

'Neil, no! It's not your place to tell.'

'If you feel like that then you shouldn't have confided in me, Saffy. I'm not losing any more sleep worrying that I'm keeping important information from the police.'

'Just give me today, OK? I'll speak to the police and when everything settles down –'

When he speaks, Neil's tone is firm. 'I'm sorry, Saffy, but I've discussed this with Mira and we're both of the same opinion. Fox will be staying with us at home where we know he's safe for the time being, and if you're not going to tell the police about what happened last year, then I will.'

43

Poppy

She closes her eyes and dips her head forward as the needles of scalding water from the shower rain down hard, pummelling her taut shoulder muscles into submission.

The detectives know everything. What she was doing outside Ash's house, the photographs of Leona she'd texted to Ash on the phone they recovered in the search. And although she gave them a full explanation and they let her go 'for now', as DI Shah put it, they seem to be nursing a crazy idea that she and Saffy are somehow in cahoots and are implicated in Leona and Rosie's disappearance.

Poppy tips her head towards her right shoulder, allowing the water to soothe the seized-up muscles in her neck.

She should have gone straight to Saffy after she left the police station. Told her how stupid she'd been, going to Leona's house to carry out Ash's bidding. But she just couldn't face it after the police grilling. Instead, she whiled away some time doing a bit of clothes shopping she couldn't afford and then went to an internet café. It was there she remembered with a jolt that she was meeting Harry tonight.

Their dinner date is the one positive thing in her day that she refuses to cancel. She intends telling Saffy everything, of course she does. But it will have to wait until tomorrow now. She needs to escape all this crap, blow off some steam, and to do that, she must get into the right mindset for her date.

The umpteenth call from Saffy comes through just as she's

sitting down at her desk in front of her propped-up makeup mirror. Is it possible the police have already told her sister what she's been hiding? Poppy lets the call ring out, turns her phone to silent and tosses it on to the bed. She can't handle her sister's wrath. Not tonight.

Ash Bannatyne turned out to be a Class A dick who pretended to be one thing and was really someone else altogether. But this guy, Harry, is a different sort of man . . . the real deal. There is something authentically dangerous about him, as if he's done and seen things most people don't get to experience in a lifetime.

Poppy turns her attention back to the mirror. She has good, clear skin, bright eyes and full lips, and she applies the cosmetics in a way that showcases her good points, rather than obliterate them. She applies a light base, some pale gold eyeshadow and a nude lipstick.

She painted her fingers and toes earlier in a shimmer-pink nail varnish so now she's nearly done. She smothers her skin in body butter and uses a liberal spray of Marc Jacobs Daisy that Saffy bought for her last Christmas.

On the way to her wardrobe, a mere six steps from her desk in this tiny room, she picks up her phone and shakes her head in irritation at the now five missed calls and two voicemail messages from her sister.

She hesitates a moment, fleetingly wondering if Saffy has news about Leona and Rosie, but then she pushes it right out of her mind. It won't be that, it will just be Saffy trying to keep her usual tabs on her, asking a hundred questions about what the police have just spilled about Poppy and what she did.

She wants to keep Harry a secret for now, because Poppy knows only too well that no man can ever match up to Saffy's stringent vetting procedure. And this guy, this brooding, handsome man, wouldn't even try.

She opens the wardrobe and takes out the silky bias-cut dress she'd impulse-bought from a little boutique to cheer herself up when she'd left the police station. The clothing label is secured by a plastic tag that hangs just under her armpit. If she's careful, she'll be able to tuck it neatly out of sight and return the dress after wearing it. Then choose something else with the refund.

What's left of this term's student loan won't stretch to a new wardrobe, but if tonight goes well and Harry asks her out on more dates, she wants to wow him every time.

They had arranged to meet for a pre-dinner drink so Poppy gets the bus to the swanky cocktail bar she's walked past with her mates many times looking for happy hour prices, but never ventured in.

Inside, Harry is waiting. He looks good enough to eat, she thinks as she approaches the tall glass table where he sits on a bar stool. He has on a distinctive shirt, smart trousers, and wears an expensive-looking watch on his wrist. His hair is slicked back and, as Poppy leans forward to kiss his cheek, she smells an enticing mix of sandalwood and bergamot.

'Well, don't you just look a million dollars.' He lays a warm hand on Poppy's bare upper arm and she feels the now familiar tingle of electricity shoot through her body. 'I waited until you got here to order drinks.' He taps the cocktail menu. 'Let's see . . . fancy a Moscow Mule?'

She laughs, delighted. 'I'll try anything once.'

Over drinks, he asks her stuff about herself and then he says, 'So what's happening in Poppy's world . . . anything interesting?'

'This and that. Nothing interesting.' She smiles through the lie, trying not to think about the increasingly dire situation and the police interest in both her and Saffy. She's certainly not going to admit she's been interviewed formally by two detectives today.

'Have you heard about this local family going missing?' Harry says, taking a sip of his drink. 'Awful business.'

Poppy's heart sinks. She wants to forget all about it, pretend today never happened. Not to dissect it endlessly over her Moscow Mule.

'I've heard something about it but I try and avoid the news where I can. So depressing.'

'Agreed. I knew all that stuff trending online mustn't be anything to do with you.'

She frowns. 'Huh?'

'You told me your sister's name is Saffy, right?' He takes his phone out of his pocket, swipes a few times and holds the screen to face her. 'This woman, also Saffy, is currently trending on social media. They reckon she's got something to do with the missing local family.'

Poppy stares at the screen, her hand starting to shake. She puts down her glass and takes his phone, unmutes the video and watches it through twice.

'Oh God.' A wave of painful longing flows through her. 'Oh no.'

Saffy looks so vulnerable on the short reel. Poppy can see her anxiety behind what must appear to most people as a display of arrogance or nonchalance. Her heart squeezes. She has let Saffy down by not telling her the truth, by not updating her on the outcome of her own police interview. Her sister won't know that speaking openly to the press like this only makes her look guiltier than ever in police eyes. She has let her sister down at the very time she needs her the most.

She can't do anything about what's now been posted online, but she can put right her failure to tell Saffy everything. She looks at Harry, his concerned eyes on hers, full of unspoken questions.

She hands the phone back. 'It's . . . Look, you're right. This is my sister on the video.'

'That was posted a while ago.' He begins to scroll again. 'There's more stuff on now.'

'It's too awful. I don't want to see any more,' Poppy says. 'I'll explain everything to you, but not right now. I'm sorry, but I must go to Saffy.'

Harry's eyes are wide as he stares silently at his phone screen.

Poppy's mouth instantly turns dry. 'What is it?'

'A local news channel just posted a livestream from outside your sister's house. Two detectives have just arrived there.'

Poppy slides off her bar stool and grabs her clutch purse. 'I've got to go. Saffy . . . she's in trouble. Sorry. I need to be there for her.'

'Hey, slow down! Is that wise? To just turn up with the press –'

But as Harry continues to protest, Poppy is already half-way across the bar and she doesn't look back.

44
Saffy

At the sound of the doorbell, Saffy jumps up from the sofa. She rushes down the hall, snatching open the door without looking through the spy hole, and by the time she wonders why Poppy hasn't used her door key, she's looking at the two detectives and a gaggle of press still baying for a comment at the gate.

She'd been waiting for them to make contact all day, but it had completely slipped her mind for the last hour or so with the press interest and Neil's call.

'Oh, it's you again!' She freezes for a moment as they both stare back with cold eyes. 'This is the worst time for you to turn up, it's like a feeding frenzy. You can see that they're –'

'I'm afraid we need to speak with you as a matter of urgency, Saffy,' Shah says. 'And I don't think you'll want to hear what we have to say on the doorstep.'

Her skin starts to crawl and she stands aside to let them both in. Saffy glares at the yelling press and closes the door. 'It might have been an idea to call ahead. Your visit here will be posted online within a few minutes.' She sniffs at their lack of reaction. 'You'd better come on through.'

Saffy's phone starts ringing in her hand and Poppy's name appears on the screen. She turns it to silent and slips it into her jeans pocket.

'Aren't you going to answer that?' Shah says, her expression grim.

'No. Let's go through.'

When they reach the living room and take their seats, Saffy looks at them both in turn. Their sombre faces. They've no doubt seen the video trending online. Have come here to reprimand her for saying that stuff about Ash. But all she did was express an opinion. They can't arrest her for disliking someone publicly. 'Well . . . what is it? What's happened?'

Shah clears her throat. 'I'm sorry to have to tell you, Saffy, that a body has been found in woodland about a mile away from the Bannatynes' house. Officers were –'

'Whose body?' she wails and stands up, holds her head. She feels nauseous. Cold, then hot.

'Try to stay calm,' says Shah.

'Who is it? Not little Rosie. Oh no, please, God . . . no.'

'We're waiting for forensics but we believe the victim to be Ashley Bannatyne.'

Saffy feels the blood drain from her face. She sways on her feet. 'What?' she whispers. 'But . . . how can it be?'

The detectives stare at her, coolly evaluating her reaction. Undisguised suspicion shadowing their faces.

Ash is *dead*? How could he be when he's clearly been behind this whole thing? 'Where was this? Where was his body found?'

'The body was discovered in woodland, close to the location of Holme Pierrepont Country Park.'

'Can you say . . . Can you tell me how he died?'

'The victim had suffered multiple stab wounds, but at this point, we have no further information about cause of death.'

A lump hits the back of Saffy's throat and she clamps a hand over her mouth, squeezing her eyes shut to beat back the need to be sick. She forces a breath in and out again before she opens her eyes to see the hard glare of the detectives still on her.

She gathers herself and says, 'So Leona and Rosie are still missing? There's no sign they've been hurt?'

The detectives watch her, but say nothing.

'I . . . I can't believe it. I can't believe it's him,' Saffy murmurs, sitting down, nursing her pounding head before looking up.

'Have you anything you want to tell us?' MacFarlane says. 'In the light of this news?'

Saffy shakes her head, puzzled. 'I . . . I've told you everything I know. How would I know anything about the body? I'm more shocked than anyone.'

'Really?' MacFarlane says. 'You see, the traces of blood found in the house the day the family went missing have now been confirmed as belonging to Mr Bannatyne.'

Saffy frowns, trying to comprehend what she's being told. The blood in the house belongs to Ash? The vision of Leona struggling, fighting against her husband and hitting her head flashes into her mind again. She's made assumptions that have skewed her entire thought process.

Shah says, 'And a large kitchen knife was found to be missing during the search of your own property.'

Saffy makes a noise of disbelief. 'Surely you don't think that's anything to do with them going missing and –'

'We are no longer dealing with just a missing persons situation here,' Shah says, her voice grave. 'With effect from today, this case has now been escalated to a full murder investigation.'

MacFarlane steps forward, a grim expression on her face. Shah opens the living room door and MacFarlane lays a firm hand on Saffy's upper arm, indicating for her to move into the hallway.

'Why are you looking at me like that?' Saffy hears the volume of the shouting press increase as they move towards the front door. 'Hey . . . no! What are you doing? I'm not going out there with you. Not like this!'

MacFarlane stands in front of Saffy.

'Saffy Morris, I am arresting you for the murder of Ashley Bannatyne. You do not have to . . .'

Saffy feels like she is underwater, the detective's voice slowing down into distortion. She feels cool air on her face as the door opens; the instant wave of yelling hits her ears as she walks, Shah's firm grip on her upper arm, MacFarlane leading, and then Saffy feels a hand on the top of her head and she is inside a vehicle.

Speeding away from home.

Speeding away from time spent with Fox.

Speeding away from freedom.

45

Leona

'It's so exciting, Wes's family has bought a big piece of wood-land near the watersports centre. Can you imagine, having your very own wood?'

Saffy's forehead creased; more irritated than impressed.

'There's an old cabin in there that Wes's dad says we can have as our chill-out space. It needs a bit of work, but there's a log burner in there that'll keep us dry and warm in winter and we can get some booze in.' Leona waited but there was no reaction from Saffy. 'Wes's mum, Mags, says she has a couple of old rugs and a sofa we can have that she's been trying to get rid of for ages. We're going there tomorrow to spruce the cabin up a bit and we wondered if you'd like to come, too.'

Saffy raised a cynical eyebrow. '*We?* Wes knows you're asking me?'

'Yes, *we*. I told him you're good at practical stuff whereas I'm a bit hopeless. He says another pair of hands would be welcome.'

Leona watched as her friend picked up a magazine and started to idly leaf through the pages. 'I'll have to see what I've got on tomorrow,' Saffy said.

The next morning, Leona woke bright and early. She tapped on Saffy's bedroom door before opening it slightly. The curtains were still closed and the room dim, but Leona had heard Saffy visit the bathroom just ten minutes ago.

'Morning, Saff. Just wanted to say, wear old clothes today that you don't mind getting dirty. We need to leave in an hour.'

Her request was met with a grunt from under the bed-clothes before Leona closed the door softly.

Ninety minutes later, they were following Wes and his dad and ten-year-old kid brother, Kieran, on an overgrown path that meandered through a pretty wood. It was mid-morning and the bracken and the ground beneath their feet felt crisp and dry, sunlight dappling down from above the tall trees.

Leona felt an excitement rising in her, a warm, contented glow of being with others. With people she knew and cared about and who cared about her, too. People who actually wanted her around.

She hung back a little to speak to Saffy. 'I'm glad you came! You get to meet Wes's family, too.' They stand aside as Kieran zooms past holding imaginary handlebars and making rev-ving noises. Leona laughs. 'He's such a bundle of energy!'

'With too much confidence and sass for his own good.' Saffy scowled, watching as Kieran swaggered past again to catch up with his big brother. 'He's the sort of kid that'll be in trouble with the police at fourteen.'

'Aw, he's harmless enough, Saffy,' Leona laughed. Her friend could be such a stick-in-the-mud.

Kieran looked a lot like Wes and liked to hang around with the older boys. It was true he was always getting into trouble at school and with the Sharpes' neighbours. His misdemean-ours were labelled as mischief by his parents but he could be a bit cheeky, so Leona knew Saffy would probably disapprove of him.

She left Saffy to her grumpiness and caught up again with Wes. This felt like family life . . . or what her idea of family life had always been. She felt the prickle of Saffy's irritability behind her. Leona had tried to avoid her friend feeling left out, and in doing so, had surely annoyed her just the same as if she had pretended everything was cool between them and just gone ahead and done her own thing.

Leona shrugged off the grasping tendrils of Saffy's resentment and quickened her step until she caught up with Kieran and Wes. 'When we get the cabin tidy, we can have a picnic on the riverbank and you can ask a couple of your mates over. That's OK, isn't it, Wes?'

'Sure it is!' He winked at Leona and ruffled his brother's hair. 'We're gonna have some great times here. All of us like one big family.'

Leona turned with a smile but Saffy just tramped on behind, her eyes firmly fixed to the ground.

The cabin was smaller than Leona had imagined it, but apart from the overgrown foliage outside and the fading, unstained wood, it was in better condition than she'd expected.

'It's so much bigger in here than it looks from the wood,' Leona said once they got inside.

'Just like a Tardis!' Kieran gasped, looking around.

'Wait until you see the den in the basement, son,' Wes Snr ruffled Kieran's hair.

'Is it big, Dad?'

'Aye. We didn't bother with planning permission or anything inconvenient like that,' Wes Snr quipped. 'This is our own private land, so nobody will be any the wiser.'

The interior was dusty and the floor covered in crisp old leaves that had blown in from a broken window. As could only be expected, it smelled a little fusty and Mags, Wes's mum, threw open a couple of windows to get some fresh air circulating.

For the next couple of hours they swept, cleaned windows. Mags had brought some small bottles of water and a battery-operated radio and Leona felt happy in her work.

'I could probably get a generator running outside and then you could boil a kettle and have a light,' Wes's dad said, thinking aloud.

'That would be ace, Dad,' Wes said. 'We could set up a gaming corner in here, whaddaya say, Kieran?'

'Cool!'

Wes Snr frowned. 'How many times? I don't want you encouraging Kieran with that crap. He's gonna be a professional football player, he's not going to fritter his life away like you do. Right, son?' He pulled Kieran a little roughly to him.

'Right, Dad!' Wes Snr got him in a headlock and Kieran gave a warrior roar, repeatedly play-punching him in the stomach.

Leona watched as Wes's expression darkened and he moved away from his father.

Surprisingly, Saffy seemed to instantly set up a rapport with Mags Sharpe. They scrubbed, dusted, carried in a rolled-up faded rug together. 'This carpet came from Persia, very expensive in its day,' Leona heard Mags telling her.

Saffy appeared to be all smiles in her role as Mags's little helper and Leona felt a little squirm of jealousy. She and Mags had built an understanding through their love of nursing and yet today, Mags seemed to be only interested in Saffy.

'She'll just feel threatened,' Saffy said when Leona shared her concern about Mags taking no notice of her.

'Threatened by what, though?'

'I dunno. That you might end up marrying her darling son and taking him away from her, maybe.'

But the more time she spent around the Sharpes, Leona saw it was not Wes who was the 'darling son' but Kieran.

Wes brushed past her as he headed for the door. 'Come outside,' he muttered to her.

Leona turned and followed him out. Down the steps from the narrow deck and back on to the rough ground. Wes walked to the edge of the trees and tucked himself furtively behind one of them.

'Isn't the cabin great?' Leona said brightly when she reached him. 'It's going to look so nice when –'

Wes pulled a packet of cigarettes and a lighter from his inside pocket.

'What are you doing?' Leona glanced back at the cabin before continuing. 'I thought you'd given up! What about your fitness levels?'

'Don't you start!' Wes snarled.

'Sorry, I . . .' She took a step back. She'd never seen him like this; his features looked somehow twisted. 'I didn't mean anything by it, I just –'

'Shut up,' he hissed, lighting up. 'You don't know what it's like . . . how he makes me feel.'

Leona felt a little shaken by his aggressive reply, but understood the reasons he was upset. Stressed. 'You mean your dad?'

'Who else?' Wes took a deep drag of his cigarette and stared into the thick curtain of trees in front of them. 'I hate him, but he's right, isn't he? I am a failure. I'd have been picked up by one of the big clubs by now if I had a real chance of making it.'

'That's not true, Wes. You *will* make it. I really believe in you and –'

'Leona? Where are you?' Saffy's voice called out close by. 'Hello?'

Wes groaned. 'Great. Just what I need.' He turned his back as Saffy appeared in front of Leona.

'Oh, there you are! I just . . .' Saffy's voice faded as she took in Wes's obvious annoyance and her friend's worried expression. 'What's wrong?'

Mutely, Leona shook her head, eyes widening to warn Saffy against speaking out of turn.

'What's wrong with Leona?' Saffy moved to confront Wes face to face. 'She looks upset.'

'How should I know?' he snapped, blowing smoke towards her. 'Ask her yourself, she's right there.'

'Nothing's wrong.' Leona gulped, taking Saffy's arm and pulling her gently away. 'I'm fine. Go back inside, Saffy.'

Saffy stood her ground and Leona's hand fell away. 'You don't look fine. What's up?'

'You heard her, she's fine.' Wes turned, his eyes burning dangerously in a way Leona hadn't seen before. 'Now get lost.'

Saffy looked at Leona and she nodded. 'I'm fine,' she said in a small voice. 'Really. We're just talking. I'm coming back inside soon.'

Slowly, Saffy took a few steps before glancing back at her. Leona nodded. 'I'm OK,' she mouthed.

When Leona turned back, Wes had gone. Just the smell of cigarette smoke hanging in the air in the space where he'd stood.

46

Poppy

In the cab, she's struggling not to shout at the driver to go faster. Poppy stares into space as people dressed up for the evening walk by, talking, laughing. The bright lights of the bars and restaurants on the other side of the road morph into a neon blur through the filter of her tears.

Harry had insisted on getting an Uber and coming with her and she'd felt glad of his support. They're about half the way there when her phone rings. She snatches up the call. 'Neil? Have you seen that –'

'Saffy's been arrested,' Neil says, sounding out of breath.

'What?' Poppy grabs a handful of her hair and looks around wildly.

'She just rang me as she was leaving the house with detectives. She's across all the social media channels saying she hopes Ash is dead or something like that.'

Harry twists around in his seat and watches her.

'I've seen all the stuff online,' Poppy says. 'But . . . why has Saffy been arrested?'

Neil falls silent for a moment before speaking. 'The police found Ash's body.'

'What?' Poppy glances at Harry, her eyes wide. He touches her arm and gives her a questioning look. 'Ash is . . . *dead*?'

Full of dread, she looks at Harry and sees the colour has drained from his face. He blinks rapidly, his eyes dark and troubled.

'Police found his body in woodland and two detectives came to arrest Saffy at home for his murder. In full view of all the press gathered there, too,' Neil continues.

'Oh God. Oh no . . . what a shit-storm! Poor Saffy.' Poppy pinches the top of her nose and murmurs, 'OK, I'm on my way over there but I'll divert to the police station. I'll –'

'Poppy, trust me, they won't let you see her, you can't do any good there. She asked me to let you know what's happened, but she called me so I can get a solicitor for her. This process has just got to run its course until the police realize they've taken a wrong turn somewhere along the line.' Neil's voice softens slightly. 'If you like, you can come over here to wait for news. Fox would love to see you and –'

'Thanks, Neil, but . . . I'm with someone.' She looks at Harry, and for a second she is nonplussed by his expression of what looks like pure panic as he stares wide-eyed at the driver's headrest in front of him. Poppy shivers and averts her glance before he sees her looking.

'Who?' Neil suddenly sounds concerned. 'Who are you with?'

'I'll call you later. Just let me know if you hear anything else from Saffy.'

'What did Neil say, exactly?' Harry asks, after Poppy hangs up. 'What does he think about it all?'

'The police have found Ash's body in an area of woodland and they've just arrested Saffy.' As she says the words, her hands shake a little. Ash – the man she'd slept with for months, spent hours talking to and, at one misguided point, even thought she might have a future with – is dead. And her sister is in custody.

'Poppy?' Harry touches her shoulder. 'Are you OK?'.

'Yeah, sorry. I'm all right. Neil says there's no point me going down to the station. But he agrees that the police are

268

seriously mistaken if they think Saffy is involved in Ash's death.' Her chest is thudding. 'I don't know what to do for the best.'

'We'll go to my place, we can wait there for news. It's only ten minutes from here,' Harry says firmly, issuing the driver with a new destination via the app and offering twenty pounds cash for the inconvenience. 'You can get your thoughts together there in peace. Don't worry,' he squeezes her hand. 'We'll sort this mess out together.'

She laughs sadly as a solitary tear rolls down her cheek. 'My life is so messed up you would not believe it.'

'Hey, that makes two of us.' He slides his arm around her shoulders and pulls her to him as the cab makes a U-turn in the road. Poppy buries her face in the warmth of his neck and closes her eyes.

'I'm scared though, Harry. I'm really scared,' she says.

'About what's going to happen to your sister?'

'About all of it.'

As the cab picks up speed on a bigger road, Poppy tells him what's been happening. Starting with, 'I had a brief affair with Ash Bannatyne,' and ending with, 'The police questioned me about my involvement with him at the station this morning.'

Harry lets out a low whistle. 'You're a dark horse, that's for sure.'

'Not that dark. I didn't kill Ash, if that's what you're wondering.'

Harry gives her a strange look. 'No. I know you didn't.'

After their fifteen-minute journey, the cab turns into a small new-build estate at the edge of Hucknall, a small market town about seven miles north from the city centre. The driver slows to a halt outside a row of attractive townhouses.

Harry fishes keys out of his pocket and opens the apple-green front door of the middle house in the row. He ushers Poppy inside. 'Cloakroom is on the left if you need it, or straight down the hallway for the kitchen. I'll make you a coffee. Or something stronger maybe?'

'Coffee will be fine, thanks,' Poppy says, sitting on a small two-seater couch by a set of narrow patio doors. 'If Saffy rings I want to have my wits about me.'

'Good call,' Harry says and she hears him filling the kettle at the sink. Poppy turns just in time to see him furtively open a drawer and sweep a small, neat stack of documentation from the worktop into it.

She turns quickly back to the window and only twists around again when she hears him groan.

'What is it?' Harry is standing in front of the open fridge.

'No milk. All things considered, I don't think we can get through the evening without coffee.' He sighs, closing the fridge door. 'I'll have to pop down the road for some – it'll only take me ten minutes there and back.' He leans forward to kiss her cheek. 'Operation Milk underway. Make yourself at home. I'll see you soon.'

A few seconds later the front door opens and closes. Poppy runs to the front window and watches as Harry walks down the road looking at his phone.

Poppy likes Harry. Poppy *really* likes Harry, but something is not right. That look she caught on his face when he heard Ash was dead . . . She feels it in her gut.

She rushes back down the hallway into the kitchen and opens the drawer she saw him push the documents into. She takes out a stack and leafs through it.

There's a signed tenancy agreement for this house, receipts for rent deposit paid and various furniture items . . . She stops short her search at a single piece of paper bearing a dark red wax seal at the bottom. A UK deed poll certificate. Poppy stares at it, reading it several times. Harry Farmer, formerly known as Harris Fielder.

So Harry changed his name a year ago . . . but why?

Poppy flicks through the remaining paperwork. Every second counts and she has no time to stop and reflect and wonder. Not right now.

Mindful of the few scant minutes she has left, Poppy speeds up, leafing through various receipts, letters and then . . . then the walls seem to close in around her.

A release order for Harris Fielder from a Greek prison eighteen months ago. Poppy holds her breath, her eyes scanning for details of the original crime committed, but it bears only the date and conditions of his release. Trembling, Poppy snaps photographs with her phone before continuing.

A handwritten letter . . . bearing an official prison authority stamp from twenty months ago.

Harris,

I don't want you anywhere near Rosie. I'm married now and Rosie considers Ash to be her dad. As a convicted criminal, the UK courts will never allow you custody, so please don't come back over here hoping for something that will never happen. We've moved on in your long absence, and having never even met you, Rosie is far better off without you in her life.

If you really care about her as you claim, you'll leave us alone.

Leona

Poppy snatches her phone up again and takes a couple of snaps of the letter.

Wow. She's managed to find herself yet another compulsive liar.

She can feel her heartbeat in her throat, a growing tightness in her chest, but Poppy steels herself to continue.

There's more regular paperwork until she gets to the final item in the pile. A brown A4-sized envelope. There is no writing on the exterior and she turns it over to find it has been opened and resealed, but the glue is soft to allow for easy re-opening and closing. There is something inside that feels slightly stiffer than letters.

Poppy feels suddenly cold as she slides a finger under the glued flap before reaching in to pinch out the contents. She pulls out photographs. Some grainy images, but most are crystal clear, four to a page printed on glossy photographic printer paper.

All of them feature the Bannatyne family. They have been taken from a safe distance at various times of day and in all weathers outside their house. Many are of Leona and little Rosie but there are also a couple of sheets at the end of Ash. Close-ups of his face, of him talking on the phone before he gets into his car. Grinning in that arrogant way he had that Poppy had once found so attractive.

She feels sick. Her legs are shaking as she picks up her phone and opens the camera app to take snaps. There's a noise at the front of the house and she freezes. Her phone hovers in mid-air as a key jangles in the lock. Harry is back!

Poppy begins to stuff the paperwork messily back into the drawer.

Thump, thump, thump . . . her heart bangs against her chest as the front door opens and shuts again. 'Only me!' Harry calls out brightly.

In Poppy's haste to move quickly, the bottom few sheets of photographs fall to the floor. She can hear Harry kicking off his shoes in the hallway.

With seconds to spare, Poppy scoops up the photographs, roughly folds them and slides them into her clutch bag.

When Harry appears in the kitchen doorway, she is there to take the milk from his hands.

'You look a bit flushed,' he says carefully. 'Any more news?'

'No! Nothing at all.'

His gaze pins to her just a couple of seconds too long. His eyes are dark brown, deep and warm, but as he turns slightly and the light changes, they turn almost black.

'Everything OK?' He looks around the room, his eyes settling back on her.

'Sorry, I got swallowed up looking online for updates,' Poppy says quickly and stops before her voice starts to shake. She takes a couple of breaths and continues, 'Saffy is everywhere on all channels. Telling the world she basically hopes Ash is dead. Which he now is.'

Harry blinks. 'I'll make the coffee, shall I?'

She watches as he flicks the button to re-boil the kettle and pulls two mugs from an overhead cupboard.

Poppy runs through the new facts she has about him.

Harry . . . *Harris* . . . is a convicted criminal. He is Rosie's biological father who has been denied parental access by Leona. He's been following the Bannatyne family around and taking photographs. He has a cast-iron motive for abducting them, and killing Ash.

Poppy feels heat channelling into her head. The reason she could sense that thrilling danger around him is because Harry is genuinely dangerous. And he might also be a killer.

He pulls the coffee canister towards him and murmurs, 'Spoon.'

His hand reaches for the drawer right next to the one she messily pushed the paperwork into, in contrast to how he'd placed it in there. Poppy wants to throw up.

Harry makes the coffee and adds a splash of milk, pushing a mug across the worktop to her.

Poppy takes a sip and closes her eyes briefly. She doesn't know how the hell she's going to get out of this situation.

'I'll need to go soon, need to –'

'Don't worry, everything is going to be OK. You're in no state to go anywhere,' Harry says. 'You can stay here all night. In the spare room, if you like. Until we hear what's happening with your sister.'

'I love you've said that, but honestly, there's no need.' The scalding mug is burning her fingers but she keeps it in her hands to help her focus. 'I'd better get back home because that's where Saffy will expect me to be. I'll call you first thing in the morning to let you know what's happening.'

Harry smiles his big, wide smile and puts down his coffee. Then he takes her hand and squeezes it . . . just a tad too hard.

'Did I make that sound an optional offer?' He brings Poppy's hand up to his mouth to kiss her fingers. 'It's not. You're staying here with me. End of.'

47

Poppy

Behind the safety of the locked bathroom door at last, Poppy feels as though she's going to throw up at any moment. Her legs are wobbly and her heart rate is off the scale.

It's been hell sitting down there for the past thirty minutes with Harry. Trying to appear normal while wondering if she's trapped herself here, in a house with a killer. Meanwhile, her innocent sister is being interrogated by detectives. Each time Poppy looks at Harry, she can't help wondering if he has Leona and Rosie holed up somewhere in a dank, dark basement.

It has crossed her mind to simply run from the house, but she needs to be cleverer than that. The police are clearly resolved to try and tie Saffy to Ash's death and the family's disappearance. There is still time for them to come for Poppy too, if they truly believe she and Saffy might have worked together to abduct the family.

It's clear from his prison sentence that Harry is a seasoned con. With his links abroad, he can just up and leave the country before Poppy can even begin to try and convince the police to take her seriously. She needs something solid and damning.

In the cab when she took the call from Neil, Harry looked rattled by the discovery of Ash's body but he collected himself quickly. Her one advantage is that for now – she thinks – he's relatively unsuspecting that she knows something is off. Poppy must try to keep him onside for a little while longer, at least until she has a good idea exactly what it is he's done . . . and what has happened to Leona and Rosie.

She sets the tap running and splashes cold water on her face before sitting on the closed loo seat and opening her clutch bag to study Harry's images of Ash. Each A4 sheet of photo paper features four smaller-sized images. Close-ups of Ash's face. The images are minutely different and have clearly been snapped in quick succession. It's obvious that Ash, relaxed and looking in the opposite direction, is completely unaware he is being watched.

The back of Poppy's neck prickles as she hears a creak on the stairs. The bathroom door is locked and bolted, but before she opens it, she must conceal the photographs more carefully. Roll them tighter and place her makeup items and hairbrush on top in case Harry has a crafty glance inside.

'What you up to in there, Poppy?' Harry says in a strange low voice, tapping lightly on the door.

Poppy jumps up, startled he's here. Right outside the door.

She assumes a groggy tone. 'I'm OK, my stomach feels a bit upset. I won't be long.'

'The tap has been running for ages.'

How long has he been listening out there?

'I've been splashing my face.' She walks over to the sink. 'There. It's off now.' Harry does not reply and the silence feels deafening. Poppy tries to quickly conceal the photos in her bag but soon realizes she can't roll them tightly to fit snugly in the bottom of her bag or he'll hear the paper crinkling. No, she must get rid of him instead. 'Go back downstairs, Harry. I'll be out soon.'

Outside on the landing, Harry gives a frustrated sigh. Poppy listens for his receding footsteps, but there is nothing.

Then the door handle rattles, and Harry calls out impatiently, 'Come on, Poppy. Let me in.'

Her head is pounding as she pushes the photographs clumsily into her bag and pulls back the lock. Pasting a smile on her face, she opens the door just as the clutch bag's strap slips from her shoulder and it falls to the floor. The spring catch flies open and the photographs fall out.

Harry's powerful physique fills the doorway. He stares, cheeks inflaming, at the photos scattered around her on the floor.

Poppy fights the urge to start babbling, to try and make up some plausible story on the spot. She has no excuse.

She has been caught in a lie and there is absolutely no way out of it now but to face this man who she barely knows and yet has so willingly trusted and allowed into her life.

48

Saffy

She feels bruised and battered when she finally emerges from the police station.

Saffy has been released 'pending investigation', which means there'll be more of the same to come. Except there is no respite because it keeps happening. The detectives haul her back to the station, question then release her, always with the implied threat that they will likely need to speak with her again so she shouldn't go far. Although this time feels more serious because she was actually arrested.

It's eight fifteen and although it is not yet dark, the light is fading, the sky turning from an intense blue to a moodier purple tinge. Saffy checks her phone and finds one text from Poppy two hours ago that reads:

I'm coming to get you!!

But Poppy isn't here and a rising feeling of desperation fills her chest. She needs to do something – anything – to help herself. But what? She has no clue what happened to Leona and Rosie when she left the house that day. Saffy would have bet her life that Ash was the aggressor who'd forced Leona and Rosie to leave the house against their will. But now Ash is dead and things have completely changed.

Is it possible Leona somehow got the upper hand and managed to turn the tables on him? But if so, why are she and Rosie still missing?

Think. Think. Think. Who might be able to shed new light on the situation?

Saffy herself is the last person to have seen the family together. As far as she knows, she's the only person who received any messages that day, and now there is no trace of them.

A face hovers on the periphery of her mind's eye. The neighbour who'd waved at Saffy when she'd first arrived at Leona's house, and who'd rushed off to avoid speaking when Saffy had called out to her in the supermarket. The same neighbour who, according to the newspaper report, initially reported the missing Bannatynes to the police.

Leona had mentioned her name once in conversation. *Tania Torkard.* She knows exactly which house she lives in and, with very limited options, Saffy is suddenly seized by the desire to speak to this woman who perhaps had sight of the family most days and may have a better overview of Leona's state of mind than Saffy herself has.

Time can erode the closest friendship. A gentle, barely noticeable *tick, tick, tick*, as the trust, love and loyalty softly dissolve, taking with them the happiest memories.

Saffy crosses the road from the police station and walks to the bus stop just around the corner. On sick leave without pay, she's way over her budget to consider more cabs, but the service into West Bridgford is a good one with buses running every twenty minutes. Saffy takes the short bus ride, staring out of the rain-streaked windows at all the people going about their business. Doing the ordinary, monotonous stuff that everyone complains about. Travelling to and from work, shopping, phone calls . . . busy, busy, busy with all the things life demands. And yet, as Saffy knows, it's a life that can grind to a halt in a flash. All those irritating tasks lifted from you in an instant and replaced by a far more hellish existence.

Leona's street is a three- or four-minute walk from the bus stop. Saffy is the only passenger getting off and the road is quiet with few passing cars. She walks at a decent pace, trying to ignore the voice in her head that casts doubt on her decision.

At the police station, the detectives had questioned her in detail again about her 'unauthorized entry' – as Shah insisted on calling it – to Leona's house.

'I'm trying to understand why you entered the house in the first place,' Shah said. 'You've said you were looking for the journal Leona told you about. What made you think you'd be more successful at finding it than our trained officers?'

'I got the impression you weren't taking me seriously when I told you about the journal,' Saffy said bluntly. 'You seem to find it difficult to imagine Ash could have done anything wrong.'

'Not so,' said MacFarlane. 'We're obliged to keep an open mind, but all information is noted and considered.'

Saffy kept quiet. That hadn't been her experience to date.

'I find it curious you'd go to such lengths as to break into a property to duplicate our search,' Shah pressed her. 'Could it have been you were looking for something else you wanted to conceal?'

'Like what?'

Shah gave a small shrug. 'You tell me. Something you hoped we might not find in the search, perhaps?'

'No,' Saffy said.

'Can you explain this?' Shah's face darkened as she pushed a plastic bag towards her. Inside, Saffy could see a letter. 'We've been informed that you were accused of sending this to Leona Bannatyne.'

That's when she realized that Neil had carried out his

threat. Despite supporting her at the time, he'd now told the detectives of her suspected involvement. Saffy silently cursed herself. What had she been thinking of, confiding in her ex-husband, of all people, in a panicked, low moment?

She recognized the letter. It was sent by post to Leona last year. The letter was typed, but it bore a handwritten 'S' in blue ink at the bottom. Someone had written it expressly to make it look as if it had come from Saffy.

'It was found in Ash Bannatyne's bedside table drawer by the search team and has just come to light,' Shah added.

'I didn't send this letter,' Saffy said quietly, staring down at the bag without touching it.

She doesn't need to read it. She knows the wording off by heart.

'Early last year, probably unwisely, I challenged Ash – not aggressively – about his obvious dislike of my visits to see Leona and Rosie. Unsurprisingly, his reaction was passive-aggressive. He laughed and insisted I had imagined it. He also implied I needed my medication increased.'

'I see,' Shah said, wanting more.

'A few days later, I hadn't heard from Leona and I still felt confused and upset about his reaction, so I confided in Neil when he dropped off Fox on the Sunday.

'Neil told me not to let him get to me. He said, "If Ash sees he's upsetting you, he'll goad you all the more." I knew he was right and I set about putting it behind me.'

'What happened next?' Shah prompted.

'About a week later, that letter landed. It was addressed to Leona and, as you can see, it encouraged her to ditch Ash before he "got what was coming to him". Leona was very upset. Both she and Ash came round and confronted me about it.'

'What was your reaction?'

'I was mortified! I swore on my life I knew nothing about it.' Saffy hesitates, remembering the shouting, the accusations. The tears. 'Leona seemed to calm down. She said she believed me, but Ash wouldn't let it go. He kept saying, "Well, if you didn't send it, then who did?" And of course I couldn't answer that.'

'So how was the disagreement resolved?' MacFarlane asks.

'In the end, Ash told me – with no objection from Leona – that I was no longer welcome at the house. That's why I found it strange he seemed so friendly on the day they disappeared.'

When Ash had threatened to go to the police, Saffy had turned to Neil in desperation again. He had intervened. Spoken to Ash and calmed the situation. But Saffy had never been quite sure if Neil had fully believed she had nothing to do with it.

'So who do you think sent the letter?' Shah says.

As far as Saffy was concerned, there was no mystery to it. There was no doubt in her mind who had sent the vicious note.

Someone who would benefit from framing Saffy to try and turn Leona against her for good. Someone who wanted to cast doubt on Saffy's recovery from her mental health crisis.

'It could only be Ash himself,' Saffy says. 'He set me up.'

49
Saffy

Saffy turns into Musters Road. There is a police van outside Leona's property and she wonders if the detectives have already despatched officers to recover the carved wooden box Saffy had described to them. There also appears to be a cluster of press hanging around near the house, their interest no doubt boosted by the news of Ash's death.

Fortunately, Saffy doesn't need to walk past the Bannatyne house to get to Tania's, which is twice as wide as Leona's with a full block-paved front garden dotted with Buxus cones planted in modern grey troughs that sit on immaculate pale gravel squares.

Saffy opens the gate and walks up the path to the glossy white front door. A frosted plaque is secured to the brick-work on the left-hand side. It bears the number 112 and the family name of Torkard printed underneath.

Saffy rings the doorbell and steps back to wait. The upper- and ground-floor windows are all screened by white shutter blinds and Saffy can't help thinking although it's an attractive look, there's a kind of subtle 'keep away' vibe about the place. Something to do with the sparkling clean glass, the glossy white sills that bear not a single cobweb or speck of dirt.

The front door opens and there she is. Tania Torkard. Her pleasant, open expression changes to a frown. As she starts to close the door again, Saffy steps forward, and extends a hand.

'Please. Just give me five minutes of your time and then I promise I'll leave you alone. I just need to ask you a couple of questions.'

'I have nothing to say to you, Saffy,' Tania says, pushing back against her outstretched hand with the door. 'I reported the Bannatynes missing and I've spoken to the police a couple of times and I've nothing to add. They've told me you're a person of interest, so I really don't think you should be here.'

Tania has been quite happy to speak to the press about what she saw the day of the disappearance, but Saffy bites her tongue in the interests of trying to get her onside.

'Look, I know this situation is crazy. You've probably seen speculation online about me, too, but I can assure you, Tania, none of that is true. All I want is to find Leona and Rosie. Ash's death is a massive shock to me too, as I'd pretty much decided he was behind all this.'

Movement from across the road catches Saffy's attention and she sees a couple of reporters walking purposefully in their direction. Tania cranes her neck out of her front door and makes a frustrated noise.

'I suppose you'd better come in, but I can only spare a few minutes. The last thing I want is more hassle from that lot. My husband and son have gone fishing for the day to get away from it and they won't be happy if they think I'm encouraging more drama by speaking to you.'

'Don't worry. This won't take long, I promise,' Saffy says, relieved to step inside the cool, welcoming hallway with its light oak flooring and ivory walls hung with floral prints. An open shelving unit displays interesting ceramic pieces and a couple of framed family photographs.

Tania leads her through to the kitchen, an extended space that's light and airy with pale grey units and a view of the neat, mainly paved garden featuring more topiary trees in modern pots.

'I'm giving you the benefit of the doubt here, you know,' Tania says, looking wary and indicating an open app on her phone. 'There are reporters outside – all I have to do is to shout through the doorbell camera for help if –'

'Tania, I'm Leona's best friend. I'm Rosie's godmother. I love them both and all I want is to find them. I'm not a murderer!'

Tania gives her a curt nod. 'Drink?'

'A glass of water would be lovely,' Saffy says. 'Thank you.'

Tania takes a glass tumbler from a cupboard. 'I've got press ringing, messaging me online. They hang around the street and rush over if I dare to leave the house.' She presses the glass against a water dispenser set into the refrigerator door, the tinkle of liquid filling the brief silence. 'It's been a terrible shock. Stuff like this just doesn't happen around here. I can't bear to think of little Rosie, frightened and . . .'

Tania shakes her head and sets the half-filled glass on the worktop in front of Saffy.

'Thank you.' Saffy takes a sip of the cool drink. 'You're the only other person as close to this as I am. I feel like I'm literally losing my mind keeping everything inside.'

Tania indicates a small sofa close to the windows. 'Look, I know I blanked you at the supermarket, but I couldn't risk an altercation in public; I already feel violated with the press attention. I spoke to the *Nottingham Post* briefly because it seemed the only way to make them go away but I totally regret doing it. Things have just got worse and interest is picking up again now they've found Ash's body.'

'I completely get it. I've done myself a disservice with the police because I was too honest from the start about not getting on with Ash. I told them I couldn't stand him and I know he felt the same way about me.' Saffy sighs and looks at her hands. 'Regardless of that, I haven't got a clue of what happened after I left the house last Thursday. I've come here today because you're the only person I know of who might be able to shed a little more light on Leona and Ash's relationship.'

'Well, I'm not sure about that,' Tania says doubtfully.

'Ash and I have never got on,' Saffy continues. 'The strange thing is that when I got to the house on the day they disappeared, he was super-friendly. Couldn't do enough for me and –'

'Can I ask why you didn't like Ash?' Tania interrupts. 'He's always seemed such a personable guy. Phil, my husband, and Ash were both big Forest fans. They went to the odd big match together but mostly to the local pub on a Sunday afternoon to watch the footie on the big screen. The police spoke to Phil, but as he told them, Ash never gave anything away about his marriage or family life.'

Saffy considers this fresh angle of Ash as the nice guy; the decent, friendly neighbour. But he'd always struck her as someone who kept himself, and his family, quite isolated.

'I guess it was just a clash of personalities,' she says generously. 'Leona and I have been friends since our school days, and I think Ash was threatened by that. You might not have seen this side of him, but he was a very controlling person behind closed doors. With Leona at least.'

Tania gives her a look. 'Really? Why do you say that?'

The last thing Saffy wants to do is gossip with Leona's neighbours, but she's got very few options left. Tania might not agree to speak to her again, so she needs to make this opportunity count. And also, try to get Tania to look at her neighbours' situation in a new light.

Saffy relays a few well-chosen details of her recent chat

with Leona, including the bruises she'd spotted on her wrist.

Tania looks concerned. 'This doesn't match the couple I see from the other side of the street,' she says, looking thoughtful. 'I mean, I can see Ash is the organizer, rounding up Rosie for school and he always drives and locks up, that kind of thing. But Phil's a bit like that, and to be honest, I take responsibility for a lot of the everyday stuff in the running of the household and so I welcome him taking charge sometimes.'

Saffy nods. 'I get that completely, but things are different in the Bannatyne family. Ash hates Leona having friends. He doesn't like anyone visiting the house. Myself included.'

Tania frowns. 'Yet you visited them only last Thursday and you said Ash was friendly? Besides, as I told the police, Leona has another friend, a woman who visits her regularly, sometimes when Ash is home, too. So he can't have a problem with it, can he?'

'Really?' Saffy sits up straight. Leona has always had an issue with trusting people and as a result has never been an overly sociable type of person. So far as Saffy knows, she herself has remained Leona's only good friend. 'Can you describe her?'

Tania thinks for a moment then reels off a string of short facts. 'Tall and slim, late twenties, maybe? Very attractive though with long, dark hair. Nice car too. A silver sporty number, maybe a Mazda or something. Cars aren't my strong point, I'm afraid.'

An unpleasant buzzing sensation starts to creep across Saffy's skin as a person appears in her mind's eye, clear as a hologram. 'You're saying this woman visits Leona regularly?'

Tania nods. 'At least a couple of times a month. She sometimes brings her little boy with her, too.'

289

Fighting nausea, Saffy bends forward and pulls her phone from her handbag. Her heart rate ramps up a notch as she swipes the screen a few times and then, without speaking, turns the phone around so Tania can see the photograph she's pulled up.

'Yes, that's her!' Tania says with a small smile. 'He looks such a sweet boy. I've seen Rosie jumping up and down in excitement at the door whenever they arrive. I do hope little Rosie is OK . . .'

Saffy had taken the photograph herself last year at a local party venue.

A lovely snap of Fox on his third birthday with his daddy and Leona's visitor: aka Mummy Mira.

50

Poppy

Poppy's legs begin to shake as she looks up at the dark, foreboding shape that fills every inch of the bathroom doorway. Harry is silent as he glares at her, the shadows on his face lending his black eyes a dangerous glint.

Poppy looks down at the scattered photo sheets but does not move to pick them up. Her legs feel wobbly now, as if they might not hold her up if she moves them. 'I found them in the kitchen drawer when you went to the shop earlier,' she says. 'Along with a deed poll certificate showing your real name and a letter from Leona about your daughter. You're Rosie's dad.'

Harry makes a fist and thumps the doorframe. Poppy shrinks back as the walls vibrate, but she's already in way too deep to just stop talking and pretend nothing has happened until she can escape.

'Snooping, the first chance you get,' he growls. 'Thanks for the vote of confidence.'

'I was looking for a teaspoon to make the coffees while you were out.' The lie rolls easily off her tongue. 'But I'll be honest, I knew there was something odd about you, something you weren't telling me. I liked you, Harry.'

Harry doesn't respond and she chews on her lip, trying to think. She cannot physically barge past him. She cannot leave the room unless he allows her to. Her only option is to blag her way out by sounding more confident than she feels.

'There's not really any point saying any more about it, is there? I want to leave now.'

Harry does not budge, but he speaks in a low, dangerous voice. 'What the hell gives you the right to go rooting through my personal belongings?'

'Maybe I shouldn't have rifled through your personal papers, but it's a good job I did, right?' She indicates the strewn photographs. 'I'd have liked nothing more than to be proven wrong. With all the craziness happening – Leona and Rosie missing, Ash dead, my sister constantly questioned by the police – I can't afford to take chances. I was just trying to take care of myself. I don't know who you are at all, Harry.'

Harry moves quickly. Before Poppy can try to dash past him, he takes two giant steps forward and suddenly he's in front of her, so close she can smell his aftershave and hear his laboured breathing. She yelps and jumps back, but her back hits the sink behind her and she stumbles.

Harry raises his hands and Poppy flinches, but instead of striking her he brings his large, solid hands down firmly but gently on her shoulders to steady her.

'I didn't exactly lie to you, Poppy, not really. My name *is* legally Harry Farmer now and you never asked if I had connections to Leona or Rosie so I didn't have to deny it. In the same way you never volunteered to tell me you were attacked and nearly died.'

Poppy stares at him. Furious, nervous and silenced all at once. 'Still, I haven't just got out of prison, like you.'

'You know, I went down for fraud, not murder or abduction.' Harry scowls and lets his hands drop by his side. 'I was at a low point in life. I'd lost my hospital job and got a small pay-out. I got sucked in and scammed by a fake investment deal. I was an idiot. I learned my lesson and I left Harris

Fielder behind with the whole sorry mess in Greece. I never want to be that guy again.'

'But it can't be a coincidence . . . That night in the pub, you said you'd come straight from the airport. Pretended you were a stranger who'd just bumped into me. Now I've seen Leona's letter refusing you access to see Rosie, I know you must have hunted me down as a way in to getting close to her.'

Harry holds up his hands. 'Guilty. I came back to the UK months ago, not the night I met you. I admit I did know you were Leona's best friend's sister, but I really liked you, too. I'd been watching the Bannatynes a while. I followed Ash on a few occasions and some of those times, he was meeting you.'

Poppy's eyes widen. 'You followed *me*, too?'

'Only once. It didn't take long to put all the pieces together. I saw Leona with Saffy in a bar, saw you at Saffy's house . . . It's amazing how much you can learn about people and who they spend their time with in a matter of a few focused hours of observation. I've been a bit intense, I know. Anyway, aside from your connections with Saffy and therefore Leona, I really liked you, too.'

Disconcerted by this new offhand transparency, Poppy makes a derogatory noise in her throat and folds her arms. 'I bet you did.'

'I swear it's true. Look, let's go downstairs, have a drink and talk about everything.'

Poppy feels heat flood into her face. 'I think it's time for me to leave.'

'You don't think . . .' Harry breaks off, surprised. 'Surely you don't think I'm a danger to you?'

She gives him a considered look from her barefooted five-foot-two position and keeps her voice steady. 'You probably don't know what it's like to feel afraid and vulnerable, Harry.

293

You don't have to actually strike someone to make them feel scared and short of breath. Please move out of my way.'

'Oh, I'm sorry. OK?' He stands well back from her, holding his hands up as if in surrender. 'Will you at least let me explain my side of things before you go?'

Poppy tucks her clutch bag under her arm and walks forward. She stops next to him and narrows her eyes. 'Answer this question truthfully. Do you know the whereabouts of Leona and Rosie?'

'That is a categoric "no",' he says instantly.

'But you've just admitted to watching their house and taking pictures like a total creep.'

'Hey, I might have been the crappiest dad on the planet so far, but that's in the past. I want to be present in Rosie's life from now on and there is no way I'd put her through the terror and trauma of something like this. Poppy, please. You must believe me.'

He doesn't seem dangerous right at this very minute, she thinks, apart from the unknown depths of those dark eyes. Still, the fact remains that Harry has the most to gain out of getting rid of Ash and Leona. Leaving Rosie vulnerable and alone and ready to be reunited with him, her missing biological parent.

Poppy closes her eyes briefly, her heart sinking at the thought of little Rosie, confused and afraid. *Please God*, she gives a silent prayer. *Please let Leona and Rosie come home safely*.

'Rosie doesn't know you!' she turns on Harry. 'You're a stranger to her. Ash was the only father she's known.'

There's a second of shocked silence when Poppy thinks she's gone too far. When a shadow falls across Harry's face and his jaw tightens. And then his expression softens and he looks down, his eyes no longer black but the soft brown she loves. And they are shining with tears.

'You're right. I know you're right. But please, Poppy . . .

please, just listen to me. I tried the regular routes to see my child, but Leona cut me off dead at the first pass. Some might say I deserved that, and maybe I did. But I couldn't just walk away and accept her decision without a fight.' He shakes his head, appealing for her understanding. 'Watching Rosie, getting a sense of their routine and habits, was the only way I could learn about their family set-up and see my daughter.'

'You can't just stalk people like that because you don't like what they say.' Poppy scowls. 'Just like you can't act like a bully boy if someone spends a little longer in the bathroom than you'd like.'

Harry laces his fingers over the top of his head. 'Touché. But rightly or wrongly, I decided I wouldn't be fobbed off or made to just go away and be quiet. I confess I did want to be a problem for Leona, but did that extend to hurting her or her family? Never.'

Poppy watches him. The dark, sad eyes, his hunched shoulders and downbeat expression. This is her chance to leave and call the police, but something is stopping her from doing so. He looks like a man who is telling the truth.

'They think my sister might be a murderer when in actual fact *you're* the one with a rock-solid motive for wanting to get rid of Ash . . . and Leona, too.'

'If you want to go to the police, I can't stop you. But think carefully, because once you involve them, you'll just delay everything getting sorted out and that could be disastrous. They'll see me as an ex-con who is hell-bent on revenge because Leona turned down visitation with my daughter. But that's not who I am. I admit, I've made some massive mistakes in my life, I've hurt a lot of people, but I want more than anything to get past that and make a fresh start. I want the chance to get to know my little girl. Poppy, could we work together to get the people we love back safely?'

Poppy moves around Harry and steps on to the landing. He doesn't try to stop her, just tracks her movement with pleading eyes. Annoyingly, his words about the police making instant assumptions about him and haring off at another tangent ring only too true to her. Somewhere, Leona and Rosie must be praying to get back home, unless . . . unless it's already too late for them.

'Poppy, please. I swear I've got nothing to do with Ash's death, but if you go to the police, you'll be effectively slowing everything down and wasting so much time. They'll go through the motions and probably arrest me too, question me for days and . . . well, you get the picture. Time in which Leona and Rosie could easily be harmed too. Think about it. Together, we can find out the truth and that will help Saffy, too.'

Poppy thinks about sweet little Rosie, who used to make pretty beaded necklaces and gift them to her, who'd beg her for a bedtime story when she stayed over. Little Rosie who believed Poppy when she once told her she was a real-life Disney princess. Where is Rosie now? How scared must she be?

'You've seen the photos from the drawer, yeah?' Harry continues, sensing her hesitation. 'Well, I have more on my phone. And just when you thought you'd seen the extent of my psycho-stalker behaviour, I'm going to confess something else to you, Poppy.'

'I'm not sure I want to hear it.'

'Trust me, you definitely do, because it's our best chance yet of working out how we're going to get Rosie and Leona home and your sister out of police custody.'

Poppy bites her bottom lip. 'I'm listening.'

Harry smiles. 'The Bannatynes aren't the only people I've been watching.'

51

Saffy

Monday

Saffy is on the bus again. This time she gets off at the Phoenix Business Park interchange at Cinderhill and begins the two- or three-minute walk to the low-rise, plush modern offices where Neil's accountancy firm is based.

It's a bright, warm morning and she unzips her lightweight jacket as she tries to step up the pace. She feels sluggish and tired. It was late when she got back home last night. Soon after Tania's bombshell revelation about Leona's regular visitor, Saffy made a great effort not to show her devastation and quickly made her excuses to leave Tania's and to head back home.

If she hadn't been to see Tania, she might never have known about Mira's secret connection with Leona. Saffy had almost stopped breathing when Tania had confirmed that Mira and Leona were apparently good friends.

On Friday, when Saffy had gone to Neil's house and shared the news of the Bannatynes going missing, there had been no suggestion that Mira had any connection or knew the family other than vaguely.

Saffy's chest burned with resentment all night long that Mira has been taking *her* son to play with Rosie. *Mummy Mira.* The mysterious 'ship game' Rosie had spoken about that Saffy didn't recognize . . . it now makes perfect sense.

She barely had any sleep at all and even then, her rest was haunted by dreams of Fox crying to stay with Mira when Neil dropped him off.

Has Mira already spoken to the police, admitting her connection to the family? Does Neil know his fiancée is friendly with Leona?

As she approaches the building now, she spots his dark grey Lexus parked underneath a sign reading: *Director Parking Only.*

She has timed her arrival here to coincide with the end of Neil's customary morning briefing to his staff, so is hoping she'll be able to see him right away.

Saffy enters the pleasant, light-filled reception and walks up to the desk. The foyer is empty of other visitors. The receptionist, wearing a cerise-pink suit, sits to attention when she sees her and scrabbles to move something on the desk. Saffy catches a glimpse of a phone screen bearing what looks like an active game of Candy Crush.

'I need to speak to Neil Cardle urgently,' Saffy says politely. 'If he's not available, I'll wait here as long as it takes.'

The receptionist, clearly slightly irritated with the interruption to her game, looks at her screen and sniffs. 'Can I take your name, please?'

'Saffy Morris. Please stress it's urgent.'

She raises an eyebrow and picks up the phone. 'Bear with me a moment.'

While she speaks in low, urgent tones, Saffy wanders over to the large, floor-to-ceiling windows that look out on a courtyard with a water feature. When she first met Neil, he worked in a scruffy little building in Sherwood. His office – one of three – was accessed by a battered wooden door that led straight off the street up a vertigo-inducing flight of stairs

298

to a one-room space with a desk, chair and a grim little shared loo just off the landing.

He'd started off on his own, preparing accounts for sole traders and start-ups at affordable prices. His break had come a few years later when one of his clients hit the jackpot and developed his IT project-management business into a franchised chain.

Neil had been invited to join an established firm of accountants and he'd taken his successful clients with him, working his way up to being senior partner in the premier accountancy company in the East Midlands. His success had exploded just as their marriage fell apart.

'Ms Morris?'

Saffy snaps out of her reminiscing and returns to the desk. She can tell by the receptionist's expression it's not good news.

'I'm so sorry. I did try, but Mr Cardle is in meetings all day. Then he's heading straight out to dinner with clients. He says he'll contact you later today. Sorry.'

'Fine. If that's the way he wants to play it.' Saffy moves over to the modular seating at the side of the reception desk and sits down. 'Looks like I'll be keeping you company here all day.'

'I'm sorry, you won't be able to stay here.' The receptionist frowns.

'Watch me.' Saffy folds her arms and stares at the wall clock opposite. 'It's OK, I won't be any trouble. You can go back to your game now.'

The receptionist's face flushes and she sits down at her desk, beginning to furiously type without looking at her again.

The burning in Saffy's throat gets her through the first twenty minutes. But when she's been sitting there for more

299

than half an hour, she begins to wonder if she can carry out her threat after all. She feels exhausted from lack of sleep. It also occurs to her that if the receptionist calls the police, this could compound the problems she's already having.

Then something happens that makes her forget about her plan altogether. The glass doors open and a harassed-looking woman she instantly recognizes enters the foyer. She's wearing jeans and a loose tunic top with lots of silver bangles on both arms. She looks slender and agile and Saffy can't detect her pregnancy bump at all.

Saffy's mind races. What excuse can she give for being here?

She stands up and smiles. 'Hello, Mira. How nice to see you!'

Mira's perfectly made-up face falls. She looks from Saffy to the receptionist. 'Oh! I didn't expect to see you here. Are you waiting to see Neil?'

'I am. I've been waiting a while and I'm prepared to wait a few hours longer, if necessary.' She looks around quickly, just in time to catch the receptionist rolling her eyes at Mira. But that's OK because she's just had a better idea. 'Are you here to see Neil, too?'

'No, no. I just brought his lunch in. He left it on the side this morning.' She holds up a small coolbag. She glances at the receptionist. 'I know he said he's super busy today.'

Saffy feels a stab of annoyance. Why should she spare Mira the discomfort of being challenged? In that moment it feels like she's spent her whole life tiptoeing around people. In reframing her thoughts, she realizes Mira's appearance here could afford her a better option. Saffy might find out more by putting Mira on the spot rather than trying to shock Neil into submission.

She stands up. 'Actually, I've just realized you might be better placed to help me, instead.'

'Oh! I . . . I can't really. Not today. I have an appointment in town later and –'

'It won't take long. I'll walk out to the car with you.'

Mira turns to the receptionist. 'Can you let my fiancé know Saffy was here and that she left with me, please?'

'Of course. I understand,' the receptionist says pointedly.

They think they're so clever with their coded looks and not-so-subtle hints.

Once they are in the car park and away from the doors of Neil's offices, Mira turns to her. 'Look, Saffy, this is a bit awkward, but I don't think it's a good idea for me to spend any time with you. Neil is extremely concerned for Fox's well-being in the middle of all this trouble you're in with the police, and in the interests of transparency –'

'Is Neil concerned that you were so friendly with Leona, visited her regularly with my son?'

Mira's mouth sags and Saffy knows immediately that Neil is unaware of her connection to the Bannatynes.

'Just out of interest, have you disclosed to the police that you visited the house just a few days before the family disappeared?'

'Saffy, I . . . It's true I've popped over there a couple of times, but it was just to let Fox and Rosie carry on their friendship more than anything. Leona and I got on but I know nothing about what happened to them. Nothing at all.'

'Then you've nothing to be worried about, have you?' Saffy takes out her phone. 'I have DI Shah's direct line in my contacts if you want to clear your conscience.'

'I've nothing on my conscience,' Mira says tightly.

'Neither do I, but ever since the police found out I'd been at the house, they've had me in a headlock. I was at the police station last night again, answering their questions. Neil and the police certainly need to know about your secret friendship with Leona.' Saffy gives her a little smile. 'You know, in the interests of transparency.'

Mira's face pales and she touches her stomach lightly. 'Saffy, please. I . . . I've been feeling very low energy and, well, I'm sure you appreciate it's not a good time for me to be taking on more stress.' She reaches for Saffy's hand. Touches it lightly. 'I know you'll understand, Saffy. I wasn't close to Leona, not really. Not like you are. We bumped into each other in town about a year or so ago and Rosie made a bee-line for Fox. Leona said she'd really missed seeing him, so I offered to pop round so Fox and Rosie could play for an hour or so and . . .'

Her voice tails off when she notices Saffy's steely expression.

'You need to tell Neil and the police, Mira. Otherwise, you leave me no option.'

It wasn't beyond the realms of possibility that Mira knew more than she was letting on about Leona and Rosie's disappearance.

'But I don't know anything and Neil will go nuts!' she cries out, running a hand through her thick, dark hair with its expensive caramel highlights.

They reach Mira's silver sports car, the one Tania had admired from across the road from Leona's at least twice a month.

'There's only one way I'll agree to saying nothing for now,' Saffy says, running a hand along the flank of the metallic paintwork.

'Anything! What do you want?'

'Information,' Saffy says slowly. 'About something I found at Leona's house.'

'I don't have any information. I don't know anything, I already told you that —'

'It's a simple enough question, Mira. Did Leona tell you she was pregnant?'

'Oh God! How do you know about –'

'What did she tell you exactly?'

Mira shakes her head and unlocks the car. 'I'm sorry, Saffy. She swore me to secrecy. This really is none of your business and –'

'You know it's not Ash's child, I presume?'

'What?' Mira's eyes widen, her hand gravitating subconsciously to her own stomach.

Saffy hardly dares to breathe. She can feel she's so close to Mira opening up.

She bluffs impatience. 'Was Leona having an affair?'

'I don't know and that's the honest truth, but . . .'

Saffy waits.

'Leona never expressly said that, but . . . I did wonder a couple of times if she was seeing someone. The odd comment she'd make about going out when Ash was working away and this little grin she sometimes gave me when I'd ask who she was texting. That sort of thing.'

Saffy thinks about the WhatsApp messages she got last Thursday. When this nightmare started. Why would Leona text me instead of Mira, if they were close? 'You believe Leona was having an affair?'

Mira bites her lip and nods. 'I can't be a hundred percent certain, but yes. I think she was having an affair and I think, judging by the way he spoke to her when I last visited, Ash might have started to suspect it, too.'

52

Poppy

She opens her eyes and looks around Harry's tiny spare room, squinting against the light flooding into the room. She reaches for her phone and sees it's after ten.

She still has so many doubts about Harry, but after what she'd found last night, she feels a little more convinced he was perhaps telling her the truth about wanting to turn his life around.

Harry hadn't been joking when he said this room was a mess. Last night, before she could get into bed, she'd had to move a pile of clothes. The floor was already choked up with boxes, so she'd opened the small, rickety wardrobe door to stow them away when a pile of candy-coloured packages caught her eye. She'd abandoned the clothes and taken a closer look.

Birthday presents. Five of them. All wrapped beautifully and with tags written.

To Rosie, Happy 3rd Birthday! All my love, Daddy

To my beautiful daughter, Rosie. Happy 5th Birthday! All my love, Daddy

Poppy had felt an involuntary prickle in her nose. There was something so inherently sad about it all. Sure, Poppy totally got Leona's reaction in blanking him. She'd brought

Rosie up alone while Harry – Harris back then – went gadding off abroad, back to his Greek fiancée and landing himself in the nick. But that didn't change the fact he was little Rosie's father and one day when she got older, she would probably want to get to know him.

Poppy had placed the clothes carefully on top of the gifts and closed the wardrobe door. She'd been so tired and in no position to wrestle with a moral dilemma such as this one.

But as she had drifted off into a much-needed sleep, it occurred to her that perhaps Harry wasn't the marauding killer she'd briefly suspected he might be.

Poppy sits up now, staring at the notifications on her locked screen. There are no messages or missed calls from Saffy or Neil, but that just makes her feel more uncertain. This is probably the longest her sister has gone without calling her or demanding to know what she's up to by text. Since Saffy found out about her affair with Ash and her tendency to have casual sex, Poppy has obviously been downgraded in her list of priorities.

In one way it's a relief, but Poppy is surprised to find that she feels slightly uncomfortable that Saffy must have changed her opinion of her quite profoundly.

The call connects but goes straight through to her sister's voicemail. Poppy's starting to think Saffy doesn't want to speak to her at all, but that's not an option. She needs to see her soon to explain developments.

Poppy yawns and runs a hand through her tangled hair, then pulls the curtain to look outside. It looks out over the street, the bigger detached houses on the other side looking like Toy Town properties with their identical wooden porches and burgeoning window boxes.

She listens for movement in the house but all is quiet. Maybe Harry has slept in, too.

They were both so knackered last night, talking until after two a.m. What he had to tell her was illuminating. And shocking.

Harry had eventually persuaded her to go back downstairs and talk instead of rushing off and contacting the police after their bathroom altercation. They'd called a truce while Harry made a fresh pot of coffee and Poppy agreed to sit next to him on the sofa while he scrolled through a mass of photographs on his phone.

'Were these taken outside Ash and Leona's house?' Poppy had said, looking at a man she'd never seen before outside the house.

'Yes,' Harry said. 'I only saw him there once, but I was able to follow him home that night. It was over an hour's journey in the car. He lives in a sprawling remote farmhouse near Wymeswold.'

Poppy threw her hands up. 'OK, I give in. What's this all supposed to mean to me?'

'I'm not sure,' Harry said, causing Poppy to groan and rub her forehead. She'd thought this was supposed to be significant. 'It doesn't mean anything to me yet, either. I just have a hunch about this guy.'

'A hunch about what, exactly?'

Harry had selected one of the photographs and pinched it bigger so that the man's face filled his iPhone screen.

'I think Leona was having an affair with this man before she went missing.'

Poppy made a noise of surprise. 'How do you work that out?'

'Because he came round when Ash was out and then Leona drove out to Lowdham and met him in a coffee shop two days before they all disappeared. Maybe Ash found out and became violent towards her.'

So, Ash had been right to be suspicious after all. Those few mornings she'd watched the house, she might've bumped into Harry, who was also watching. 'According to Saffy, Ash was controlling Leona. Knocking her about. I find that difficult to believe because . . . well, *as you know*, Ash and I had a fling and he was never controlling or violent with me. Not a hint of it.'

'Not a monster like me then.' Harry winked but Poppy remained stony-faced. She hadn't felt ready to fully forgive him for his lies and inappropriate behaviour at that point.

'So how do we find out who this guy is?'

'That's the problem. I've done some cursory research, can't tie the farmhouse to a name.'

'Have you done a reverse image search on Google?' Poppy says. 'You can load up an image and Google will try and match it to other photographs that have been posted online of that person. If you get lucky it might also include a name.'

Harry gives her a look. 'Hey, I might be thirteen years older than you but I'm not an IT dunce. Not yet, anyway.'

'No need to get touchy, I'm just asking.'

'Answer is yes. I've done a reverse image search on Google. Similar types of faces came up, but sadly not his specifically. But . . .' Harry yawned. 'I guess we can pick this up in the morning.'

Poppy rubbed her eyes. 'Yeah, I've got double vision. Definitely time for bed.'

'Is that an invitation?' Harry had grinned widely. She allowed him a small smile before responding in a droll voice, 'In your dreams.'

'Spare room's a bit of a mess but the bed's made up. If you like, you can sleep in my bed and I'll –'

'Spare room will be fine, thanks.'

Harry stood up and extended a hand to pull her off the sofa. 'I'm sorry you had to find out who I really am the way you did, Poppy. I would've told you.'

'Yeah, right.'

'Seriously. It's just one of those things, you know? You start to get to really like a person, you both get on well and somehow it gets harder to risk the truth.'

Poppy said nothing but she couldn't help thinking of the secrets she herself had felt obliged to keep from Saffy. Grudgingly, she took his hand and he pulled her up to standing.

'Look, do you think we can put the crap aside and focus our energies on finding Rosie and Leona?' Harry said. 'Realistically, it's the only way you'll get the detectives off Saffy's back and two heads are most definitely better than one.'

It was probably true. After what Harry had shown her tonight, they might be closer to the truth than the detectives were.

'Maybe.' Poppy had still felt put out. 'I'll sleep on it.'

She'd slept just in her knickers last night, so she finds a man's stripey dressing gown in the wardrobe and wraps it around her before padding along the short landing to Harry's bedroom. The door is open and the quilt is in a tall pile in the middle of the bed but Harry isn't there.

Downstairs, she finds him in the kitchen making coffee.

'Perfect timing,' he says, adding a splash of milk and handing her a mug. 'How did you sleep in the storage cupboard?'

She smiles. 'The spare room was fine, thanks. I slept well. Listen, Harry, I have to leave very soon because I can't get hold of Saffy. She told me last night she was home from the police station, released pending further investigation.'

'OK. Are we . . . you know, cool?' he asks sheepishly. 'I mean, you're not going to just disappear and tell the police everything I told you?'

Poppy shakes her head. 'No. You were a prat last night and you should've been honest with me. But I do agree that the best chance of sorting this mess out is if we work together.'

Harry blows out air. 'Thank you. And I really am sorry. So you're heading to Saffy's house now?'

'I need to make sure she's OK and I want to be honest with her from this point forward. Tell her everything.'

He pulls a face. 'About me, you mean?'

Poppy nods. 'If you're feeling brave enough you could even come with me this morning.'

He hesitates and Poppy laughs. 'Seriously, I'm just joking. I don't expect you to come, but we need to decide what our next move is. And how we're going to find out who that guy is you snapped.'

Harry takes a deep swig of his coffee. 'Let's do this. I'll put my big boy pants on and face your sister. Will that finally convince you I'm an OK guy who wants to put stuff right?'

Poppy wrinkles her nose. 'I don't know about that, but it'll be a start.'

53

Saffy

She sits on the bus and stares out of the window but doesn't notice the people, the places she passes. All she can think about is that Leona is pregnant with her lover's baby and there's a good chance Ash found out about it before they disappeared.

Since leaving the office block car park and her conversation with Mira, Saffy's head is buzzing with what Mira told her about Ash. In return, Saffy agreed not to tell Neil about Mira's visits to the Bannatyne property. For the time being, at least.

Infuriatingly, Saffy doesn't know any more details because Mira suddenly started to feel 'unwell' and had to rush off.

When Saffy gets back home, she steps into the hallway and sees Poppy's coat discarded on the stairs and her size four ankle boots which have been kicked off carelessly at the door. She barely glances at them and stares instead at the trendy white trainers placed neatly next to Poppy's footwear. They look big. About a size ten.

'Saffy, you're back!' Poppy appears in the hallway.

'I was going to call you. It was my next job.' Saffy shrugs off her jacket and hangs it on the bottom stair post. 'Who do the trainers belong to?'

'It's great the police released you.' Poppy gives her a hug. 'Did they honestly believe you'd murdered Ash?'

'Yep. They seemed pretty convinced of it until they had to

accept there's no evidence. They've released me "pending investigations", apparently. It means they haven't got enough to charge me but they don't think I'm completely innocent either.' Saffy stops talking and frowns. 'The trainers?'

'I've brought someone with me. A friend,' Poppy says, indicating the other room. 'Come and say hello.'

Saffy follows her and stops dead at the living room door. 'What the hell are *you* doing here?' She glares at Poppy and then points at Harris. 'What are you doing with *him*, here in my house?' Her entire head feels like it might blow off. The letter she found in the box ... the lover, the pregnancy test. This man fits it all.

'Saffy!' Poppy cries, rushing to her side. 'You look like you're going to collapse! Sit down.'

For all Saffy wants is Harris out of her house and away from her sister, she feels faint and very sick. She sits down, never taking her eyes from the unwanted visitor.

'Give him a chance to explain, Saffy,' Poppy begs. 'Please. There's so much stuff you don't know about Harry.'

'Harry? There's stuff *you* don't know about him. His name is *Harris Fielder* and he abandoned Leona when she fell pregnant with Rosie. He's Rosie's father!'

'Our split was mutual,' Harris says calmly, staying in his seat. 'We both wanted to end the relationship, but I didn't know Leona was pregnant when I left.'

'You were engaged to a woman in Greece and you never told her!' Saffy can feel her cheeks burning.

'Fair play, I was wrong, OK?' Harris holds up his hands. 'But Leona never got in touch, never let me know she'd had a baby ... so it's not fair to imply I abandoned Rosie, too.'

'That's an outright lie. Leona told me you ghosted her when you found out she was pregnant.' Saffy spits out the words and Harris looks aghast. 'You were already engaged when you began a relationship with her.'

'I behaved badly, but it's just not true I shirked my parental responsibilities,' Harris says faintly, looking at Poppy. 'I swear it's not true.'

'So then why come back after all this time demanding to see Rosie?' Saffy sees his obvious surprise in her knowing. 'I found a letter from you at Leona's house.'

'I served time in Greece for fraud,' Harris says calmly. 'I've not made the best decisions in life, but I want to put that right now. I want to get to know my daughter. Before I went to prison an old colleague got in touch and gave me the low-down on our classmates who he saw on Facebook. One of them kept in touch with Leona, so he passed on that she had given birth to a little girl just a few months after I emigrated, showed me pictures from her private Facebook profile. Rosie looked uncannily like me. I did the maths and contacted Leona. She admitted it but then I was sentenced and sent to prison for five years. I served three. When I came out, I wrote to Leona again and her circumstances had changed. She'd got married and . . . well, she told me to sod off, basically. Wouldn't agree to any access at all.'

'A good call, I'd say.' Saffy sniffs, a little stunned Leona had never mentioned Harris's contact even before she met Ash. 'Did it never occur to you that contacting her might cause trouble between her and her new husband?'

'Not relevant any more though, is it?' Poppy says. 'Ash is dead. Ash the bully, the abuser – according to you, Saffy – is dead. So who killed *him*? That's what Harry and I are concerned with at present, not what happened six years ago when Leona was pregnant with Rosie. We want to know what's happening to them right now.'

Saffy stares at her sister. The mess she's got into with this man she has aligned herself with. The terrifying way she seems to trust him when he's obviously a cad, a liar and, if Saffy's suspicions are correct, possibly a murderer. And yet she's acting as if they are a team trying to discover the truth about who killed Ash.

Despite her low opinion of Harris, Saffy does not feel afraid of him. She's determined to get answers.

'Were you having an affair with Leona, Harris?' she says bluntly. 'Was she carrying your baby when she went missing?'

Poppy gasps. 'Saffy, what the hell?'

Harris lets out a harsh laugh. 'You're joking, right?'

'Do I look like I'm joking?'

'Look, I understand you're defensive of Leona,' Harris says to Saffy, shuffling to the edge of his seat and picking up his phone. 'But there are things you're not aware of. Can I show you something? I'm trying to identify this man.'

Saffy moves gingerly towards the sofa. She doesn't sit next to Harris but chooses to peer over his shoulder.

The reaction is visceral when she sees the photograph. Blood freezing then boiling in her veins, a curdled noise trying to escape her throat that she manages to swallow down at the last second.

Harris looks up at her from his seat. 'You OK?'

Poppy walks around the sofa and peers at her face. 'Saffy? You've gone really pale.'

'I'm fine,' Saffy says, the words emerging strangulated and high. 'I'm tired. So tired. I'm going upstairs to have a lie-down.'

Poppy and Harris exchange a glance as she turns to leave the room.

'Saffy?' She stops walking as Poppy appears suddenly at

her side and lays a hand on her arm. 'Did you recognize the man in the photo?'

Harris holds up his phone and again she catches sight of the sandy-coloured hair, the light blue eyes and pale skin. She feels confused and utterly exhausted. She can't trust a thing her mind is telling her.

'No, I don't,' she says and looks away. 'I've never seen him before in my life.'

54

Poppy

'What was all that about?' Harry says, looking aghast. 'Saffy seemed in a state of shock when she saw the photo.'

'She definitely does know something, I'm certain of it.' The expression on Saffy's face when Harry showed her the photograph on his phone said it all. Poppy inclines her head, listening to Saffy's footsteps upstairs and then the shower turning on. 'She looks exhausted. I'll give her ten minutes to finish her shower then I'm going up there to get it out of her. Can you ping those shots of the guy over to my phone?'

Harry nods. 'Sure, I'll do that now.'

Ten seconds later, three images AirDrop into Poppy's iPhone.

She swipes through the images. Gazes at the strong jaw-line, the smiling face and the hooded blue eyes. Her eyes linger on the last shot where he is turning, his strong profile clearly in view.

Five minutes later, the shower still humming, the front door suddenly opens and bangs shut again. Poppy rushes into the hallway but there's nobody there.

'Saffy?' she calls upstairs. There's no answer and she starts to climb before Harry calls out, his voice urgent.

'Saffy's getting into a cab.'

Poppy jumps back down a few steps and rushes to the door. She opens it just in time to see a car pulling away. Poppy runs out in her bare feet, calling out Saffy's name and waving.

'She must have ordered an Uber upstairs and left the shower on to put me off the scent,' Poppy gasps, back inside. She snatches up her phone and calls Saffy. Once, twice, three times the call goes to voicemail.

'Saffy, call me, please! We need to know who the guy in the photo is. Just let us know where you are and we'll come and get you.'

Harry walks away from the window and sits down. 'Why would she just take off like that without saying a word?'

'She knows who it is, in that photo. That's a certainty, but I don't know why she's done a runner.' Poppy makes a noise of frustration. 'Great. She's turned her phone off now so I can only leave a voicemail.'

'Why wouldn't she just tell us?' Harry says, frustrated. 'We could have taken her where she needs to be.'

'I don't know, Harry. I haven't got a clue.' Poppy stands up. 'I'm going up to turn the shower off.'

She runs upstairs, turns off the shower and walks into Saffy's bedroom. The bedcovers are unruffled despite her saying she wanted a lie-down, and there's nothing out of place in here. Saffy obviously just waited under the cover of having a shower, then ordered her Uber before making her escape.

She hears Harry climbing the stairs but he doesn't come into the bedroom.

Poppy looks around in case Saffy has written anything down or left a note, but there's nothing. She stands in the middle of her sister's bedroom feeling vulnerable and at a loss. It doesn't make any sense how her mood changed after seeing the photo.

'Poppy!' Harry shouts. 'In here. I found something.'

She rushes across the landing into the spare room/office. She sidesteps piles of her own textbooks and looks at Harry sitting at the desk. In front of him is Saffy's laptop. 'What is it? What have you found?'

'It was open at this when I came in. I touched the mouse pad and it jumped up,' Harry indicates the screen. 'This must've been the last thing Saffy looked at before leaving the house.'

Poppy studies the Google map on display. Then she puts the coordinates into her own phone and studies the 3D landscape, pinching it in and out, searching the surrounding area.

'I know this place,' she murmurs. 'Saffy told me she used to hang around in the woodland here as a teenager, and there's a kids' playground nearby where we sometimes used to take Fox and Rosie.' She looks at her phone and then at the bigger image. 'Something happened here. A tragedy of some sort, but Saffy's always been weird talking about it . . .' Poppy's phone pings but she doesn't break her focus on the map. 'Why on earth would she have pulled this up on her laptop?'

'Maybe she was just reminiscing,' Harry says. 'If she used to hang out here as a kid.'

Discomfort begins to roll around Poppy's stomach. She points at the screen. 'Look at that – the location search happened just before she left the house. This must be connected to the photograph you showed her.'

55

Saffy

The cab drops Saffy off at the entrance to the country park. She waits for it to leave before beginning the 300-yard walk to the small clearing that is shielded from the unmade road, in the acre of private woodland to her right.

When Harris had shown her the photograph, Saffy had gone into a sort of shock. Poppy and Harris's voices faded out and all she could do was witness the old memories resurfacing.

She had found the small area she was looking for on Google Maps in Holme Pierrepont Country Park, noted down the coordinates and fed them into the map on her phone.

She's been grappling with a nagging thought since seeing the photo and connecting that with what the police told her yesterday about the rough location Ash's body was found. Finally, the pieces of the jigsaw are fitting together and she feels hollow inside.

Saffy walks until she is deep into the woodland. At first, birdsong accompanies her along with sunlight that has the strength to permeate the tall, leafy trees. But as she gets further into the wood, her surroundings grow steadily darker and cooler, and now, there is only the sound of breaking twigs beneath her feet and rustling leaves around her. With no obvious paths this far in, she is completely alone.

The years seem to melt away, her chest growing tighter

with each step as she recalls her feelings that day. She stops walking for a moment and listens. The rush of the river, faint but unmistakable.

A shiver runs through her, vivid memories of the past bearing down like a freight train.

She continues, periodically glancing at Google Maps on her phone until she unexpectedly runs out of charge. She's heading in the right direction, though, she's fairly sure of that. This is always how they found it, before the days of maps and apps, by setting off on foot from the road in the vague direction and having faith they would stumble across it at some point. They always seemed to find it easily, but the woodland is overgrown now after so many years. The paths that had been so well-trodden back then are virtually invisible to Saffy now.

After walking for another six or seven minutes, in a wide arc, Saffy catches a glimpse of something solid and wooden. She stops and peers through the thick layers of beech and oak trees. Nothing there, apparently, but flora and fauna. Except Saffy knows she's close now.

She walks on, never taking her eyes from the general area she feels sure she needs to be. Another glimpse through the trees. Then suddenly, there it is. A sliver of a man-made structure that jars the eye here in the midst of nature. Saffy moves a little closer before taking cover behind a mature oak tree that has a wide, gnarled trunk. She stares at the weather-worn cabin, nestled in so closely to the trees that the foliage surrounding it caresses the walls.

The roof of the cabin is covered in grass, planted there many years ago when Saffy was a teenager, now overgrown and spindly but providing excellent camouflage from other curious teenagers or exploring walkers. A line of beech trees planted close to the front of the cabin provides a further effective screen that helps the structure to blend seamlessly with its environment. It renders the structure invisible to all but the most inquisitive passers-by.

Saffy inches closer. At first glance the cabin appears to be derelict. The window frames are in a very poor state and clumps of grass and earth hang from the damaged roof.

Anyone else happening upon this place would no doubt dismiss it as dangerous to enter and assume it's probably filled with rats and other undesirable wildlife.

But Saffy is not fooled. Upon closer inspection she can see that the walls and door are sound. The windows themselves are intact and nowhere can she see holes or cracks where the rain and wind might tear the place apart.

There is no movement, no sign of life coming from the cabin, but Saffy does not walk up to the front entrance. Instead she walks in a big circle around the back and stands for a little while, studying the structure from the other side.

After waiting a few minutes until she's satisfied there is no sign of life in the cabin, she creeps up to the rear door and turns the handle. It's locked . . . or at least it appears to be. But Saffy tries out a complicated manoeuvre seared into her memory.

Handle up as far as it will go then down twice, hard.

The first time the door stays fast, but the second time, Saffy puts extra weight behind the upwards movement and pushes down a little harder than before. She feels the door shift a little and then, slowly, slowly, it creaks open.

Saffy listens. No sound, no movement.

Using her shoulder, she pushes gently and then shoves a little harder and manages to force the door open a couple of inches more each time.

Saffy slips inside, the smell of damp and mould assailing her nostrils. The interior is very dim but she can discern the main features. The log burner over in the corner, the small, scratched table and chairs, the crummy old sofa and the arm-chair, covered with sackcloth.

Old memories flit around her like fireflies, too fast for her to catch and keep them. Softly, she pads further inside and gently pushes the door closed behind her, listening all the time, on alert for the slightest sound.

Cast aside in the middle of the floor is an old Afghan-style rug, its tassels matted and stuck together. Next to the rug is the reason she came here.

Exactly as she remembers it.

56

Saffy

Saffy crouches down and stares at the steel ring of the trapdoor.

For so many years, she has buried deep what happened on that long, hot afternoon towards the end of the summer holidays. Leona and Rosie missing and the events of the last few days have overshadowed everything, and it's only since the discovery of Ash's body that this place has crept back into her mind.

Sitting here, it's impossible to fight the past. She's back there; can almost feel the heat of the sun on her shoulders and bare arms.

She had just turned nineteen and felt lonely and miserable on her first visit here. On her actual birthday, she'd lied to save face. Told Leona she'd been invited out for tea, but in fact, once her friend had gone out with her boyfriend, Saffy, feeling abandoned, had gone up to her bedroom and crawled under the covers, her heart heavy and sad. Every day, her best friend seemed to fall further and further under the spell of Wes Sharpe, whereas Saffy and Leona's own connection seemed to wane and fade in the shadow of their relationship.

But Leona did not fail Saffy completely. She had planned a nice birthday surprise. On Friday, they were going shopping together.

'I'm going to treat you to the best belated birthday lunch,

too!' Leona had said, linking her arm with Saffy's and resting her head on her shoulder.

When the day arrived, Saffy had made a real effort to haul herself out of her low mood. She brushed her unruly hair into a neat ponytail, dressed in her new jeans and a pretty top, and even applied a little lipstick and blusher. Leona had surprised her by arriving thirty minutes earlier than they'd agreed. Saffy greeted her excitedly at the door, but the smile slid from her face as she noted Leona's flushed cheeks and sheepish expression.

'Saffy. I'm so, so sorry but I can't do today. Can we rearrange to next week?'

Saffy's face fell. 'But . . . why? I'm ready now and –'

'I know . . . It's totally my fault but I completely forgot that Wes's family are holding a surprise party today for his youngest brother Kieran. You know Kieran, don't you?'

Saffy knew him all right. He'd been an irritating pest that day they went to see the cabin.

She didn't reply, refusing to be pulled into an amiable conversation with Leona when she was about to let her down so badly. But it didn't stop Leona continuing as if nothing had happened.

'Yeah, Kieran's just passed a really important exam at his martial arts academy; he's got the next coloured belt or something. A big deal. Anyway, Wes's family are doing this surprise tea party for him.' Leona had stopped talking and looked at Saffy. She seemed to be gauging whether her efforts at softening the blow were having the desired effect. 'Thing is, he's going to Holme Pierrepont with his friends, where the river runs through, you know? And I sort of promised Wes's mum I'd help her trim up the garden with bunting and balloons so that he walks into a surprise party when he gets back for his tea, and we wondered . . . well, we wondered if you could go down to the river to bring him back to the party? You can say he's needed at home or something, otherwise he'll probably stay out all day and early evening with his mates and miss the party altogether.' Leona's smile faltered. 'I really wish you could stay for the party too, but his parents have said it's strictly family members only, so . . .'

Saffy regarded her blankly. 'So, you're saying our lunch and shopping afternoon is off because of a kid's party?' And to make matters worse, she was being used as a messenger for a party she wasn't even invited to!

'Not off as such . . . just postponed!' Leona grasped her arm. 'You understand, don't you, Saffy? I'm sorry, I really am, it's just . . . I gave Wes my word that –'

'You gave *me* your word before you gave it to him,' Saffy snapped. She wanted to just wave Leona away, say it was fine. Act as though she didn't care, even though she was hurting badly inside. But she couldn't. Her stomach felt full of acid.

'Aw, don't be like this, Saffy,' Leona pleaded. 'Kieran's a lovely lad and he's done so well, and his family just want to make a fuss of him, you know?'

Saffy thought back to when she'd been not that much older than Kieran. When they had lost her father, and her mother had been constantly ill, and Saffy had needed to stay home to look after Poppy. She could count the number of times she'd had a party thrown for her on one hand and here was that spoiled brat Kieran, getting the full works because he'd passed some lame Kung Fu exam. It wasn't even a proper school subject like science or maths.

Some kids got it all handed to them on a plate and then there were others, like Saffy, who had to fight for everything they got in life. Ending up with the crumbs left by other people.

'Are we good, Saffy? Will you do it?'

Saffy looked at her friend's face. She could see Leona's loyalty was torn, between her boyfriend and her best friend. But Saffy knew there was no contest. Wes held all the cards and Saffy's own power as Leona's friend and confidante was waning fast.

'Yeah, OK. I'll do it,' Saffy said quietly.

Leona beamed. 'Cool! I promise we'll rearrange your birthday treat. I'd much rather be out with you today, Saffy, but Wes is adamant that as his girlfriend, I need to be at Kieran's party.' She gave a little laugh. 'He thinks the world of his little brother. Sometimes I think Wes loves him more than he loves me!'

Now, with a slow, rising panic filling her chest, Saffy bends down and curls her fingers around the cold, hard ring pull of the trapdoor.

The cabin jumped into her thoughts the moment she saw the photograph. Despite the terrible memories of this place, Saffy remembers the thrilling, nervy feeling of being a teenager here. Of being a mere half a mile from the country park, full of people and governed by a hundred rules, and yet here, in the adjacent untamed woodland, kids ruled and adults were rarely seen. They might have been in the middle of Narnia, it felt so magical and remote.

Saffy pulls firmly again at the steel ring. Her fingers slip against the smooth metal and the trapdoor remains steadfastly in place.

The cabin used to be the rangers' place when the land was owned by a nearby private country club. Then, when the estate was split up in order to sell it, the Sharpe family bought thirty acres of land together with an adjoining mansion that Wes Snr had plans to renovate.

The Sharpe family kids lucked out when their builder

father kept his promise and extended the cabin down into the storage basement, leaving the main living accommodation untouched. They'd felt like the coolest kids in town the day they first saw the place and planned the secret den that would soon exist for their use.

Saffy adjusts her posture so she's able to leverage more weight above the trapdoor and wraps an old cloth lying nearby around her fingers to ensure there is no slippage this time.

Again, she grasps the metal ring, gives an almighty pull and all at once, the trapdoor lifts and slides smoothly, on mechanical runners, up and away from the opening.

Saffy looks down and sees a dim light has turned itself on, illuminating the metal ladder. A pounding starts in her ears. A working light means an electricity supply. The small humming generator she remembers in one of the rooms downstairs has clearly been maintained by someone.

All is utterly silent down there in what was the teenagers' paradise that runs the length and breadth of the original cabin rooms that she now stands in. If she can get in and out of this place before anyone returns, maybe she can leave here with some real answers to take to the police.

The space seems so much smaller and more claustrophobic than when she last climbed down here all those years ago. To be expected, of course – she is now twice the age and bigger all round – but it feels a bit unnerving all the same. Saffy begins to step back and down, feeling each hard rung of the sturdy metal ladder beneath the soles of her flat boots.

She takes it slowly, and when her foot meets the floor, she steps down on to hard tiles. The den is not enormous but it is well designed with the space well used, so feels bigger. Saffy can hear the faint hum of the generator in the cramped cubby-hole that they had called the boiler room. The main outer wall stands behind her on one side of the ladder and the door leading to the den space on the other.

Saffy's ears prick up when she detects a faint dragging sound, just for a second or two and coming from behind the door. Her heart thudding, she looks up beyond the ladder. The oblong aperture that leads back to the main cabin and the only exit gapes above her, looking darker than ever now that she's standing in the lit space.

Saffy stands frozen for a moment. There is nowhere to hide and she's given herself away now the lights are on. She grasps the sides of the ladder now, calculating how quickly she could scoot back up if someone suddenly appeared in the short corridor. But there is no further noise and tentatively, Saffy takes a step forward, reassuring herself she must have imagined it. Then she takes another step and another until she reaches the first closed door.

As her hand reaches out to slowly pull down the handle, the space around her is suddenly plunged into pitch dark. She hears the trapdoor slam shut and, staggering back, she screams in terror as the door in front of her flies open, wrenching her fingers from the handle.

Someone, large and powerful and breathing heavily, pushes her hard and viciously cracks her on the side of her head.

57

Poppy

Poppy locks Saffy's front door before getting into Harry's car. As they fasten their seatbelts, she turns to him. 'Ready?'

'Ready as I'll ever be,' he says, winking at her.

'Harry?' Poppy lays a hand on his arm before he starts to drive. 'Before we go, let's just get something straight. Our "relationship" – or whatever it was we had going on together – it doesn't exist any more, OK? I agree we need to work together to try and find Saffy and Leona and Rosie, but we're just doing that as friends now.'

Harry pulls the corners of his mouth down into a sad clown face. 'I guessed as much when you took the spare room last night. But hey, if that's what you want, then fine. I know all the stuff I told you has been a lot to take in.'

'Well, that's true enough. And in the interests of us being straight with each other, I have to say part of me still thinks you're a weirdo,' Poppy says.

'Oh, you say the nicest things,' Harry grins before his voice turns serious. 'Look, I haven't always handled things in the best way. I know that. I tend to get obsessed; I find it hard to accept I can't do what I want to do when I want to do it. I took advantage of the prison's counselling programme, can you tell?' He gives her a weak smile. 'I admit, with hindsight, it wasn't right what I did. Watching the Bannatynes. But at that point I felt desperate to see Rosie. Leona had cut me off and I felt as if I had no other options. Now all I'm interested in is finding my little girl.'

Poppy stays quiet. She can hardly criticize him. With hind-sight, she wishes she'd told Ash to get lost when he'd asked her to watch Leona for him.

Harry continues, 'Saying all that, I'm still glad I did it.'

Poppy frowns. 'Seriously?'

'Seriously. Because we've got ourselves a lead the police don't have. The mystery guy who visited Leona.'

Something clutches at her throat. 'I just had an idea.'

'Oh yeah, what's that?' Harry says, checking the road before driving away.

Poppy says, 'I'll tell you when it's done.'

She opens WhatsApp and sends a message, attaching one of the photographs.

Hey Neil, do you recognize this man?

Poppy presses send and sits back, turning her phone face down. 'I just sent the mystery guy's image over to Neil.'

'Saffy's ex, *that* Neil?' Harry says, puzzled.

Poppy nods. 'Remember that Neil came on the scene years ago. He knew a lot of the people around Saffy and Leona that I can't remember because I was so much younger. I just thought it was worth a shot, because I'm worried about what Saffy will do.'

Harry slows at traffic lights and looks across at her. 'She's a loose cannon, taking off like that. Does she think she can solve this case single-handedly? Maybe we should just leave her to it and carry on with our own enquiries.'

'Enquiries about what? We've already drawn a blank.' Poppy sighs. 'My sister has a crazy side to her, Harry. I'm worried she might do something stupid, something she doesn't want to involve us in.'

Harry blinks at her and stays quiet.

'I can't just sit here. I need to know she's OK, but –' Poppy looks down at the notification that's popped up on her phone. 'Neil's replied!' She opens the message and reads it. Squeezes her eyes shut. Reads it again.

Harry pulls over. 'What does it say?'

She turns her screen to face him so he can read the message for himself.

> Took me a moment, but Leona used to date this guy. She kept a photo of the two of them at a funfair. Can't remember his name. Saffy told me he was a nasty piece of work though. She hated his guts. Why??

Harry sucks in air. 'Oh shit,' he says. He turns to look at Poppy. 'You OK?'

'Not really.' Her eyes are prickling. 'I'm scared, Harry. Everything is so out of control right now, Saffy might do something silly. Put herself in danger.'

'Hey, come on. She'll be all right.' Harry slides a chummy arm around her. 'She's a tough old bird, right?'

Poppy nods. 'She drives me nuts, but she's all I've got, you know? She saved my life three years ago. She'll do anything to protect the people she loves.'

'Listen, tell me to get lost and that'll be the end of it. But . . . do you want to tell me what happened back then? Would it help you to talk about the attack, do you think?'

Poppy shakes her head and blinks back the tears. 'Not now, but maybe one day. I just want to find Saffy and bring her home.'

'Then that's what we'll do.' Harry puts his hands back on the wheel and pulls back on to the road. 'Your wish is my command.'

They drive in silence and although Poppy tries her best to fight it, the memory has been stirred.

58

Poppy

Three Years Earlier

There was no problem when Saffy asked if she could stay over at Poppy's flat after her Christmas work party. Poppy had a fridge full of snacks in and she planned to spend the evening watching re-runs of *RuPaul's Drag Race*, which Saffy detested and had always spoiled with her criticism of it when she'd lived at home.

After securing the A-level results she needed, Poppy had started at Nottingham Trent in September. Without consulting Saffy, she had enquired about student accommodation close to the university. Although the campus was only about six miles away from her home with Saffy and Neil, Poppy couldn't wait to spread her wings and fly towards the myriad opportunities she imagined were spread out before her. The building blocks to an exciting future life.

And holy moly, it had lived up to the hype! Having her own space was incredible. She had friends, she went out drinking and partying . . . Saffy was strict because she loved her, Poppy knew that. She'd promised their mum she'd always look after her. But jeez, it was good to have some freedom.

Saffy had come over earlier and left an overnight bag. It had been nice to chat and for it to be in Poppy's new space. But when Saffy began questioning her about her social life and commenting on what needed doing around the place, it was a relief when she took herself off for the evening.

Now, Poppy sipped at a glass of cheap rosé and bopped around the kitchen alone to Taylor's *evermore* album – louder than she'd usually play it because the guy who lived upstairs had told her he was away for a couple of days – while she opened a bag of corn chips to enjoy with the tomato salsa and sour cream dips.

Poppy looked at the full bin bag near the kitchen door and groaned. Before she'd left, Saffy had reminded her to take the rubbish out. She was like the voice of Poppy's conscience. She might as well do it now so her sister didn't give her grief when she got back. It was only one night, and tomorrow morning after breakfast, Poppy would be free to do as she pleased again.

Five minutes later, the rubbish was out and she was stretched out on the sofa with her wine and snacks and the last episode of Season 12 on too loud when she thought she heard something – a sharp crack – out in the hallway.

Poppy muted her programme and listened. She hadn't got any girlfriends coming over, and it was far too early for Saffy to be home. All seemed quiet and Poppy decided something had probably just fallen over in the hall; Saffy's propped-up umbrella, perhaps. Feeling relaxed from her glass of wine, Poppy couldn't be bothered to get up and investigate, so she picked up the remote control again and resumed the programme.

At the exact point the episode finished, she heard the noise again. This time a tap-tapping. The back of her neck prickled, every inch of her suddenly on high alert. She muted the TV again and began to slide to the edge of her seat cushion and then, like an act of magic, he was there. Right in front of her.

A man. Tall, over six feet. Broad shoulders, big arms, dressed entirely in black with gloves and a balaclava with cut-out eyes and mouth showcasing plump lips that looked horribly red and wet.

Poppy jumped up, nimble on her feet, almost succeeding in dashing right past him when he grabbed her hair and hauled her back. She screamed, feeling clumps of her hair rip out at the roots.

'Good try, bitch.' His voice was low and he spoke in a hoarse whisper as if he had a sore throat. 'But not quite good enough.'

He pushed her back on to the sofa and stood over her, so close his knees were pressed against her trembling legs. He held his arms slightly away from his body and it occurred to Poppy that he was trying to appear as big and intimidating as possible, really wanting to terrify her. It was working.

'What do you want?' she whimpered, not wanting to know the answer. 'Take what you want and get out. My sister will be back any moment and –'

'Will she really? And here's me thinking she was out for the night at her party.'

Poppy's eyes widened.

'That's right,' he continued, edging closer so she could smell his sour breath. 'I've done my homework.'

'What do you . . .' Her voice fades away. She can't finish the sentence.

'What do I *want*?' A low, eerie snarl. 'You. I want you.'

His hand slid to a narrow, deep pocket on the thigh of his black cargo trousers and he pulled out a knife with a blade that Poppy realized must be at least eight or nine inches long.

A high-pitched noise escaped her throat and she shunted her whole body to one side in an effort to escape, but he pinned her fast with his knees and held the knife above her head.

'Please, no! Please . . .'

'You're the cost, remember that. You're the cost.'

'What?'

Every few seconds, his fingers flexed long before curling around the handle again. Then he bent forward, and she braced herself. He slapped her face hard and, grabbing a handful of hair, he sheared it off at the root. Again and again, pulling back her head, and she could feel her dark blonde locks falling on to the backs of her hands like damp feathers.

She cried softly as his movements grew more frenzied and then, using the heel of his gloved hand, he pushed her forehead hard so her head snapped back further and she was looking at the ceiling, her pale throat exposed.

Poppy let out a startled whimper and then a low moan as she caught a glimpse of slick metal in his other hand before he pressed it firmly against her throat, digging in the point of the blade until she felt a trickle running down her neck.

She waited, her insides turned to liquid. She couldn't breathe. She was going to die.

He growled, 'I'm going to hurt you so bad no man will ever want to touch you again.'

His tongue flicked out between those red, wet lips and Poppy fought the urge to vomit.

He brought up his hand and sank the tip of the knife into her throat. Poppy gasped with the sharp sting of pain and the warmth of a heavier flow that seeped from her neck.

She closed her eyes and saw her sister's face. Then her beautiful nephew. The people she loved the most in the world. She felt warm and then cold. It was hard to keep her eyes open despite her fear . . .

Light flooded into the front room as a car stopped outside. She felt his iron grip falter. 'Saffy!' she whispered, tears of relief and fear filling her eyes as her neck throbbed when he released her hair. *Please God, let it be Saffy.*

Poppy was so desperate to see her sister and yet terrified for what Saffy might walk into. Terrified that she would get hurt, too.

The man waited, as if deciding what to do. A car door slammed, Saffy's voice calling out a thank you. Poppy knew it sounded louder than it should, which made her wonder if he'd left the front door open behind him when he'd entered the house.

The vehicle moved off and the room faded back to a dim glow. Saffy must have left the event early in a cab.

Saffy's heels clipped up the path and then . . . then the sound of her heels stopped and Poppy realized she'd seen the door was open. She'd know something was wrong.

Thank you, God. Thank you, God.

'If you shout out or make a sound, I'll kill her. I'll kill your sister,' he hissed into her ear.

Poppy's legs were shaking so bad. She did not move. She did not make a sound.

He looked down at her, looked back at the window. He still held her tight so she couldn't dash away from him. And she felt light-headed. Weak.

'The front door is open,' she whispered. 'My sister will know something is wrong.' Her voice sounded slurred and she was speaking too slowly. 'She'll be ringing the police right this second.'

'Shut your filthy mouth.' He pressed the tip of the knife harder to her neck as she whimpered. 'You'll spend the rest of your life hiding in terror from every man you meet.'

Then the handle of the closed living room door slowly moved down and Poppy opened her mouth to scream a warning to her sister, but he was fast. Very fast. In a split second he had bolted across to where Saffy stood motion-less, barely comprehending the scene in front of her.

'Saffy, run!' Poppy screamed, breaking the spell.

But the man barrelled into Saffy. She cried out and tried to step aside to avoid him as his arm came up and hatcheted sideways, punching her hard in the face.

He bent down, close to Saffy's face. 'Next time, bitch! You'll never know when I'm coming but I give you my word. I will. One day I'll be back when you least expect it,' he growled before thundering past her, down the hall and out of the open door.

Poppy lay in a crumpled heap, the sour smell of him still hanging in the air around her. Her head felt like it might explode as she tried to pull herself up to sitting, when Saffy limped across to her.

'Your face, you're bleeding,' Poppy said, holding out a hand and touching her sister's wet face so that her fingers were covered in the blood that coursed out of her nose.

Saffy grabbed her phone, began speaking as Poppy drifted in and out of warmth and cold. She heard the odd word and phrase but couldn't string the meaning together.

'Attacked . . . blood-loss . . . weakening . . .'

Poppy lay on the floor and ran her fingertips over the strange new tufts sprouting from her scalp. She felt shell-shocked, as if she'd woken from a disturbing dream but couldn't quite recall any of the details. And she was suddenly so, so tired. Tired enough to sleep for a long, long time . . .

'Stay with me, Poppy! Wake up, keep your eyes open.' Tears streamed down Saffy's face as she pressed some kind of cloth hard to Poppy's neck. 'Hold on, my sweet girl. Hold on. Help is on its way.'

59
Saffy

When Leona left the house to go and help Wes's mother trim up the garden for Kieran's party, Saffy double-locked the door and walked into Leona's bedroom. Poppy had gone out for the day with her friend's family and it was the first time Saffy had had a good chunk of uninterrupted time in the house on her own.

Leona had been very secretive about her relationship with Wes for the past few weeks and Saffy wanted a little snoop around her room to see if she could find anything interesting. Leona wrote in her little pink journal most days and, Saffy thought, if she could lay her hands on that, it might shed some light on what was happening in their relationship.

When Saffy had invited Leona to move in with them after the death of their mother, the girls had spent long hours in each other's bedrooms. Often in the mornings, they'd drink tea and talk about celebrity gossip while Poppy combed their hair and applied ribbons and glittery slides. Sometimes they'd chat late into the night if one of them couldn't sleep. Saffy and Leona were like sisters, joined at the hip, and Saffy always felt their lives were complete with just each other for company.

But all that stuff, that togetherness, rarely happened any

more. Leona was busy with her nursing training and Saffy with her first job as a secretary in a firm of solicitors. Leona went out with Wes most nights and slept in later on weekend mornings, playing catch-up with her rest. Lately, she'd started staying over at Wes's house, too. 'His parents make me so welcome; it feels like I finally have a family,' she'd said in a dreamy voice.

Leona had taken Saffy's old bedroom that overlooked the tiny back garden while Saffy had moved into her mum's big room at the front of the house, looking out over the quiet road. Saffy's walls were covered in posters, prints and a cork noticeboard, which she filled with inspirational quotes, but Leona's bedroom walls remained bare.

Saffy looked around the room now. Leona's bed was made and the clothes that weren't in the free-standing single ward-robe were folded neatly in piles. A marked difference to Saffy's own bedroom with its tangled bedclothes and the teetering mound of garments that she cast off daily, promising herself she'd get them laundered and hung up one of these days.

It was the children's home training, Saffy decided. Repeatedly leaving places and setting up somewhere else at the drop of a hat. Sad, really, almost as if Leona hadn't yet felt safe enough to make a space her own until now.

Saffy opened a couple of drawers but found nothing. Leona had at least showcased the odd item that meant a lot to her, like the carved wooden box she loved so much that her mother had given her before she'd abandoned her. Saffy pushed the tiny metal bead at the bottom and flipped open the secret panel at the back like Leona had shown her when they were still at school.

She smiled and lifted out the small, hardbacked journal, began leafing through it and then perched on the bed to read the neat handwriting that packed the last few pages. The words became blurry as Saffy scanned over the gist of the entries.

> *I love him so much. I can't wait to move out of here, for us to get our own place together.*
> *S acts like she's my mother and W can't stand her. But how can I just abandon her? She's my BFF.*
> *S went to bed early tonight. I think W might be right. She's jealous and bitter of what I have with him.*

Saffy's face felt rigid. She pushed the journal back and snapped the secret panel of the wooden box shut, returning it to its position on Leona's bedside table. Resentment burned in her chest. How could her best friend write those things? There was no doubt in her mind that Wes had brainwashed Leona and succeeded in turning her against Saffy.

She walked over to the window and picked up the fancy framed photograph that was perched on the narrow sill. It was the only picture on display in the room despite the girls having taken hundreds of photographs of themselves on various days and nights out. Saffy had used her copies to make a collage display on the wall of her bedroom.

The frame showcased a vibrant snap taken of Leona and Wes at last year's Goose Fair celebrations, an historical travelling funfair and a Nottingham tradition. Their faces were flushed and alive with excitement as they pressed closely together, hinting at their intimacy. The bright, dazzling lights of the rides and stalls formed a stunning backdrop against the night sky. *All the fun of the fair.* Saffy hadn't been invited, as was the case on so many occasions these days.

Wes had made a big fuss presenting Leona with the framed photo last Christmas and proudly showed her how he'd had the silver frame specially engraved.

Saffy had saved up to buy her friend a glittery top from Next that Leona had loved but been unable to buy for herself as a Christmas gift that year. Her present had gone down well but nothing had matched up to Wes's offering.

Saffy turned to place the picture back on to the sill and then, just as she was about to set the frame back in its place, her fingers slipped and it fell to the floor. The glass shattered and pierced Wes's face.

She looked down at the mess, at his fractured, ruined smile. She had no choice but to leave it there now, so as not to reveal her snooping. It had been perched precariously on the windowsill anyway, and it was entirely possible Leona would think it had just slipped off.

Saffy left Leona's room, making sure the door was closed behind her before changing into shorts and a T-shirt. The cruel words she'd read in Leona's journal were on constant replay in her mind. She couldn't seem to shake them off.

She filled her small backpack with a bottle of water, some fruit and an old paperback that was more of a prop to help disguise the fact she was so obviously alone than something she was genuinely interested in reading.

She left the house and set off at a brisk pace, turning her face up to the sun. It was a good start to the roasting hot weekend predicted by the Met Office. It was also the end of the first week of the school holidays. Saffy could almost feel the promise of good times in the air, as though collectively, people had breathed out for the summer. That was, people who had someone to share the good times with.

She left the house and headed for the country park. Families were out walking, too, little kids plaguing their parents to stop off at the ice cream kiosk at the entrance to the park. Saffy walked past the main entrance and approached the bank where older kids liked to swing on ropes and bathe in the river that snaked around the outskirts of the watersports centre.

Saffy scanned the riverbank, her eyes travelling past more families and the paddle boats for rent to where the people started to thin out. She walked up to where the river began to narrow and deepen with signs posted every few yards warning of the dangers of entering the water and prohibiting swimming in this section.

There was the odd cluster of mostly older boys here and there. Bare-chested in their swim shorts, egging each other on to jump into the water at the most precarious spots. But there was no sign of Kieran.

Saffy carried on walking, scanning the edge of the river at clearings in the bushes and rocky outcrops that provided natural risky diving boards for the brave . . . or the stupid. Saffy had never walked down this far and was struck by how much quieter it was here away from the families and younger kids.

A shout and peal of laughter alerted her to a group of boys a few yards further on. There were three . . . no, four of them. Barefooted and skinny chested, calling out to each other. They were screeching with laughter at a boy who had somehow shunted along a thick tree branch that hung over the river towards the deepest water in the centre.

She walked closer to the dense foliage and stopped a little further down from where the boys were, squinting her eyes to see a little clearer. Yes, it was definitely him. Kieran. He was the boy shuffling across the branch, clinging on like a deranged monkey and acting the fool. Loving the attention, just like his show-off big brother, Wes.

A spike of fury stabbed at her chest. She'd been sent here like a lackey to round this brat up and get him home for an

345

extravagant family party where he'd be feted and spoiled like a little prince. It was Saffy's opinion that kids like Kieran deserved to come a cropper now and then, so they didn't grow up thinking life was just one big pleasure ground.

She watched as Kieran reached the end of the branch and clambered awkwardly to his bare feet, balancing with his arms stretched out wide like an aeroplane. Impressive, really. But also incredibly stupid.

Saffy heard an urgent shout. A man's voice bellowed and she ducked behind a small cluster of tall bushes, peering through the leaves to watch.

'Hey, get down from there!' A man walking his dog stood waving a stick from the opposite riverbank. 'Don't jump in there, lad, the undercurrent will pull you straight down and carry you away.'

Kieran raised his hand and stood very still, nodding as though he was listening to the man's advice. He waited until he went on his way and the shouts of encouragement from his friends resumed.

'Do it, Kieran! Jump!'

'Jump in, yellow belly!'

Then the boys chanted in unison: *Jump! Jump! Jump!*

Kieran laughed and postured like an Olympic swimmer about to perform an impressive dive. In that moment, it occurred to Saffy this might be a good moment to step forward and tell him he was needed at home. But she was too late.

Saffy heard the crack of splintering wood before the boys seemed to, thanks to their catcalling and shouting. Kieran's face suddenly contorted with shock as he felt the substantial branch give way beneath him. His cries were swallowed up with an almighty creaking and snapping noise as the branch crashed into the river, taking him with it.

Kieran grabbed on to the branch, desperately clinging on as the river began to take him with it.

'Hold on! Hold on!' The panicked calls of his friends came now. A couple of them grabbed flimsy sticks and branches they found on the ground and tried in vain to hold them out for Kieran to grab on to. One of the boys began to wade into the water and stumbled, almost going under before the others pulled him back. For a second or two, the boys stood, frozen on the edge of the bank, paralysed by their horror and fear. Their youthful indecision. Until one shouted, 'We'll go and get help! Stay where you are . . . hold on, Kieran!'

Kieran's head twisted this way and that, his eyes wild and terrified as his friends all began to run in the same direction, yelling for help; running towards the people, towards the adults with their families much further down the embankment.

Now, Saffy and Kieran were alone in the narrow stretch. Saffy snapped out of her own shock and disbelief to rush out from the bushes at last, her heart pounding so hard it felt fit to burst. Kieran continued to struggle against the current, the bottom half of him invisible under the dark, swirling water.

'Kieran! Try and swim over here, to the side!' Saffy yelled out, waving her arms.

Kieran shrieked as the river ripped the branch from his hands and started to pull him downstream towards Saffy, who had her arms outstretched towards him.

'Help! Help!' His voice was weaker now, lost in the rush of the water. Saffy could see he was trying to swim for his life. Thrashing his arms hopelessly instead of – as Saffy knew from a school safety swimming lesson years ago – trying to relax into the pull of the water.

As vital seconds passed, she could see Kieran visibly

growing more tired and then he was moving swiftly down-river towards her. Saffy inched to the very edge of the bank, dumped her backpack and began to wade in, holding on to a sturdy bush with one hand and stretching the other arm out. Kieran was drawing closer to her now. Closer, closer . . . until by some miracle, their fingers touched and Saffy jolted her arm forward an inch or two further and grabbed Kieran's skinny wrist, anchoring the grip of her trainers in the shifting bank of silt and mud as the river deepened.

She held her breath and pulled, keeping a tight hold of his wrist, and Kieran moved, very slowly, towards her, his eyes wide and his mouth open, gasping for air.

He was getting closer and Saffy felt that she was on the cusp of hauling him out and on to the bank. She sensed movement on the opposite bank and jerked up her head in case help had already arrived. But it was only a squirrel scurrying across a tree branch before it leapt across to the next one.

Kieran started to panic again, thrashing hard in the water, and she almost lost her footing. The squirrel had distracted her and her grip had loosened slightly. Kieran began to make guttural noises in his throat and Saffy realized he was swallowing water. Filthy river water. He turned his head towards her and for a second, he looked the image of his brother, Wes.

'Relax, Kieran . . . don't fight the water!' Saffy's own breath-ing began to labour but she anchored her feet afresh and managed to gain another inch, wrapping her fingers tighter around his wrist.

'Save me! Please . . .' Kieran gasped as a sudden swell of water pushed him hard and Saffy felt her grip on his wrist loosen again. It was like one tiny step forward, two big steps back.

Kieran's face looked chalky white now, his dark eyes half closed but still pinned to hers, keeping that tenuous link with life. Silently pleading with her to continue this seemingly hopeless tug of war with the powerful current.

'I'm here. I'm holding on. I won't let go, Kieran!' Panic was like a battering ram, pummelling Saffy with the desperation to hold on, the awful knowing that she could not do so. Her own feet began to slip steadily and her body weight began to work against her. In a few seconds she might fall into the river herself, but she couldn't give up on Kieran. She had to somehow get him home . . . to his party . . . to his family . . .

Saffy tried so hard to keep hold of his hand, but the water was such an unstoppable force and she was floundering to keep her balance now. She screamed out his name, above the rush of the water.

'Kieran! Hold on. Just keep holding on . . . help is coming.'

It seemed liked slow motion as Saffy watched a bank of water shunt the boy violently from behind and Kieran's eyes widened in surprise. He opened his mouth to cry out and then . . . then the weight of him was lifted from Saffy's fingers.

'Kieran! No . . .' Saffy waded out of the river and tried to run alongside him on the bank, but she felt winded and she couldn't move fast enough to keep up. The small, limp shape that only a few minutes ago was a posturing and reckless boy called Kieran Sharpe was being carried away by the water. All Saffy could do now was watch, time standing still, until he was nothing more than a pale dot that was suddenly and ruthlessly pulled beneath the dark water.

He did not surface again.

Saffy snatched up her backpack and retreated to the trees as people began to appear on the opposite bank. Shouting, and crying out Kieran's name. Saffy found she could not move, could not speak.

She walked further down the bank and lay exhausted, staring up at the blue, blue sky. She'd held Kieran's life in her hand. The freezing water, the slick feel of his bony wrist as she'd wrapped her fingers around it.

It could have all been so different. If she could have just held on a few seconds longer, pulled him out of the water. She'd have been a hero. Leona would have been so proud of Saffy. Kieran's family would have accepted her into their fold . . . but now she'd only ever be part of his tragic, senseless death.

That's when Saffy decided to disappear. To rewrite what happened.

If she delayed her arrival until after Kieran had drowned, nobody could point the finger, or imply she should have done something different.

More importantly, Leona wouldn't be disappointed in her.

60

Saffy

Saffy opens her eyes and finds she is shivering, but not with cold. In the years since Kieran's death she has been crippled with guilt and fear for being too weak to save the boy. But she'd never once relived every moment with startling clarity like she just has . . .

She can't yet discern what's in front of her, but she's able to gauge that it is dark around her. She has a splitting headache and her shoulder hurts, but apart from that she can't feel any notable pain anywhere else in her body.

She feels exhausted from recalling every detail of that fateful day. The top third of her back rests against something hard. A wall. The rest of her body is slumped so that her chin is almost resting on her chest. She is clothed and instead of woodland around her, there is a rough carpet underneath her fingers.

Then she remembers: she is in the cabin. And she has been moved from the corridor at the bottom of the ladder.

Saffy forces her crusty eyelids fully open, blinks away the gritty feeling and looks around her without moving her head. It's not fully dark in here. A very weak light emanates from over in the corner by the door.

She is in the space they used to call the den. The furniture has gone and the floor is clear. The wall opposite her features a closed door and there is a fluorescent tube light and a large, hinged lamp attached higher on the wall. All the lights are turned off.

Saffy turns her head to try and look behind her. A sharp pain shoots around her head and she gasps, looks forward again. She makes a small noise in her throat. She isn't gagged and her hands have not been tied. That means whoever has moved her isn't afraid of her attracting attention by shouting or banging. Someone who knows this place as well as Saffy herself does . . .

She shivers, tries to shift into a more upright seated position. She manages it eventually by placing her hands either side of her on the floor and shuffling her bottom back towards the wall. All this, while keeping her head as still as possible to minimize the pain.

Saffy feels weak and thirsty like she's fading away. How much time has passed? She has no grasp of the time of day. There is no light or dark in here, no way of measuring the passage of time.

Will Poppy be missing her, wondering where she is? It's not that long since she turned up with Harris – Harry, or whatever he calls himself now – and Saffy doesn't trust him one bit. He's come from nowhere after years of being silent and that's enough to tell her he must have something to do with all this.

Instead of rushing from the house, lost in shock and the wave of guilt from her past when Harris showed her the photograph, she should have asked to speak to Poppy and explained who the man in the photograph was. But Saffy had been too ashamed to confide in her sister and now . . . now Poppy won't know where to look for her when she worries where Saffy is.

Saffy had run from Poppy and Harris, and Neil is playing happy families somewhere with his sly, pregnant fiancée and her beloved son, Fox. There are so few people left who she is close to. She's managed to push away so many. Colleagues, acquaintances at the gym, people she'd see out and about in her local shops and cafés. It had happened slowly, without her really noticing. Or caring. But that's even more reason why she must find Leona and Rosie, because now Saffy realizes more than ever what they mean to her.

She sits in a slightly more upright position and closes her eyes again. The mist that hovers on the edges of her thoughts is closing in again. Saffy swallows and her throat feels raw, as if it's been scrubbed with sandpaper. The pain isn't just in her head after all. Her throat is hurting and she is desperate for water. Her chest feels tight and hurts when she breathes, and there's a throbbing pain between her shoulder blades where she thinks she must have hit the wall.

Saffy breathes in for three and out for five. In for three and out for five. It hurts and she can't focus on it for more than a couple of rounds. She starts to drift off, her head lolling to one side. She wants to lie down now. She should lie down but she can't move. Her entire body feels like lead.

There's a sound . . . beyond the door. There it is again . . . a strange scraping, is that footsteps? A bang on the door and the sound of bolts being slid across. Then the door opens, and her breath catches in her throat as she shields her eyes from the blinding light. Saffy cries out and stares at Leona. She is standing right in front of her. *Right in front of her.*

'Thank God. You're safe!' Saffy tries to get to her feet but can't.

Leona walks over, pulls up a chair next to her and sits down. Her face looks pale and drawn. 'Hello, Saffy.'

Saffy frowns. She must be losing focus . . . Although Leona is clearly stressed, her attitude is one of resignation rather than panic and fear. 'Where's Rosie?'

A shadow crosses Leona's face. 'Don't worry about Rosie, she's fine. I'm fine.'

'Please . . . I need to know she's safe.'

'Rosie is safe. You're going to have to take my word on that.'

'They found Ash . . . he's . . .'

'I know he's dead. But Saffy, Ash being dead is the least of our worries now.'

Saffy looks up at her friend, a thread of nausea working up into the top of her throat. Something isn't right here. Nothing is making sense.

'What happened?' she says, her voice dry and croaky. 'The day of the interview when I came to the house . . . the messages that were deleted.'

Leona smiles sadly. 'Ah yes, the messages. Where it all started. I must tell you, Saffy . . . you were right all along. I sent you the messages and then I deleted them.'

Saffy brings her hands up to her face. 'I – I don't understand. Why?'

'I've been planning this for a long time, believe it or not.'

Saffy freezes. Stares at her friend and tries to absorb what she's saying. She feels sick with shock. Leona is here, in front of her but . . . but she's betrayed Saffy in some way. Has planned all this . . . it doesn't make sense. Before she can speak, Leona continues.

'Saffy, I found out you've been lying through your teeth to me all these years,' Leona says blankly. 'How could you? How could you pretend you got there after Kieran drowned when you were there all the time? What kind of a monster could watch a little boy die?'

Saffy pushes her knuckles to her lips and squeezes her eyes closed. 'I didn't watch him die, I swear I tried my hardest to save his life, but . . . I failed and I felt like it was my fault. I felt like Kieran dying was all my fault and that you'd blame me and hate me and . . . I couldn't bear to lose your friendship. So I decided to say I'd arrived later. After the accident.'

Leona looks at her, eyes dark and empty. 'You robbed the Sharpe family of closure all these years when you could have helped them come to terms with what happened.'

'It wasn't my fault. I swear, I tried to save him.'

But Leona isn't listening. 'And as if Kieran's death wasn't enough, I found out at the end of last year that Ash and Poppy were having an affair, which you must have known about.'

'I didn't! Poppy only told me about that a few days ago. I would *never* have allowed that to go on behind your back.' Saffy shakes her head. 'You know that, Leona. You know the kind of person I am.'

'I thought I did.' Leona seems to be in some sort of daze. 'I was at such a low point. Harris had been in touch asking to see Rosie and telling me he was coming back to the UK. I hid his letter but I tried to talk to Ash about it, but you can imagine his reaction. I didn't know which way to turn and then, out of the blue, someone got back in touch.'

'Wes Sharpe,' Saffy says.

'You know, I never stopped loving Wes, not really. Never got over losing him like that after . . . after Kieran died.'

'Except Kieran didn't just *die*, did he Saffy?' Both women look up as Wes walks into the room. 'You killed him.'

61

Saffy

'That's not true!' Saffy cries out. 'I tried to save Kieran, I held on to him and I told him, *"I'm here, I'm holding on, I won't let go."* I tried so, so hard, but the river –' Her voice breaks and she looks from Leona to Wes and back again. 'But the river took him, and in the end, there was nothing I could do.'

Wes begins to clap. A slow, sharp slap that echoes around the room. 'Bravo, Saffy. That was quite the performance. Very impressive.'

Resentment builds in Saffy's chest. She's opened her heart and Wes is mocking her. She looks at Leona. 'I swear on my son's life, that's the truth.'

'Ah yes. Your son, Fox.'

A chill runs through Saffy when he utters Fox's name.

'But let's keep on task for now,' Wes says dispassionately. 'Your acting skills might have convinced me if it wasn't for what happened to me four years ago. A young man approached me as I left the office and headed for my car. He was thin and his face looked hollowed out. I had him immediately pinned down as a drug addict. I dismissed him. I said, "Sorry, I have no money on me," and his reply stopped me in my tracks. He said, "I knew your brother, Mr Sharpe. Kieran was my friend."'

Saffy stares at him and says nothing.

'I took him to a small café around the corner, bought him a sandwich and a coffee. His name was Bobby and he told me

357

he'd been an alcoholic since his late teens and that he was recovering with AA. As part of the recovery process, he told me he needed to make amends. That he had something to tell me, privately, that had lain heavy in his heart for years.'

Saffy's skin prickles. She tries to swallow but coughs, the action raking her already raw throat. She looks longingly at the bottle of water on the floor by Leona's chair.

'I didn't really know my brother's school mates, just saw them as kids he knocked around with. So I still didn't recognize him. I started to think he just needed someone to sound off to. Maybe he wanted to just talk about Kieran and how he'd missed him. I was about to make my excuses to leave when he stopped me in my tracks. "I was there that day," he said. "The day he died. I saw what happened."'

Jump! Jump in! Yellow belly . . .

Wes presses his lips together. 'Bobby was one of the three boys with my brother that day, and when he fell into the water, he saw exactly what happened.'

'Kieran's friends ran to raise the alarm,' Saffy counters. 'I saw them go. They left your brother in the water, alone.'

She sees the three boys in her mind's eye. Three bare-chested, barefooted boys in baggy swim shorts. Two of them skinny, one plumper and pale, standing a little further back from the water's edge.

Wes glares at her. 'When the branch snapped and Kieran fell into the water, *two* of his friends ran to raise the alarm. Bobby said he could feel his asthma rising in his throat. He started to follow but found he couldn't keep up with the others, so he turned around and stayed put trying to watch over Kieran.'

Saffy thinks about seeing three boys running away, back to the populated area of the riverbank to get help. She never saw one of them come back.

Wes narrows his eyes. 'Here's the strange thing. Bobby said as he watched, a teenage girl came out of the bushes. When Kieran started to drift, the girl waded in, still wearing her trainers and reached out to him. And she managed to grab hold of Kieran's hand!' He watches her steadily as she puts every scrap of effort into keeping her expression blank. 'I thought, how incredible. Someone tried to save my brother that day? Someone had his hand?'

Saffy closes her eyes briefly; the guilt that has plagued her for so long is freed, squirming in her belly. The movement she'd seen out of the corner of her eye that day . . . the movement she'd assumed to be a squirrel scurrying up a nearby tree.

Had that movement been Kieran's friend, Bobby?

'And then Bobby, he kills me dead. He tells me that this . . . this *person*, this monster, who held my baby brother's hand and had just got close enough to pull him towards her and haul him on to the bank, called out his name. Then you know what she did?'

Saffy looks blankly at him, her stomach roiling and burning.

'I'll tell you what she did. Just as he looked at her with hope, she let go of his hand. Can you believe anyone would do that to an eleven-year-old child?' His face burns with thinly disguised hatred. 'Of course you can believe it. Because that person, that was you, Saffy Morris.'

'I tried to save him!' Saffy cries out, looking to Leona for support. 'I tried my best to save Kieran.'

'You let go of his hand. My brother was looking at you, so you could see the light leave his eyes as the river carried him off. Bobby heard it and he saw the sick satisfaction you took.' Wes's voice breaks and he looks away. 'You just let go of his hand. You let the river take him.'

'It's not true!' Saffy cries out. 'It's just not true!'

She shrinks back against the wall, looks pleadingly at Leona. 'There was a swell of water and it just took him and there was nothing I could do, I –'

'I don't want to hear it!' Wes screeches, his face puce, and Leona wraps her arms around herself in her seat and begins to rock back and forth.

'If you tried to save Kieran, if you had nothing to hide, why would you lie about being there at the moment he was lost to the river?' Leona says softly. 'Only a guilty person would do that, surely?'

'I wish with all my heart I had told the truth from the beginning. I made a snap decision to keep quiet . . . I thought you'd be disappointed in me, that I hadn't managed to save him. I should have said I was there and that I tried my hardest to save him.' Saffy hangs her head. 'I'm sorry. I'm so sorry I misled you all.'

'You didn't mislead us. It was far worse than that,' Wes says in a more measured voice. 'Bobby told me what he saw and –'

'Can't you see it's Bobby who is lying?' Saffy cries out suddenly. 'He was just an eleven-year-old kid back then! You can't take an alcoholic's account as the truth. His recollection is bound to be flawed.' But Wes doesn't seem to hear her.

'Bobby, he's crying in the café,' Wes says quietly. 'He's saying how sorry he is. "I'm so, so sorry, Wes. I should have told you this way before now. Told you what I saw." I asked him why he hadn't come to my family that day. Told my parents what he'd seen. He said he was afraid. Ashamed that he and the others had encouraged Kieran to climb along the branch. He'd hidden himself in the trees. See the difference between the two of you? Bobby's honesty against your denial and lies?'

'That's not true! I've suffered too all these years. I've felt guilty, every single day. I've blamed myself, racked my brains if I should have done things differently, even though the river nearly pulled me in with him. Even though I did everything within my power to save him.' Tears roll unchecked down her cheeks. She looks at Leona and sees a hopelessness that unnerves her.

Wes is unmoved. 'Bobby buried what he'd seen you do. Told himself for years and years he'd imagined it and eventually, the weight of it turned him to drink. Nearly killed him.'

'It's just his mistaken take on what happened,' Saffy says pleadingly. 'The truth is, I'm the only person who tried to save your brother that day, Wes. While Bobby watched from a safe place, I was thigh-deep in the river trying to help Kieran.'

Wes is driving his top teeth into his bottom lip and it has started to bleed.

He smiles a mean smile. 'You are the single point of interest in Kieran's death, Saffy. All roads lead back to you.'

'I didn't kill Kieran!' Saffy cries out, looking wildly between Wes and Leona. 'I tried to save him; I swear on my son's life. I tried so hard.'

'Even if you didn't kill him, you didn't save him when you had the chance.' Wes moves over to Leona, slides his arm around her shoulders. Saffy stares, wondering if she just imagined Leona's flinch. 'And for that, we – that's Leona and I – we decided you must pay the price. And Ash would be targeted too. It was our chance to get rid of him once we found out Leona was pregnant.'

'Leona? Please stop this. Nothing makes sense . . . you know I'm not a killer!'

But Leona is looking down at her trembling hands, rocking. It's as if she's a stranger, as if she despises Saffy after all their years of friendship. Saffy can't reach her, can't make her see the truth.

Saffy is shaking when Wes moves towards her, his gloved hand clutching a knife. Her eyes widen when she sees it's a Joseph Joseph knife with a distinctive yellow band around its black hilt and the bottom edge of the handle.

The very knife the police had marked as missing from Saffy's kitchen block when they carried out their search.

Wes sees her shock and grins. 'That's right. You're about to get reacquainted with your own kitchen knife. The knife that killed Ash Bannatyne, which the police will soon find embedded in your stomach. That is, when you decide you can't face what you've done and end it all.'

'I love you, Leona,' Saffy whispers, tears almost choking her. 'These past few days I've tried so hard to find you and Rosie. Tried to push the police to work faster and harder . . . I've been so afraid I would lose you both. What has he done to you?'

Leona looks up, her eyes swimming with tears. She looks at Wes and then meets Saffy's eyes. 'I'm so sorry, I've been such a fool and –'

'Enough!' Wes strides towards Saffy, raising the knife.

Saffy scrunches her knees up to her chest and holds up her hands. 'Please, Wes . . . please . . . let's just talk . . . about this.' Her words come in short bursts as she fights to breathe.

'I don't think so. I've been waiting for this moment for a long time. For way too long,' he says, his voice calm and measured. 'And I want to enjoy every second of it without having to listen to any more of your lies.'

Saffy closes her eyes and wraps her arms around her knees. This is it. This is the end. Fox's sweet face fills her mind's eye. The warmth of his small body when she embraces him; the laughter and joy he has brought to her life. Nothing and no one can ever take her love for him away from her.

'Wes, this was never the plan!' Leona screams and Saffy's eyes snap open.

Leona is out of her chair, standing between Saffy and Wes, her arms stretched out like a barrier.

'Shut it!' He prods the knife at her, but she stands firm. 'You wanted your useless husband and your so-called best friend gone as much as I did. And now you're having second thoughts?' He shakes his head at Leona. 'Far too late for that, my love.'

'Don't do this, Wes. Enough is enough,' Leona pleads, but Wes has stopped listening.

He steps to one side and addresses Saffy again. 'When they eventually find you here, it won't be too hard for them to work out what happened. After murdering a child, the guilt all got too much for poor Saffy and she had to come out here to the woods and end it all in the cabin she came to as a teenager. By which time, Leona, Rosie and I . . . and our unborn baby will be long gone.'

Saffy glances at Leona but she is staring at the floor and can't meet her eyes.

'First,' Wes continues, 'I'll rip you open and watch you bleed out. And I'll enjoy every moment, just like I did when Ash died.'

'Wes, no! He didn't tell me he was going to kill Ash, Saffy,' Leona cries out. 'He was just supposed to threaten him. Pay him off and get him out of my life. I swear I didn't know that's what he was planning to do.'

'Enough!' Wes lashes out and slaps Leona across the face. She reels back in shock. 'I said . . . shut it!'

'Leave her alone,' Saffy yells, despite the fear coursing

through her. She pushes back hard against the wall and manages somehow, despite her pounding head and dizziness, to get into a crouching position, her hands steadying her on the floor as she painfully rises to standing. 'Leona's not like you. She was never like you.' From somewhere inside her, a surge of courage comes. 'You're a coward, Wes Sharpe. You've waited until now to confront me, after you've pulled Leona into your pathetic plans.'

Wes walks forward, a manic grin on his face. 'That's not strictly true though, is it Saffy? Three years ago you and I had a brief but very memorable little chat.'

Saffy frowns. Another one of his silly games to lead Leona to believe Saffy has been in touch with him. 'I've never set eyes on you since Kieran's funeral.'

Wes puts his hand to his chest. 'I'm gutted you've forgotten already. And yet . . . maybe I can jog your memory. Your Christmas night out . . . you came home early and spoiled my little party with Poppy.'

And time stands still.

62

Saffy

Saffy can feel the blood turning to ice in her veins. She opens her mouth to respond, but a voice speaks out before her.

'That wasn't you.' Leona's words emerge as a whisper before becoming more strident. 'Say it. Tell me it wasn't you, Wes.'

A whooshing noise fills Saffy's ears and she leans back on the wall as her knees begin to buckle. The balaclava, his height. His vicious parting words.

One day I'll be back when you least expect it.

And now he is back.

A smirk spreads over Wes's face and Leona recoils, her hand clamping over her mouth.

'Poppy didn't do anything!' Saffy shrieks. 'She was barely an adult.'

'You took my brother's life. Why shouldn't you lose your sister?' Wes screams, his face contorting with hatred. 'An eye for an eye.'

All three of them start when an almighty crash comes from above them. The trapdoor! The sound of the ladder crashing down.

'We're here . . . down here!' Saffy screams as loud as she's able. 'Help!'

Roughly, Wes grabs Saffy's arm and squeezes hard as he pulls her towards him just as Leona lurches forward and scratches his face. Wes roars and shoves her away. Leona loses her balance and falls heavily against the wall, crying out in pain as her arm cracks and bends at a strange angle. 'Stay back.' Wes looks wildly around the room. 'Let me deal with this.'

'You lied,' Leona sobs, cradling her injured arm. 'You promised nobody would get hurt. You need help, Wes, you –'

Footsteps thunder down the corridor outside and the door crashes open. Wes yells and runs towards Saffy, the knife raised in his hand, but at that moment, Harry barrels into the room, knocking Wes off his feet, the knife clattering to the floor.

Wes snatches it up again as the two men wrestle, Harry successfully knocking the knife out of Wes's hand. Harry tosses it away into the corner of the room and sits astride Wes, panting and holding down his arms.

'Saffy!' Poppy rushes into the room and embraces her sister. She looks around, her face pale and shocked when she sees Leona, and Harry astride Wes on the floor. 'Saffy . . . you're hurt.'

Saffy says, 'I'm OK. How did you know . . . how did . . .' Saffy's thoughts won't join up. All she can think about is what Wes just confessed. She can't tell Poppy. Not here. Not now.

Poppy is slightly breathless. 'We found your Google Maps search. I remembered you brought me here once when I was a little kid. And Neil recognized him from the photo.' She nods to Wes. 'Leona's old boyfriend.'

Unable to move under Harry's bulk, Wes snarls, 'Get off me before I . . .'

'Before you what?' Harry presses forward and applies more weight to Wes's arms. He cries out in pain. 'I'm staying right here, mate, until the police arrive.'

'We heard you shout for help and so I rang the police

'upstairs while Harry came down here,' Poppy tells Saffy before looking at Leona.

The two women regard each other and Leona says, 'Poppy, I never knew. I swear I never knew.'

'Knew what?' Poppy frowns.

Saffy hugs her closer and suddenly Wes gives a hard, hacking laugh. 'I see your hair grew back.'

'What?' Poppy's hand moves to her head, smoothing down her hair.

'Poppy. Look at me,' Saffy says calmly even though her insides are twisting in on themselves. 'Turn away from him and look at me.'

But Saffy can see that Poppy is no longer listening. She isn't registering what Saffy is saying. She has a laser-like focus on Wes. Poppy takes a step closer to him and Saffy reaches for her hand but Poppy shrugs her off.

'Leave me,' she says in a strange, disconnected voice.

Saffy's arm falls away and she watches as her sister moves even closer to Harry who still has Wes firmly pinned underneath him. Poppy crouches on the floor next to Wes.

'What did you just say?' Poppy says in that same, odd tone. 'About my hair?'

'If you know, you know. Right?' Wes laughs, a crazy, unbridled sound that ricochets around the bare, echoing walls of the den.

'It was *you*?' Poppy says softly. 'You're the man who attacked me?'

Wes gives an animalistic howl of triumph, thrashing his head from side to side. Harry increases the weight on his arms again and the howling stops, Wes crying out in pain instead.

Poppy is shaking. 'His lips. The red, wet lips.' She backs away, her fingers knotting and unknotting in front of her face. Saffy tries to catch her eye, to beckon her away, but Poppy is transfixed, staring at Wes. She looks small and afraid. The armour that has protected her so far – that flimsy construction of courage and belief that nothing can hurt her again – has dissolved.

Saffy watches as Leona stands up. She stands silently at first, observing the behaviour of this man she'd committed to a new future with. A man whose child she is carrying.

'All along you had it planned, didn't you?' Leona says carefully. 'All along, your only real motive was to get to Saffy and to avenge Kieran's death by killing her. Ash was just collateral damage.'

Wes writhes under Harry's steel grip. 'Saffy must pay for what she did. Back then I failed, but I won't fail again.'

As if to prove his point, Wes makes a mammoth effort to free himself, bucking and twisting. Harry is the stronger man and pushes back hard but somehow, in the shift of weight, there is a split second of opportunity which Wes seizes upon. Saffy gasps as, in one fluid movement, Wes's back arches and he manages to surge up before Harry can contain him. The top of his skull smashes into Harry's face and he flails back.

Wes springs up and kicks Harry hard in the head with a heavy-booted foot. Harry yells out and Wes kicks him again. He rushes to retrieve the knife before turning and hurtling towards Saffy.

She backs up, holding up her hands, but there is nowhere to go. Wes's fist smashes into her face and Saffy hears her own piercing scream as thick, warm blood trickles from her nose on to her lips.

The room is blurred as Wes shakes her hard, screaming obscenities at her. Saffy registers his fist rising again and she squeezes her eyes shut, waiting for the impact. Then she is

368

shunted aside as Leona launches herself at Wes, clawing at his face and screaming again and again, 'I hate you! I hate you!'

'You were just a means to an end.' Wes grabs Leona's wrists and laughs as she tries, unsuccessfully, to scratch and pummel his face. He raises his voice above her frustrated yelling. 'You made it easy; you were so gullible. I never planned to be with you, never wanted that thing in your stomach that's probably not even mine.'

Saffy rushes forward to pull Wes off Leona, but before she can get there, Wes turns back to her with the knife.

'I'll kill you!' he screams, the knife stabbing at Saffy's leg just as Poppy puts her whole body weight behind a powerful charge into Wes's side. The knife clatters to the floor and Leona snatches it up, plunging it into Wes's stomach.

Saffy's knees buckle and she falls to the floor.

For a brief second or two, the room is silent and then Leona moves away from Wes and to Saffy's side. His eyes are closed and he isn't moving. A ruby pool of blood spreads from beneath his wound.

'I'm sorry,' Leona whispers to her. 'I didn't know . . . he'd lost his mind. I thought we could be happy . . .'

Banging and shouting sounds above them. Poppy rushes into the corridor and is back within seconds.

'It's the police!' she cries out.

63

Saffy

The community nurse says the tendon injury behind Saffy's right knee is healing nicely. Wes had inflicted several nasty wounds, but it was the tendon that suffered the most long-lasting damage.

'I'm sick of not being able to walk properly,' Saffy complains to her. 'Not ideal when I look after my young son –'

'Be patient, tendons can take months to heal,' the nurse says. 'No climbing mountains or skydiving for a while, but apart from that, you're doing fine.'

Saffy laughs. 'Don't worry, adventure pursuits are the last thing on my mind.'

The nurse grins. 'Right, I'll see you next week. Oh, I nearly forgot.' She reaches into her apron pocket and produces a clutch of mail. 'The postman gave me these on the way in.'

When she's gone, Saffy feels grateful she's making good progress mentally and physically. She's feeling a little stronger each day, and it leads her to wonder how Wes Sharpe is feeling this morning. While the horror of what's happened, given time, will eventually start to fade for her, Wes's reckoning for his wicked deeds is getting closer with every night's restless sleep in his cell in HMP Nottingham.

He is charged with the murder of Ash and a string of other offences including assault and actual bodily harm.

371

'With the level of planning involved in Ash's death, he's not likely to see freedom again for a long, long time. If ever,' DI Shah remarked when she called to tell Saffy he'd been charged. 'Although, when various assessments have been carried out, he could spend some of that time in a secure hospital rather than a prison.'

Saffy prays that wherever he ends up, she's right, and it turns out to be for *ever*.

They'd heard just last week that Leona will not be charged for stabbing Wes. She'd acted in self-defence and in the defence of another. But she was arrested in connection with Ash's death and, because of her part in what amounted to months of conspiring, she has been refused bail and is currently in custody.

But last week, when Shah made a flying visit to the house to return Saffy's garnet necklace, she told her that it is possible, once investigations are completed, that the case against Leona may be dismissed.

It's strange, but Saffy's mind is increasingly choosing to remember the good days with Leona, the laughter, the kindness she once showed to her, to Poppy and to Fox. That kindness and love was real at that time, regardless of what came after. Regardless of the fact that Leona has since turned against her so completely.

Saffy has accepted she will never know just how Wes Sharpe got inside Leona's head and convinced her to embark on his devastating plan for them to be together. But Leona *did* buy into it. She became invested in ruining her one-time best friend regardless of the effect on Fox and Poppy.

In the absence of the truth, Saffy chooses to believe Leona didn't know the full extent of it: that Wes planned to kill Ash to get him out of the way and to kill her to feed his obsession and avenge Kieran's death.

She sighs and sifts through the handful of letters the nurse brought in. An electricity statement, what looks like it might be a get-well card, a generic piece of 'To the Householder' mail and . . . she peers at the handwriting before tearing the last one open and taking out a folded document and a single sheet of lined notepaper.

Saffy reads the letter first, a small sound of disbelief escaping her throat. She stares down at it. Reads it again. And again.

Saffy,

I can't undo the damage and hurt I've caused you and I know my apologies will mean nothing. Just know this: Wes nearly destroyed me, too. My heart breaks when I think of the attack; what he put you and Poppy through.

I never knew the full truth of what he was planning, Saff. I never wanted you or Ash hurt. If I could turn the clock back, I would. I can never repay you for taking Rosie in until I'm out of this place. She loves you like a second mum, always has.

Will you come and see me so I can fully explain everything that's happened? I'm enclosing a visiting order here and I pray you'll give me this chance, for old times' sake.

I love you.
Leona

Saffy refolds the letter and tucks it back in the envelope with the visiting order. She has so many questions that still keep her awake at night. Questions only Leona can answer.

But Saffy doesn't know if she can do this. She doesn't know if she's strong enough.

The back door opens and Rosie flies in. In one breath she says, 'Auntie Saffy, we went to the park and Pops pushed me

373

as high as the sky on the swing and it was too high really but I loved it!'

'What?' Saffy feigns annoyance, making Rosie giggle. 'Right, Poppy's in real trouble now!'

Poppy walks in laughing. 'Little Rosie snitch-face. You said you wouldn't tell!' She looks at Saffy. 'Cup of tea and a biscuit?'

Saffy smiles. 'Lovely.'

Poppy has been taking Rosie to see her mum in the prison's family centre. And sometimes, Neil and Mira take her out for the day with Fox. Regardless of what's happened, everyone is trying to make things as easy as possible for Rosie.

And looking at her now, with her flushed cheeks from the fresh air and her happy smile, Saffy thinks they must all be doing something right.

64

Poppy

When she's washed and dried her hair, she takes a piece and winds it around the heated barrel of her new styling wand, waiting a few seconds before allowing the long, golden curl to spring free.

Poppy is getting to know her hair again. Getting to love the feel of its softness and the fragrant shampoo smell around her face.

Since she's been able to put a face to her attacker, to learn, from Saffy, about his life, Poppy has been cut free of the ties that have bound her. The police have been proven wrong. Her attacker had not been a stranger who'd arbitrarily walked into her flat one night, the only clue to his face being intense eyes and those vile lips.

Her attacker's name was Wesley Sharpe. A man who lost his brother and became obsessed with finding someone that he could blame. Specifically, he believed that Saffy was to blame. That she'd had it within her power to save Kieran, but deliberately chose to let go of his hand and leave him to perish. Saffy, who had her faults but who underneath, had the kindest, purest heart. Wes Sharpe had tricked and used Leona in order to commit murder and violence in his unhinged quest for revenge.

Poppy finishes curling her hair and studies her reflection.

She dresses in jeans and a modest top and waits for her flat-mates. They're all going into town for a few drinks and when it gets late, she will come back here with them. She no longer needs to be the Poppy who would wave them off and stay behind to hunt down an unsuitable man. The Poppy who needed to prove she was a survivor and had no fear. Who felt she must take risks with men she barely knew to prove to herself that she remained fearless and unaffected.

A weight has been lifted.

The light catches her neck and Poppy traces the faint, silvery scar from the serious vascular injury that nearly killed her three years ago.

Thanks to Saffy's quick thinking, stemming the blood loss and summoning the emergency services that night, Poppy had survived.

She owes Saffy a lot. Her annoying, controlling sister who she loves more than life. And that's why she's moving back in with Saffy and Rosie and, when he's there at weekends, Fox too. In between her studies, Poppy will help Saffy care for the kids and she'll pull her weight without complaining.

Because that's what families do.

65

Saffy

Two Months Later

After a pleasant drive through South Derbyshire to the hamlet of Foston, Neil navigates the Lexus up a long driveway and parks in front of the Victorian country house with its ornate Jacobean facade.

'Hard to believe it's a prison, isn't it?' Neil gives a low whistle as he appraises the building. 'I suppose if you've got to do time, there are worse places.'

'That's a matter of opinion,' Saffy remarks. 'Foston Hall is a prison all the same, and Leona doesn't deserve to be there.'

'And that's another matter of opinion.' Neil parks and turns off the engine. 'When all's said and done, Wes couldn't have carried out his plans without her help. So, when you go in there and listen to her tale of woe, you'll do well to remember it was Leona who sent you those deleted messages and Leona who willingly framed you as the main suspect for a missing family who weren't really missing. She's not a saint, Saffy.'

'I know that,' Saffy says, gathering her belongings and opening the passenger door. 'The visit lasts an hour. See you soon.'

Neil takes out his iPad and wiggles his fingers. 'Take your time. I'm looking forward to catching up on my spreadsheets.'

Inside the prison, Saffy is shunted through the process.

Waiting, then the presenting of visiting orders, searches, more waiting and then, finally, filing into the visiting hall with the other friends and families.

Saffy scans the large room but can't see Leona at first. Until a painfully thin woman with scraped back hair and bad skin raises a frail hand to attract her attention.

Saffy picks her way through the small tables, feigning a benign expression when she's actually shocked to her core.

'I can't believe you're here at last.' Leona stands up, keeping one hand on the table for support. 'Thank you for coming, Saffy. Thank you so much.'

'Of course I came.' The two women embrace for a moment before sitting down. 'I had to, right? We both need answers. But first . . . Poppy told me you lost your baby. And I want to say I'm so sorry for that.'

Leona nods and lowers her eyes. 'Thank you,' is all she says.

Saffy takes the opportunity to make a quick study of Leona, the dark clothes that hang off every part of her skeletal body. The breakout of angry, inflamed spots on her cheeks that look like an allergic reaction. But the saddest observation she makes is of Leona's beautiful feline eyes, now puffy and red-rimmed, the stunning hazel colour faded to a dull brown with no sign of light at all. She's been through a lot. As she herself has. As Poppy has.

'Obviously, I got your letter,' Saffy says when Leona finally looks at her. 'It took me a little time to decide whether to come or not, but in the end, we have so much history between us. So many good years.'

'So many good years,' Leona murmurs. 'So much love and respect. And now . . . I've thrown it all away.'

'Why? That's the question I most want answered,' Saffy says. 'Why did you betray me?'

Leona sighs. 'The only way I can explain how it happened is to start at the beginning. And it all began about a year ago.'

Saffy shifts in the uncomfortable plastic chair and laces her fingers on the scratched wooden table in front of her. 'I'm listening,' she says.

66

Leona

One Year Earlier

She'd had another argument with Ash that morning and it felt like a watershed moment when Leona finally admitted to herself she was sick to death of her life. More than that, she was sick to death of her husband, but she'd known that for a while. It was another matter what she could do about it, but she knew that, somehow, she must get herself and her daughter away from Ash.

The handsome, caring man who'd swept Leona off her feet was nowhere to be seen. High on love and a feeling of safety for herself and little Rosie, Leona had married Ash in haste. He had turned out to be a narcissist and a bully but also an expert gaslighter who had the ability to twist her into knots within minutes if she dared to complain about the way he spoke to her, or the things he expected her to do.

'What are you talking about?'

'Are you serious? It's all in your head.'

And his favourite and recently most used: 'You really should make an appointment to see the doctor.'

Now, Leona had reached the stage where she felt she had nobody to turn to. She'd neglected her friendship with Saffy in favour of her marriage. With Ash, there had never been enough room for both. She had become friendly with Mira,

Neil's partner, but it was the kids that bound them together. They hadn't got a great deal in common other than that.

But Leona was getting desperate. She'd never felt as low as she did right now. She had only recently discovered that Ash had got himself into trouble financially, funding a lifestyle they could not afford. In fact, he'd pulled them close to financial ruin. Their joint savings were gone and there was no money left to continue renovating and decorating the house that he'd pressured her to buy, even though they had only just managed to get a mortgage big enough.

Incredibly and in spite of all this, Ash had been pressuring her to give up her nursing job at the City Hospital for months now. 'I'm earning enough for both of us,' he'd boasted, pouring himself another large glass of the expensive red wine he got delivered by the box from an online retailer. 'I want to start my own consultancy business soon, so you can deal with all the admin side of things.'

'But I love my job,' Leona had countered. 'All my years of training will be for nothing if I leave.'

Ash had laughed, his delusion complete. 'It's hardly brain surgery, is it, honey? Private consultancy is big money, it can benefit us far more than the pennies you earn.'

She hadn't let on that she'd discovered the letters from the bank. Had observed him each time he'd taken a call from the bank and wandered off down the garden with a pale, anxious face. Back in the days of living in care, Leona had perfected the art of noticing everything and saying nothing. Nobody liked a child who sought out confrontation, and Leona had very much wanted to be liked. Loved, even.

She knew she had to confront Ash at exactly the right time when she had everything she wanted to say lined up in her head and felt strong and confident enough that he couldn't browbeat her with his unpleasant and demeaning questions.

Leona had noticed a few red flags relating to Ash's health recently. His appetite for drinking was increasing almost daily and he'd developed a strange high colouring in his cheeks. Often, heart palpitations had him getting up and pacing around the house in the middle of the night. Leona wondered if she waited a little longer, he might just keel over and all her problems would disappear.

And then, almost overnight, Leona's life changed.

Just before the end of her shift, the ward manager called her over. 'We've got a difficult patient in treatment room one. He's got a nasty cut to his hand that needs dressing, but he's already complained two health assistants are too rough and inexperienced. Would you do the honours?'

Leona agreed but groaned inwardly. Her shift finished in forty minutes but she'd be expected to finish this patient's treatment before leaving.

She entered the room and stopped, her feet rooted to the floor as shock numbed her for a moment. When she came to her senses, she closed the door behind her. 'Wes?'

'The very same. You haven't changed a bit, Leona. Just got even more beautiful.'

She'd batted away his compliment, embarrassed. And yet . . . the butterflies were instantly back and she felt like the schoolgirl she was when she first set eyes on Wes Sharpe. Back when she thought she'd never stand a chance with a guy like him.

'I understand you have a cut that needs treating on your hand,' she said to cover up her shock.

He held up his hand and she could see it was sore and caked in blood. As she gently inspected the injury, he never took his eyes off hers. His hair was darker and longer now. He'd filled out since his youth – as she had – and his teeth looked veneer-perfect, but he was there. Underneath it all, she could still see the boy she'd known and loved with all her heart.

'I've never stopped thinking about you in all these years, you know,' Wes said softly as Leona sat down and opened a drawer full of bandages, gauze and antiseptic cream.

A flood of heat channelled through her and she smiled to cover her nerves, setting out the dressings she needed on the table between them.

'What we had, the love I felt for you . . . I never found that again,' Wes said, sliding his good hand over Leona's.

She left her fingers under his for a moment before taking her hand gently away and resuming her preparations for the treatment of his wound. 'So, as you can see, I stuck with nursing as a career. What about you? What have you been up to since I last saw you?'

Leona had been inconsolable for weeks after Kieran's death. She'd told Saffy, 'I can't stop thinking, at the very moment he was drowning, we were tying up balloons and pinning coloured bunting to the hedges. Wes is tortured that Kieran was alone when he died. We'll never know exactly what happened.'

Saffy had stayed quiet and held Leona's hand. She'd stroked her hair and made her endless cups of tea and a cup of hot chocolate each night before bed. She had been the textbook good friend.

But the thing that had upset Leona even more was the fact that suddenly she'd found it impossible to reach Wes emotionally. They'd been so close, but after the tragedy, he had completely shut down and retreated into the bosom of his family. Every day she'd called him or gone round to the house, but the answer from his parents had always been the same.

'So sorry, Leona, he's just not up to visitors right now. The

GP has put him on medication, he's not himself. None of us are.'

The day of Kieran's funeral, Leona and Saffy had been told the indoor service was already full, but Wes's uncle had spotted Leona and taken them through with him. He'd left them standing at the back of the chapel. At the end of the service Leona had run desperately to the front pews.

'Wes, please! I love you! I need to see you!'

People had looked aghast, nudging each other, staring at her with shocked expressions.

It hadn't done her any good. Not long after, the Sharpe family had sold up and moved away and Wes had never contacted her again.

'I went into freelance IT consultancy and I've worked away for a long time,' Wes said simply. 'Just came back to the area a few months ago. I knew I had to find you.'

'How *did* you find me?'

'It was easy with social media, didn't take long. Your public details showed you were a nurse, even the name of this hospital on Facebook. And here I am.'

She didn't know what to say apart from, 'I'm married, now. I have a daughter. You?'

'Never married. No kids.' He waved a hand as if none of that mattered to him. 'You and I, Leona, we were robbed of our love. Of our chance to be happy together. I was too young and I allowed it to happen but . . . I've never forgotten you. And I knew I'd never find anyone I loved as much as I loved you.' He touched her hand again. 'As much as I *love* you. It's never dimmed.'

A warmth spread through her. She'd never forgotten Wes Sharpe, either. Never quite healed from the pain of losing him. Instead, she had settled for less. Rosie's deadbeat dad, Harris, and then Ash.

'I missed you too,' she says softly. 'I'm not sure I ever stopped missing you.'

A shadow flickered over his face. 'I've never forgotten you. I don't suppose I can tempt you to join me for dinner when you're finished here?'

There was a beat of silence. Ash would be expecting her back, but Rosie had a sleepover tonight at a school friend's house. Ash had started getting a cab to and from work and usually got back late after his weekday drinking sessions. Leaving Leona to go back to an empty house to stew in her own problems.

But here, with Wes, she felt warm and wanted, like she had choices again. It was a welcome relief.

'I'd love to go for dinner with you,' Leona said.

67

Leona

One Year Earlier

It was as if they had never been apart. After Leona stopped being scared of what Ash would do, that is. After she'd stopped feeling guilty and stopped fighting her old longing for Wes.

Leona knew she was falling under his spell all over again, but it felt so good. She didn't want to stop the sweet relief after all the crap, the deceit and the narcissistic behaviour she'd had to put up with from Ash.

They saw each other sporadically for a couple of weeks. Time was difficult to carve out for Leona. She had Rosie to think of and couldn't underestimate Ash, as even though his drinking had worsened, he was an accomplished functioning alcoholic, more than capable of putting on a perfectly normal facade when necessary. His trusty 'successful businessman' mask never slipped despite the rest of his life crumbling around him.

After getting closer to Wes again, Leona became seized by a powerful urge to just run away from it all. But Wes had other ideas.

One day, while Ash was away working in the North-East and Rosie was at school, Wes took her to his apartment on the river for the first time.

Leona watched as Wes swiped a key card and pressed floor six.

'Top floor?' She raised an eyebrow, impressed.

'Penthouse.' He smiled and held up the key card. 'Nobody else can access that floor without one of these.'

The lift opened into an impressive, wide space full of light. Wes punched in a four-digit code on a pad and they walked through a door.

Leona found herself in a vast glass living area with floor-to-ceiling windows affording an incredible view of the river and an expansive grassy area known locally as the Hook opposite and Lady Bay beyond. An air-conditioning unit whirred softly on the wall, maintaining a comfortably cool temperature despite the sticky heat outside.

'This place is incredible,' Leona murmured, looking around at the stylish cream furniture and polished wooden floors. 'You've done an amazing job with the interior.'

Wes laughed, 'Sadly, I can't take the credit, the place came fully furnished. But all this,' he waved his arm around the space, 'is incidental. The view is what I came here for.'

He took her hand, and they walked over to the glass. The Trent glittered like liquid pewter, sunlight bouncing off the still, sparkling surface.

'This place is a shrine to me. When I see the river, I feel Kieran's spirit of adventure. A young life ended far too soon when it could have been so different.' He stared out at the water as if he could see something there that Leona couldn't. 'It also serves as a reminder of unfinished business.'

Leona looked at him, puzzled. 'Unfinished business?'

Wes nodded, his face contorting as if he were in physical pain. 'No matter what it takes, nothing will stop me avenging my brother's death. I can never rest while his murderer is walking around, still living. Still laughing.'

'Sorry, Wes, you've lost me,' Leona said carefully. 'I still think about Kieran a lot, too. The horrible way he died, but . . . nobody murdered him. He drowned in the river. So incredibly tragic, such a terrible waste of his life, but . . . at the end of the day, it was an accident.'

Wes turned to face her, placing his hands gently on Leona's shoulders.

'That's what I thought too, Leona, but it turns out we were all deceived by a devil. A devil in human form. Saffy Morris lied to us all. I have proof she was there when Kieran took his last breath. She could have saved him, you see. But instead, she chose to let him die.'

68

Saffy

Present Day

'I tried so hard to save him,' Saffy whispers, her eyes welling up as she looks pleadingly at Leona. 'There's not a day goes by in all this time I haven't thought about Kieran, too. Not a day I haven't vilified myself for staying quiet about being there instead of telling his family. And to think . . .' a tear rolls down her cheek, '. . . to think of the hurt and the pain that's been caused by that single decision. The attack on Poppy would never have happened if it hadn't been for my lie.'

Leona shakes her head. 'You were always too hard on yourself, Saff. Taking the blame for everything. The way your mum treated you in favour of Poppy.' She reaches for Saffy's hand. 'Wes would have blamed you anyway, don't you see? He could never accept that Kieran's death was an accident, and when Bobby came along, he had everything he needed to make things right again in his eyes. But it wasn't your lie that screwed everything up. It was all Wes's doing.'

Saffy says, 'When did it start, his drive for revenge?'

'He became so ill after Kieran's death. I went to see his elderly mum a few weeks after Wes and I met up again. Wes Snr died, so Mags and Wes are the only ones left now – and she explained to me that they had to have him sectioned a few years after Keiran died. It took Wes a long time to get well, a long time until psychiatrists deemed him fit to return to normal life. But, as Mags said, Wes learned to hide his illness well. He hadn't recovered, he had just become adept in concealing it.'

'Had he been in hospital all that time?' Saffy asks.

'In and out of private clinics. Don't forget, his parents were wealthy. They paid for the best care and also for medical support. But just before he found me again, he became obsessed with avenging Kieran's death. His mum said they now know he'd quietly begun to plan in great detail when he came back home. The first hurdle was locating me and restarting our relationship. The police found dozens of notebooks full of detailed strategies, some of them written out hundreds of times and repeated word for word.'

'What happened, on the day I received the deleted messages?' Saffy says.

'Wes had planned exactly what would happen, but I added a few of my own things to convince you of my situation at home. I'm ashamed to tell you this stuff, but nothing can change between the two of us until we're honest, right?'

'That's right. I want the truth. No holds barred.'

'First off, it's true I was very unhappy with Ash. We married too quickly and, as usual, I didn't spot the signs that he was a raging narcissist. Saying that, he wasn't the monster I made him out to be, either. He was just a weak, selfish man.'

Saffy waits.

'When you and I met up for a drink the week before we went "missing", the bruises on my wrist were actually smudges created with black and blue powder eyeshadows. Very convincing. But you've always seen me as a weak person since we were teenagers, so I knew you'd jump to the right conclusion.'

'That's not true. You're strong and –'

Leona holds up a hand. 'I know I've allowed myself to be fooled and manipulated by men over the years, but somehow you accepting that view infuriated me. Sounds silly now, but I wanted you to . . . I don't know, expect more of me for once. But you believed it so easily.'

'So Ash wasn't abusing you?' Saffy says faintly.

'Ash could be cutting, but the stuff about my weight and controlling me wasn't true. I lost weight because I lost my appetite. I was torn between planning stuff with Wes and staying loyal to you. I hated myself for what I was doing, but by that stage, I felt I had no choice but to go through with it.'

Saffy thinks back, the details clicking into place. 'I found the pregnancy test and the letter from Harry in your carved wooden box. The magazine article about controlling partners you'd marked with a sticky note.'

Leona nods. 'Red herrings . . . Wes said I needed to leave evidence trails to back up my story.' Leona looks down. 'But I'd forgotten the pregnancy test was wedged in there. I took off my wedding ring after sending you the messages. I know how eagle-eyed you are with stuff like that.'

'You certainly went to town.'

'Yes, and I'm sorry. Even the garnet pendant that you lost – the upholsterer found it wedged down the sofa when we had it re-covered. I was going to return it to you, but by that time I was back in touch with Wes and he said to hold on to it. That we could make use of it.'

'I was so surprised when you gave up your nursing career because Ash wanted you to. Especially when I found out he'd lost his job.'

Leona nods. 'By that time, it didn't matter. Ash was in deep money problems, which Wes said was a good thing as he'd pay him off to just go away and leave us alone. And leaving my job helped it look as if Ash was controlling me in every area. Wes suggested I could resume my career once we'd set up home together.'

It's a lot of information for Saffy to take in, but she's just about keeping up. 'When I left the house to pick up Fox, what happened?'

Leona hunches over her hands on the table. 'Wes was already up in the attic when you came over. Ash hadn't been home long when you arrived, and Wes installed himself before that, came in through the back gate.'

Saffy is alarmed by the thought. The noise she'd heard up in Rosie's room . . .

'I took Rosie out into the garden and Wes made Ash an offer he couldn't refuse. Except Ash did refuse it and the situation got heated. Wes had a taser and . . . well, you can imagine. By the time Wes had finished, Ash was in no state to argue.'

'So that's what the blood was about? But how did you get out of the house without the neighbours seeing?'

'Yes, Ash lost quite a bit of blood. But he was OK . . . at that stage, at least. I had to keep Rosie out of the hallway, which was difficult, but as soon as it got to the end-of-school time, the neighbours started disappearing to pick up their kids and there was a bit more traffic, which was actually useful because Wes had hired a big transit van that just looked like a regular delivery van and it was less noticeable on a busier street.'

'Then what?'

'Wes drove the van in front of the house and Rosie and I slipped into the front seat. It was one of those vehicles that has a separate front and rear, so Rosie couldn't see what was happening back there. By that time, Ash was conscious and could walk, and somehow, Wes got him down the path and through the sliding side door of the van. Within minutes, we were on our way with the house door slightly ajar and everything as we'd left it. We didn't think about the Tuscan chicken in the oven and the smoke alarm, but afterwards Wes said it was a nice touch.'

'Where did you go? The days you were supposedly missing?'

'One of the outbuildings in the farm at Wymeswold,' Leona says. 'It's in the middle of nowhere and surrounded by private land. Wes's mum, Mags, she's astute but has problems with her mobility, so she didn't know myself and Ash were staying there. Just Rosie, who Wes explained was a friend's daughter who needed looking after for a few days. Mags spoiled her rotten and Wes had ordered soft toys and craft sets from Amazon to keep her busy.'

Saffy shakes her head. 'I can't believe Wes almost pulled it off. With your help, he almost did it.'

Leona looks down at her hands. 'I don't know how I didn't see he was psychotic. I think I was just so relieved to be heading towards a new life with Rosie and Wes. It felt like my only chance to escape Ash and start afresh.'

'He never told you he intended to hurt Ash?'

'Oh God, no! I despised Ash, but want him dead? Of course not. The crux of the plan was for me to lure you to the house to ensure you'd be suspected of knowing something about our disappearance. Then, when the police became convinced you'd played an integral part in it, we'd make you an offer. In return for us clearing your name with the police, you would confess that you knowingly let Kieran drown.'

Saffy gives her a pained look. 'Sounds like Wes planned it, but you had no problem in going along with it all.'

'It sounds brutal, I know. But after Wes had told me you had essentially killed his brother, told me what Bobby had witnessed that day, I was horrified. I convinced myself you'd deliberately let go of his hand. Wes pointed out other stuff, said you must have lied for your sister to cover up her affair with Ash.' She sighs. 'He just had this really compelling way of explaining everything. He was so believable, you know? Setting everything out like a story and fitting all the pieces together. It made sense at the time. How you wanted to ruin our relationship back then, how you'd always hated every man I met. How you despised Wes in particular.'

'I saw his darkness, Ash's too. I —'

'You don't have to explain, Saffy. Wes led me to believe that making you confess and paying off Ash to leave us alone would be enough. But I was naïve because all the time, he had nothing but murder in mind.' Leona shakes her head sadly. 'In here, I've had plenty of time to reflect. I've realized through my own therapy sessions these last few weeks how much my childhood experience of living in care affected my choice of partner. I've always been blind to control and co-dependency and reframed it as security and contentment. The question is, can you ever forgive me?'

The two women regard each other. Saffy leans forward and takes Leona's hand. 'This isn't all your doing, Leona. I have accountability, too. Starting with not being honest with you about Kieran. But also never wanting you to settle with some man who I didn't think was good enough. I admit they were never good enough in my eyes.'

'I've been weak,' Leona admits. 'Always going for the wrong sort of man and yearning for the connection of a deep and meaningful romantic relationship, whatever the cost.'

'We've both had painful lessons to learn,' Saffy says. 'I've wasted so much time living in fear, waiting for the worst to happen . . . wanting to protect the people I love even if that means smothering them. Namely you and Poppy.'

'How *is* Poppy?' Leona asks. 'I've been so grateful to her for bringing Rosie here to see me, but we've not reached a level of conversation where we can talk about Ash yet.'

'Poppy is OK. Since memories of the attack have flooded back she's struggled, but crazy as it sounds, we see that as a good thing. She no longer has to come to terms with an unknown assailant. She has some closure.' Saffy smiles. 'Another surprise is Harry. He is a good friend to her. She's found a strong, reliable figure who's helping her redefine what a good man should be. But Poppy swears there is only friendship there, nothing more. She says she wants to take some time to just get to know herself again.'

'Harry has surprised us all, I think. Thank you for agreeing to his supervised visits with Rosie. He says he's satisfied with just a couple of hours a week at the moment, happy to take it. I can't ask more than that.'

Saffy nods. 'Likewise, Neil has been brilliant. He's kept to his word and I'm having Fox over every other weekend now.'

Leona hesitates and then says, 'Mira's been visiting me, but . . . well, she and I won't ever be great friends.' Leona falters, 'Like you and I used to be, I mean. Like I'd give anything for us to be again.'

Saffy looks at her then. This woman she has shared so much with. They've laughed and cried . . . they've been there for each other for so long.

'I'm willing to try and rebuild our friendship and trust if you are,' Saffy says, ignoring the clammy grip of fear that tightens around her throat instead of giving in to it. 'Fox and Rosie love each other. Maybe they can be our guide.'

It feels right, feels good that they are back here together

again. A fresh start with their kids, with Poppy and even Harry. How long it will take, whether they'll ever find the trust they had again, who knows. But they're both willing to try.

Starting today.

69
Saffy

Saffy heads back to the car park and when the Lexus comes into sight, she stops walking. Neil is in the driver's seat as she left him, but there's also someone sitting in the passenger seat.

Neil gets out of the car and walks over to her.

'Saffy, there's someone here who wants a word with you.' He shifts his weight, one foot to the other. 'I'm going to have a walk around the perimeter and give you both five, OK?'

Saffy frowns. 'Hang on. Who's in the car?'

'You'll see when you get there,' he says, a tad awkwardly.

She watches as Neil slopes off without looking back at her. She walks over to the car, and it is Mira who gets out of the passenger side. It's only now that she notices the familiar silver Mazda parked in the next bay.

'Oh, it's just you!' Saffy grins. 'Neil was being so mysterious!'

'Saffy. Thanks so much for agreeing to talk,' Mira says. 'Let's take a seat over here.'

They walk over to a nearby grassed area and sit on a wooden bench at the edge of a flower bed.

'How are you?'

'I'm doing OK. Still limping, but getting better. How are you feeling?' Saffy looks pointedly at Mira's now sizeable baby bump.

'I'm well, thanks, and baby Iris is doing fine.'

399

'Iris? What a lovely name.' Fox and Iris. It has a beautiful ring to it, Saffy thinks.

A beat of loaded silence, then Mira says, 'I have something to tell you, Saffy. Something that has been preying on my mind and I want to offload.'

Saffy waits. After everything that's happened, nothing can possibly surprise her now. 'Gosh, OK then. Fire away.'

'Neil told me that last year, you were very upset at being blamed for a letter sent to Leona and that he took it upon himself to tell the police about it.'

'Yes, that's right. I suppose he did what he had to do.' Sounds like Neil has been sharing Saffy's worst bits with Mira again, as he had done about Poppy's attack. 'I know in my bones Ash sent it, but of course there's no way of proving that now.'

'Ash didn't send the letter to Leona,' Mira says, her voice shaking. 'I did.'

Saffy looks at her, nonplussed. 'You sent it? Why would you do that?'

Mira holds up her hands. 'I'm sorry. I'm so sorry, I can't apologize enough. It's not an excuse, but I was jealous of how you and Neil seemed to be close. He was always talking about how well you'd done to recover from your crisis.'

'Was he?' Saffy is surprised.

'Yes. At least it felt like he was, and I was insecure back then. I sometimes thought you two might get back together.'

Saffy raises an eyebrow. 'Well, that was never going to happen.'

'This particular time, Neil mentioned that you were put out because Ash made you feel unwelcome at the house and Leona had also said something similar to me when the kids played together. She said you and Ash couldn't stand each other.'

'That was true enough.'

'Anyway, this one day, Neil was late home because he'd stayed for a chat at your house after picking Fox up and I was angry. Ridiculously angry . . . and I just wrote that spiteful letter to Leona as if it was written by you and I mailed it before I could change my mind.'

Saffy stays quiet and considers this before saying, 'And you decided you had to tell me now, after all this time?'

'Yes,' Mira says. 'Because I know what you're doing for Rosie and I think it's marvellous. I'm not a bad person, Saffy, and I'm very sorry for what I did to you. I love Fox and I'm in a good place now. Neil and I are good together. I want Fox and Iris to be close and I want us to be on good terms, too, and . . . That spiteful letter I wrote is just always there in my mind. But Neil said he could forgive me, if you will do the same.'

Saffy looks down at Mira's hands and sees they are trembling.

'Thank you, Mira,' Saffy says. 'I forgive you.'

'What? Do you mean that?'

'I do.' Saffy sighs. 'I once told a lie and, as you say, it was just there the whole time, for so many years. I wish I'd had the courage to just tell the truth and break its power. Eventually I did, but it's caused so much heartache. None of us is perfect and all of us are human and sometimes, it's just so hard to give ourselves a break.'

'Thank you. That's very generous of you, Saffy.'

'After everything that's happened, I've realized what good people I have around me, and that includes you.'

Mira touches her hand shyly. 'That's very sweet of you, Saffy. Very generous.'

They both look up as Neil appears in front of the car after doing his five-minute disappearing act.

'Right. I'll go and see Leona now,' Mira says, standing up. 'Take care, Saffy, and I hope to see you very soon.'

Saffy stands and embraces her. 'Bye, Mira. Speak soon.'

When Mira walks off towards Foston Hall, stopping to embrace Neil, Saffy and Neil head for the car.

'She's had so many sleepless nights over this,' he says. 'Thanks for being so gracious.'

'Far worse things have happened recently,' Saffy says, getting into the passenger seat. 'She didn't have to tell me, but I'm glad she did.'

Neil sits in the car and looks at her. 'I thought now might be a good time to suggest we agree equal share of custody of Fox,' he says, just like that. 'That OK with you?'

'Er . . . yes!' Saffy laughs. A joyous sound. 'Really? An equal split?'

'Yep. I'll get my lawyer to look at the process of getting it rubber-stamped in the family court. If you're happy and it's what you want.'

'Happy? I'm absolutely delighted.' Saffy looks at her ex-husband and feels a genuine affection. 'Thank you, Neil, for always being there. This has made my day, my week, my year . . . my whole life!'

He smiles and buckles up. 'It's a good start for me making up for the fact I decided to dob you in with the police. For a letter you never sent. Even though I thought I was doing it for your own good, to get things out in the open. Sorry about that.'

Saffy turns slowly to look at him. 'Congratulations, Neil.'

'Huh . . . for what?'

'For finally learning how to apologize. I knew you'd manage it one day.'

'Ha ha, very funny!' He rolls his eyes and starts the car. Then he says something Saffy never thought she'd hear.

'Today, let's surprise Fox and pick him up from school together.'

'That's truly the best idea I've heard all day,' Saffy says, fastening her seatbelt. 'Let's go.'

Acknowledgements

It takes many talented people to bring a book to publication and I'm very lucky to be surrounded by some of the best.

I'd like to give special thanks to my editor Joel Richardson who believed in this story from its first brief concept. I'm so grateful to the whole amazing team at Penguin Michael Joseph including: Stephanie Biddle, Clare Bowron, Riana Dixon, Emma Henderson, Ellie Hughes, Nick Lowndes and Stella Newing.

Huge thanks as always to my agent Camilla Bolton and to Jade Kavanagh and the rest of the team at Darley Anderson and Associates Ltd.

I am incredibly lucky to have the unwavering support of my husband Mac and my daughter and social media manager Francesca at FKN Social who has transformed my online presence.

Last but not least, a heartfelt thank you to all my wonderful readers. Your loyalty and support truly mean the world to me.